BLOOD MAGIC

"An intense and suspenseful tale. For anyone who enjoys werewolves and romance, *Blood Magic* is a must-read . . . Eileen
Wilks is a truly gifted writer. Her newest novel is truly a work of
art as her words paint a picture of a modern-day Romeo and Ju-
liet."   —*Romance Junkies*

"A tantalizing glimpse into the past of one of the series' most
enigmatic characters, Lily's shape-shifting grandmother. Wilks's
storytelling style is so densely layered with plot complexities and
well-defined characters that it quickly immerses readers in this
fascinating world. There is no better way to escape reality than
with a Wilks adventure!"   —*RT Book Reviews*

"Another great addition to the Lupi series, Eileen Wilks's *Blood
Magic* is an engaging paranormal tale full of action and adventure
that should not be missed!"   —*Romance Reviews Today*

"Terrific."   —*Midwest Book Review*

MORTAL SINS

"Filled with drama and action . . . This story is number five in the
World of the Lupi series and is just as good as the first."
—*Fresh Fiction*

continued . . .

"Held me enthralled and kept me glued to my seat . . . The characters and world are intriguing, and the solution to the murders is unusual and thought provoking . . . Ms. Wilks has a skill with description and narrative that truly brings a world and its characters alive." —*Errant Dreams Reviews*

"Fabulous . . . The plot just sucked me in and didn't let me go until the end . . . Another great addition to the World of Lupi series." —*Literary Escapism*

"[Lily and Rule are] a crackling couple . . . [Wilks manages] to translate that indefinable tension, that absolute and utter chemistry that happens between real couples . . . onto paper." —*Romance Novel TV*

NIGHT SEASON

"A captivating world." —*The Romance Reader*

"Filled with action and plenty of twists." —*Midwest Book Review*

BLOOD LINES

"Another winner from Eileen Wilks." —*Romance Reviews Today*

"The magic seems plausible, the demons real, and the return of enigmatic Cynna, along with the sorcerer, hooks fans journeying the fantasy realm of Eileen Wilks." —*The Best Reviews*

"Intriguing . . . Surprises abound in *Blood Lines* . . . A masterful pen and sharp wit hone this third book in the Moon Children series into a work of art. Enjoy!" —*A Romance Review*

"Savor *Blood Lines* to the very last page." —*BookLoons*

"Quite enjoyable and sure to entertain . . . A fast-paced story with plenty of danger and intrigue." —*The Green Man Review*

MORTAL DANGER

"Grabs you on the first page and never lets go. Strong characters, believable world-building, and terrific storytelling . . . I really, really loved this book."
—Patricia Briggs, #1 *New York Times* bestselling author

"As intense as it is sophisticated, a wonderful novel of strange magic, fantastic realms, and murderous vengeance that blend together to test the limits of fate-bound lovers."
—Lynn Viehl, *New York Times* bestselling author of the Darkyn series

"[A] complex, intriguing, paranormal world . . . Fans of the paranormal genre will love this one!"
—*Love Romances*

FURTHER PRAISE FOR EILEEN WILKS AND HER NOVELS

"I remember Eileen Wilks's characters long after the last page is turned."
—Kay Hooper, *New York Times* bestselling author

"If you enjoy beautifully written, character-rich paranormals set in a satisfyingly intricate and imaginative world, then add your name to Eileen Wilks's growing fan list."
—*BookLoons*

"Exciting, fascinating paranormal suspense the will have you on the edge of your seat. With a mesmerizing tale of an imaginative world and characters that will keep you spellbound as you read each page, Ms. Wilks proves once again what a wonderful writer she is with one great imagination for her characters and the world they live in."
—*The Romance Readers Connection*

"Destined to become a big, big name in romance fiction."
—*RT Book Reviews*

"Fantastic . . . Fabulous pairing . . . Ms. Wilks takes a chance and readers are the winners."
—*The Best Reviews*

"Fun [and] very entertaining!"
—*The Romance Reader*

"Should appeal to fans of Nora Roberts."
—*Booklist*

"Eileen Wilks [has] remarkable skill. With a deft touch she combines romance and danger."
—*Midwest Book Review*

Books by Eileen Wilks

TEMPTING DANGER
MORTAL DANGER
BLOOD LINES
NIGHT SEASON
MORTAL SINS
BLOOD MAGIC
BLOOD CHALLENGE
DEATH MAGIC
MORTAL TIES

Anthologies

CHARMED
*(with Jayne Ann Krentz writing as Jayne Castle,
Julie Beard, and Lori Foster)*

LOVER BEWARE
(with Christine Feehan, Katherine Sutcliffe, and Fiona Brand)

CRAVINGS
*(with Laurell K. Hamilton, MaryJanice Davidson,
and Rebecca York)*

ON THE PROWL
(with Patricia Briggs, Karen Chance, and Sunny)

INKED
(with Karen Chance, Marjorie M. Liu, and Yasmine Galenorn)

MORTAL TIES

EILEEN WILKS

BERKLEY SENSATION, NEW YORK

THE BERKLEY PUBLISHING GROUP
Published by the Penguin Group
Penguin Group (USA) Inc.
375 Hudson Street, New York, New York 10014, USA

Penguin Group (Canada), 90 Eglinton Avenue East, Suite 700, Toronto, Ontario M4P 2Y3, Canada
(a division of Pearson Penguin Canada Inc.) • Penguin Books Ltd., 80 Strand, London WC2R 0RL,
England • Penguin Group Ireland, 25 St. Stephen's Green, Dublin 2, Ireland (a division of Penguin
Books Ltd.) • Penguin Group (Australia), 250 Camberwell Road, Camberwell, Victoria 3124, Australia
(a division of Pearson Australia Group Pty. Ltd.) • Penguin Books India Pvt. Ltd., 11 Community
Centre, Panchsheel Park, New Delhi—110 017, India • Penguin Group (NZ), 67 Apollo Drive,
Rosedale, Auckland 0632, New Zealand (a division of Pearson New Zealand Ltd.) • Penguin Books
(South Africa) (Pty.) Ltd., 24 Sturdee Avenue, Rosebank, Johannesburg 2196, South Africa

Penguin Books Ltd., Registered Offices: 80 Strand, London WC2R 0RL, England

This is a work of fiction. Names, characters, places, and incidents either are the product of the author's
imagination or are used fictitiously, and any resemblance to actual persons, living or dead, business
establishments, events, or locales is entirely coincidental. The publisher does not have any control over
and does not assume any responsibility for author or third-party websites or their content.

MORTAL TIES

A Berkley Sensation Book / published by arrangement with the author

PUBLISHING HISTORY
Berkley Sensation mass-market edition / October 2012

Copyright © 2012 by Eileen Wilks.
Excerpt from *Ritual Magic* by Eileen Wilks copyright © 2012 by Eileen Wilks.
Cover art by Tony Mauro.
Cover design by George Long.

ISBN: 978-0-425-25492-9

BERKLEY SENSATION®
Berkley Sensation Books are published by The Berkley Publishing Group,
a division of Penguin Group (USA) Inc.,
375 Hudson Street, New York, New York 10014.
BERKLEY SENSATION® is a registered trademark of Penguin Group (USA) Inc.
The "B" design is a trademark of Penguin Group (USA) Inc.

PRINTED IN THE UNITED STATES OF AMERICA

10 9 8 7 6 5 4 3 2 1

ALWAYS LEARNING   PEARSON

ACKNOWLEDGMENTS

Special thanks go to M. David Lugo, cemetary manager at Mount Hope, who helped me get some of the details right.

I also want to send a shout-out to my Watercooler sisters (you know who you are). Thanks for the hand-holding, commiseration, and for celebrating with me when it was time to break out the confetti.

ONE

LILY Yu hadn't planned to visit the graveyard at sunset. It just worked out that way.

Mount Hope's main gates closed at three thirty, but the pedestrian gates stayed open. People liked to stop by after work, the guy at the cemetery's office had said, especially on the deceased's birthday or other important dates. No parking available at this hour, though, except for what you could grab along the street.

Lily pulled her government Ford to the curb and checked her rearview mirror. The white Toyota that had been following her drew close, then cruised on by. She would wait. No point in making them anxious by getting out before they could park. It was bad enough she brought them here when the light was going.

Not that they would be spooked by the setting sun, no more than she was. The dead weren't scary. It was the living you had to watch out for.

While the Toyota hunted for a parking place, Lily transferred her penlight from her purse to her pocket. The day was slipping down toward dusk, and twilight's a tricky bugger. In the daytime you know where you are and can see

where you're going. At night you know you can't see, not
without help—electric help, most likely, from the city, a
flashlight, whatever. You know, so you take precautions.

Twilight blurs the edges. In the shadow time, it's easy to
mistake what you see, to step wrong, thinking there's light
enough to keep going. Back when she worked homicide,
Lily had arrested people who went that one terrible step too
far, confused by a personal twilight of drugs or emotion.
People who never set out to be killers.

But some take that step on purpose. Some damn well
know where the lines are and cross them deliberately. Like
the bastard whose hearing she'd testified at today.

Goddamn copycats.

The Toyota backed itself into a spot between an SUV
and a pickup halfway up the block. Lily grabbed her purse,
checked for cars, and climbed out of her Ford. Traffic was
sparse enough she could cross right away, so she did. By
the time she reached the cemetery side of the street, two
men had gotten out of the Toyota.

One was slim and pale, with a round face and glasses.
He looked like he ought to have a pocket protector tucked
away somewhere. The other was a head taller, eighty
pounds heavier, and looked like he ought to have a couple
of tattoos and a rap sheet. Geek Guy wore a cheap sports
shirt. Tough Guy wore a black T-shirt. Both wore jeans,
athletic shoes, and sports jackets.

Lily wore a jacket, too, and for the same reason. It might
be a few days short of January, but this was San Diego. The
air was crisp, not cold. But people get upset if you walk
around with your shoulder harness showing.

The men crossed the street between a dark sedan and a
delivery truck. Geek Guy made a quick gesture with one
hand. Tough Guy set off through the gate at an easy lope.
Lily followed Tough Guy—also known as Mike—and was
in turn followed.

They hadn't been tailed here, but it was just barely possible their enemies knew she planned to come and had
someone waiting. Highly unlikely, but possible. A month

ago she'd picked up a map of the cemetery. Theoretically, Friar could have somehow learned about that and kept the place staked out ever since.

Or so Scott had said when she told him she was coming here. Lily considered this one of the safest things she'd done lately. Friar's organization had been badly damaged in October when he'd managed to get a lot of people killed and had seen his long-laid plans blow up in his face. She doubted he had the resources to keep a sniper in place 24/7 for a month. She doubted even more that he had any idea she'd picked up that map in the first place.

He did, however, have one resource they could neither predict nor evaluate in any meaningful way, so she could be wrong. If so, well, she had backup.

Sometimes it really is all in the name.

For months she'd struggled with the need for bodyguards. No—be honest, she told herself as she set off down a narrow road that twisted through the cemetery, heading generally where she needed to go. She'd hated it. She'd hated dragging guards everywhere, hated the loss of privacy . . . hated, most of all, that one of them had given his life for her. The need for them was real, but her acceptance of the necessity had been a grim thing, testy and prone to muttering.

Last week Rule had shaken his head at her mutters and said, "I don't get it. Didn't you ever call for backup when you were a regular cop? That didn't make you crazy."

"Backup," she'd repeated slowly. Then said it again as a weight shifted, not disappearing but settling into a more comfortable place, like slipping on her bra or shoulder holster. "Backup, not guards. They're my mobile backup."

Trailed by half of her mobile backup—Geek Guy, aka Scott White, who was a lot more interested in guns and knives than computers—Lily left the road for the soft grass, moving between the resting places of the dead.

Her target lay in the newest part of the cemetery. Mount Hope was old for this side of the country, an accumulation of graveyards the city had assumed responsibility for over the years, with lots of established trees and old-fashioned headstones. Here, though, it was what they called garden-style, with neatly trimmed grass and markers set flat into the ground, each with a little holder for flowers.

The grass was damp and springy and perfumed the air. In other parts of the country, people associated the smell of freshly cut grass with summer. It evoked winter for Lily. That's when the rains came, when grass grew lush and green and was in need of cutting. This year December had been unusually wet, bestowing nearly five inches of rain on them. Lily walked on soft grass between the graves of people she'd never known, heading for the one she had.

She hadn't brought flowers. It would be tacky to bring flowers to the grave of a woman you'd killed. Especially when you didn't regret it.

Lily counted rows, turned, and counted graves. She didn't see Mike nearby, but she hadn't expected to. Lupi were good at tucking themselves away where you couldn't spot them.

And there it was. Lily stopped.

She hadn't brought flowers, but someone had.

Not an expensive bouquet. More like the kind you pick up at the grocery store, with a few dyed carnations supplemented by baby's breath. Pink and red carnations, in this case. There was an inch of water in the glass cylinder holding the bouquet.

Was this the right grave? Maybe she'd lost count. She knelt by the headstone laid flat into the ground, frowned at its unexpected decoration, then used her penlight to read the inscription on the plaque.

Helen Annabelle Whitehead

When Lily killed Helen a year ago last month, she hadn't known the woman's last name. She hadn't known much about her at all, save for a few vital facts. Helen had lived up to the common wisdom about telepaths—she'd been batwing crazy. She'd tortured and she'd killed; she'd tried to open a hellgate; she'd intended to feed Lily's lover to the Old One she served. She'd also been doing her damnedest to kill Lily just before Lily put a stop to that and the rest of the woman's plans.

So . . . no regrets, no. Lily had done what she had to do. And Helen hadn't had a spouse, lover, or any living family, so Lily didn't even carry the burden of having brought grief to those who might have loved the woman.

Yet here she was. She wasn't sure why. In some murky, underneath way it was connected to what she'd done yesterday, when she and Rule had stood in line for a ridiculous amount of time at the County Clerk's office. They'd left with a marriage license good for the next ninety days.

The wedding was in March—two months, one week, and two days away.

Yesterday had been the immediate catalyst for this visit, but the decision to come here had grown up organically in Lily's mind over the last several months. She'd found out where Helen was back in June, but hadn't come. Last month she'd swung by Mount Hope's office and gotten directions and the map, but hadn't gone to Helen's grave. She hadn't been ready.

Ready for what? She wasn't sure. She was here, and she still wasn't sure why.

Mount Hope had been San Diego's municipal cemetery for about a hundred and fifty years. Raymond Chandler was buried here. So was Alta Hulett, America's first female attorney, and the guy who established Balboa Park, and a lot of veterans. So was Ah Quin, who was remembered as one the city's founding fathers . . . at least by its Chinese residents. And so were those who'd been buried at the county's expense, though budget cuts meant the county was likely to cremate, not plant, these days.

Helen had died a virgin, a killer, and intestate, but taxpayers hadn't had to pick up the tab for disposing of her mortal remains. The trustee appointed by a judge had seen to that, paying for it out of her estate.

Turned out Helen had socked away well over a quarter

million. Telepaths had an inside track on conning people, didn't they? If they could shut out the voices in their heads enough to function, that is—which Helen had been able to do, thanks to the Old One she served. That's how she'd met her protégé, Patrick Harlowe . . . who'd also died badly, but not at Lily's hands. Cullen Seabourne had done the honors there.

But Lily had killed again since then. Helen was her first, but killing and war went together, didn't they? Even if most of the country didn't know they were at war, the lupi did. Lily did. And so did her boss, head of the FBI's Unit Twelve . . . head, too, of the far less official Shadow Unit.

In the run-up to the war, Lily had killed demons, helped a wraith reach true death, and ushered a supposed immortal through that small, dark door. This last September she'd tried and failed to kill a sidhe lord. And in October, just before the first open battle of the war, she'd shot a man. Double-tapped him.

That man had just shot a fellow FBI agent—a lying, treacherous bastard of an agent, but at that point he'd been on Lily's side. There had been other lives on the line: four lupi, another FBI agent, and the twenty-two people the bad guys intended to slaughter. Lily had sited on the shooter's head—his body had been blocked by the van he'd driven—and squeezed off two quick shots. She'd killed him cold, not hot, killed him to stop him from killing others.

That was training. Most cops never had to use their weapons, but when you took up the badge you knew you might be called on to take a life. Lily had never doubted she could. Not since she was nine, anyway. The man who'd raped and killed her friend while she watched, tied up and waiting for him to do the same to her, had been arrested and tried and convicted. He'd gone to prison for life, which was all the vengeance she was supposed to want.

But for months afterward, she'd dreamed of murder.

Lily had always known she entered the police force to stop the monsters. She was beginning to understand the other reason she'd needed that bureaucratic harness.

"Goddamn morbid sort of thing to do, isn't it?" said a gravelly voice. "Hanging out at the grave of someone you killed."

Lily jolted, then twisted to scowl at the intruder. "Oh, hell. I thought you were gone."

"Guess you were wrong." The man standing disrespectfully atop a nearby grave wore a dark suit with a wrinkled white shirt and a plain tie. He was on the skinny side of lean, with his dark, thinning hair combed straight back from a broad forehead, and he was pale. Pale as in white. Also slightly see-through.

Al Drummond. Her very own personal haunt.

TWO

WHAT had she ever done to deserve this? Lily ran both hands through her hair. "Go away."

"Ah . . . Lily?" Scott said.

Scott, of course, hadn't seen or heard anything, except for her talking to empty air. "It's Drummond, dropping in again for a visit." Al Drummond, former FBI Special Agent . . . the lying, treacherous bastard who'd been shot by the man Lily had killed last month. Scott knew about him.

The dead might not scare her, but they could be damned annoying. "If you're here to give me more of your pearls of wisdom—"

"No. At least . . ." He paused uncertainly. "I don't think so."

Drummond had been many things in life. *Uncertain* wasn't one of them. The novelty of it interrupted her more thoroughly than his words, stirring an unwanted curiosity. "What, then?"

"I don't know." He crossed his arms, scowling. "You think I picked you to fix on? You think this is my idea of a great way to spend eternity—popping in to watch you brush your goddamn teeth? What the hell are you doing here, anyway?"

Lily stood. Whatever she'd hoped for today, it wasn't happening now. Not with Drummond hanging around. "In what way can that be considered any of your business?"

"Just curious. It makes things easier for me, but somehow I don't think that's why you came."

"What do you mean, it makes it easier for you?"

"Easier for me to show up. Places like this, the veil is thin."

Amusement jabbed at her, half funny and half painful. "I wish Mullins could hear you talking about 'the veil' like some TV psychic."

He snorted. "That would chap his ass, wouldn't it? You like to hang out at the graves of people you've killed?"

"How do you know whose grave this is?"

"I can read."

"And you know who Helen was."

"Did you think I didn't do any digging before I set out to get you?"

Drummond might have gone spectacularly wrong, but he'd been a good agent before that—savvy, smart, and thorough. Of course he knew who Helen was, knew that Lily had killed her. God only knew what else he'd dug up about her. "Go away."

"Don't get all huffy. I've got a proposition."

"Does it involve you leaving me alone?"

"And where the hell would I go?"

"How should I know? Obviously you don't have to hang around me every minute. You were gone for over a month."

"A month?" That rattled him. "I was . . . I think I was sleeping. But not the whole time. I was at the courthouse with you just now when—"

She scowled. "I didn't see you." Supposedly Drummond couldn't see or hear the world without manifesting, at least to the drifting-white-mist stage.

"You didn't look up, and I was . . ." His mouth kept moving, but all she heard was silence. He stopped, scowled,

and tried again. Midway through, his mouthed words became speech again. ". . . show up all the way in some
places. And talking is goddamn hard, too, so stop interrupting."

"You're not really talking, you know. No movement of
air, which is why no one else hears you." It had to be some
kind of mindspeech, however much it sounded like regular
speech to her.

He snorted. "Like I hadn't figured that out. Listen, I
think I know what I'm supposed to do. Why I didn't just die
or go to hell or whatever." His eyes burned with intensity.
"I'm supposed to be your partner."

It was so ludicrous she had to laugh. "Yeah, that'll happen." She collected Scott with a glance and started for the
road. Drummond tried to grab her arm. His hand passed
right through her, of course, so after a disgusted grimace he
kept pace beside her. At least that's what it looked like—as
if he were walking, his feet pushing against the ground the
way hers did.

"Look, I get that you don't like me," he said. "So what?
I've worked with a lot of assholes. If it gets the job done,
you live with it."

"You're a little limited in what you can do right now."

"Maybe, but I can do things you can't. Anywhere within
about three hundred feet of you, I can check things out.
Check things out on either side. For example, there are
three ghosts here—pretty tattered, not much for conversation, but they're here. And on your side of things, I know
where your wolf man is. He's hunkered down right over
there." He stretched out an arm to point at a dip in the
ground.

One finger on that hand glowed faintly from the wedding ring he still wore. It caught her attention, that ring.
Unconsciously she rubbed her thumb over the ring she
wore—an engagement ring, not a wedding ring, but the
same sort of token. Rule's ring.

She looked away. "His name is Mike."

"Whatever. The point is, I can help."

They'd reached the narrow road that wound among the graves. She stopped. "And you think I should trust you."

"I dealt straight with you. Once I saw what they were doing, I dealt straight with you."

True. He'd risked his life to rescue twenty-two homeless people, then given it to save a friend. And after he died, he'd found the death-magic amulet so they could destroy it.

But first he'd betrayed the Bureau, nearly killed Lily's boss, conspired in the murder of a U.S. senator, and damn near ended Lily's career along the way.

Lily studied him a moment, then took out her phone.

He frowned. "Who are you calling?"

"A friend. She hears dead people all the time." Lily had only chatted with one dead guy. This one. As for the big, fat "why" of this screwed-up situation . . . well, the expert she was about to consult used the analogy of a house. Most people didn't see or hear the dead because their houses lacked windows and had only one door—a tightly locked, one-way affair. That door didn't open until the person died. Because Lily had died once, her door didn't lock anymore. It was a tiny bit ajar. Mostly that didn't matter, but she'd been present at Drummond's death, and somehow that had allowed their energies to get tangled up together.

At least that was the theory. It didn't explain everything. Lily had been present when a lot of people died that day, including the man she'd shot. None of the rest of them had taken to tagging along with her.

She scrolled down to "Etorri" in her contacts list and selected "Rhej."

The Rhejes were the clans' wise women, or maybe historians or quasi-priestesses. They were all Gifted . . . and the Etorri Rhej's Gift was mediumship. Lily had never heard the woman's name because the Rhejes weren't called by their names, but last month she'd given in to curiosity. Rhejes didn't actually hide their names and Lily had the woman's phone number, so it hadn't been hard. The name of the Etorri Rhej was Anne. Anne Murdock.

Anne answered right away. Lily apologized for disturbing her, then said, "He's back."

"That ghost?" Anne was clearly surprised. "What was his name—Hammond?"

"Drummond. He just showed up again. He's glaring at me right now."

"He still seems coherent?"

"In the sense you used the word, yeah."

Anne made a little huff of frustration. "I wish I could talk to him. I haven't met a fully coherent ghost since I was seven, and she left soon after my mother spoke with her."

Lily knew what Anne meant by "coherent," because they'd talked soon after Drummond showed up. Most ghosts were more of a habit than a person—some ingrained action or fear or moment that played itself out over and over, a ripple cast by the soul's departure rather than the soul itself. Others seemed like real people, able to interact, but in a limited way. They often didn't make a lot of sense to those few of the living who could see and hear them.

But there were a few rare exceptions. Fully coherent ghosts, the Etorri Rhej called them, and the experts didn't agree on what they were, how they came to be, or much of anything else, except that they were different from the rest. A coherent ghost seemed to be the whole person. He or she remained aware of the living world, seemed to perceive it through the same senses as the living, and used language the way the living do. Coherent ghosts were like the rest in one way, however. They were tied to something—a place or an object or, very rarely, a person.

How had Lily gotten so lucky? "He says he's tied to me, but he was gone for over a month."

"I'm afraid I can't explain that."

"Neither could he. He also says he thinks he's supposed to be my partner."

"Are you asking for advice?"

"Is there any way to sort the good ghosts from the rotten, lying sons of bitches?"

Anne chuckled. "Only the same ways we sort the living.

If you want to know if he's lying, that's certainly possible. He could equally well be telling the truth, or the truth as he understands it. We may not know much about coherent ghosts, but we've no reason to think they're any less muddled than the rest of us."

Lily hesitated over her next question—but dammit, she wanted to know. "So could he, uh, think he needs to help me out because of unfinished business? And once he does, he can . . . go on?"

"I don't buy the 'unfinished business' explanation for ghosts in general. Almost everyone leaves some kind of unfinished business behind, but hardly anyone lingers as a ghost more than a few moments. However, some of the more coherent ghosts strongly believe they *can't* cross over. Either they're right, or the strength of their belief itself holds them here."

"So Drummond might be supposed to work with me, and he can't, ah . . . cross over until he does that. Or pays a debt or something. Or he might be stuck here because he believes he's stuck here."

"Pretty much, yes. I'm not much help, am I?"

Not really. "One more question, and this may be outside your area of expertise, being more a matter of . . . ethics, I guess. Does this obligation thing go both ways? Does Drummond being tied to me give me any sort of obligation to him?"

Anne was quiet for a long moment. "I can only tell you what my mother told me, which is what her mother told her, and on back for generations. We have no more duty to the dead than we do to the living. And no less."

That was not what Lily wanted to hear. She thanked the Rhej anyway, disconnected, and looked at the man—or what remained of a man—scowling at her.

"Well?" he demanded. "Did your friend tell you anything useful?"

"Maybe." Making Drummond go away for good was high on her priority list. If he thought he had to help her out in some way . . . but she hadn't exactly gotten a guarantee about that. "You were at the courthouse, you said. You know what Brian Nelson did."

"Yeah." He scowled. "Goddamn copycats."

That echo of her own thoughts creeped her out. "That's right. He and three of his gang wanted to raise death magic, so they captured two young women and slit their throats. They'd heard about what your pal Chittenden did. They were copying him."

His expression shut down. "You want me to tell you I was wrong?"

"Oh, I figure you know now that you were on the wrong side. What I want to hear is that you've changed your mind about magic and the people who use it."

He was silent.

"That's what I thought." She started walking again.

"Okay, so we won't be partners. I'm still a resource, and you're wasting me. I've got twice your experience. You can't ignore that."

He was right. That, too, was annoying. She stopped and looked at him. "Mostly you haven't hung around long enough to be much use. You pop in; you pop out."

"I . . . can be more available now."

She waited. He didn't elaborate, so she asked, "Is the 'why' to that one of those things you can't explain?"

"Since I don't understand it myself, the answer would be yes."

"You told me you never met Friar." Robert Friar, who'd started a war—or was resuming one begun over three thousand years ago. Robert Friar, who'd seen the slaughter of hundreds of people on his own side as a great way to take down the lupi, the Gifted, and everyone else who stood in the way of the one he served. Like the U.S. government.

"Just his buddy, Chittenden."

"But you researched him. If you dug into my background, you must have checked him out, too, before throwing in on his side."

"Sure, but I doubt I know anything you don't. I used the Bureau's files, talked to a couple people."

"I'm asking for your professional opinion, not the details of your background check. Given what you learned then and what you know now, would you say he's a sociopath?"

"Huh." He thought that over, frowning and silent for a long moment. "Could be. There's no record of the usual markers, like torturing baby bunnies when he was a cute little toddler. But sociopaths aren't identical. Could be he's what they call *high functioning*."

"Really good at hiding what he is, you mean."

"That, yeah, but also with better impulse control. Most sociopaths aren't good at restraining themselves."

"Most of the ones we know about. The ones who get locked up."

"True." He cocked his head. "You're trying to get to know Friar better."

She nodded and started walking again, but slowly. "Him and the one he serves." The Old One who wanted to take over the world and remake it according to her standards. The one they never named, because that could draw her attention. The Great Bitch had to act through local agents because she was barred from their realm, thank God. Or thank the Old Ones who'd opposed her, like the lupi's Lady, who'd shut the door on themselves in order to lock *her* out.

"That's why you came here." Drummond sounded pleased, like he'd turned a puzzle piece around and finally saw where it fit. "Not to poke around in your own psyche, but to try and dig into hers. Helen Whitehead's. Whitehead belonged to that Old One you told me about."

"She did. And she seems to have been a sociopath, too."

Drummond's eyebrows lifted. "Yeah?"

"As was, possibly, one Patrick Harlowe . . . the other agent of *hers* that I know about."

"That doesn't say good things about the Old Bitch."

"It doesn't, does it? If—" A muffled gong sounded in her purse—the ringtone for calls forwarded from her official number. She dug out her phone. "Agent Yu here."

It was T.J., aka Detective Thomas James, the man who'd

trained Lily when she was a shiny new homicide cop. As he talked, Lily gave her watch one wistful glance. She owed T.J. a lot more than one delayed supper, though, so she spoke briskly enough when he paused. "Sure. I'll be there in fifteen." She put her phone away and glanced over her shoulder at Scott ten feet behind her. "Did you hear?"

"Only your side, and that your caller was male."

Had Scott been a bit closer he'd heave heard T.J. just fine, but there were limits even to lupi hearing. She was gradually learning what those limits were. "An old buddy of mine from Homicide has a suspicious death. He wants me to see if magic was involved, but off the books. Unofficial." Lily was a touch sensitive, able to feel magic tactilely, often able to identify what type it was—and unable to work it or be affected by it. If there was any magic on the body or the scene, she'd know. "I'll be heading to 1221 Hammer, apartment 717."

She texted Rule on her way out of the cemetery, letting him know she'd be late. Mike passed her before she reached the gate, moving at the lupi version of an easy lope—about as fast as she could sprint, in other words. And, to her annoyance, a filmy white shape drifted right along with her. When she reached her car, it solidified. Sort of.

"Sounds like we've got a case," Drummond said.

"One of us might." She unlocked the car and climbed in.

"Dammit, I can help."

"Or you can trip me and laugh when I fall down."

His features grew even more sour than usual. "I'll be around when you change your mind. Uh . . . I can't manifest at Clanhome unless you call me."

Manifest. That was a word she never would have heard from Drummond when he was alive. "You can't do it there?"

"No. It's like . . ." His fingers opened and closed as if he were scratching at the air. "That's closed to me, is all. Unless you call. Wherever you are, if you call me, I can manifest."

"Huh." Nokolai Clanhome was where she and Rule were living these days. As were a lot of others.

Rule's people had always lived under threat, but they'd felt that their children were safe. Even during times of fierce persecution, lupi children had lived unmolested among humans who might have tossed them onto the fires along with the witches, had they known what they were. And the clans might fight among themselves, but kids were exempt. In all the years that Leidolf and Nokolai had been enemies, neither clan had worried that the other would strike at their children. Even mean, mad old Victor Frey, the Leidolf Rho who'd tricked Rule into assuming the mantle, then died before he could take it back, had left Toby alone.

Though the latter, Lily suspected, might be because Victor had known his history. Four hundred years ago, Leidolf and Nokolai had acted in rare and complete accord, along with Wythe. They'd acted with the explicit backing of every other clan . . . every clan but one. Bánach clan had been feuding with Cynyr. Bánach clan took the eight-year-old son of Cynyr's Rho hostage—took him unharmed, but refused to release the boy until Cynyr submitted.

Bánach clan no longer existed.

Victor Frey had been vicious and maybe crazy toward the end of his life, but he had been Rho. No hatred, however fostered and festered, was as important as the survival of his clan. Toby had lived in North Carolina the first eight years of his life, deep in Leidolf's territory. Victor had left Toby alone.

Robert Friar wouldn't hesitate to take children. He wouldn't hesitate to kill them. There had been kids at those Humans First rallies. That none had been killed was a matter of luck—luck and the furious defense of the lupi the Humans Firsters wanted gelded, imprisoned, or dead.

And so, in addition to bringing in extra fighters, Nokolai had gathered as many of its children as it could into Clanhome—children, and sometimes their mothers, and as many of their female clan as would come, too. Isen had also opened Clanhome to the children of their two subordinate clans in North America—Laban and Vochi, both of whom lacked the resources to house and defend all of their children at their own Clanhomes, though for opposite reasons.

"Is that why you haven't pestered me this past month?" Lily asked. "Because I've been living at Clanhome, and you can't manifest there?"

"No." He shrugged stiffly. "There's stuff I don't understand about this being dead business, but that's not why I was gone. I can manifest some places easier than others, but I can do it pretty much anywhere if you call me."

She needed to go. Still she paused, looking at the ghost of a man who'd been her enemy and was now determined to be her partner. Or whatever. "Tell me something."

He looked wary. "If I can."

"You killed that woman, or arranged her death somehow. The one with the Fire Gift. The one who killed your wife."

His face didn't change, but for a long moment she thought he wasn't going to answer. Finally he spoke, his voice entirely level. "I did."

"Did you enjoy it?"

The pause was even longer this time, and his voice was different. Husky. "Oh, yeah. I fucking loved it."

THREE

BEING dead sucked.

He hated it when she went in a car. You'd think the plane trip back here from D.C. would've been worse, but somehow a plane—at least a big one like the 757 she'd flown in—established its own space, a locus he could hang onto. He'd been able to hold together okay in the plane.

But cars were a bitch. Al Drummond sailed along behind the white Ford like he'd been tied to the bumper. He didn't have to work at it. That wasn't the problem. All he had to do was relax, and she pulled him with her.

He didn't feel the wind, the pressure of air zooming past, shoving at his hair and face and skin, making his eyes stream. That would've been fine. That would've been great, but he never felt the air anymore. It was the sheer speed that tattered him, made him into something that didn't feel, didn't have eyes to stream, didn't have ears to hear or any goddamn way to experience the world. Most of the time he felt like he had a body, even if it wasn't the same kind he'd had before he died. But not when Yu went zooming around in a damn car.

You were gone for over a month . . .

He'd lied to her. That didn't bother him. He was a good liar. It wasn't enough to just smooth your face out to official blankness. Any moron could learn to do that, but a good cop learned to lie, too. But it had been luck, not skill, that made this particular lie work. He'd been shook up enough for it to show, so she'd put his hesitation down to that.

And if she hadn't, so what? He wasn't going to tell her where he'd been.

Yu was right, damn her. He'd thrown in on the wrong side.

Twenty-seven years of law enforcement. Twenty-seven years of stakeouts, bad food, and the slow, painstaking build of cases some asshole of a defense lawyer couldn't shred. Plenty of failures along the way, but some triumphs, too. He'd been a good cop.

And he'd thrown it away. Wiped it out. It didn't take a genius to spot the when and why. The job had reached out in the person of Martha Billings and killed Sarah. He'd reached back to return the favor. Most people would say that's where he stepped wrong, where he made the decision that destroyed him. He didn't agree. It hadn't felt like a choice, like being faced with a decision he could choose or reject. Martha Billings had killed Sarah. Martha Billings would die.

She had, too. Burned to a crisp. Just like Sarah.

And Yu wanted to know if he'd enjoyed it. That memory was one bright, hot spot of pleasure in the endless gray his life had become the moment he learned Sarah was gone.

No, killing Billings wasn't where he'd taken a horribly wrong turn. Maybe that had been wrong, but only in the unstoppable way that cancer is wrong. Staying on the job after he killed her, though, hiding what he'd done—that's what twisted him. He should've done what he had to do and turned himself in. At the time, he'd thought that getting himself thrown in prison would've handed Billings a post-mortem victory. At the time, he'd felt that stopping Billings wasn't enough. He had to stop everyone like her, too.

At the time, he'd been bumfuck crazy. Which was why he hadn't noticed the other reason he stayed on the job. So he could piss on it.

The job had killed Sarah, and he'd wanted revenge on it, too. Only he hadn't known that's what he was doing, not until a month or so after he died, when he'd done what he'd told Yu was impossible. He left.

Getting himself fully, properly dead turned out to be harder than he'd thought.

Not that he'd seen extinction as the only possibility, but he'd been pretty sure that's what would happen. His world—the only world left to him—was about two hundred yards in diameter. Get three hundred feet away from Yu in any direction and everything turned fuzzy. Keep going and it got . . . not dark. Darkness was a lack of light, and out there in the gray it was like vision itself didn't exist. Out there was *nothing*.

Nothing had sounded like a damn good place to end up. He'd expected to become nothing, too, when he left Yu, though he'd conceded it was possible he'd get that white light people yammered about, the one that hadn't shown up when Big Thumbs pulled the trigger. Or maybe . . .

He hadn't really let himself think about that "maybe." He didn't deserve it. But it was like a rope—there were two ends to it, and if the end he held was grimy and black with guilt, the other end was as shiny and right as any of the angels he didn't believe in.

Mostly, though, he'd expected to die for good. Drummond hadn't believed in God for years, much less an afterlife . . . though Sarah used to tell him he wasn't a true unbeliever, just too mad at the deity to give Him the time of day. She'd been at least somewhat right. He figured that any God who let the sort of shit happen that he'd seen over and over wasn't worth much. Sure, you could blame it on free will and people being assholes, but if so, God had done a pisspoor job of creating when it came to man, hadn't He?

So he'd left, walking off into the gray. Pushed ahead

even when he didn't have any sense of a body, when there was nothing left of darkness or light, no whisper of sensation, barely the memory of it. Slogged on until he couldn't tell if he was moving anymore, until even the blasted whatever-it-was that tied him to Yu grew so faint he couldn't find it.

Maybe he'd stopped then. Maybe he'd kept going. He had no way of knowing. But still moving or just plain still, he'd waited. And waited.

At some point—it had seemed like hours, but might have been weeks or minutes, given how little time meant in the gray—he'd known he'd been wrong about that "maybe." Wrong that it might be even a little bit possible. Wrong, too, about how desperately he'd wanted it to happen anyway.

If Sarah had had any way of coming to him, she would have come then.

He'd broken down then, broken apart. Sobbed like a baby, and if he hadn't had eyes and a body to sob with, that made it worse. There was no Sarah. There would never be a Sarah for him again.

There was no anything . . . but him.

People think they know what *alone* means. Shit, he'd thought he did, thought he was more loner than not. He hadn't had the least damn clue. Broken, bereft of bones, breath, sight, hearing, touch, he'd known that the gray was hell, and he'd waited for hell to eat him.

It hadn't.

Not that he knew what had happened. Maybe, like he told Yu, he'd slept. At some point he'd drifted back to himself, wisping around like a bit of fluff so insubstantial that gravity was a lesser force than the eddies of air he floated on. He'd come back soft and slow and gentle, and found himself lying on a bed in one of the guest rooms in Yu's D.C. house. He'd come back knowing two things.

While he was away or asleep or whatever, someone had talked to him. Not Sarah, and he didn't think it was God, but someone. And he had to help Lily Yu.

However little either of them liked it.

What I want to hear, she'd said, *is that you've changed your mind about magic and the people who use it.*

People like her. People like her boss, who he'd tried to kill, and her fellow agents in Unit Twelve, and that damn werewolf she intended to marry. People like most of her friends and at least one of her family, according to the reports he'd read when he checked her out.

People like Dennis Parrott. Not that he'd known about Parrott's charisma Gift back when he was busy pissing on everything he'd spent a lifetime fighting for. Dennis Parrott had found him easy prey, twisting him around until it made perfect sense to kill Ruben Brooks because he was in charge of the magic-users in the FBI. Perfect sense to conspire to kill a U.S. senator—not that he'd known exactly how Parrott planned to do it, but that was no excuse—and frame Brooks for the murder. Perfect sense to do whatever it took to rid this country of magic.

Whatever it took . . . until he learned that his associates thought that meant killing twenty-two people to make death magic. Parrott and Chittenden had kept him in the dark about the death magic. They shouldn't have been able to do that, but he hadn't been at his best, had he? When he did find out, it had been almost too damn late. When he found out . . .

Al Drummond didn't deny one ounce of the blame that was his. He'd earned the hell that hadn't eaten him. But magic made the playing field too damn uneven.

And Lily Yu wanted to know if he still hated magic?

God, yes. Just like he hated the gun laws in this country that made it too fucking easy for bastards to blow each other away along with whoever else might be standing nearby. Didn't mean he hated guns—just the ones used by goddamn idiot losers who had no business being handed power like that.

That's what he hated about magic. That it could be wielded by losers at least as easily as by the good guys. That it could—like all power—turn a good guy into a loser.

He should have told Yu that. She didn't trust him, which

proved she wasn't an idiot. But he needed her trust. He needed her, period. Needed her more than he'd needed his mother's tit as a baby.

Just went to prove . . . if there was a God, He had one sick sense of humor.

FOUR

~

"I'M fine, Mother. Really." Beth Yu dropped to the floor, lifted the bed skirt, and peered into the crowded darkness under her bed. Nope. Not there. Which meant it had to be Deirdre . . . again. "The apartment may be small, but you saw it. It's in a perfectly decent part of San Francisco, and . . . he did? Well, you can tell Uncle Feng to butt out of—"

That, of course, was a mistake. While she listened to "Respect Your Elders" speech number twenty-seven she pushed to her feet and headed to the door of her closet, aka bedroom. Through superhuman organizational ability she'd managed to make room for her desk, but that's about all it held. That and a small file cabinet and the twin-size bed she'd swapped out her old bed for so she could wedge the desk in. When you were freelancing from home, you had to have a desk.

The door to closet number two—Deirdre's room—was three steps down the hall. She opened it and frowned at the debris covering every surface. Was it only two years ago that she'd lived like this, too? Back then, it had seemed deliciously hedonistic. Liberated. Now it just looked stupid. You couldn't find anything in a space this messy. Like shoes. *Her* shoes, which Deirdre liked so much she kept borrowing them, maybe because she couldn't find any of her own.

Beth stepped into the one spot of carpet that showed between piles of cast-off clothing and started digging.

When her mother paused for breath, she said, "I'm sure my uncle meant well, but I hate that he got you all worried. There's nothing wrong with this neighborhood. People can get shot anywhere. No one was killed, and it isn't like it was a gang shooting or something—"

Another mistake. Usually she handled her mother better than this. She started tossing clothes around as her mother explained how very stupid it was to assume it wasn't gangs when the police didn't know who'd done it, and if the victim wasn't dead yet, he probably would be soon, and if he didn't die, he'd probably be paralyzed. How was that any better? Not that she wouldn't far prefer to have a paralyzed daughter to a dead one, but this wasn't about her feelings, it was about Beth's safety.

Beth sighed and pulled out the big guns. "I really think this neighborhood is safe, but you're right, I have to be careful. I'll ask Lily to check those crime statistics for the area again. Maybe they've changed. I know she said they looked pretty good when I moved here, but . . ."

It worked. It worked so well Beth ground her teeth. Citing her sister calmed her mother as nothing else could these days. It was as irrational as it was infuriating. "You want to call her yourself? Oh, of course. I know . . . " Where were those damn shoes?

"And just what do you think you're doing in my room?"

She must have been listening to her mother more than she'd thought. She hadn't heard the front door. Beth looked up at the skinny girl lounging in the doorway. Deirdre had short, shiny blond hair, a nose stud, five piercings in one ear and three in the other. She didn't trust even numbers. "Looking for my—hey!"

Beneath the ragged hem of Deirdre's jeans were the sky-high hot pink wedges Beth had bought when she got her first check as a freelance website designer. She waved at her roommate's feet. "Take 'em off. No, Mother, I didn't mean you. Deirdre borrowed my shoes and I want to wear them, so . . . listen, can I call you back? It might be late, but—okay, tomorrow, then. Love you."

She disconnected quickly.

"You don't need your shoes now," Deirdre informed her. "It's Tuesday. You're going to the dojo. You don't do kung fu in wedges."

"I don't do kung fu at all, and I wear shoes to get to the class, which is not held in a dojo. Today I will wear *those* shoes. Which are mine."

Deirdre rolled her eyes and stepped over two newly redistributed piles of clothes. "You weren't this selfish in college."

"I wasn't buying my own stuff in college. Do you know what I paid for those?"

"They were on sale." Still, Deirdre sat on her bed—and a red sweater, a yellow and green skirt, and a pair of jeans—and unbuckled one shoe. "So who's the target?"

"I don't know what you mean."

Deirdre waved a vague hand. "You're wearing a new sweater—which I love, by the way, and when did you get it?—and you're desperate for your fuck-me wedges. There is a target." She handed Beth one shoe, and her narrow face lit in a grin. "Oooh. Are you finally moving on Sean?"

Beth slid the shoe on. "Sean and I are just friends."

"These are not just-friends shoes." Deirdre dangled the second shoe by its skinny strap.

"Anything more would be inappropriate, now that I'm working for him." Beth reached for the shoe.

Deirdre jerked it back, out of reach. "Nuh-uh. Not until you come clean. And you aren't working for Sean. He's a client, or his firm is, which is not the same thing at—hey!"

Beth had tackled Deirdre back onto the bed, snatching her shoe in the process. Beth rolled off, sat up, and bent to fasten the shoe in place. "He doesn't see it that way, plus he's hung up on the age difference."

"Hence the shoes and the sweater."

Beth couldn't help sliding her friend a grin. "Hence the shoes and sweater. "

Deirdre squealed. "Go you! He's one heavenly hunk of man, and what's a couple of years? Besides, older guys can be so considerate."

It was twenty years, not a couple, and Beth knew that ought to matter. It didn't. It just didn't. "He's picking me up in . . . Jesus. Any minute now." She bolted to her feet and hurried to the bathroom. She needed to check her makeup.

Deirdre pattered after her. "You need a spritz of my Opium—no, too obvious. He'd get his defenses up, and this is clearly an ambush. I know! That 'come hither' spell!" She dashed back to her room.

Beth didn't roll her eyes because she was redrawing her eyeliner. "I don't have time."

"It's super quick. I just need to find my grimoire—oh, here it is!" A muffled crash suggested she'd pulled it out from under something that hadn't been entirely stable. She appeared in the bathroom door a second later, leather-bound book in hand. "And don't give me any shit about not wanting to take unfair advantage. You know I only do white magic."

Beth wouldn't object on those grounds at all . . . since this spell was no more likely to work than any of her friend's spells. Deirdre was a complete null. On some level she had to know that, but she didn't believe it. Plus her "spells" were derived more from her own freewheeling creativity than any existing tradition. Beth had to smile. "I know you do. No compulsion involved, huh?"

"This is no more of a nudge than those shoes," Deirdre assured her, and began chanting what might have been Latin. Or maybe Sanskrit. She'd gone through a Sanskrit phase awhile back.

Just as Beth finished her mascara, Deirdre slapped the journal closed. "There!" she said happily. "He'll be paying attention now."

And that was Deirdre. A flake, but so openhearted you couldn't hold it against her. "Thanks," Beth said, and gave her a quick hug just as her phone chimed that a text had arrived. She checked and, sure enough, it was Sean, letting her know he was there.

Be right down, she sent, and grabbed the backpack with her workout clothes. Sean was courteous, but not insane about it. The apartment she shared with Deirdre and Susan—and wasn't it funny that one of her roommates had the same name as her oldest sister? They were alike in other ways, too. The apartment the three of them shared was on the fifth floor and parking was impossible, so Beth didn't really miss her car. Much.

Five floors hadn't seemed bad when her old college buddy mentioned needing a new roommate just when Beth decided she had to get out of San Diego. San Francisco was so crazy expensive she'd thought she couldn't swing it, but splitting the rent three ways made it work. Their third roomie was a complete workaholic—hence the likeness to Beth's oldest sister— so they didn't see her much.

After she moved in, Beth had realized she wasn't in as good of shape as she'd thought. But stairs made for a cheap workout. She could run up all five flights now. Running down them was easy.

When she hit the sidewalk, Sean's Beemer was nowhere in sight. He'd be circling the block. He hated it when others double-parked, so he wouldn't do it himself.

San Francisco was a lot colder than San Diego. Beth set her backpack down and slipped on her jacket, but didn't zip it. That would negate the effect of the sweater. She petted the buttery smooth leather and smiled. It was brand-new. A Christmas gift from Sean, and if he wanted to believe it was just a friendly way of looking out for her, he could go on thinking that . . . for a little longer, anyway.

A bicyclist whipped by, legs pumping. Two high school girls hurried across the street. An older man and woman walked past, talking about where to eat that night, and a young, dark-skinned guy with hair frizzed out to his narrow shoulders stopped, scowled at nothing, and turned and went the other way. The supremely well-built if rather homely

man who lived two doors down came out of his building
and glanced at his watch. Beth's eyes were busy, keeping
track of all of them, as she picked up her backpack.

The particular flavor of martial art she'd picked was
called Bojuka, an amalgamation of boxing, jujitsu, and ka-
rate. You wore street clothes to practice, not a *gi*, and it was
strictly for self-defense, not sport. Bojuka was all about
repelling an attack, and the first step was learning to stay
aware, to spot danger before it was on top of you. She was
getting better at that.

One year, one month, and two weeks ago, Beth hadn't
been able to repel any kind of attack that went beyond ver-
bal. Snark she could handle. People with guns, knives, and
muscles that had received a testosterone boost, not so much.
She'd been kidnapped through magic, but held by brute
force to be used against her sister.

She didn't want to ever feel that helpless again.

A shiny black and chrome Beemer turned onto her street
at the light. It was a monster of a motorcycle, brawny and
tough and sleek all at the same time. A lot like its rider.

Beth's heart gave a happy little jump as she slipped her
backpack on. She couldn't see Sean's face—the helmet's
visor obscured everything but his jaw and that lovely mouth
of his. But she didn't have to. She might not know his body
in the thoroughly tactile way she wanted to, but she knew
the look of it.

He pulled up to the curb, the Beemer's motor rumbling
like a ton or so of happy cat. "Hi, geek boy," she said,
swinging her leg over the seat. "You looking for a good
time?"

He flashed her a grin over his shoulder. "Helmet, party
girl. We don't play till the protection's in place."

She rolled her eyes but twisted around to unfasten the
spare helmet that was hooked to the tail. As soon as she'd
strapped it on, he took off . . . slowly. He drove carefully
when she was aboard, though she had talked him into taking her out of the city and opening it up twice.

Beth slid her arms around Sean's warm, solid middle

and leaned with him as he took the corner. Their class was held in a strip mall a good twenty minutes away, so she settled in to enjoy the ride.

She was glad she'd picked Bojuka in spite of the inconvenient location of the class. In spite of the fact that it had been Lily's recommendation, too. First because she had to quit resenting her sister. Both her sisters, really, but she was used to resenting Susan. Susan was the oldest, the brain, the good girl, who'd become a doctor and married a man with the right kind of ancestors. It was traditional, really, for the younger kids in a Chinese family to resent their overachieving eldest sibling, and who was she to buck tradition? But Lily . . . for years, Lily had been the rebel. The one who'd disappointed their mother, the target of Julia Yu's anxiety and nagging. Lily hadn't rebelled by getting in trouble—she was way too straitlaced for that—but by becoming a cop. An awesomely good cop. One who went around catching bad guys and saving people, and the country, too. One who was supposed to get a medal from the president herself in a few months.

In short, both of Beth's sisters were incredibly competent women. She was the cute one.

She did cute very well. It just wasn't enough anymore.

But the main reason she was glad she'd picked Bojuka was warm and solid along her front. If she'd gone for judo or something, she'd never have met Sean Friar. And that didn't bear thinking about.

FIVE

NIGHT checked in early at the end of December. It had been dark for hours by the time Lily curled up on one of the long leather couches with her warmed-up lasagna. The news was on—something about the sidhe trade delegation that had recently arrived in Washington via the Edge Gate—but the sound was turned down low, so Lily could ignore it. The air smelled of spices and tomato, ashes and woodsmoke.

The fireplace was dark and cool now. She'd missed the fire, just as she'd missed sharing dinner with the man now sitting at the big dining table, surrounded by paper piles and focused on whatever business shit he'd called up on his laptop.

Lily ran her thumb along the band of her engagement ring. She had to quit putting this off. The wedding was two months, one week, and two days away. Tonight, she promised herself, after she ate. She'd bring it up tonight.

Rule looked pretty involved with his business shit. "Where's Toby?" she asked, taking her first bite of lasagna.

"He and Emmy are spending the night at Danny's."

"But he had a spend-the-night here just last night."

"It's Christmas vacation," Rule said without looking away from the computer.

Until recently Lily hadn't known she had a parenting style. After Rule gained custody of his son last summer, she'd learned that she did, and it was very different from Rule's. Her parents had seen sleepovers as a privilege to be earned, certainly not something that could happen two nights in a row. As for mixed-sex slumber parties . . . Lily had to grin, thinking of her mother's reaction to that notion.

But Toby was not interested in girls as girls. He liked Emmy the same way he liked Danny and Michael and half-a-dozen others. That would change, and Rule would know when it did. The hormonal tumult of puberty was as unsubtle in its scent, Rule said, as it was in its effects.

Lily stopped shoveling in pasta long enough to sip some of a Merlot Rule had thought she'd enjoy. This was the lasagna's second warm-up, but it was still good. After all, it was, as Toby would say, *Carl's* lasagna. Isen's houseman kept the freezer stocked with dishes like this for when he was off, like tonight.

Having Carl around was a huge perk, she admitted. Not enough of one to entirely balance out the loss of privacy, but a huge perk all the same.

There were others. She didn't have to dust or vacuum or scrub the bathroom—was, in fact, strongly discouraged from doing any of that. Carl had a roster of young clan members eager to earn spending money who did most of the cleaning. Plus she could grub around in the dirt whenever she had the urge and the time, and if the gardens here weren't born of her planning or planting, destroying weeds was always satisfying.

In spite of the obvious perks, Lily didn't want to live with Isen. She didn't like the long commute. She didn't like the sense of being a perpetual guest, and she couldn't get used to the lack of privacy. But Rule would be much more at risk if they stayed at his San Diego apartment. So would Toby. So would the guards who tried to keep the three of them safe. That's why, three weeks ago, Rule had sublet his old place.

No going back. The only direction anyone had was *forward*.

At least here she could go for a run without wondering if someone was going to shoot her or the guard keeping pace with her . . . and that was the point, wasn't it? She and Rule were prime targets for the enemy, and Friar was still out there, plotting and planning on *her* behalf.

Which was why she needed to talk to Rule. They were targets, and they were getting married in two months, one week, and two days, and the whole world knew about it. The guest list included her entire family, of course. Also a state supreme court justice, a U.S. senator, and a few more state movers and shakers plus some Washington types—including Lily's boss, the head of both Unit Twelve and the Shadow Unit dedicated to fighting *her*. Plus a whole lot of lupi. Nokolai's Rhej would be one of Lily's maids of honor; their sorcerer was Rule's best man.

Rule wasn't an idiot, she told herself. He must have thought about how dangerous it was to hold the wedding at the posh resort where they'd put down that huge deposit. He'd probably be relieved she brought the subject up.

Why didn't she believe that?

Maybe because the invitations had already gone out. Then there was the spreadsheet he'd created. And the detailed seating plan. Lily sighed and took a healthy swallow of wine.

Unlike her, Rule was happy here. When she first realized that, it had disconcerted her considerably, but once she thought about it she understood. He'd probably prefer to have his own house, but living at Clanhome . . . yes. He spent a lot more time surrounded by clan now, and lupi need to be around clan.

He didn't seem very happy tonight.

Lily studied her lover, friend, and mate as she finished her meal. He wore what he usually did at Clanhome: jeans. Period. No shirt, no shoes. She was used to seeing him in dressier clothes, but he was eye candy either way, long and lean and powerful. His dark hair was untidy, as if he'd been running his hand through it a lot, and as usual was overdue for a trim.

As she watched, he ran a hand through it again. Gold glinted on one finger.

Lily smiled. A couple months ago, she'd said something to Rule about him wearing an engagement ring, too. She'd been joking. He'd loved the idea. She ended up telling him he didn't get to buy it for himself and he'd have to put up with whatever she could afford. She'd had to dip deep into savings, but she'd gotten a custom ring for him, gold and platinum with a little diamond, and given it to him for Christmas.

He freaking loved that ring. "I talked to Arjenie today."

"Oh? She's well, I hope." His eyes remained trained on the computer screen . . . both of his lovely, dark eyes. No more pirate's eye patch. The other wounds he'd received in October were healed, too, leaving not a trace of scar tissue to mark that battle.

But not all scars showed, did they?

"Yeah, she's fine." He seemed fine, too. Preoccupied, but fine. He'd kissed her when she got here, told her about the lasagna, and said he was digging through a stack of reports he'd been putting off. Between arranging the upcoming All-Clan and his duties as Ruben's second in the Shadow Unit, Rule didn't have much daytime left for handling the finances of two clans.

He hadn't asked what made her so late.

She'd told him anyway. He'd listened and nodded and poured her the glass of wine she was still sipping. There'd been no magic at T.J.'s scene or on the body; it looked like the coroner would have to determine cause of death. Maybe it really had been a heart attack that hit right after a major argument with T.J.'s suspect. She'd told Rule about Drummond's reappearance, too, though not in depth. More like a teaser to see how he responded.

He'd agreed that it was good to know Drummond

couldn't show up here at Clanhome, poured a glass of wine for himself, and dived into his neglected reports. Where he'd been buried ever since.

Lily swirled the dark red wine in her glass. One of the tricky things about being part of a couple was knowing when to poke and probe and when to leave the other one alone. Truth was, she was better at the poking. She wasn't chickening out on the talk she needed to have . . .

Yes, she was. Lily sighed, took a last swallow of wine, and put down her glass. "I need to talk to you about the wedding."

"Oh?" He did at least look up.

"I think we need to move it here, to Clanhome."

"No."

"That's it?" Her voice rose. "That's it—'no'? Not 'I don't agree, but let's talk.' Not 'I don't agree, and here's why.' Just 'no.' "

He tunneled a hand through his hair. "Hell. I did that all wrong. I don't agree because that would be letting the bastards win. And I don't want to talk about it tonight. Not tonight, but we'll talk."

She looked at him a long moment. "Okay."

" 'Okay'? That's it?"

"We'll talk, but it can wait a day or two. Where's Isen?" Rule got along well with his father, but there was some strain, living in his father's house. His Rho's house. Maybe they'd argued.

"He went for a run."

"Training or four-footed?"

"He Changed first."

Her eyebrows lifted. "Again? Is he . . . Hannah's death hit him hard." Harder than Lily had expected, but she hadn't known that the previous Rhej had been Isen's oldest lover as well as his friend, not until after she died. Ham and eggs, Laurel and Hardy, lupi and secrets—they went together every damn time.

"It did, but that's not the reason." He sighed and, at last, really looked at her. "Today is Mick's birthday."

Mick . . . Rule's half brother, several years older. Mick, who'd killed and conspired to frame Rule for it, longstanding envy ripened into madness by an ancient staff and the crazy telepath who'd wielded it. Mick, who had died the same night Lily killed Helen. Died saving Rule's life.

She felt as if she'd been punched in the stomach. "I didn't know. I should have." Rule had mentioned Mick's birthday last year—not the exact date, but that his father had gone off by himself for two days on the anniversary of his second son's birth.

"Isen didn't want you thinking about it. You would have been careful with him. That would have annoyed him."

Was Rule talking about his father or himself? Didn't matter, she decided, and set her glass down and stood.

Rule had the sexiest eyebrows she'd ever seen on a man. Even when they drew down like they did now in a go-away frown, they were a total turn-on. "I'm okay, Lily."

"I know. But 'okay' is a pretty roomy place, isn't it? Room for all sorts of stuff you do not want to talk about. I get that."

His fingers tapped on the table rather the way a cat's tail twitches when it's annoyed. "Think you know me pretty well, do you?"

"Yeah, I do. Especially the parts that are a lot like me, like when you work really hard so you don't have to think about something. The problem is, now that I've forced you to talk about the thing you weren't thinking about, it's going to be harder to cram yourself down into those reports."

"It will be easier once you stop talking about it."

She nodded as she reached him. "That's one option, but it will be a bitch, won't it? Pretending you give a damn about, uh . . ." She tilted her head to read the heading on one page. "EPS."

His mouth tightened—but maybe that was because he'd had to work to keep it from twitching. "Earnings per share is a vital part of analyzing a stock's potential."

"I'm sure it is." There was just enough room, she judged,

and slid one leg over his lap, and sat. "Kind of crowded here."

His hands came automatically to her hips. Large, warm hands, their heat all on the surface at first. . . . "Lily—"

"I was thinking you might have to up the ante, go for physical distraction since I've made the mental sort harder." She threaded her hands together at his nape. "I was also thinking that this is the first time we've ever had the house completely to ourselves."

Oh, yeah, his did twitch this time. "No Carl."

"No Isen."

"No Toby." His hands shifted slightly, but the motion seemed more restless than caressing. "It seems more appropriate to distract myself with work than with pleasure."

Lily had never lost a sibling. Both her parents were alive. She didn't really know what Rule was feeling, but . . . "My father's mother is extremely alive, but his father died before I was born. Grandmother has observed his birthday every year."

"I didn't know that."

"When I was a kid, it was a mandatory family thing. We'd go to Grandmother's every April sixteenth and eat ourselves sick—Chinese food for dinner, followed by an array of American-style desserts starring an enormous birthday cake. She and my father would talk about Grandfather. She wanted us to know him, but she also wanted a party. Birthdays, she says, are for celebrating life, and neither grief nor death erases the life someone lived." She smiled slightly. "Mother is more traditional, which is funny, since she's third generation, while Grandmother is so very Chinese. Have I told you about Qingming?"

"I don't think so."

"Mother observes Qingming every year by taking flowers to the graves of her ancestors—first her grandparents', then her parents' graves. So that's how I honor my grandparents on her side, because that's how she does it. But every April sixteenth, I have a Grandfather cupcake."

"Did you do that this year?"

"Yes. Should I have told you?"

"Probably. As I should have told you that today was Mick's birthday." He was silent a moment, and still, his eyes losing focus as he looked inward. "Mick was an asshole sometimes. He wrapped up all his problems in me so he wouldn't have to deal with them."

She said nothing, but she listened hard.

"He wasn't an asshole all the time." Rule's sudden grin delighted her. "He knew how to have fun. When I was twenty, he took me to Tijuana for my birthday."

"Maybe I shouldn't hear the details of that celebration."

"Among other things, I learned that it is possible for a lupus to get drunk. It takes real dedication and the condition is extremely short-lived, but it is possible."

"Do I want to know how you achieved that?"

"Five quarts of tequila downed as fast as I could swallow."

"Did they come back up as fast as you could vomit?"

"I staggered and giggled for a few minutes, felt queasy a couple more, then both nausea and intoxication faded."

"That's it? No hurling, no hangover?"

"I did have to piss most urgently."

"Life is just not fair."

"Lily."

"Yeah?"

"I love you."

She smiled and tipped her head and kissed him—softly at first, but as his breathing quickened she put more effort into it. When she straightened, one of his hands had shifted well north of her hip, while her hands were enjoying all that lovely bare skin along his shoulders and chest. Her smile this time was wicked. "I promise I won't be careful with you."

Words could be overrated. He omitted them entirely in his reply.

She was bare to the waist and extremely distracted a few moments later when her mate abruptly straightened, his head tipped ever so slightly. It was a posture she recognized.

"What did you . . . oh, God. Isen." Rule must have heard his father returning. She looked around frantically for her shirt—saw it on the floor, but not her bra—

"Not my father." He pushed his chair back, his face still distant. Listening.

She clambered to her feet, bent, and snatched her shirt—and there was her bra, under the table. She snatched it up. "What, then?"

"You didn't hear it? No, obviously not." Rule grabbed his phone from the table. "Something just blew up."

SIX

⟞

"SHIT." Lily hooked the bra around her waist, twisted it, slid her arms in, and yanked it up.

Rule tapped the screen on his phone. "Isen didn't take his phone with him. Or his guards."

"Double shit." Bra in place, she reached for her shirt.

The phone—the landline—rang. Rule had his phone to his ear. He gestured at her to take it. "If it's Pete, put him on speaker."

She hurried to the old-fashioned stand the phone rested on and snatched up the receiver. "This is Lily."

"I need the Rho," the second-in-command of clan security told her.

"He's on a run. Alone. Rule wants me to put you on speaker." Lily did that, set the receiver down, and tugged her shirt over her head. "Rule is talking to someone on his mobile, but he—"

"I called Hammond," Rule said, sliding his phone in a pocket as he joined her. "He lives near the draw where Isen often runs. He'll cast for Isen's trail. Pete, what happened?"

"Don't know yet, but there's a fire halfway up Big Sister."

"Halfway?" Rule asked sharply. "Which side?"

"East. It's not big yet, but I can see the glow from here. Hang on." Lily heard a voice in the background, then: "You heard?"

"Two patrols near Big Sister have reported an explosion," Rule said, "and are on their way to investigate."

"Yes. Lily said Isen's on a run alone."

"He's alive." Rule said that with calm authority. He would know, of course. If his father had been killed, the full mantle would have descended on him. "I don't know where he is, but he's alive. Call full alert. I'm switching to my earbud. Call me on my mobile." He touched the disconnect button.

An explosion and fire on Big Sister. Lily had stuffed her feet into her shoes while Pete reported. Now she raced for the bedroom she and Rule shared. Big Sister was the tallest peak in Clanhome. The view from the top was spectacular, but getting there was a bitch and a half. Halfway up, though, wasn't a bad hike even for the two-legged.

She grabbed her purse and shoulder harness. "Benedict's cabin?" she called. Benedict had a propane tank up there. That would make a nice, big boom.

"That's on the west face, not the east."

She knew that. Or should have. Lily ran back to the great room. Rule stood just this side of the entrance hall. He'd opened a small door set into the wall, revealing what looked like the control board for a security system. He wore his earbud, and his face said "listening" again. "Good. I want Cynna here, fast. Triple the detail on Toby. Send Cullen to deal with the fire. He's to take a squad with him to—yes, just one. Every other squad mobilized, but hold them at their meet-points until we know more. Pick someone with a good nose and set him on Isen's trail."

The lights went out as Lily passed Rule, stepping into the entrance hall. Full alert meant the Rho's house went dark. She paused, letting her eyes adjust, and used the moment to slip on her shoulder harness. "The fire's a diversion."

Rule's voice came from right behind her. "I think so, yes. Or possibly Isen took his run up on Big Sister and precipitated an incident." He moved past her, a whisper of sound and warmth in the dark. A second later she heard a door open.

It wasn't completely black. The windows in the great room weren't draped, so some light spilled in from that end of the hall. But the moon was only a couple of days past new, so that wisp of illumination was too thin for human eyes. Lily trailed her fingers along the wall to guide her.

"Here," Rule said, giving her a target.

She brushed past him and entered Isen's study—where it was truly, deeply dark, being a completely interior room. When the light was on, it was a cozy and inviting room with floor-to-ceiling bookshelves, a desk in one corner, a small bassinet in another, and four cushy chairs grouped in the middle. The walls and ceiling were reinforced with steel. The trapdoor that opened on the emergency escape tunnel was hidden beneath a fine old Persian carpet.

Lily stopped just inside and waited for Rule to shut the door and turn on the lights.

"I'm leaving the door open until Cynna gets here with the baby," he told her. "I'll have to switch to the landline then, but until . . . yes." The last was apparently addressed to Pete. "I see. Lily, call Benedict. His mobile number is star four. Brief him. Pete can't raise the patrol that was on Big Sister at the time of the explosion."

Rule was in full Rho-mode, which meant tossing out orders, not requests, but Lily wasn't going to quibble over phrasing. Benedict had to be told, and she wasn't useful otherwise at the moment. She moved farther into the room, feeling for the desk. She'd need the landline; there was too much metal in the walls for her mobile phone.

She found the desk and the phone, propped her rump on one and lifted the receiver of the other, causing the number pad to light up. She tapped the star key, then the four, and waited.

Benedict was Rule's oldest brother, the head of security

for the clan, and absent. That was highly unusual, but so
was being gifted with a second Chosen by the Lady, which
was the reason he wasn't at Clanhome. He'd traveled across
the country to spend the holidays with Arjenie's family.
Then, right after the holiday, they'd had to go to D.C. Benedict's Chosen was Arjenie Fox, a researcher for the Bureau
with a secret heritage: she was part elf. She hadn't seen her
father in years, but he'd told her a lot about the sidhe, so
when the trade delegation showed up in Washington, Ruben
had summoned her.

Benedict was also the only Nokolai other than Rule who
could carry the mantle if Isen were killed, since Toby was
too young. That made him a major potential target for their
enemies. If Isen and Rule were killed, Benedict would be
the clan's only chance to survive.

She could just barely make out Rule's bulk against the
rectangle of paler darkness that was the doorway. She couldn't
hear him much better than she could see him. He was talking
to Pete, but keeping his voice so low she'd need lupi hearing
to make out the words.

"Yes," a deep voice said in her ear.

"This is Lily. We've got a situation. Between five and ten
minutes ago there was an explosion halfway up Big Sister—
the east face—resulting in a fire Pete described as not very
large. We're on full alert. The patrol nearest the incident
can't be raised by phone. Two other patrols are headed
there to investigate, and Rule is sending a squad with Cullen to deal with the fire. Rule and I are in Isen's study.
Cynna and the baby will be here any minute. Toby's at
Danny's—Eric Snowden's son—with his guards tripled.
Isen's whereabouts are unknown, but he's alive."

"His guards?"

"He went for a run without them."

A moment's silence. "Mick's birthday."

"Yes."

"Hold a moment." He didn't wait for her to agree—
typical Benedict—but he wasn't gone long. She heard him
telling someone about the explosion, then she heard Arje-

nie's voice, though she couldn't make out the words. Then he spoke to her again. "I've informed the guards. We're vulnerable if we attempt to leave the hotel, so we'll stay here for now. Arjenie's going to increase the power to her ward, and I'll attempt to contact Mika and see if he's willing to stand watch."

"Okay. Rule, Benedict and Arjenie are staying put. He's going to see if Mika will keep an eye on things. Anything else I should pass on?" He didn't answer. Maybe he'd shaken his head, forgetting that she couldn't see him. But if he'd had something to add, he would have, so she said, "I'll call when I can and there's more information." She disconnected.

Then there was nothing to do but wait in the darkness. And think.

It wasn't that hard to sneak onto Nokolai Clanhome. It was too big. Over six thousand acres meant miles of perimeter to patrol, and even with the recent influx there weren't enough guards to survey the entire border at every moment. A single person could cross easily if he or she was fit enough for the terrain and savvy or lucky enough to miss the patrols. The trick was remaining unseen, unheard, and unsmelled once you got here. Lupi patrolled in pairs—one two-footed and armed, one four-footed, with onboard armament and a really good nose.

If you wanted to penetrate very far into Clanhome—say, all the way to the small village at its heart—you'd want a diversion. Especially if you were leading a small group bent on mayhem. The problem was, the diversion their intruder had chosen didn't make sense.

Big Sister was a relatively easy target for an outsider. The peak itself was on Nokolai land, but part of its rumpled skirts lay in the state lands that abutted the clan's acreage, and the terrain was rougher on the Nokolai side. Hard to patrol. A bomb set off there would certainly pull the nearest patrols that way, potentially opening a route . . . but to what? Lily pictured the area in her mind, but she couldn't come up with a target that was both close enough to Big

Sister for the absence of nearby patrols to matter, and far enough away that the intruders wouldn't be spotted by the patrols converging on the fire.

Fire. Maybe that was the key point. Maybe the intruder was counting on the fire to get big enough to require most or all of Nokolai's fighters, leaving the village relatively undefended. If whoever it was didn't know about Cullen's knack with fire, that would make sense. . . . except that this was winter. An unusually wet winter. There was more to burn on the east face of Big Sister than the west—more trees, brush, and general growth—but none of it was dry enough to catch readily.

Maybe Big Sister hadn't been the first choice. What was it Rule had said? Isen might have "precipitated an incident." Or someone else could have, like the missing patrol. Someone who spotted the intruders or was spotted, which somehow resulted in setting off the bomb in a less than ideal spot.

And she was diving off into pure speculation now, when what she needed was facts.

Faint but not distant, she heard yipping. That meant someone had approached the house who was supposed to be here.

"Cynna's here," Rule said abruptly—and in his normal voice, which meant he was talking to her, not Pete. "With Ryder. Toby's team reports all quiet there. Still no word from the missing patrol, but the others should reach the area any minute now. If . . . yes?"

Lily heard the front door open and a woman's voice murmuring softly: "Shh, now, we're going to see Uncle Rule and Aunt Lily, and yes, I know you want to finish eating and you will in just a minute, promise . . ."

"Hell," Rule said. "Warn Cullen. Cynna's here, so I'm switching to the landline now."

Lily shoved to her feet. "What?"

"Rick," Rule said—apparently to the dark shape that suddenly bulked in the doorway, blocking what bit of light there was. "Any problems on the way here?"

"Nothing," said a young lupi Lily knew slightly.

"Good. Take your post. Cynna, once you're in here, we'll turn on a light."

"Good, because while Ryder doesn't mind the dark, I bump into things. Lily?"

"Back here," she answered as dim forms moved against the paler shape of the doorway. Cynna was a good friend and fellow FBI agent, currently on extended maternity leave. She was also the new Nokolai Rhej, as vital to the clan in her way as its Rho. "You've been told what happened?"

"An explosion and a fire up on Big Sister." Her voice moved as she came into the room. "Cullen's off to—" She stopped, blinking as the overhead light came on. "Wow, that's bright. Cullen's going to go put the fire out."

Cynna looked a bit like a blond Xena who'd gotten carried away with body art. Lacy patterns decorated pretty much every exposed inch of her skin, and most of the unexposed regions, too. Anyone who knew much about tattooing would realize the designs hadn't been applied with a needle, however. It took magic to imprint lines that spiderweb-fine.

At the moment she wore jeans and a button-down shirt and carried a blanket-wrapped bundle that was beginning to bleat like a distressed sheep. "Firebug Asshole interrupted Ryder's dinner," she added, plopping down in one of the chairs and unbuttoning her blouse with one hand. "That's about all I know."

"We don't know much more," Lily told her. "Isen's off on a run. He went alone, which is why Rule's in charge. Rule, you learned something just as Cynna got here."

His face was about as closed as the door he'd just shut. "One of the nearest patrols got close to the fire, but had to retreat. Our intruder has burned some grass, a couple of trees, and one hellishly large amount of wolfbane."

SEVEN

WOLFBANE, aka monkshood, blue rocket, devil's helmet, aconite. There were over two hundred species in the genus, many of which had been used medicinally for hundreds of years. Landscapers still planted it ornamentally. It was a deadly poison.

The roots of several species contained a highly toxic alkaloid that the Japanese once used for hunting bears and the Chinese in war. In Ayurvedic medicine, aconite was said to increase the fire *dosha*, and traditional Chinese medicine considered it a remedy for "coldness" or lassitude. In Western medicine, it had been used for everything from a local anesthetic—contact with the sap caused first tingling, then numbness—to a treatment for various heart problems. Certainly it acted on the heart. It stimulated the cardio-inhibitory nerve in the medulla oblongata, reducing both heart rate and blood pressure, but there was a wee tendency for the heart to slow too much. In most mammals, though, respiration stopped before the heart did.

Werewolves were not most mammals, but wolfbane affected them, too. It made them sick. Deeply, miserably sick. Hence the name.

"What symptoms?" Lily asked urgently.

"Aaron is still puking his guts out," Rule said. "Will wasn't as badly affected and was able to drag Aaron away from the smoke and call Pete. No paralysis."

That was a relief. There was a woman—currently in prison and stripped of her Gift—who'd devised a way to combine wolfbane with other ingredients to create a smoke that paralyzed lupi. Best if that innovation did not spread.

Lily looked at Cynna. "How close does Cullen have to be to tell the fire to quit burning?"

"It depends on how big the fire is, but the closer the better. He won't be able to get very close, will he? Unless . . . how steady is the wind?"

Rule answered that one. "Too fitful up on the slope to predict. Unless it steadies so that Cullen and the others can approach from upwind, we'll have to wait for the wolfbane to be consumed before we can deal with the fire."

Lily gave him a look. "You've got plenty of clan who aren't lupi." Clan who were female, in other words. The daughters of lupi were human but were considered clan, and there were more than the usual number of adult females at Clanhome now.

Rule got a funny expression on his face, as if he'd taken a swig of what he thought was water and found out was vodka. "You're right. I didn't think of it, but . . . still, it would take them awhile to get up there, and the wolfbane should have burned up by then."

"Unless Firebug Asshole scattered wolfbane all over the place, so that wherever the fire spreads, there's wolfbane around to burn."

It took Rule five seconds to nod. Every instinct was arguing against it, she knew. Lupi didn't precisely coddle their women. At least Nokolai didn't. Southern California sprouted wildfires in the summer the way Iowa grew corn, and Lily knew that some of the female clan had been on fire lines before. But the instinct to protect went deep. Sending women out now, exposing them to possible attack from whoever had invaded Clanhome . . . no, that hadn't occurred to Rule, and it took him a moment to accept the necessity.

Still, he called Pete and told him that Mellie would be in touch shortly about an escort for the female firefighting crew she would put together. Then he called Mellie. Mellie Blackstone was fifty-something, tough as nails, and owned a small construction company. She was also on Nokolai's council of elders.

All of the lupi clans had councils except Etorri, which was too small to need one. Lily hadn't understood the function of these councils at first, save for the obvious: they advised the Rho. In a few clans they also managed the clan's financial affairs; in others they had ceremonial duties; in a couple they were responsible for overseeing the clan's youth. They also took on the day-to-day duties of the Rho if he were incapacitated or unavailable. Wythe's elders had kept the clan going until their mantle found its new holder in Ruben; Leidolf's elders were responsible for a great deal now that Rule held that clan's mantle, given how little time he was able to spend there.

But the most vital duty of a Councilor was never stated outright, which was why it had taken Lily awhile to figure it out. They had to be able to argue with their Rho. Not simply advise, but disagree loudly, firmly, even fiercely.

Most lupi are deeply reluctant to argue with their Rho. Many simply can't. The ability to do so if necessary was the most essential qualification for becoming an elder. Lily had eventually realized that this, rather than egalitarianism, was why all of the councils except Leidolf had at least one female member, and some had several. The mantle didn't include or affect female clan. Lupi did not—ever—harm women. So a tough-minded woman could look her Rho in the eye and tell him he was being an idiot when even strong-minded male Councilors might find it hard to offer more than tepid disagreement.

"I guess Mellie has firefighting experience," Lily said when Rule ended the call.

"She used to be a fire-jumper, and she'd kick my ass if

she knew I had to be prodded to think of her for this," he said wryly. "I'd appreciate it if you didn't—hold on." He touched his phone again, accepting a call.

It must have been good news. The tension in his shoulders eased. All he said was, "Good," before disconnecting, but when he looked at Lily his eyes were smiling. "Isen's on his way. He's fine, unhurt. Hammond found him at Snake Draw, all the way at the east end. Down there he couldn't see the glow from the fire, so he didn't know. They're headed back at a run."

Lily felt her own shoulders relaxing, too. The east end of the draw was maybe four horizontal miles away, but the first part of the return trip was anything but horizontal. Still, lupi were fast. Isen would be here soon.

"Excellent!" Cynna said, and, "Say, could one of you get me a diaper? She's about finished, which means she'll go to sleep, then in ten minutes she'll stink the place up. Regular as a clock," Cynna said proudly. "Thanks," she added to Lily, who'd retrieved a diaper and some wipes from the stash in the bassinet, and went on, "I was wondering if there was any way Firebug Asshole could have known that Isen wasn't here at Clan Central. That he'd gone off alone."

"I don't see how," Rule said, "unless we postulate a Nokolai traitor."

"And that's unlikely, I know," Cynna said, "but if the goal wasn't to pull attention away from an attack on Isen— or on me or you or Lily—what was it? Why hasn't something happened?"

"It's only been fifteen minutes or so," Lily began, then stopped. Cynna was right. If the firebug knew what he was doing, he'd have acted by now. The more time passed, the better their chances of finding him. Or her. Or them.

"Maybe it has," Rule said slowly, "and we just don't know it yet."

Lily drummed her fingers on her thigh. "When you want to figure out a perp's goal, you start with what actually happened."

Rule's gaze sharpened. "We went on full alert."

"Which meant lights out here, you and me tucked up in this room, and a squad sent to fetch Cynna and Ryder."

"A squad that reported no problems along the way."

"Rule." Cynna sat bolt upright, dislodging Ryder and leaving her breast entirely bare. "You also sent Cullen to deal with the fire."

Rule's face went tight. He reached for the phone—but even as he did, it rang. "Yes." A pause. "I agree. Send the closest two squads there, stat. He doesn't go in until they're in place. I'll call him to make sure he understands that." He ended the call and looked at Lily. "Someone or something triggered the wards around Cullen's workshop."

HINDSIGHT works a treat. Lily clambered up the steep path as quickly as she could and added up all the ways the perp had outsmarted them.

The key was the workshop's location. Cullen didn't always make things go boom, burn up, or stink to high heaven while investigating whatever magical conundrum had his attention, but the chances of one of those three things happening in any given month were good. There was a large sinkhole where his previous workshop had been. Still, some of the things he could make, some of the ideas he was working on, could be vital to the clan, so Isen built him a new one. That one was on Little Sister . . . the mini-mountain Lily was currently climbing. And the closest peak to Big Sister.

The saddle connecting the two was riven with crevices and such a tumbled confusion of rock that even a mountain goat would prefer to go the long way around. The intruder could be confident that no one sent to investigate the fire on one peak would stumble across him on the other, and there was no one on Little Sister to notice him. There were a few homes near the base of Little Sister, but none farther up, where the workshop was sited.

None that anyone lived in, that is. Hannah's old cabin was about two hundred yards from the workshop, but despite the current crowding at Clanhome, no one had moved in. It was still filled with her things, and because she had no living relatives, it would stay that way until Isen gave permission for them to be removed. So far, he hadn't.

Isen was in the steel-reinforced study now. Rule had run ahead so he could check out the perp's trail, and Lily was nearly at Cullen's workshop. Two lupi kept pace with her. She had her weapon, her purse, and a flashlight. She couldn't see in the dark the way they could.

She did know a few things about the intruder now. It looked like he'd acted alone—and yes, the intruder was a *he*, and he was human. His scent had told the lupi that. He was a thief, maybe a pro, and he liked motorcycles.

Cullen was fast, even two-footed. He'd reached his workshop maybe fifteen minutes after his wards were breached, and he'd followed orders. He hadn't gone inside . . . but he had nosed around outside, including looking in a window. That's how they knew the intruder was a thief—something was missing. José had shown up at the workshop with his squad while Cullen was cursing the thief, but he didn't send one of his wolves in to check out the workshop. By then, Isen had gotten home, and he'd altered Rule's orders. Nokolai had an explosives expert. Pete had sent for him when the whatever-it-was exploded on Big Sister, but he lived in a small town nearby, not on Clanhome. Isen had wanted everyone to wait for the expert. Even a really good nose might miss something if he didn't know what he was sniffing for. This guy did.

Lily couldn't fault Isen's caution. The intruder had already shown he knew how to blow things up. Plus the delay gave her to time to get to the scene before it was completely contaminated by Cullen and the others. Maybe. If she hurried.

The expert was there now.

While José and his squad had been waiting for the expert, though, they'd been busy. The four-footed contingent had found the intruder's scent quickly—fresh, male, and human. The wind was with them, too, so they had scent in the air and on the ground. They'd taken off after him. The thief had had less than twenty minutes' head start at that point. Not enough, not when he was human. They'd expected to catch him, and they would have—if not for the second fire. And the motorcycle.

The second fire was started with plain old lighter fuel, not explosives, and laid smack-dab on the trail the thief had taken. Laid with the wind in mind, that helpful wind that had carried his scent to them. The wolfbane-contaminated smoke took out five of the twelve-man squad immediately. Five of the others were affected to a lesser degree, leaving only two at full strength. Still, one of them managed to pick up a scent trail on the other side of the fire.

That's when the klaxon went off.

Lupi do not all react the same way to the same dose of wolfbane. The nausea is universal, but the degree varies, the duration varies, and some lupi have other symptoms. José was one of those who lost their sense of smell. He hadn't inhaled much smoke, so he was queasy rather than incapacitated, but his nose was horribly and infuriatingly dead.

There is little that makes a lupus crazier than losing his sense of smell. Maybe that had led José into error, or maybe he'd have done the same thing had his sniffer been at full strength. He ignored the klaxon as an obvious attempt to lead them away from the real trail—the scent trail he could no longer detect, but two of his wolves had it. He and the remaining squad members took off down that trail, crossing onto state land.

Then they heard the dirt bike . . . half a mile of very rough country away. Right about where the klaxon had gone off.

When they got there, both motorcycle and thief were gone.

Smart thief, Lily thought as she crested a rise, breathing hard. The klaxon had been a double-dip of deceit. What kind of fool would set off a klaxon to announce his location while pursued by wolves? One who knew something about lupi, who knew they'd trust their noses over their other senses. Rule was investigating that deceptive scent trail now.

A man stepped out of the darkness in front of her. "Lily."

She couldn't see his face well without shining her flashlight in it, and that would be rude. But she did lift the light slightly. "Ah—David, right?" She'd met the leader of this squad at some point—tall, with a blocky build and reddish brown hair, but mostly what she remembered was the mustache. Very few lupi kept any facial hair.

"Yes. This is the perimeter Merowitch suggested should be safe."

Merowitch was the explosives guy. "He's in the workshop still?" When David nodded, she said, "I need to talk to Cullen."

"He's at the workshop."

"Dammit, he was told—"

"Not inside," David said quickly. "But Isen didn't tell him to stay away from the workshop—just not to go inside. He, ah, takes orders very literally. And only," he added with justified exasperation, "from his Rho or Lu Nuncio. Or so he informed me."

That sounded like Cullen. "Does he have some reason to think that's safe, or is he just being an asshole?"

"He did some kind of spell and said he didn't find any explosives—but he thought we should all wait on Merowitch's okay, just to be sure. But if he isn't sure, he shouldn't be there."

"I'll take care of it," she assured him, and raised her voice. "Cullen? I'm heading down there to talk to you."

A voice floated up from the darkness. "Like hell you are!"

"Lily?" David said, worried. "You can't—"

She patted him on his arm as she passed him and kept her voice raised. "If it's safe enough for you, it's safe enough for me."

"Dammit, David, can't you stop one little bitty human female?"

Either David had caught on or he was truly appalled. "You want me to physically restrain a Chosen? Rule's Chosen?"

"She's not going to shoot you," Cullen called back. "I don't care what she says, she won't shoot."

That made Lily grin as she picked her way down the path. "I don't threaten what I won't do." There were trees on this side of the ridge—pine and scrub oak, mostly—and the trail down was steep and skid-inducing, with scree and pine needles. She kept her flashlight on the ground right in front of her, but farther down she could see light through the branches. It wasn't very bright, but it gave her a target. She could hear something, too—Cullen cursing as he hurried up the trail toward her. The light brightened as he got close, resolving into a small ball of pure light floating just ahead of a half-naked man who could have given nine out of ten Hollywood stars a run for their money.

Ten out of ten, if he hadn't been scowling so hard. "Did it even occur to you that I wouldn't be down there if it wasn't important?" Cullen demanded as he came to a stop in front of her.

"Important and urgent aren't the same thing. Are you going to behave, or should I tell Cynna?"

"Cynna would understand. If there was a firebomb, I could put it out, couldn't I? But there isn't. I did a quick Find spell."

She didn't say a word.

"I may not be a Finder, but my spell's pretty good."

She kept looking at him.

"And don't tell me I proved anything by coming up here to stop you. If something did blow, I'd heal. You wouldn't."

She glanced back over her shoulder, where David and the rest of the squad waited—all of whom were every bit as good at healing as Cullen—then looked back at him, eyebrows raised.

"All right, all right. But it was important enough to take a small risk." Cullen ran a hand through his hair—something he'd been doing a lot of, judging by the way it was spiked up all over. "You don't have to mention this to Cynna."

"I need to know about the prototype that's missing."

"Yeah, well, I need to know how the rat bastard got through my second ward, which I can't figure out from up here."

"We can start there. What does your second ward do?"

"Stops kids."

"I'm pretty sure the perp isn't a kid."

Cullen waved one hand impatiently. "It takes too much power to outright block people with a ward. If I could figure out how they used to do it, using ley lines to—never mind. The point is, I can keep out fleas and scorpions. Flies are harder. So are kids. You tell kids they can't go somewhere, they're immediately going to want to check it out. Can't have that. Aside from the sheer nuisance of having them sneak into the workshop, it isn't safe. So I added a second ward. If someone crosses it, a wall of flames springs up around the building."

Lily's eyes widened. "You'd risk burning nosy kids?"

"It won't burn anything."

"I thought you couldn't do illusions."

"It's real fire. It just doesn't burn anything."

"But—"

Cullen rolled his eyes. "Look, let's skip the explanations. You wouldn't understand 'em anyway. I've got three wards on the workshop. The first one's the keep-away. There's layers to that one, but it's basically a single ward. It makes anything with a nervous system deeply reluctant to go farther. A motivated adult—or a kid being egged on by his buddies—can summon the determination to keep going. Or you can hit it at a run and be through before you have time to stop." He stopped, his scowl returning. "The rat bastard wasn't running, so he—"

"You know that how?"

"Tracks. He left some clear prints, so I know he walked through the first ward. But like I said, if someone's determined enough, he can do that. But then he should have set off my second and third wards. The third ward worked. That's strictly a warning to me that there's an intruder. But the second one didn't. No pretty flames."

"Pretty flames that don't burn," Lily said. "Maybe he knew that and kept going."

"It's real fire," Cullen said again. "Even if he somehow knew it wouldn't burn him, he'd have a hard time talking himself into walking into it. He wouldn't just see it and hear it—he'd feel the heat. It should have at least slowed him down. But that doesn't matter, because the ward wasn't triggered."

"You're sure? With the way your workshop's tucked away in this cleft, you wouldn't have seen the flames from Big Sister, and since they don't burn anything there would be—"

He snorted in disgust. "What do you think I was doing just now? I can see the power loss if one of my wards gets triggered. That one wasn't, so I was looking for signs of tampering."

"Did you find anything?"

"No, but someone dragged me away before I could finish."

"Okay. We'll come back to that. Tell me about this prototype the rat bastard stole."

"Have you listened to me at any point in the last month?"

"You've been working on a thingee that shields tech from ambient magic. You thought you had it figured out, but the device didn't work."

"Oh, it works, aside from a little problem with sporadic discharge. Unfortunately, the side effects preclude using it."

"Did you tell me about side effects? Because I don't remember that. I remember you found out it had a problem when you did a demo for some bigwigs from a tech company."

"The demo didn't go well." He brooded on that a moment. "T-Corp knew it wasn't ready for production—I told them about the unpredictable discharge—but they wanted a demo anyway. I agreed. We'd tested it plenty here at Clanhome. How was I to know it would affect nulls that way?'

He definitely hadn't told her this part. She'd have remembered. "What does it do to nulls?"

But she'd lost him. His head came up, alert and listening. Without a word, he spun and sprinted back down the slope, nimble as a deer or a cat—more like the cat, she thought sourly, since he could see in the dark. "Am I about to be blown up?" she asked the empty air.

"Merowitch gave the all clear," David said from behind her—right behind her, though she hadn't heard him approach. "I imagine that's why Seabourne took off."

Cullen might have taken two seconds to mention that. "I need to get down there before he tramples over any evidence the thief left."

EIGHT

LILY had never been to Cullen's workshop. He discouraged visitors of any sort, but especially her. That wasn't personal. The minute trace of magic her touch siphoned off made no difference normally, but there were some spells and charms that were fragile enough during some stages that even the slightest alteration might affect the outcome.

On the outside, it wasn't much to look at—a plain cinderblock rectangle with a shingled roof. There was no electricity, and water was supplied by a cistern that had been filled through a combination of magic and muscle. Eventually the building would be connected to Nokolai's water supply, but that was delayed for now. Too much other construction going on.

On the inside, it was a cluttered visual cacophony. Aside from the intricate circle inscribed in the center of the cement floor, it looked like a junk room with a few odd outbreaks of order. And it smelled like . . . everything. The scents were too many and jumbled for her to sort—herbs, ashes, leather, ozone, coffee, all mixed in with stinks both organic and chemical.

No wonder it had taken Merowitch awhile to check the place.

Lily had wrested an agreement from Cullen: she'd stay in the doorway if he would refrain from touching things. The door where she stood was set precisely in the center of the north wall. She could see well enough; a pair of mage lights bobbed around on the ceiling. There were three windows placed with equal precision in the middle of each of the other walls. Two of the windows held window boxes where a few brave herbs struggled for survival. In addition to being a sorcerer—which meant he could see magic—Cullen was Fire Gifted. Not a good match for growing anything but flames. Cluttered shelves sprouted along the two longest walls, almost as miscellaneous as their contents—three of them wood, two metal, one plastic, and one an incongruously elegant glass étagère.

The corners of the room held a ratty old recliner, a woodstove, a sink, and a cage. On one side of the circle laid into the floor was a long table—counter height, not dining. On the side nearest Lily was a perfectly ordinary looking pair of filing cabinets and a desk. The top of the desk held a lizard—alive—three Nerf balls, an ornate spoon, a surprisingly healthy aloe plant, a litter of papers, two pencils, a paperback book by Douglas Adams, a broken clock, a bottle of ink, and a small cauldron. And Cullen's grimoire.

It was large, covered in black leather, with a runic symbol of some kind on the front. Anyone looking at that would guess what it was. "Why didn't he take your grimoire?" she asked.

Cullen was squatting in front of one set of shelves, frowning at its contents. Apparently that wasn't enough. He leaned forward to sniff them, too. "He didn't see it."

"A lookaway spell?"

"Yeah. Though the one you're looking at is a fake." He rose to stand with his hands on his hips, scowling around at his invaded domain.

"I take it he didn't find the real one, either."

"I don't keep it here." He dropped to his haunches suddenly. "If that dung-begotten abortion of a thief got hold of my—" He started to reach under the table.

"No hands!" Lily reminded him firmly. "No touching."

Cullen swung his scowl around at her. "And how the hell am I supposed to know if he found my copy of Czypsser's grimoire if I don't look?"

"Smell?"

"Shit, the whole place stinks of him!"

She frowned confused. "Does he have an unusually strong odor, then?" The perp couldn't have been in here long. "Or did he touch a lot of things?"

"No." Cullen grudged that answer. "Go investigate somewhere else for a while." He turned away and stalked over to the glass étagère.

"Have you found anything else missing?"

"No." Cullen bent to study one of those outbreaks of order: an empty shelf. His worn-to-a-thread jeans looked ready to give up the battle for intactness any moment. His running shoes were equally ragged, and his spice brown hair stood up in spikes. He was as pretty a bit of eye candy as any woman was likely to see, and he was in a rage.

Not just pissed off. He'd been that earlier. Maybe it was a lupi thing, set off by the smell of an intruder in his space? Whatever the reason, he all but vibrated with anger. "Not," he added crisply as he stopped scrutinizing the barren shelf, "that I can tell for sure without *touching* things."

She nodded. "Makes sense, if he's a pro."

"A pro?" Brilliant blue eyes focused on her. His lovely mouth sneered at her. "He left behind my copy of Czypsser's grimoire! Do you know what that thing's worth?"

"He came here for one thing, got it, and got out. Didn't let greed make him linger because he knew he didn't have much time."

His eyes were even wilder than his hair, the blue flame-bright—and starting to darken. The pupils seemed to be growing as black ate into the irises. "If the rat bastard is a pro, he'd better be ready to be professionally eviscerated. When I—"

"Cullen."

"—get my hands on him I'm going to ask real nicely how he got past the flare ward, and if I like his answer maybe I won't—"

"Cullen!"

Cullen stopped midword. Closed his eyes, took a deep breath, and ran both hands through his hair. Again. "I'm okay."

The black had receded from his pupils, so she believed him. "Good. Let's step outside. I need to call the CSI team in. While we wait for them, I've got some questions about your prototype."

He fell into step beside her. "When I think about all the hours and hours of work I put into it, and then some—"

"Best if you don't think about all those hours right now. Think about how you're going to condense what you know about the prototype so you don't drown me in explanations." She paused on the other side of the doorway. David and one of his squad had taken up positions there. She checked her phone. No bars. She put the phone back and pulled out her flashlight. "Looks like I'll have to head up out of this ditch your place is in to use my phone." She glanced at David. "You'll keep the scene secured until my CSI people get here?"

He nodded. "I checked with Pete. Until further notice, I'm under your orders."

"Good. That includes keeping Cullen out." She started for the trail she'd come down a few minutes ago. "Cullen?"

"No one put me under your goddamn orders," he grumbled, but he followed. He even brought the mage light with him.

It provided plenty of light, so she flicked her flashlight off and stuck it back in her purse. "So what's the side effect that makes the prototype not ready for prime time?"

"It can create persistent, temporally displaced illusions in nulls."

"Temporally displaced . . . unpack that for me."

He shrugged. "Memories. Vivid, hallucinogenic memories of shit that never happened. Usually shit that couldn't have happened, like flying rats in goggles and aviator jackets."

"Flying rats."

"With wings. Dressed up like World War I pilots." He sighed. "That one came from the VP in charge of development. The really weird part was how little it bothered him. He clearly remembered seeing those rats flapping along beside the plane when he flew in that morning—he'd had a window seat—but the memory didn't strike him as odd. After we talked things out, he agreed that there couldn't really be any flying rats, so it had to be a hallucinatory memory, but he seemed to think I was making a lot of fuss about something pretty trivial. So did the other two."

"The other two?"

"I did the demo for four execs from T-Corp. Three of them were nulls, not a whiff of magic to 'em. One was a practicing Wiccan—Air Gift, not strong, but well trained. The Gifted guy didn't experience any hallucinogenic memories. The three nulls did. The fabricated memories all involved events that really occurred on that day between seven and four hours prior to the demo."

"If they didn't recognize the, uh, fabricated memories as bizarre, how did you find out about them? No, wait—I want to know that and a bunch of other things, like what the prototype looks like. But I need to call the CSI team first." She reached for the phone in her jacket pocket. "Do you have a photo of it?"

"No photo."

"What does it—"

"I'm afraid you can't call CSI," Rule said from the shadows partway up the slope.

She frowned at him. "Sure I can. If I don't have any bars here I'll head up the hill."

"Isen forbids it. That means less to you than to the rest of us, but this isn't a Unit matter. No magic was used in the crime."

Her first reaction was to call it in anyway. Rule was

wrong; MCD could only investigate felonies committed using magic, but she was Unit. She could investigate anything connected with magic, including the theft of a magical object. But if he wanted to, Isen could make investigation impossible. If their Rho told them to, every lupus at Clanhome would insist there had been no explosion, no intruder, and nothing was missing. Every damn one of them, including Cullen.

Including Rule.

"Cullen," she said, her voice tight, "how about you go burn something while I chat with Rule?"

"Oh, stop and think, Lily," Cullen said crossly as he brushed past her. "It's obvious why Isen doesn't want outsiders involved."

Not to her, it wasn't. "Well?" she said to Rule.

He sighed. "How did the thief know where to find the prototype?"

Ah, shit. Double shit. She should have thought of that.

There were other possibilities than the obvious. The thief might have conducted aerial surveillance. Photos that showed Cullen going to and from the workshop, for example, would locate it. But that was not the only way for him to find out. Not the easiest way, nor the most certain. Not the likeliest way. Her stomach hurt when she said it out loud. "Isen thinks there's a traitor in the clan."

"He believes it likely, yes. Or among our guests. Isen has called all three clans present at Clanhome to the meeting ground."

Her eyes widened. "All of them? Will everyone fit?"

"Some of the tenders are excused to care for the children, as are those guards needed for patrol and those still fighting the fire on Big Sister—which was under control but not out, the last I heard. Otherwise, every adult must attend. He asked that I include my Leidolf guards. I agreed, with the stipulation that Leidolf be questioned first."

Rule was Lu Nuncio to Nokolai—heir and enforcer, basically. Obedient to his Rho. He was, however, also a Rho in his own right. Rho to Leidolf, Nokolai's longtime enemy.

Two-mantled, some were calling him. Even at Nokolai Clanhome, Isen couldn't command the Leidolf guards. He couldn't order his son to bring them. He could only request. "Why first?"

"Most of those present will already be blaming my Leidolf guards. They must be shown quickly and publicly to be untainted. Lily, we need to go to the meeting field *now*."

"In just a minute. First I need to—"

"This isn't the time to argue. We have to go. My father is very angry."

"He would be."

"You don't understand. You've never seen him deeply angry."

No, she hadn't. She'd seen Isen laughing, kind, ruthless, annoyed, tender, and ready to kill. But deeply angry . . . "How mad is he? Are you worried he'll lose control?"

He hesitated. Only for a second, but that scared her as his words hadn't. "No. Of course not."

CULLEN accompanied them. The guards didn't. They were among those excused, which reassured Lily somewhat. Isen might be throwing a Rho-sized hissy, but he hadn't stopped thinking entirely. He'd left essential personnel on duty.

Some of them, anyway. The guards were guarding the scene, not investigating it. That's what Lily should have been doing instead of tramping back down half a mountain. That and calling in the crime scene techs, dammit.

For several minutes none of them spoke. Lily was thinking hard and not liking the answers she turned up. She figured the others were in the same boat.

It was a brisk, clear night. The sky was heavy with stars the way you only see it this far from the city. The moon was a thin fingernail clipping lodged high overhead. That would have been plenty of light for the two men with her, but fortunately Cullen had remembered that it wasn't enough for her. He'd held onto one of the mage lights and kept it bobbing a few paces ahead, giving her a good view of the ground and throwing weird shadows. The wind was soft, brushing at her hair and cheeks with airy caresses. It smelled of burning.

It would take them about twenty minutes to reach the meeting field, going at her slow, human pace. Might as well make use of that time. "Did you learn anything from the perp's scent trail?" she asked Rule.

"Yes. José and his squad followed the strongest scent trail. Usually that means the most recent, but not this time. The thief had laid a false trail earlier by taking off his shoes and going back and forth barefooted along one stretch. Had José been less distracted by his own loss of smell, by the sudden blare of the klaxon, he'd have seen that the footprints changed from shod to bare."

"Clever. He expected his pursuers to trust scent over sight. He knows something about lupi."

He nodded grimly. "Too much."

"There may be a traitor, but don't lean on that idea too heavily. Yeah, the perp could have learned about lupi from a confederate here at Clanhome. Or he might know someone who knows a lot about lupi—an *ospi* friend or girlfriend or whatever—or maybe he hacked into the FBI database. There's a lot about you there. Or he could just be damn good at research. He's a planner. Cullen."

He didn't answer. She glanced back at him—he was trailing slightly behind her and Rule, frowning faintly as if he found the ground ahead of him perplexing. She suspected he didn't even see it. "Cullen," she repeated.

His frown tightened as he looked up. "What?"

"Who knows about the prototype?"

"That it exists? Four executives at T-Corp and whoever they told. Also most everyone here at Clanhome—most all Nokolai, anyway. No one was supposed to speak of it outside the clan, so our guests aren't supposed to know, but some of them probably do."

"People will talk," Lily agreed. "And kids repeat stuff they hear—especially if they think it's a secret."

"Which is why," Rule said evenly, "silence was part of

the agreement between Laban, Vochi, and Nokolai. They are bound not to reveal anything they learn while staying here, except to their Rhos, should they ask. Children can't be bound by such an agreement, but the Laban and Vochi children have had no opportunity to speak with anyone outside Clanhome since they arrived."

Laban and Vochi were subordinate clans, which was basically a feudal setup. Their Rhos were subject to Isen the way a minor lord used to be to an earl or a count or whatever back when titles were more than an attraction for the paparazzi. Back when titles were connected to real duties and responsibilities . . . duties that flowed both ways. "Vochi's supposed to be good with money," she said after a moment.

"Abe trained me."

"Abe's the Vochi Rho."

"Yes." Rule's voice was tight. "I have a degree, but that only gave me the blocks to build with. Abe taught me how to build, what to watch for, how much fluidity to retain under various conditions, how to . . . he taught me so much. I can't believe—" He cut himself off abruptly.

That his teacher had betrayed Nokolai. That's what Rule meant. That's why Isen was so furious. The Vochi Rho could have learned all about the prototype from his people living here. He could have learned everything the thief had needed to know.

Lupi didn't have the same priorities as humans. To them, the possibility that a subordinate Rho had betrayed that relationship was a much bigger deal than the loss of a device that was potentially worth millions, maybe hundreds of millions. Or would be if it worked. Did the thief know it didn't work right? Lily tabled that question for now. It was vital, but not as urgent at the moment. Lupi took a really hard line on betrayal. No shades of gray. If a member of Nokolai betrayed the clan, that was treason. If a subordinate Rho violated his agreement with Nokolai's Rho, that was treason. In their world, treason had only one possible punishment.

If she wasn't really smart—and probably lucky, too—someone was going to die. Maybe tonight. "Laban would be in the same position as Vochi to learn stuff," she said carefully. "And they're a lot more competitive than Vochi."

Cullen snorted. "I doubt Leo knows how to balance his checkbook, much less how to sell the prototype. Rich in fighters, Laban. Poor in everything else."

That's what she'd been told. Nokolai's two North American subordinate clans were opposites. Laban was small, contentious, and bred good fighters. Vochi was small, wealthy, and bred too many submissives. "Vochi like money games. They're good at them."

Rule bit off a one-word reply. "Yes."

"The thief stole the prototype of a device that doesn't work."

"That . . . doesn't sound like Abe." Rule's voice loosened slightly. "Treachery doesn't sound like him, either, but to steal something that doesn't work—to betray everything for an object without value—Isen needs to hear this." He started to move ahead. Stopped.

"Go," Lily told him. "Cullen can walk me down. If we run into trouble, he'll burn it. It'll do him good. Go."

He hesitated a moment longer, then nodded and took off.

Lily and her fire-happy escort moved on in silence at the best pace her human feet could keep on the rough slope. It was maybe five minutes before Cullen spoke. "The prototype does work."

She sighed. "Yeah. I know." It was possible the thief knew about the side effects, too. And wanted them. She didn't know why, but maybe that's what had kept that abstracted look on Cullen's face. Maybe he'd been trying to figure that out.

After a pause Lily added obliquely, "Abe matters to him."

Cullen sighed back at her. "Yeah. He does."

Lupi were very black and white about treason. Traditionally, it had only one punishment: death. And traditionally, it was the Lu Nuncio who carried out that sentence.

NINE

～

RULE stood at the center of the meeting field on his Rho's right hand beneath glowing mage lights that blotted out the brilliance of the stars overhead. His heart beat slowly because he willed it so . . . but it was hard.

His Rho was angry. The stink of that anger rolled through him. He felt it in the very pulse of the mantle—a hard pulse, steady but a shade too fast. Out of sync with his own. This was something a Rho could do, use the mantle to pull any of his clan into an intimate rhythm. Rhos did it most often to steady a clan member whose control was slipping. Rule had done that himself. You didn't have to pull on the mantle very hard, not one-on-one. Control your own heart rate, allow the mantle to flow out, and the heart rate of the other fell in with yours. Fast, if you wanted to move them into action. Slow, if you wanted to calm them. Rule had never tried to spread his control over so many at once, but Isen had, many times. Rule had experienced it from the other side.

He should be experiencing it now. Standing so close to his father, his Rho, while Isen pulled firmly on the mantle, no amount of training was enough for him to separate his pulse from that demanding beat. But he carried a mantle, too. And Leidolf did not beat at Nokolai's command.

He felt dizzy. Disoriented. He was Nokolai.

And he was Leidolf.

He'd known that since the Leidolf mantle was forced upon him. Known with his head, at least, that the trace of Leidolf blood he'd inherited from a great-grandmother had made it possible for Victor to force the mantle on him. Victor had meant to destroy him with it. He'd failed.

Now he stood beside his Rho, surrounded by clan—by Nokolai—and his heart didn't beat with Nokolai. It beat for Leidolf. He held it to a slow, steady rhythm, and that was hard, but not as hard as it should have been.

He was Leidolf. He knew that in his heart now. Literally. He was Leidolf, and Nokolai did not command him unless he allowed it.

Isen was playing a dangerous game tonight.

"Bill Peterson," a voice called from the left.

"On duty," Pete said firmly. "Excused."

Rule's nostrils were flared, open to the night. The air was soft and cool and thick with scent—dust and skin, sage and grass, fear and anger, a whiff of menstrual blood from a young woman nearby. Most of all, it was heavy with the massed scent of lupi.

Nokolai. That was the strongest smell, the scent of clan reassuring even now. But Leidolf as well, a scent carrying so many of the same notes, yet arranged to a different tune. That smell, too, contented him, where it used to wake his nape to bristles. Also Laban. A musky lot, Laban. And Vochi. Quiet, unthreatening Vochi. Leidolf, Laban, Vochi . . . each was clumped up together not far from the center of the field.

Nokolai Clanhome was crowded these days.

"Josh Krugman," another voice called. "And Celia Thompson."

"On duty," Pete replied loudly, his voice crossing the response from the woman standing near Cullen saying the same thing. "Excused," they both said, one right after the other.

In normal times, most lupi did not live at their clanhomes. Nearby, yes, if they could, but lupi had to earn a living just as humans did, which for most of them meant living elsewhere. Some worked at Clanhome, either as guards or for the nursery or at the clan's construction firm. Others owned their own small businesses elsewhere or worked for human employers or companies. But a large number worked at companies owned by the clan in the three coastal states that comprised Nokolai's territory.

This was unusual. Until the Supreme Court stopped the government from administering the drug gado to any lupi it caught, Rule's people hadn't dared live together in large numbers. Most clanhomes couldn't house even half their clan's members, and clans hadn't considered it safe to have too many of their members working at the same place.

Nokolai was different because of Isen . . . and Vochi.

Isen had known for a long time that lupi couldn't continue to live secretly. The world had changed too much. He'd planned for the day they came out into the open; he'd worked with Wythe clan to make that happen, using the country's legal system. Even before that, though, he'd been preparing. First he'd created a pretext for gathering forty or fifty clan to him—the fiction that Clanhome housed a religious cult. In addition to the homes here, he'd built dormitory-type housing for "visiting brethren." After Nokolai went public, he'd added a second dormitory and additional houses.

Nokolai could, at need and with some crowding, house their entire clan.

Even so, and even now, not all Nokolai lived here. Many remained scattered in California, Oregon, and Washington, keeping their ears perked and their eyes open. That was both strategy and necessity. War was expensive. Nokolai was a wealthy clan, but even it couldn't afford to fully support all of its members for a long stretch. Not when a large chunk of that wealth came from the businesses it owned, where its people worked.

The decision to operate businesses that employed clan

had been Isen's. But he couldn't have implemented it without Vochi's help.

Vochi had always been a small clan, suffering even more than most from the limited fertility common to those of the Blood. It had always thrown too many submissives, too few fighters. Add to that a peculiar interest in accumulating wealth, and Vochi could have been the skinny kid in glasses getting picked on by the jocks . . . or, during times of clan strife, the skinny white guy who got caught on the wrong turf when the Crips and the Bloods were slugging it out.

Vochi knew this. They'd first submitted to Nokolai sixteen hundred years ago. Nokolai had defended Vochi ever since, and Vochi had done much in return for Nokolai. They were the reason Nokolai was the wealthiest clan—their acumen and, more recently, Isen's understanding that money meant power in the human world. And for better or worse, that was the world lupi lived in.

In, but not of. They had much in common with humans, but they were not human. The clans could not be run the way humans ran their societies.

Human crowds reminded Rule of flocks of birds or children, unable to tolerate stillness for long. He stood beside his father at the center of roughly three hundred mostly still and silent people. Mostly, because there were humans in this crowd, too—female clan, who were as quiet as they could manage. But most were lupi, with a wolf's instinctive understanding of the value of stillness. Most were Nokolai. Their Rho had called for quiet. They obeyed. Even with that hard pulse stirring them, they could hold quiet and wait . . . for now. As long as the rhythm didn't pick up.

But not all here were Nokolai. Laban, Leidolf, and Vochi had each gathered into a knot of their own, surrounded by Nokolai. They would be feeling the tension. They were close enough to smell Isen's anger. They'd hear the massed heartbeats around them, like a distant ocean. Leidolf would react to this differently than the other two. Rule held their heartbeats to a slow, steady rhythm. They were alert, but calm in their stillness.

Laban and Vochi were still, too—for a wolf's reason. Fear.

The gathering was not, however, completely silent.

"Your find didn't work?" Lily said to Cynna, her voice very low.

Cynna shook her head. "Mountains are tricky. I can find through dirt, but even small amounts of quartz will distort things unless I have a really good pattern. Which I don't. I'll work up a more complete pattern, but that will take time."

"Emanuel Korski," someone called from the rear of the crowd.

"On duty," Pete said loudly. "Excused."

"Matt Briggs," another voice called from up near the front of the crowd. Pete responded with the same two phrases: *On duty. Excused.*

Lily drummed her fingers on her thigh. "About Laban . . . they haven't been subordinate to Nokolai for very long, in lupi terms."

"Less than thirty years this time," Cynna whispered back. "But they've submitted several times over the years to different clans. This is their third dance with Nokolai."

"Because they're combative. They have trouble controlling themselves, so they need a dominant clan to sit on them. Vochi, on the other hand, throws a lot of submissives. They need a dominant clan for protection."

"Andy Carter!"

"On duty. Excused."

Six of them stood in the center of the meeting field—Rule and his Rho at the very center, with Pete at Isen's left. Cullen stood behind them beside a short, angular woman with iron gray hair, thick glasses, and skin that remained luminous in her seventh decade—Isadora Bourque, the chief tender, who answered for those tenders excused from the meeting, just as Pete was for the guards.

Lily and Cynna stood to Rule's right with their heads together to conduct their soft-voiced conversation. Lily had not run out of questions. No one else would answer them here and now, but Cynna was Rhej. Isen couldn't command her silence, and by answering Lily's questions she gave tacit permission for them to continue. Isen was ignoring the whispered conversation. If Cynna had chosen to sit down and paint her toenails, he would have ignored that, too.

But he hadn't had to permit Lily within the small group in the center of the field. Lily had assumed she would stay with Rule, but Isen didn't have to allow it. He had. There was a reason—with Isen there was always a reason, often several—but Rule had no idea what it was. Isen hadn't given him any private word, any guidance at all.

His heart beat steady and slow, out of sync with the rest.

Perhaps no one but he and Isen and Cynna heard Lily's next question. She kept her voice very low. "But the Vochi Rho himself is a dominant, right? He'd have to be."

"Right."

"And Vochi has been subordinate to Nokolai for centuries but has never been . . . what's that word? Oh, yeah—*subsumed*. That's why Leidolf doesn't have any subordinate clans. They used to, but they subsumed them."

"Becka Whitbourne," a voice at the east side of the crowd called.

"On duty," Isadora announced in her gravelly voice. "Excused."

The obvious way to locate a traitor was to see if someone failed to appear. Isen wasn't calling roll, however; he was calling absences. Or having them called out.

Visitors—both *ospi*, or clan-friends, and nonresident Nokolai—had been told to report to Pete. There were currently three clan-friends and two nonresident Nokolai at Clanhome, and they were accounted for. Mason and the two adults currently helping him at *terra tradis* were excused, of course. Adolescents couldn't be left unsupervised. Nokolai's guests from the other three clans had been told to assemble up front; Nokolai had been told to gather in the groups they were assigned under the emergency evacuation plan. Evacuation drills were held once a year, so this was a familiar way to assemble. Group leaders had been informed of the fire and the theft and told to pass that information on. Isen hadn't called for silence until they were all in place, and now the group leaders were announcing any who were absent.

So far, the absences were all excused to other duty.

"That's right," Cynna said. "Bad habit of Leidolf's—or of their mantle."

"And Nokolai hasn't wanted to subsume Vochi. Are they worried it might make them throw submissives?"

"It's not that intentional." Cynna chewed on her lip while someone else called out two names and was answered by Isadora. "I'm not sure I can explain it, mainly because I don't really understand. I think you have to be a mantle-holder to really understand. But usually a subordinate clan gets subsumed when the mantles mesh too closely. The dominant clan doesn't do it on purpose. It just happens. Nokolai's a good dominant for Vochi because their mantles don't mesh. Same with Laban."

Another name was called out. Isadora responded, then looked at Isen and nodded. "All of mine are accounted for."

Lily's voice dropped even lower. "And Leidolf meshes with everyone?"

"Leidolf just swallows," Cynna whispered back. "Doesn't matter if they mesh or not. Sooner or later, they subsume any subordinate clans. I think it's the high-dominant thing. Their first Rho was high dominant."

Two more names were called out. Pete responded loudly, then said much more quietly, "All of mine are present or excused."

Rule had expected to hear that. It brought him no relief.

Isen spoke, his deep voice rumbling up as if it came from the soles of his feet, magnified by his barrel chest. "Group leaders! Are there any others missing from your groups?"

Silence answered him. Rule focused on his breath. In, out. Slow. Deliberate. Calm.

Isen held that silence for a long moment. The pulse in the mantle stayed steady . . . steady, but too fast. Not calm.

When Isen spoke again his voice dropped to a low growl. "We are at war. We are at war with the Great Enemy. The Lady's enemy. And we have been betrayed."

There was a reaction this time. Not words, but a soft susurration, from dozens of indrawn breaths. A quivering in the air. Isen had named the stakes. War. Betrayal. He had told them there would be no clemency.

Isen flattened his voice. "I would speak first with the Leidolf Rho."

Rule stepped out from his father's side and moved to stand in front of him. He stood nearly a head taller than Isen. He looked into eyes shadowed by heavy brows set in a face carved by time and will into stone. His Rho's face.

But now, tonight, he was Leidolf. "I greet Nokolai's Rho."

Isen moved his head in the barest token of a nod. Rhos did not dip their heads. That would suggest a baring of the nape. "I greet Leidolf's Rho."

Rule inclined his head the same fraction of an inch. "Leidolf agrees that this is a time of war. The loss of the object Cullen Seabourne has been working on could be a blow to all the clans."

"Will you ask your people what, if anything, they know of this theft? Of this thief? Will you ask them here and now?"

"As a favor, and so that none here will be distracted by suspicions that take them on the wrong trail, yes. I will ask." Rule continued to face Isen and spoke quietly. "Leidolf! To me."

There were sixteen Leidolf at Nokolai Clanhome—the guards who took turns protecting Rule and Lily. Sixteen men who moved toward him with silent ease . . . and he felt them. That had never happened before. He hadn't known it was possible, but he felt his Leidolf clansmen moving toward him. It was nothing like what he felt through the mate bond, a sure and certain sense of where Lily was. It was far more subtle, more like feeling the faintest wisp of a breeze

on a hot day. Something stirred behind him, and he knew
what it was, that was all.

He turned. He let his gaze touch each of them briefly,
and he *knew* them. Knew them personally, yes, and of
course the mantle recognized them. But for the first time,
his knowledge and the mantle's recognition blended into a
seamless whole.

He knew them, and they were his. "Leidolf," he said, his
voice raised enough for Nokolai and the other clans to hear.
"You will answer truly and fully now. If I have given you
orders on some previous occasion which might cause you
to withhold information or mislead or lie, you will disregard those orders. Do any of you have personal knowledge
of this theft or of this thief?"

Some shook their heads. Some said no. A few did both.

"Have any of you spoken to someone not present tonight
about Cullen Seabourne's workshop?"

Most of them spoke their *no* aloud this time, firmly. So
that Nokolai would hear. One didn't respond. Rule's heart
gave a single hard thud in his chest. He controlled it quickly.
"Scott. You didn't answer."

"I wasn't sure how to answer. LeBron and I talked about
it some. He's not here."

This time the relief was real and vivid. Rule turned to
look at Isen. "LeBron died saving my *nadia*'s life. I can't
call on him to testify for himself, so I will speak for him.
He did not betray Leidolf or our alliance with Nokolai. I so
pledge on the honor of Leidolf."

Isen didn't react. Others did. Breaths sucked in, feet or
bodies stirred. Rule could have made the pledge on his own
honor. That he'd backed it by Leidolf's meant it could only
be disputed if Isen were willing to call Clan Challenge.

It was probably overkill. Rule didn't care. LeBron's
name would be honored, not smudged by doubts.

Isen nodded again, a fraction more deeply—
acknowledging a favor. "Nokolai accepts Leidolf's pledge
and thanks you for your help. Does the Leidolf Rho have
further comment or questions at this time?"

"Leidolf has no more to contribute at this time. We are on your land. We acknowledge your rights and responsibilities in this matter."

"Then I would speak with my Lu Nuncio."

Rule had switched roles with his father many times now, going from Lu Nuncio to Rho and back. It had sometimes been tricky in the way that a puzzle can be, but never truly difficult.

Tonight it was.

The Nokolai Rho wished to take him out, use him, then stuff him back into the lesser role when it suited him? And do so publicly, demonstrating to all that Leidolf answered Nokolai's bidding. That was . . . Rule drew a slow breath. That was entirely proper. When Rule first was thrust into the leadership of Leidolf, his Rho had spoken to him about the problems inherent in being Rho to one clan and Lu Nuncio to another. He had agreed that here at Clanhome he would be Lu Nuncio to Nokolai, not Rho to Leidolf. Tonight Isen had agreed to his assumption of the other role so he could clear Leidolf of complicity, but that did not abrogate their original agreement.

Isen had noted his hesitation. No doubt of that. Others might have as well. "I have thought of one thing Leidolf might do to assist. I would send my men to guard Toby, releasing more of your men to assist in other ways."

"I accept your offer."

Rule turned and gave quick instructions to his men. As they melted away into the crowd, he faced Isen again. This time he dipped his head low, baring his nape. "My Rho wishes to speak with me?"

Isen's face held no emotion. "Change."

TEN

~

RULE'S heart gave a single, frightened leap, but he obeyed.

The moon was new and hidden now behind the curve of the earth. It didn't matter, not for Rule. Her song was as much a part of him as his pulse. He didn't rush, not wanting to pull others into the Change with him. He *listened* and opened himself to moonsong, distant and muted and impossibly pure, and it slid through him like falling water. The earth answered easily, shooting up through him, and the two met and ripped the world apart, starting with his body.

The pain was instant and intolerable—and over, the memory of it lingering faintly like an afterimage of the sun imprinted on the retina. Then that, too, was gone. He stood on four feet in a world vastly different from what he experienced on two, his vision both expanded and contracted. Expanded, because wolves have a full 180 degrees of vision, compared to a human's 100 degrees. Contracted, because wolves are myopic—unless something moves. That they'll spot quickly even at a great distance, though the object itself may be an unidentifiable blur.

Even two-footed Rule's sense of smell was better than a human's, but in this form smells burst upon him, wrapping him in a more deeply dimensional world. The air was alive, textured with information more layered and complex than any of Rembrandt's paintings. His ears pivoted, helping him read that world. He heard Isen's heartbeat now as well as feeling it pulse through the mantle. He heard the throb of all the other hearts timed to it, and realized his own heart had fallen into that rhythm the way a rock obeys gravity.

Rule stood on four feet and felt a whine try to rise in his throat. This was worse as wolf. Far worse. Wolves live wrapped in instinct, and his were at war. Rule remained four-footed but pulled himself more into the man.

Sometimes thinking helped.

His own men were away from the crowd now, no longer surrounded by the scent of the clan who had been their enemy for so long. They would do well enough even if their hearts did beat faster for a bit. But he didn't want to be compelled into the rhythm. He was Nokolai and obedient to his Rho, but he was also Leidolf, and he would not be compelled. He turned part of his attention to his breathing once more. His breath answered him, but his heart didn't want to obey. Fear was clutching at him with clammy hands, trying to wrest control. He knew what the order to Change meant. He knew.

This was the form for Challenge . . . or judgment.

Isen signaled for Rule to resume his place at his side. He obeyed. Quietly Isen said, "Pete. Name two squads who are all on the field now that you trust completely."

Pete paused. "Seven and Eight."

"Squads Seven and Eight!" Isen boomed out. "Change!"

They did. Two of the newer wolves were inadvertently caught up in it. They immediately lowered themselves to the ground in apology.

"Seventh and Eighth squads—disperse so that at least one of you stands with each group."

Wolves began to move through the crowd. As they did, Isen turned slowly, letting his gaze sweep over the gathering. He made a full circle before he spoke again. "I require you now, all of you, to think. To remember. Who have you spoken with about Cullen Seabourne's workshop? About what he has been working on? You've discussed it with other Nokolai, of course. But perhaps someone who is not Nokolai was curious. Perhaps one of our guests. Such curiosity is natural, but you were told not to discuss this outside the clan, so you will remember if someone asked. Think about this. Call it up in your memory."

Silence. Several moments of it, hearts beating together . . . but not all of them. Not Laban. Not Vochi.

And not female clan.

The pull of that demanding pulse continued to build. *Ba-thump, ba-thump, ba-thump . . .*

Isen raised his voice once more. "Everyone who remembers being asked about these things by someone outside Nokolai will come forward now." Then he lowered his voice. "Pete. Make room for them. Forty or fifty, I suspect. Don't move Laban and Vochi."

Pete moved away and began directing those groups closest to the center to other parts of the field. Others began moving up in ones and twos. It wasn't silent now, not with so many moving forward or back, the inevitable *excuse me*s, feet shuffling as some shifted to allow others to pass. Lily was asking Cynna something again. She kept her voice so low that Rule caught only a few words over the noise . . . enough to guess her question. She wanted to know what happened to a subordinate clan that screwed its dominant.

Cynna's whispered response was clear to a wolf's ears. "Anything. It can be anything, up to and including clan death, if the dominant gets two other dominant clans to agree that a betrayal took place. But if the Rho of the subordinate clan admits his guilt, it's kept between those two clans. It's all on him then, see? Not his clan."

Ba-thump, ba-thump, ba-thump . . .

Lily asked what happened to that Rho.

Cynna whispered, "He submits and is killed."

Lily didn't ask any more questions. She waited. Rule waited.

Most of those making their way forward were female clan.

That, too, he'd expected. Women were the obvious targets for someone out-clan to question. Female clan obeyed their Rho, but they were human, not lupi. They obeyed the way a human obeys a policeman or doctor—from habit, from respect, from the assumption that the cop or physician knows what's best. They knew that disobedience had consequences, but they didn't have a gut-deep certainty that it was *right* to obey. And the consequences of disobedience were different for them.

Lupi didn't harm women. Ever.

A lupus who erred in a minor way was chastised physically. He might be given some onerous job as well, but the physical defeat was what mattered. It proved that he wasn't *allowed* to disobey; those with authority over him could force his obedience, and there was comfort in that. Comfort, too, in the simple expiation of guilt—first pain, then healing, both physical and emotional.

Women couldn't be punished physically. The idea was deeply repugnant. Besides, it would bring fear, not comfort. For a minor transgression, a female clan might be given chores, a stern talking-to, something along those lines.

Serious disobedience was rare, but it happened. When it did, shunning was the usual consequence for both male and female clan. During the shunning—which traditionally lasted from one day to one week—no one would speak to you, look at you, acknowledge your existence in any way. No one except your Rho. He was the only one who knew you were alive, who might—if he chose—meet your eyes for a moment.

Rule had been shunned for three days before he was named Lu Nuncio. Not because he'd disobeyed. His father had wanted him to understand in his gut how serious a punishment shunning was.

It had worked. Rule had had nightmares off and on for a year.

If a transgression was so severe that a week's shunning

couldn't expiate it, the punishment was death or removal from the clan. Of the two, lupi considered death more merciful, but both were extremely rare. In Rule's lifetime, his father had had two Nokolai lupi killed for major offenses. None had ever been banished.

But five female clan had.

One had been a thief. She'd stolen from the clan itself. Two had been simply troublemakers and liars who couldn't refrain from stirring up those around them. Another had nearly caused the deaths of two children through a combination of willful disobedience, arrogance, and stupidity. Each of those four had been driven to the destination of their choice, given a couple thousand dollars, and cut off forever from Nokolai.

The fifth one had caused the tortuous death of a Nokolai lupus out of petty vindictiveness.

Twenty-two years ago, Nevada, Texas, Georgia, and Mississippi still had shoot-on-sight laws for lupi who were in wolf form, though they were being challenged in court. Most other states still had laws on the books for locking up lupi in either form, but by then the lockup was only until they could be turned over to the feds. The federal government was enthusiastically pursuing its more humane policy toward Rule's people: catch them, brand them, dose them with gado, then allow them to lead "normal" lives.

Gado weakens lupi, depriving them of both strength and healing. It also blocks moonsong, preventing the Change. Lupi go crazy if deprived of the Change for too long. Different lupi react differently to the drug; for a few, the effects of a single dose linger for months.

Sheila had been angry at Carlos, a fellow clansman and former lover, and had turned him in to the feds. He'd been caught, branded, and dosed. Nokolai found Carlos after the feds released him, and hid him. That was no easy task back then. The brand on his forehead wouldn't heal until the gado was out of his system, and MCD liked to keep a close watch on branded lupi, hoping to catch others.

It hadn't helped. Four months later, Carlos still couldn't hear moonsong. He'd committed suicide.

Sheila was gone by then.

Isen couldn't let her repeat her crime. She could have taken vengeance on too many others by reporting them to the government, up to and including Isen himself. She'd proven herself capable of doing just that. So he'd had her smuggled into Cuba, where she was given the equivalent of five hundred dollars and left to survive. Or not.

Rule thought about Sheila as he stood beside Isen and watched clan obediently gather in front of their Rho. Any lupus who had done what Sheila had would have been put to death. But his people did not hurt women. Ever.

With one exception.

Their Lady understood her people. She'd never told them to protect women, no more than she'd instructed them to love their children, fight their enemies, or revel in the bliss of running four-footed. They did those things because they were as she'd made them. Because she knew this, one of the very few laws she'd given them was that any clan member who willfully and knowingly assisted the Great Enemy was to be put to death. Any clan, male or female.

The Lady's law must be followed. Isen had no choice. Neither did Rule.

What happened tonight depended on many things. It was possible a male clansman had revealed details about Cullen's workshop and his project, but it was far more likely to have been a female clan. But who had she spoken to? What were her motives? Speaking when she shouldn't might result in benefit to the enemy, but stupidity wasn't punishable by death.

Rule breathed slowly and carefully and told himself he was not nauseous. His body would heal nausea, so what he felt was tension, not illness. Isen understood the difference between accidental aid and intentional. He was no fool.

But he was very angry.

"Squads Seven and Eight!" Isen called out. "Do you

smell guilt? Is anyone in your group lying by remaining behind?"

Rule couldn't see what the four-footed guards did. Vochi blocked his view to the right, Laban to the left, and those who'd been brought up front for questioning blocked the rest. He didn't turn around to look—not until Isen began to turn in a slow circle. Then he kept pace, staying at his Rho's side.

At the back of the crowd to the south, a wolf yipped. To the east and much closer, another one did. Two reluctant witnesses had been identified.

"Bring them forward," Isen commanded. Then, in an ordinary voice, he said, "Lily."

She was behind Rule and to his right. "Yes?"

"I told you once that a Rho does not question his clan directly. That was an exaggeration, but the basic principle is true. This is not yet a matter of trial and accusation. I would like you to ask the questions."

Rule's hackles lifted. His ears flattened as he swung his head around to look first at his Rho, then at Lily. He shook his head once. *No.*

Lily met his eyes, her own dark and serious. "It will be all right," she told him.

He shook his head again.

She walked up to him, knelt, and threaded her hand into the fur along his neck until her fingertips touched skin. "It will be all right," she repeated, but this time under the tongue, so quietly that only he would hear. "You won't have to kill anyone tonight."

He stared at her, astonished that she understood. And upset that she didn't.

"Oh. That's not quite it, is it?" She bent and put her mouth close to his ear, her voice so soft now it was barely more than a breath. "You won't have to disobey your Rho, either."

ELEVEN

"LILY." Her name was a low rumble, like thunder in the distance. Isen's voice was pure, deep bass. Most of the time it seemed to rumble up from the depths of his barrel chest, as if his lungs were located so deep in his body the sound had the time and space to echo around in there. It was a voice well suited to menace when he wanted it to be.

Lily wished she knew for sure he was aiming for menace instead of hitting it naturally at the moment. She straightened, keeping one hand resting on Rule's back. "I would very much like to handle the questioning. Thank you." Not that he was doing it to please her. No, he had something else in mind, and maybe she'd guessed what that was. One of his goals, anyway. Isen wasn't a two birds with one stone kind of guy. More like one stone, two birds, a rabbit, a fox, and maybe that deer will trip over the fox and we can get him, too.

Which Rule knew very well. And he was still scared. Scared his Rho would ask something of him he couldn't do.

Something was going on Lily didn't understand, but she knew what questions to ask. She spoke to Isen. "I'd like to give the witnesses some directions first."

His bushy eyebrows lifted a millimeter. "Very well." He raised his voice, addressing the tense group who'd come forward. "You will do as the Chosen bids."

The Chosen. Lily ran her thumb over the other ring she wore. Not Rule's ring, but the one that held the charm the clan had entrusted to her when she accepted her place in the clan. The lupi had considered her Nokolai from the moment the mate bond hit, but the charm marked her acceptance of that joining.

The *toltoi*, they called the little charm. The *toltoi* wasn't magic. Not exactly. Lily felt something when she touched it, something so faint it almost wasn't there, and that faint trace didn't quite feel like magic. She didn't know what it was, and that was annoying, but she'd gotten used to not knowing. Mostly.

Lily turned to look at her witnesses.

Maybe forty people waited to do as she bid. Six of them were male. All of them were anxious. "First," she said loudly, "does anyone have information that's urgent? Not just important, but urgent?" Some shook their heads. None spoke. "Okay, then. I want everyone who spoke with or was questioned by someone from Laban to move to your right. Everyone who spoke with or was questioned by someone from Vochi, go to your left. If you've been questioned by people from more than one clan, get in the middle and sit down. If you've been questioned by someone not from Vochi, Laban, or Nokolai, get in the middle but don't sit down."

You sure couldn't do this with witnesses anywhere else. They all did just what she'd told them to do. There were a few murmurs as they determined where the perimeters of each group lay, but otherwise they were quiet.

It was spooky as hell. "Thank you," she said, taking a quick count. Only six on the Laban side. Thirteen—no, fifteen on the Vochi side. Nine sat in the middle and eleven stood. "I'm talking to the ones standing in the middle now," Lily said. "If any of you are up here because you talked to or were questioned by someone from Leidolf and only Leidolf, go sit . . ." She looked around. "Got sit on the west side, near Cynna."

Everyone who'd been standing in the middle began moving. They were careful not to encroach on the open area where Isen, Lily, Rule, and the others stood. Once they'd gotten themselves over by Cynna she asked, "Is there anyone who was questioned by someone who is not clan? Not from any of the clans?" She waited. No one spoke or moved. "Okay. I'll probably want to talk with each of you one-on-one, but not quite yet. You can sit down while you wait, if you like, but stay in your groups and don't talk to each other."

So much for the willing witnesses. The two reluctant ones had arrived, escorted by two very large wolves, who prodded them to stand directly in front of their Rho. One was thirty-ish, blond and blue, five-three, about one-twenty-five. That one-twenty-five was arranged in a traditional hourglass shape. She looked miserable. The other was younger—maybe twenty—with a narrow face, long dark hair, very straight, and olive skin. Five-nine, but about the same weight as the other woman. Long and lean. Lily couldn't see her expression clearly. She kept her head lowered, letting that long hair curtain her face.

"Isen," the miserable one said, "I didn't do anything wrong!"

"No?" he said. "You won't mind answering Lily's questions, then." He made a small gesture with one hand. Rule moved to stand between the two women.

"Cullen, would you bring the mage lights lower?" The lupi might go by scent, but Lily needed to see faces. "Thanks," she said as the lights bobbed down to hover at head height. "We haven't met," Lily said to the two women, "but I guess you know who I am. What are your names?"

"Sherrianne," the blond said. "Sherrianne Jacobson. I'm Sam's daughter."

Lily blinked. Sam was a dragon . . . but obviously there was another Sam.

"Sam Posey," Isen said. "He's running the vineyard now,

but he lived here for many years. Sherrianne grew up at Clanhome, but moved away as an adult. At her father's urging she returned soon after the hostilities began—she and her son, Will. He's *ospi*, not lupus, and she and her ex share custody. I believe Will is with his father for the holiday?"

Sherrianne nodded unhappily. "Can we talk privately?"

"You will talk to Lily now."

Lily said, "In a moment." Sherrianne might have started out reluctant, but she was longing to confess now. Whether her confession would be helpful remained to be seen, but Lily wanted to let her build up more steam. She looked at the dark-haired young woman. "And you?"

She didn't look up. Her voice was low. "Brenda Hyatt."

"I've seen you around Clanhome."

Brenda didn't answer—but for the first time she glanced up at Lily. Her eyes were dark and brimming with emotion. Anger, certainly. Defiance, too. She looked down again quickly.

Defiance came with the territory at a certain age, but Brenda was beginning to interest Lily. "How old are you, Brenda?"

"I don't see why I have to answer your questions."

Lily smiled. Oh, yes, Brenda interested her greatly. "If you aren't impressed by Isen's order, maybe my badge will mean something to you. Special Agent Lily Yu, Unit Twelve, FBI. You can think about your rights and responsibilities as a citizen while I talk to Sherrianne." She gave a little jerk of her head, indicating that the other woman should follow her.

There was no way to talk privately, of course. Not with so many lupi ears nearby. But she'd give the woman some semblance of it. Lily stopped a few feet away.

Sherrianne followed. Rule kept pace with her. He would act as a lie detector. Human experts dithered over how to detect lies, or if it was even possible. Lupi were quite sure it was—for them. The blend of stress, fear, and guilt from a lie had a subtle chemical signature they could detect when in wolf form. It was easiest if the liar was a lupus confronted by his Rho or Lu Nuncio; supposedly lupi never lied successfully then. Humans were harder to read, but high-stakes lies were easier to detect even for a mere human. They produced more emotion.

Sherrianne must have known some of this. She kept glancing down at Rule—not very far down, since he made a really large wolf—but she didn't look scared. Not happy, but not scared.

Lily stopped and faced her witness. "You want to tell me why you feel guilty?"

Sherrianne leaned closer and started to whisper something.

"I'm not lupi. You'll have to be louder."

Sherrianne sighed heavily. "I guess they're going to hear me anyway."

"Some of them will, I imagine."

Another sigh. "This is so embarrassing. I was saying that it's not about the workshop. Not really. It's about him." Her gaze slid to the left, where Cullen stood. "Cullen. He's married, you know."

"Yes, I do." The only married lupus on the face of the planet. That would change in March, but right now Cullen was it.

"And I—well—people told me he *meant* it. That he's being monogamous. I didn't believe them, and I wanted . . . I mean, look at him. Who wouldn't? But at first I couldn't even meet him. He's always either at his workshop or he's with Cynna and Ryder, so I asked people about his workshop, what he does there, and when he's likely to be there and all. I thought I could, you know, pull off a meeting that way. That's why I felt guilty, because I'd been talking to people about his workshop. But I didn't do anything wrong."

"I don't think you're telling me everything."

Sherrianne's blue eyes opened wider. "I am!"

Rule shook his head.

"You aren't."

She gave Rule a dirty look, as if he'd tattled. "I guess

some of it was because of Cynna. It's not very reasonable for her to expect him to be faithful, is it? But I like her, and I . . . I wasn't able to meet him on the way to his workshop—"

Rule was shaking his head.

"Oh, all right! I did run into him, and he told me to go away, but everyone says he's really rude about being interrupted, so it wasn't like he'd really turned me down. So I . . . I sort of made friends with Cynna, because that's where he spends a lot of time. With her and Ryder."

Rule nodded. She was being truthful now.

"You feel guilty because you used Cynna in order to get access to her husband, who you want to seduce."

"That's such a judgmental way of looking at it."

"Seems pretty accurate to me. Have you talked to anyone outside Nokolai about Cullen's workshop or what he does there?"

"No! Not even once."

Rule nodded again.

"Just for the record . . . how did your use-Cynna-to-seduce-her-husband plan work out?" Lily knew the answer. She wanted Cynna—and the clan as a whole—to know, too.

"It didn't. He said . . . it didn't work at all." Sherrianne smiled at Lily and shrugged. If a whiff of embarrassment clung to that smile, the main flavor was relief that her confessing was over. She'd been raised clan, after all. Wanting to have to sex with someone wasn't bad. The embarrassment was probably because she'd pushed so hard, and maybe because she'd used Cynna. But in the end she'd taken no for an answer, hadn't she? She hadn't crossed the line.

Rule nodded again.

"Okay. Thank you for your cooperation. You can go now."

Instead she turned toward Cynna. "Cynna—"

Cynna's face was stony. "Not now."

"But I want you to know that I—"

"Sherrianne," Isen rumbled. "Go. Now."

She sighed and obeyed.

Lily turned to look at the other woman. The young, angry, defiant one, who'd been watching everything Lily and Sherrianne said and did closely. "Brenda. Come here, please." She wouldn't like that, being told to come here like a child.

Her lips tightened before she remembered to duck her head and hide again. She walked slowly over to Lily.

"Were you raised here at Clanhome, too?"

"No."

Lily waited, but Brenda was smart or stubborn enough to stay silent. "Isen?"

"When Brenda was five or six," Isen said, "her mother experienced a religious conversion. She was born again, and her views on sexuality changed accordingly. From that point on she wanted to limit Brenda's time with us. She's a fair-minded woman. She allowed Brenda's father to see her, but only away from Clanhome. After Brenda turned eighteen, she decided to get to know him—and us—better. She visited her father here several times, then last May asked to move in with him for the summer. We were delighted."

Lily had an urge to ask Isen what Brenda's favorite color was, what she'd gotten for Christmas last week, how old she'd been when she lost her first tooth. He might know. He seemed to know everything about every member of his clan. "So she's been here since May?"

"No, she went off to college in September, but then the events at the Humans First rallies made her unsafe there, so she returned here. At first she seemed to resent that, but I don't believe she does now."

Being spoken about instead of to had the expected effect. Brenda went from a simmer to a boil. "I don't see what any of that has to do with anything! What do you care where I lived when I was little?"

"That's how investigations are," Lily said blandly. "I ask all sorts of nosy questions that, in the end, turn out not to lead anywhere. But every now and then one ends up mattering a lot. Who's your boyfriend here?"

Brenda blinked. "What—I don't know what you mean."

"Would you rather I said *lover*? I suppose it does sound more adult. You have a lover here, don't you?"

That didn't make her hide behind her hair. Instead she gave her head a proud little toss, shaking her hair back. "None of your business."

"It is, you know. Especially if he isn't Nokolai. And he isn't, is he, Brenda?"

She didn't answer, but she didn't hide, either. Her head stayed up. Her eyes defied Lily to pry anything out of her.

She was so very young. Lily didn't make it a question this time, but a statement of fact. "Your lover asked you about Cullen Seabourne's workshop."

Brenda didn't answer, but Rule did. Briefly his ears and tail drooped. He nodded.

She shook her head. "Sorry. I don't get it."

"He means," Isen said, "that she felt guilt over your question."

A nod plus drooping tail . . . " 'Bad dog' equals guilt, huh?"

Rule snorted. That could mean anything from laughter to disgust, but this time probably meant something along the lines of "Don't be ridiculous." Lupi did not like to be compared to dogs.

And she was sidetracking, big-time. The next part would be . . . tricky. She thought she knew what Isen was doing, but if she was wrong, things were apt to skip the handbasket and go straight to hell. She looked steadily at Brenda, letting the silence drag out. Finally she spoke quietly. "Brenda. Look to your left."

More out of surprise than any desire to obey, she did, then frowned at Lily. "What?"

"See all those people sitting over there? Over forty people came forward when Isen asked. Forty people who aren't worried about talking about who asked them questions about Cullen's workshop. You're worried about it, though, aren't you? So worried you won't admit you discussed it with your lover. You're protecting him. You think you won't be hurt, but he might be."

"He didn't talk to me about it," she said quickly. "It was someone else. I didn't want to get h-her in trouble, that's all."

She was such a bad liar. Lily didn't need Rule's slow headshake, not with the way the girl stumbled over the pronoun. "You think he needs protection. You're afraid he asked too many questions. That his interest wasn't simple curiosity."

Silence.

"Do you think I can't find out who he is?"

"It wasn't him. I told you that. It was a woman. She's not connected to the clans at all. I sold her the information. I was angry, like Isen said. I didn't like being here instead of at university, so I-I sold the information."

Rule was shaking his head.

"Stop," Isen growled. He walked up to them—no, it was more like a slow stalk, ending three feet from Brenda. He didn't say a word, but slowly she turned to face him. Slowly her expression changed as defiance faded into fear.

Isen continued to stare at her as he boomed out, "She has confessed! She admits she sold the information about the workshop to a human. She has betrayed Nokolai willfully, knowingly—"

"No!"

The slim young man whose shout answered Isen stood among the Laban contingent.

The young man started toward them. The man to his left grabbed his arm. "Hank—"

He shook his clanmate off and kept coming. "She's innocent," he said loudly. "The Chosen is right. She hopes to protect me. I was the one who sold the information, not Brenda. She had no idea I would do that."

Lily released the breath she hadn't realized she'd been holding. She'd been right. This is what Isen had been going for—not poor Brenda's bungled confession, but the one they were about to hear.

Of course, things were still going to be tricky. He was lying, too.

TWELVE

~⁀

HANK Jamison was twenty-seven—an adult, by lupi standards, but a very young one. He was tall and slim and beautiful, with large, dark eyes and an extra helping of the physical grace all lupi possess. He looked like a Renaissance poet who moonlighted as a swashbuckler. He should have been banned from all contact with women under the age of forty.

Hank insisted calmly and definitely on his guilt. His Rho had nothing to do with this, nothing at all. He'd been greedy. He'd wanted money, and someone—he refused to say who—had paid him well to give up Cullen's secrets. He asserted all this without a quiver of emotion.

Hank's physical control was good, and he was smart enough to clam up once he'd made his announcement. Rule smelled no guilt on him. He wouldn't, though. Hank was lying, but Rule wasn't his Lu Nuncio, and he was trying to protect both his lover and his Rho. No guilt for him there.

An hour after Hank's confession, Lily was on her way back to Isen's home with Isen and Rule, who was two-footed again. Cynna had left to get Ryder from the tenders; Cullen had left for his workshop to run some kind of test.

He was still obsessed with why his ward hadn't made flames whoosh up. And Hank was in leg-irons at the guard barracks. He wasn't locked up because there was no way to imprison someone at Clanhome. Lupi didn't believe in that. Step far enough out of line and you might get dead, but you wouldn't be locked up.

Brenda Hyatt would be formally removed from Nokolai. The ceremony of expulsion was different for a clan female than it was for a lupus since the mantle wasn't involved, but it went by the same name: *seco*.

Lily had checked a few things with the other witnesses before Isen dismissed everyone. As she'd suspected, Brenda hadn't been the only one Hank had talked to about Cullen's device. Just the most cooperative.

As they were leaving the meeting field, someone brought Isen his phone. He used it to call Leo, the Laban Rho . . . who wasn't answering. As they neared Isen's house he put his phone up without leaving a message.

"Does that make him look more guilty, not answering your call?" Lily asked.

"Leo never answers my calls right away." Isen opened the big front door.

"Doesn't he have to answer when you call?"

"He has to obey."

Rule filled in that sparse answer. "It's as you and Cynna were discussing earlier. Laban is subordinate, but their Rho is very much a dominant. Leo will call Isen back—I assume you left a callback number?" he added to his father.

"Of course. I believe I'd like coffee. Would you two care to join me?"

"Sure," Lily said. Might as well. She wouldn't be getting to sleep anytime soon. "So he's playing some kind of dominance game?"

Isen headed off toward the kitchen, so it was Rule who replied. "More a way of balancing dominance and status. The two are connected, but they aren't the same thing. Leo's status is subordinate to Isen's, but he's dominant, so he prefers to be the one calling, not the one called upon.

Isen tolerates this, and generally Leo is careful not to test
that tolerance. He calls back quickly. You may have noticed
that Isen didn't leave a message."

"That matters?"

"I could leave a message for Leo, if I were calling as Lu
Nuncio. If Isen did, it would send the wrong signal. As if
their status were equal."

Lupi status games made her head hurt. "You think he'll
call back, though. Even though he must suspect it has to do
with Hank. He has to wonder if he's in a lot of trouble."

"Leo is sometimes foolish, but he's Rho. His clan is potentially at risk. He'll call." Rule sank onto the long sofa
that faced the fireplace. He leaned forward, propping his
elbows on his knees.

Lily settled next to him. She could hear Isen talking to
Carl—a dispute over which of them would make the coffee.
Isen might be Rho, but the kitchen was Carl's territory. She
turned her head to look at Rule.

He was weary. Weary and worn and barely aware of
where he was, and that wasn't like him. Sure, it was past
midnight, but Rule was a regular Energizer Bunny. He
never needed much sleep. So whatever was eating at him, it
wasn't physical . . . which left plenty of other possibilities.
It might fall to him to carry out whatever sentence Isen
passed on the Laban Rho.

But what she saw on his face didn't look like dread of an
ugly duty. It looked more like bewilderment.

She was missing something.

"You suspected Laban all along, didn't you?" he asked
abruptly.

"If money was the motive, yeah. They fit."

"But Vochi's the one who cares about money."

"No, Vochi understands money." How to put it? "Subordinate clans have to re-up every time they have a new Rho,
right? And Vochi's Rhos have been doing that for hundreds
of years. Same decision, over and over. They must like
things the way they are. Why would they risk losing that?
They've *got* money. They know what it can do and what it

can't. While Laban . . ." She shook her head. "They've been subordinate to Nokolai for less than three decades. Not long in your eyes, maybe, but plenty long enough to see that having money has helped Nokolai. That money can mean strength. They may not understand finance, but they understand strength. They had a lot more motivation than Vochi."

Carl emerged from the kitchen. He was wearing pajama bottoms. It was the first time Lily had had any inkling there was a lupi anywhere who owned pajama bottoms. "Eat," he said with his customary brevity, and handed Rule a plate with two thick sandwiches. He looked at Lily. "Need anything?"

"Ah—no. No, I'm good." She hadn't Changed twice the way Rule had. Lupi needed fuel after Changing. She should have thought of that . . . but so should Rule.

Carl headed back toward the kitchen. His room was off it. Isen passed him, bearing thick pottery mugs.

Lily frowned at him. "What's going to happen to the Laban Rho?"

"Undetermined." He handed her one fragrant mug. "Until I speak with Leo, I won't make that decision. Though I know part of it. He will attend Brenda's *seco*."

That was fair. Leo ought to witness the consequences of his actions. "That won't be all, though."

"No." Isen set another mug on the floor by Rule, who was working his way through the sandwiches—not as if he wanted or even tasted them, but as a chore he needed to finish quickly. Isen took his own coffee to the armchair set at right angles to the couch. "I can require his death, of course. That would be simplest and possibly best."

"You seldom settle for simple."

"I won't discuss this with you, Lily."

His voice was as pleasant as it was implacable. She believed him. She sipped coffee and thought. After a short silence she said, "Do I get to question Leo?"

Isen's eyebrows lifted. "Of course you would ask that. I should have expected it. I am not at my best tonight. Things keep happening that I didn't anticipate, but should have."

Rule set his empty plate on the floor and picked up his mug. "You anticipated better than I did. So did Lily." He glanced sideways at her. "You guessed, didn't you? That's why you assured me I wouldn't have to kill anyone tonight. You knew what Isen was doing."

"I hoped I did, and yes, that was part of it." Women had to be protected. That was the lupi code. In spite of that, Isen had convinced them—even his son—that this offense was grave enough and he was angry enough to order death. But maybe only the lupi had feared this. Brenda hadn't been afraid for her life, had she? Hank had. He'd confessed to protect her.

Rule was watching her. "You were going to arrest people, weren't you? Me?"

"I was thinking more of protective custody. If Isen decided someone needed to be dead, I'd take her in custody. That was a last resort, though. It would've been tricky to pull off without Isen feeling forced to go all Rho on me."

"Tricky?" Isen smiled faintly. "That's one word for it."

Rule looked at his father. "You expected Lily to do something along those lines, though. That's why you kept her nearby—so I'd realize you weren't going to order an execution right away. I didn't get the message, though. I wasn't . . . I don't understand why I didn't see it."

"You were distracted," Isen said. "That is my fault. I didn't think about what calling on the Leidolf Rho in such a situation might do."

Lily frowned. "What do you mean?"

"You couldn't have guessed," Rule said. "I didn't understand what was happening myself at first."

Isen shook his head. "I should have seen the possibility."

"I still don't," Lily said pointedly.

Isen sighed. "Rule has spoken to me about a certain frustration he's felt about being Rho to Leidolf. He experienced the mantle, but not the clan."

She gave Rule a quick glance. "Yeah. He's mentioned that." Not the way Isen put it, but he'd talked about frustration. Rule had been raised Nokolai. That clan had his heart, while Leidolf had been his enemy until that mantle was forced on him. As Rho, Rule meant to do right by Leidolf, but he wanted that more with his head than his heart. "It bugs him that he doesn't feel connected to Leidolf the way he thinks he should."

"Not a problem anymore," Rule said dryly.

"No, clearly it isn't." Isen paused, sipping from his mug. "I didn't expect you to hold your heartbeat separate. I should have. You couldn't allow Leidolf to be mastered by Nokolai."

"No." Rule's expression turned inward. What he found there wasn't giving him joy.

Lily looked back and forth between the two men. "I don't understand."

Isen rubbed his beard. "Perhaps you didn't know that a Rho can control his clan's heart rate. I was keeping Nokolai's elevated—a somewhat risky option, but I have the experience to handle it. This made Nokolai viscerally aware of my anger and created expectations . . . they knew something would be required of them. Something drastic. Our guests would have been aware of the massed heartbeat of Nokolai, increasing their sense of isolation and risk."

"I get it." Lily nodded. "Brenda didn't think she was at risk—not physically, anyway. I had my doubts about that, too, but all the lupi seemed to think you might order her killed. The heartbeat trick made them believe it."

Isen nodded and sipped. "Unfortunately, I was genuinely angry. I wasn't thinking as clearly as I believed. I didn't realize Rule could hold his heartbeat separate from my calling. To do so, he had to *be* Leidolf."

"Um . . . that's a problem?"

Isen tipped his head to look at Rule. "How much of a problem do we have?"

Rule continued to lean forward, looking at the floor, not his father. "I don't know. I'm in control, but . . . not comfortable."

Lily wanted to shake answers out of one or both of them, but Rule's distress was too vivid. He wasn't avoiding answering. He was consumed by something going on inside him, something that Isen didn't need named. Maybe something that wasn't Lily's business . . . no, not that. If Rule had a problem, she needed to know. But maybe she wasn't the one who could help. "This is a Rho thing?"

Rule turned his head to look at her, straightened slowly, and took her hand. "I've been Leidolf Rho for months now. I've gone back and forth between Rho to Leidolf and Lu Nuncio to Nokolai with no real difficulty. That's no longer the case."

"You must have noticed," Isen said, "that Rhos do not enter the clanhome of another clan often. If they must visit for some reason, they don't linger."

"I thought that was a security thing. Or status. Or both."

"Certainly those are part of it. But neither the Vochi Rho nor the Laban Rho would have any security or status concerns about guesting here, at the Clanhome of their dominant. And yet they aren't here." He stopped and looked at her, waiting for her to work out what he meant.

Isen could be annoying that way. Just like Grandmother. "Friar can't eavesdrop here," she said slowly, "for the same reason the Great Bitch can't use her super-duper clairvoyance to watch what's going on at Clanhome. Friar's clairaudience Gift comes from *her,* and *her* magic doesn't work here because clanhomes have some kind of connection to the mantles." She considered that a moment. "Is it anything like a sidhe lord's land-tie?"

He smiled to congratulate her, but it was a weary thing, bereft of his usual mischief. "I don't know enough about the land-tie to say for sure, but the differences seem to outweigh the similarities. Sidhe lords draw power from their land; I don't. They are said to sense the lives contained on their lands. I don't. But Nokolai claims this land. The mantle is part of that claiming. It reacts to certain kinds of power, which is how I would know if someone touched by *her* entered Clanhome." He paused, looked at Rule, and finished softly, "Just as I know if the Rho of another clan is here."

"But we've been here since October!" Trouble pulled Lily's shoulder muscles taut, as if she might need to punch someone. As if that could help. "What changed? Is it just because Rule used the Leidolf mantle to keep his heartbeat separate?"

"That's part of it." Rule said that much, then stopped. He seemed to be hunting words, so she stayed quiet, giving him room. "You know about the agreement I made with Isen after the Leidolf mantle was forced on me."

She nodded. "Here at Clanhome you're Lu Nuncio to Nokolai, not Rho to Leidolf."

"I haven't had a problem holding to that agreement—until now." His shoulders lifted in a small shrug. "Now the genie is out of the bottle, and I can't get it to go back in."

"He means," Isen said softly, "that he can no longer step outside of his role as Rho to Leidolf. Not because he used the mantle. Because it's no longer a role."

A role happened in your head, not your heart, didn't it? Somehow, tonight Rule became Leidolf in his heart or his gut or wherever identity is born. Somehow, that meant he was Rho all the time. She looked at him. "Does that mean that when you were out on the field and you ducked your head and said you were answering your Rho, you were only pretending to submit?"

Rule snorted, but he didn't look amused. "*Pretense* is the wrong word. I can no more pretend to submit than I can pretend to walk. Either I do it or I don't. I'm still Nokolai, still Lu Nuncio, so I still submit to my Rho, but it was . . . I can no longer stop being Rho."

"And that's a problem because of your agreement with Isen."

"Yes, though agreements can be renegotiated if both parties are willing. The real problem arises from one of the reasons for that agreement." He ran both hands through his hair, then glanced at his father. "I don't know what it feels like to you, but I feel as if I'm surrounded by a repeller field."

"Rather like having something lodged in my teeth that I

can't, for all sorts of excellent reasons, even try to dislodge."

Lily took a sip of her coffee, puzzling through what they'd said. "The Nokolai and Leidolf mantles don't like each other."

Isen gave her that tired smile that wasn't like him. "Nothing so personal, nor is it proximity that's the problem. The Nokolai and Leidolf mantles exist in very tight proximity in Rule, after all. But something about the link between mantle and clanhome makes it uncomfortable for one Rho to be in another's demesne. Some believe the Lady did this on purpose, to discourage clans from settling too near each other, which would lead to fighting. Others think it's an accidental byproduct. I lean toward the latter opinion. Had the Lady meant to discourage fighting in this way, the discomfort would be more general. As it is, only a Rho experiences it."

A brief silence fell. Lily sipped her cooling coffee and followed the logic until she arrived at . . . "Do we move back into your apartment, or will it take too long to break the sublease?"

His brows flew up, then drew down in a scowl. "The apartment isn't safe."

"That wasn't what I asked."

"I'm not going to—" He broke off, looking toward the front of the house.

"Ah, Seabourne is back," Isen said. "I wonder why?"

Lily didn't know what they'd heard that she hadn't, but she was used to that. A moment later a perfunctory knock landed on the front door. She heard it open. Quick footsteps pattered down the hall, then Cullen stood in the entry, scowling. He looked directly at Isen. "I figured it out. I don't know if you want me to say anything in front of them." A graceful wave identified Rule and Lily as "them."

Isen sighed and took a sip of coffee. "Indeed, I'm far from at my best. I have no idea what you're talking about."

"I know why the second ward didn't activate." Cullen paused for a long, significant moment . . . then sighed. "I was hoping this was one of your convoluted schemes. I guess not. There was only one possibility, really. It doesn't make sense, but it's the only thing that does make sense."

"Which you aren't yet doing, I'm afraid."

Cullen walked into the room and plopped down on the hassock near the window. He spoke directly to Isen. "I told you when I was setting the wards I'd make sure you were exempt. I can't lock out my Rho or my Lu Nuncio. Or Cynna, for that matter, and I didn't want to be bothered putting the wards up and taking them down every time I went in and out. So when I created them I built in permissions. You, Rule, Cynna, and I are permitted to cross without triggering the wards."

Lily sat up straight. "Wait a minute. Are you saying Rule or Isen stole your thingee? Or Cynna?"

"Don't be ridiculous. Isen would've stopped me if he'd been behind this, and there's no way Rule would run a deal behind Isen's back. The thing is, there's only two ways to build permissions into wards. You can set patterns into them that represent the people who are permitted to cross, but that's harder than it sounds. Cynna could do it," he added. "She's fantastic at patterns. But it would be a big job, and at the time she was absorbing so many of the memories of the clan . . . I didn't want to bother her, so I used the second option. I asked Rule and Isen for a bit of their blood."

"Yes," Isen said. "I remember."

"So do I," Rule said. "But I don't see what this has to do with the thief, since you've graciously stricken us from your list of suspects."

"It means that those of your blood can probably cross, too."

Those of their blood . . . the list was pretty damn short. Toby and Benedict. That's all Lily knew about for either Rule or Isen. As for Cynna, she didn't have any siblings, and her mother was dead. Her father was alive, but he was in Edge. "Those of your blood, too, I assume," she said to Cullen.

"Presumably. But a cousin wouldn't be close enough. At least I don't think so. Besides, Stephen is lupi, and the thief was human." He ran a hand through his hair. "Hell. I guess we'll have to ask—"

Isen's phone sounded.

Rule's father had never set up individual ring tones for his callers, so the twittery music didn't tell her who was calling. But it had to be the Laban Rho. Who else would call at this hour?

Isen picked up his phone, but then he just looked at it as if he'd forgotten what it was, or how to operate it, or why he might want to. Before Lily could entertain any serious worries about incipient senility—which lupi didn't suffer from—he thumbed the button. "Hello."

Not for the first time, Lily wished for lupi hearing. No doubt Rule could hear the caller just fine. Maybe Cullen could, too, though he was farther away. All she had to go on was the peculiar look on Isen's face—and the way Rule suddenly went rigid beside her.

Isen was very polite to his caller. "Yes, I am. Ah. Yes, my brain is almost beginning to function again. I can't say I was expecting your call, but it isn't the surprise it might have been." There was a long pause as the other person spoke. "No, I assure you I did not. You won't know what my word means, but you have it." A short pause. "You do? Interesting . . . ah. You do realize that he . . . Perhaps so. Rule?" He held his phone out.

Rule didn't move. "What's going on?"

"You heard," Isen said gently. "He wishes to speak with you."

Still Rule didn't move. He spoke slowly. "He said his name is Jasper."

"Jasper Machek."

"And he's . . ." The sentence drifted off as if Rule had no idea how to finish it.

"Yes." Isen confirmed that the way a kindly doctor might say, *Yes, the biopsy did test positive for cancer.* "He is."

Rule took the phone. "This is Rule." A pause. "We won't discuss that now, I think. You told Isen you wished to make a deal . . . ah." Rather a long pause, then, "That complicates matters." He listened some more, then glanced at Lily, gesturing with his free hand as if he were writing. "Yes," he said, "just a moment," as Lily pulled her notebook and a pen from her purse and handed them to him. He jotted something down. "In the Marina District? I'll find it . . . No. I can't agree to that." Another pause. "I don't believe I will explain at this time. I will bring another with me who may be able to help . . . No, that's not negotiable." A longer pause. "Very well. I can reach you at this number, if necessary? Until later, then."

He returned the phone to Isen and stood as if he were about to do something. But he didn't. He just stood there. "That was the thief. He wishes our assistance."

Cullen's eyebrows flew up. "Our assistance?"

"He didn't make it far with your prototype before someone in turn stole it from him. A remarkably popular item, for something that doesn't work correctly. He lives in San Francisco," Rule added. "We're to meet him there at one thirty tomorrow. He wanted Cynna to come—he's aware of her Gift—but of course that wouldn't be safe."

"Rule." Lily stood and put her hand on his arm. "Why are we going to help this thief?"

"Is that what we're going to do? I don't know . . . but we'll go." He didn't say anything for a long moment. "It seems he's my brother."

THIRTEEN

~~

LILY drew in crisp, chilly air through her nose as her feet slapped the asphalt in an easy rhythm. In the eastern sky behind her, stacked layers of cloud smoldered in crimsons and purples that stained the bulging shoulders of the humped earth. Lower down, Isen's home sprawled almost invisible in the early morning darkness.

One of the perks of living at Clanhome was all the options for where to run. One of the downsides was that the long commute into the city meant Lily was mostly stuck with using the road. The sun arrived late to land cradled by mountains, and Lily usually had to run early.

Not alone, however. Just over a month ago Cynna had asked if Lily would mind company a couple of times a week on her runs. Lily had said sure, though she hadn't expected Cynna to keep it up. For one thing, Cynna was a new mother. For another, she hated running. Or so she'd always claimed.

But so far Cynna had stuck with it. The little house she shared with Cullen and their new daughter lay about half a mile west of Isen's place, so Lily had that first half mile on her own to warm up, and the last half mile to push herself.

She and Cynna ran together for two miles, total, which was Cynna's target. Not that Cynna been able to run the whole way right off the bat. At first she'd made it to the turnaround point huffing and puffing and waving for Lily to keep going while she walked back, but she ran both ways now. Good progress for such a short time. Of course, Cynna was a tad competitive. She hadn't liked it when Lily kept going and she couldn't . . . which was one reason she'd wanted to join Lily. Motivation.

Sometimes Rule or Cullen joined them. And sometimes Rule started out with Lily, but didn't get beyond that first half mile. The chance to stop and see Ryder for a few minutes, even if she was sound asleep, was too good to pass up. Cullen had no trouble finding someone to stay with Ryder if he wanted to run, not when they were surrounded by baby-crazy lupi. Lupi loved kids—all kids—but babies just lit them up. Give one of them a chance to spend time with a three-month-old bundle of drool, stinky diapers, and adorable little gurgles, and he'd rearrange his whole week if that's what it took.

Baby-craving was so universal that custom forbade anyone actually offering to babysit. This was to keep new parents from being pestered to death. Cynna said that every new mother ought to get to spend the first few months at a clanhome. The only tricky part was making sure she didn't leave anyone out. She kept a list.

Rule and Lily were exempt from the counting and listing. Everyone assumed that close friends got extra baby time, so they didn't take offense. Isen was exempt, too. Who could be upset when the Rho spent time with his newest clan member? So Lily had seen a fair amount of little Ryder lately. She'd gotten pretty good at diapers. Burping was still not her strong point, but she could clean a teeny tiny baby butt with the best of them.

Ryder did have some adorable little gurgles.

This morning, though, she was alone as she neared the path that led to Cynna and Cullen's place. The lights were off in the stucco cottage, which could mean everyone was asleep, but she doubted it. Probably Cullen was awake, even if Ryder wasn't. Possibly he hadn't gone to bed at all. Rule hadn't.

Cynna was up. Lily hadn't been sure she would be, not with everything that had happened last night, but she was waiting where she usually did at the edge of the road, her pale blond hair almost glowing in the dim light. Lily was surprised by the lift of relief she felt.

"Hey," Cynna said as she fell into step alongside Lily.

"Hey, yourself. I wasn't sure you'd be here this morning."

"Of course I'm here. Who knows when I'll get another chance to pump you?"

"Um." Good Lord. Was that why she was relieved— because she knew Cynna would pump her? Did she actually *want* to talk about stuff? She never talked about stuff. Well, sometimes with Rule, who was a sneaky bastard and could wriggle her around into saying things.

"I guess you're going to San Fran, huh?"

"Rule's going, so I am." The mate bond limited how far apart they could be. It was not consistent about this, but San Francisco was five hundred miles away, well beyond what they could expect to be okay. "Ruben thinks I should go."

"Yeah?"

"He's got a hunch." Lily had called her boss last night. Ruben Brooks had a precognitive Gift that was off-the-charts accurate. When he had a hunch, everyone—up to and including the president—paid attention.

"That's handy, since you have to go anyway. How's Rule dealing with his surprise sibling?"

And that answered her question. Her stuff this morning was all about Rule, and Rule wasn't talking. "He's not. At least that's what it looks like. You know how I don't talk about stuff? He's doing that times ten. Times ten on the logarithmic scale."

"Is that a math word? Don't talk math. He's all shut down?"

"Not exactly." Rule closed down when he didn't want to talk about something. Usually Lily understood and respected that . . . well, she tried, anyway. But this was different. "He didn't ask any questions. Did Cullen tell you that? This Jasper Machek calls and says he wants us to come to San Francisco and help him out, and Rule didn't ask one question."

"Not everyone deals with a shock by asking questions."

"I know, but he still isn't asking questions. He's avoiding them. Did you know that Isen knew about this Jasper guy? Not a lot, maybe." Lily had run a check on Machek. It turned up plenty that Isen hadn't mentioned. "But he knew Rule's mother had had another child a few years after she handed Rule over. He knew Rule had a brother, and he never told him. And Rule's cool with that. So cool he left the room when I started asking Isen questions about Jasper."

"Just walked out?"

"Not in a rude way. Suddenly he had things to do."

"Huh." Cynna fell silent.

Rule had said he needed to arrange their trip, including the security. A nice, valid activity, only there was no reason for him to go outside to do it. Lily had just started on her questions when Isen's phone rang again.

That time it was the Laban Rho. Isen had told Leo that he was busy at the moment. No, he didn't want Leo to call back. He was to wait on hold until Isen was ready to speak with him.

"I can leave," Lily had said.

"No, I want him to wait. First he'll be patient. That won't last long. Leo has never mastered patience. Then he'll be increasingly angry. That will last longer, but eventually he'll move from anger into dread. That's when I'll talk to him."

Isen had kept the other Rho waiting on hold a full thirty minutes while he talked to Lily about Jasper . . . and Jasper's mother. When Isen deemed Leo sufficiently steeped in dread, he'd dismissed Lily. "If you can find Rule, tell him I want him. If you can't, have someone track him down. He may be running."

She hadn't found Rule. She hadn't found out what Leo's fate was, either. When she came back inside, Isen had retreated to his study, and when he closed that door no one was supposed to disturb him for anything short of an emergency. Badly as she wanted to know things, she couldn't call it an emergency. She'd gone to bed.

Cynna broke the silence. "Lupi have a word for them, you know. For their half siblings on the mothers' side."

Lily snorted. "Human?"

Cynna flashed her a grin. "Yeah, but this word is just for that relationship. For out-clan siblings. They call them *alius* kin."

"I've seen that word somewhere. Maybe in one of those journals the Rhej—I mean Hannah—had me read." Before Hannah died, Lily wasn't supposed to use her name. Now she was, because "the Rhej" meant Cynna. Thank God Cynna had told her to ignore all that no-naming-the-Rhej business. Bad enough, she'd said, that the lupi mostly wouldn't use her name anymore. She didn't want to stop hearing it entirely. "I thought it just meant kin."

"I don't know what *alius* kin would mean to someone who knows real Latin, but lupi translate it as *otherkin*."

Kin who are other. Not us, not clan. "Like they aren't real siblings."

"It makes sense, if you look at the history. It used to be rare for lupi to be raised by their mothers. If the mother was married, it wasn't to the baby's father, and if she wasn't, out-of-wedlock babies were a BFD for centuries. So it was normal for lupi to grow up not knowing their mothers' families at all, and only natural they didn't feel a close bond. Kin, not clan, you know? Chances were good their human half siblings didn't even want to know about them, much less call them 'brother,' so it went both ways." She shrugged. "A lot of lupi are raised by their moms now, at least part of the time, but the attitude has held on."

Lily thought that over. Rule had never wanted to know if he had any *alius* kin, had he? He'd never asked. And yet they were going to San Francisco. Jasper called, and she and Rule were headed for San Francisco. She didn't think it was just about the prototype. "That's part of it, maybe."

"But not all?"

Lily was pretty sure some of it—maybe most of it—had to do with the mother this Jasper Machek shared with Rule. The one who'd handed a two-week-old baby to Isen and walked away, uninterested in whether her son lived or died. Learning about Jasper meant learning something about that woman, didn't it? "Her name was Celeste Babineaux. Rule's mother, I mean. She was twenty-nine when she had Rule."

"Did Rule tell you that? Or Isen?"

"Until last night, I didn't even know her last name."

"Rule did, though, didn't he?"

"I don't know. He'd been told her name, but I don't know if he remembers." It seemed like he'd have to, but he always flew the "off-limits" banner on the rare occasions the subject of his mother came up, and she'd never pushed.

Last night she'd pushed . . . but it was Isen she'd talked to, not Rule.

Celeste Babineaux had been a French expatriate living in California, and—in Isen's words—the most staggeringly beautiful woman he'd ever met, then or since. She had also been bipolar. At least that's the diagnosis she'd eventually received, after being in and out of sanatoriums and treatment centers and such for much of her life.

Isen had paid for those stays, some of them extended. Even after Celeste married a man named Michael Machek, Isen had paid for her treatment. His eyebrows had lifted when Lily expressed surprise at that. "She was my son's mother. Of course I helped her when she needed it. Bipolar is such a recent way of understanding one type of mental illness," Isen had added. "It wasn't the doctors' fault they couldn't do more for her back then."

"Don't you think Rule needed to know that his mother had a mental illness?"

Isen had shrugged. "He didn't want to know about her. There was no medical concern—he couldn't inherit her condition—so I didn't force the knowledge on him."

"It could have made a difference in how he thought about her. It could have had a lot to do with why she abandoned him."

"You oversimplify. Do you think Rule felt abandoned? Do you see that kind of early trauma in him today?"

Maybe not. But he hadn't just missed out on knowing about his birth mother. He'd missed out knowing about his brother. "Does he have other half siblings you haven't mentioned?"

"No." Isen had smiled with sly amusement. "Although Benedict has two that he may not have mentioned to you. He sees them when he visits his mother's tribe."

No, he'd never mentioned them. Not that Benedict was exactly chatty, so that wasn't surprising. But Rule had never mentioned them, either.

Otherkin. Kin, but not clan. Lily frowned at a landscape she didn't see, her legs moving automatically. When Cynna spoke, it startled her.

"After Cullen told me about Jasper, I asked him if he had any stray brothers or sisters I didn't know about. He said no. You knew that his mom was Wiccan, right?"

Lily nodded. "She taught him spellcraft, didn't she?"

"And kept him from burning things down until he was old enough to get a handle on his Gift. You maybe don't know that she was forty when she had him. She used a strong-ass fertility charm to help her get pregnant while she was involved with his dad. Those aren't supposed to work, but either hers did or she got lucky. She wanted a lupus baby."

So different from Rule's experience . . . "Rule told me once that his name was Anglicized—that the original version was Reule. A French name. Nokolai was French before the clan immigrated, so I assumed that's where the name came from. It didn't. That's what his mother named him."

"You learned that last night?"

"Isen and I talked quite awhile. Isen called him Rule because it was easier for people to pronounce, so that's what he grew up with. But his mother named him Reule. It means *famous wolf*."

"Wow. It seems like she put some thought into his name. It also seems like there's a lot you haven't told me, if you and Isen talked so long."

Lily's breath huffed out impatiently. "I'm not sure how much to say. Rule doesn't talk about his mother, but I think it's okay if I do. But somewhere there's a line between what's okay to say and what isn't, and I'm not sure where that line is."

"I hate to say this," Cynna said, "I really do. I'd rather nag you into telling me everything, but . . ." Her breath was coming fast and hard now, so that she had to start dumping her words out in bursts. "My own rule is that . . . if I think it would make Cullen mad . . . for me to repeat something . . . that's okay. I can talk about stuff that . . . makes him mad if I want to. But if it would hurt him or . . . make him feel exposed . . . I don't say . . . anything." She slid Lily a look. "But hey. You can . . . talk about how you feel without . . . violating any . . . confidentiality deal."

"Confused." And shut out, which she didn't like, but she understood. Rule needed time to come to terms with what this newfound brother meant to him. Only she wasn't sure he knew that. "We're nearly to the turnaround point."

"Thank God."

They'd marked the one-mile point with a small stack of rocks. When they reached it, Cynna said she wanted to pause and stretch out a bit. Mostly she wanted to get her wind back, Lily thought, but that was okay. There was a long, flat rock she could use to stretch her hamstrings. She balanced on its edge and dropped her toes slowly.

The clouds stacked across the morning sky had lost their

earlier blood-and-fire glory by then, fading to soft pink in the east with myriad grays and steel blues overhead. Rain by noon, she thought. She wouldn't be here to see it.

"I wish I was going with you," Cynna said.

"I guess you could, if you decided to. Neither Rule or Ruben can tell you no."

"The upside of being a Rhej is that no one can tell me no. The downside is that this forces me to be a grown-up and tell myself no sometimes." Cynna hugged one leg close to her chest. "Ow. That hurts so good. Sometimes it's hard to tell what the grown-up thing is, though. This is probably the safest it's going to get for a while. Friar's organization is a mess."

"We think so, anyway."

"And Jasper-the-thief wanted me there."

"Which could be a strong argument for staying here."

"That's what Cullen said. Along with a lot of other shit." Cynna lowered that leg and hugged the other one. "Why is my left butt cheek always stiffer than my right? Anyway, I couldn't make up my mind, so I tossed a coin."

"I guess San Francisco lost."

"Yeah." Cynna switched legs.

"Well, if you're here you can connect with the CSI squad. Now that the internal clan stuff's been cleared up, Isen agreed that I could call them in. They'll be here about ten."

"I can do that." Cynna lowered her leg slowly. "I'm going to have to resign from the Bureau, you know."

Lily stopped moving. "Shit."

"I don't have to do it right this minute. I've got another two months of unpaid leave. But I'm not going to be able to go back to active duty. I won't be able to go where I'm needed. If I was still an apprentice I could, but now . . ." She shrugged.

Lily couldn't think of what to say. She'd nearly lost her position with the Bureau in October, and that had all but wrecked her. "Have you talked to Ruben yet?"

"He said he'd find a place for me if I wanted, maybe in

Research. But research isn't my thing. Or I can be a consultant. I'll probably go with that. I don't want to stay in the Bureau just so I can be on the payroll. I don't need to, either. Nokolai would pay me a salary if I wanted, you know."

"I didn't know that."

"Usually a Rhej gets housing and utilities from her clan, but being a Rhej isn't a full-time job, so most of them work at regular jobs, too. Hannah did when she was younger, and I expected to. But with this war, that's going to change. We've been talking about it."

" 'We' being the Rhejes?"

Cynna nodded. "They're an incredible bunch of women. I thought it might be hard for them to accept me. They loved Hannah. She was the eldest, and they all . . . but they've been great. Anyway, there are two of us who don't have apprentices—me and the Etorri Rhej—and she and I have talked several times. We agreed that we can't risk the memories. She's quitting her job, and I won't be going back to the Bureau."

Lily was silent a moment. "Are you okay with this?"

"You know, I am. I don't like being denned up at Clanhome, and I'll miss being an agent. But I'm not a cop all the way down the way you are. I'm not giving up something that's fundamental to me. And then there's Ryder. I knew things would change once she was born, but I didn't know how much of the change would be in me. In what I want." She shook her head as if she'd run out of words. "Anyway, the reason I told you today instead of some other time is that I wanted you to know where I'm coming from. I want you to promise me something."

"If I can."

Cynna's grin flashed. "Smart answer. I don't think this one will stretch you out of shape. If you decide you need me in San Francisco, call me. Cullen won't. I'm pretty sure Rule won't, either. Not that I can promise I'll come if you do, but I want to know. I want it to be my choice, not the default setting everyone picks for me."

"Damn, you are turning into such a grown-up."

Cynna's grin widened. "I am, aren't I? So will you do it?"

Lily nodded. "It's a deal."

"Good. Thanks. I guess you need to get back."

"I really do. Check-in's at ten, and I've got a ton to do before then." Lily started off at a slow jog, but Cynna seemed to have her breath back, so she moved into an easy lope. After a bit she said, "Things keep changing, don't they?"

"All the fucking time," Cynna agreed. She sounded annoyingly cheerful about it, though.

FOURTEEN

~

RULE was leaving the house when Lily returned. He told her he was heading over to Eric Snowden's to get Toby, touched her face as if he, too, regretted the lack of a private moment, and left at a lope. By the time Lily showered, called Ruben, called the local FBI office to delegate some of her cases, and texted her parents that she'd be out of town for a while, he was back.

So was Toby. So were Emmy and Danny. Rule vanished into the study with Isen, and Lily ate breakfast with a noisy and inquisitive crowd. The three kids charged back out as soon as they finished downing the pancakes they'd drowned in maple syrup. It seemed the self-defense refresher course planned for their age cohort had been moved up to today.

Lily approved of the clan's custom of teaching basic self-defense to its kids. She suspected that today's class was at least partly to keep them busy, maybe wear them out a bit. They were all wired after last night. But it would also reinforce the idea that being young and small might mean taking orders and running or hiding if necessary, but it did not mean they were helpless.

As soon as Toby and company left, José told Lily about

the arrangements for their trip. The bulk of the guards who'd accompany them had left while Lily was still asleep because they were driving up. But Scott would fly there with her, Rule, and Cullen.

Scott was Leidolf. So, she realized, were the guards José named who'd already left. That had to have something to do with Rule's newly found sense of himself as Leidolf, but what? Lily put that on her mental list of things to discuss later, when she and Rule were alone.

At ten till nine she finished packing—she'd gotten really quick with that—and rolled her suitcase out to the living room. Cullen sprawled on one of the couches, a battered duffel near his feet and a cup of coffee in his hand. He nodded at her. "José is bringing the car around."

She glanced at the hall that led to Isen's study. "Rule still in with Isen?"

"Yeah."

In addition to the steel plates in the walls, Isen's study was soundproofed. No point in asking if Cullen had heard anything. Lily parked her suitcase by the hallway and started for the kitchen. "I'm going to grab a cup of coffee."

"Don't bother. This is the last of it."

"You took the last cup?"

"Is that a rhetorical question?"

She sighed and plopped down on the hassock. Maybe Isen had given Rule the brief report she'd printed off for him and they were talking about it. The Bureau didn't have a lot on Jasper Machek, but what they did have made interesting reading. "How did you rig the coin toss?"

"I don't know what you're talking about."

"Right. You're fine with Cynna coming with us if she wants to. You didn't do a thing to influence that coin she tossed."

He grinned. "Nothing anyone can prove."

Lily wasn't about to tell Cullen that she approved, but she did. She'd call Cynna if they needed her in San Francisco, but her promise on that score didn't mean she couldn't stress the danger. Cynna shouldn't be kept penned up at Clanhome every minute . . . but there was a chance this whole deal was a setup designed to get as many of them as possible away from Clanhome, where they could be ambushed. Cynna was nursing. Where she went, Ryder went. Best if she sat this one out, at least for now.

"Last night I kept getting interrupted when I was questioning you," she said, pulling out her notebook and flipping it to the next blank page. "You said you didn't have a picture of your prototype, so I need a description." An omission she'd noticed with a cringe when she reported to Ruben.

"A skull."

She stared. "It looks like a skull?"

"It *is* a skull. The runes are written on it in black ink—specially prepared, but you don't need to know about that. And of course the yellow quartz is adhered in a carefully composed pattern that—"

"You used a human skull for your prototype?"

"You're really slow on the uptake this morning. Maybe you did need that cup of coffee."

"You can't be ignorant of the laws about using human relics in magical practices. If you—"

"Of course I know the law," Cullen said testily. "The skull's over seventy years old, which exempts it from most restrictions. It's been blessed and certified clean of taint or ties to its original owner. I bought it from the Catholic Church. Paid a pretty penny, too."

"The Catholic Church sells skulls."

"At a huge profit, but they're the most reputable supplier around, plus the only one that can offer sufficient quantity, so if you're worried that I hadn't considered how many I'd need if—"

"No. No, that wasn't my concern. Why in the world did you use a skull for your prototype?"

"Congruence, first of all, plus bone has useful properties. There's an element of theater, too, of course. The magically ignorant require a touch of showmanship to believe something is working the way it should. Skulls impress the hell out of them."

She shook her head. "You've got a weirdly malfunctioning magical device. It's made from a human skull. You don't think there might be a connection?"

He frowned. "That's what Cynna said, but there is no theoretical support for the idea. The skull tests neutral in every way that matters—mortal ties, transference, elemental imbalance—"

Her phone ran through the opening bars to the theme from *Jaws*. She grimaced. "Hold on a minute." She pulled it out.

Cullen grinned. "If your mother ever finds out what ringtone you gave her, you are toast."

"If anyone ever tells her, he's toast. Remember that. Hi, Mother," she said. "I guess you got my text."

"Of course I did, though I've told you I don't like text messages. They're too impersonal. I wanted to make sure you talk to your sister while you're in San Francisco."

"Oh. I probably will go see Beth, but I'm going there on a case, not for pleasure, so—"

"You have to talk to her about this man she's seeing. He's older than she is. A lot older," Julia Yu said ominously. "I don't know why she had to move there in the first place. I said it wouldn't work out well."

"She's seeing someone in particular?" Lily said, surprised. Beth dated a lot, but she hadn't mentioned anyone special. A whiff of guilt drifted in when she realized she hadn't talked to Beth lately. A few texts, yeah, but she hadn't called in . . . three weeks? Maybe more. Given the way Beth flamed through relationships, that was plenty of time for her to be head over heels. "Beth falls for someone every other month. I don't think we need to worry."

"This one is different. She didn't tell me about him."

"What do you mean?"

An impatient sigh. "She's mentioned him, but she doesn't say she's in love. It's there in her voice, but she hasn't said it, and when I ask, she says he's just a friend. Clearly this one is different."

"What's his name? How much older is he?"

"Sean something-or-other. He's over forty."

That was a pretty big age difference. Not as big as the one between her and Rule, but Lily's mother didn't know that. Rule looked about thirty. Still . . . "I'll ask her about him if I get the chance. I can't promise. I don't know how this case is going to go, but . . ." The study door opened. "I've got to go, Mother."

It wasn't that easy. Things never were with her mother. While Julia Yu explained how necessary it was for Lily to find out everything she could about Sean something-or-other, Lily listened with half an ear to Rule ask if the car was waiting. Cullen assured him it was, stood, and cocked an inquiring eyebrow. "Anything we should know before we leave?"

Rule raised both brows. "You couldn't have heard us."

"I didn't. That's why I'm asking."

"There is news, but it's for Isen to speak of."

As he said that, Isen joined them. "Got to go, Mother," Lily said hastily. "Bye." She disconnected quickly.

Isen was looking cheery again. The twinkle was back. "Lily, you'll like this part of my news. Young Hank acted on his Rho's orders, so Nokolai does not hold him responsible for his misdeeds. He won't be allowed to remain here, but he will be released without further punishment."

"You're right. I do like that."

"You'll also be pleased to hear that I decided the situation did not require Leo's death."

She'd bet he was pleased about that, too. Isen could be ruthless if he thought it necessary, but he preferred to be devious. "Good."

"Leo was under the impression he was being clever. He thought I'd appreciate his, ah, sneakiness. In his mind, by selling worthless information—he knew the prototype had problems—he benefited his clan, thereby benefiting Nokolai as well. I explained the flaws in his reasoning."

"You did more than that."

"True. However he may have justified his actions to himself, he deceived and betrayed Nokolai. I can no longer trust him. I required him to pass Laban's mantle to his heir—"

The quick "son of a bitch!" came from Cullen.

"—who will be joining you in San Francisco to assist in your investigation."

FIFTEEN

～

LILY snapped her seat belt in place. "I've never wanted to punch your father more."

Rule smiled at his *nadia*, seated between him and Cullen in the backseat of Isen's oversized and armored Lincoln. No doubt it was perverse of him to find her aggravation comforting. "It's not an uncommon reaction."

"There is no reason for him to be so tight-lipped about his reasons!"

"He did explain."

Lily snorted. "Oh, yeah. He's just making things easy for me."

"That's Isen for you," Cullen said. "One considerate son of a bitch."

Isen had informed Lily that it would be convenient for her to have Tony around to question in person. True, but Lily's skepticism was justified. There was more to Isen's arrangement . . . not that Rule assumed he knew all of that "more," but he knew some. "You will want to talk to Tony about the deal his father made with whoever wanted the prototype."

"Of course I want to talk to him. Isen didn't get any information about that from Leo. At least that's what he claims." She shot Rule a look. "You were with Isen for a couple hours. You know more about this."

"Most of our discussion this morning involved clan politics. Isen's manner of handling Laban's betrayal will have repercussions."

"Why?"

"It's meddling," Cullen said. "Meddling in an internal Laban matter."

"It's okay for Isen to kill Leo, but it's meddling if he makes him step down?"

"Pretty much, yeah."

Rule could tell how little Lily understood that. "A subordinate clan owes obedience to its dominant, but is governed by its own Rho. Isen was well within his rights to require Leo's death, but telling him he must pass the mantle to his heir . . . he has the authority, but some will question whether he has the right. Only a Rho makes decisions concerning the mantle."

"Yet killing Leo would have the same effect—the mantle would go to his heir. Plus Leo would be dead."

Rule nodded. "And that's how Isen will present his decision, as the symbolic death of an oath-breaking Rho. The Rho 'died'; the man did not. Some will still see it as a usurpation of the Laban Rho's authority. Ah . . . this isn't a perfect example, but think of how testy local cops get when your Bureau intrudes on what they consider their turf. The feds have the authority to do so, but local officers sometimes think they abuse that authority."

"Then there's the Civil War," Cullen said cheerfully. "States' rights and all that—what powers belong to the federal government and what belong to the states. People still get hot under the collar about that. Laban is subordinate to Nokolai, but it still has rights."

Rule nodded. "It doesn't help that Tony was Leo's heir, and Isen didn't allow him to change that before passing the mantle on."

"What does that have to do with it?"

Rule and Cullen exchanged a look. Rule answered. "Until this past July, Leo's heir was his older son, James, but he suddenly replaced James with his younger son, Tony. It's widely believed that the two of them argued and Leo wanted to teach James a lesson, and that Tony, the younger son, is a temporary placeholder for his brother."

"What's wrong with Tony?"

"Nothing," Rule said firmly. A little too firmly, maybe, and she raised her brows at him. He sighed and gave a partial answer. "Tony doesn't have a son. And yes, I've told you that's essential for a Lu Nuncio, but it's a cultural requirement, not a distinction the mantle makes."

Cullen put in helpfully, "It's like the way Jasper Herron named Myron the Lu Nuncio for Kyffin. Myron's a lousy fighter."

She nodded slowly. "A Lu Nuncio is supposed to be proven in battle, but Jasper made his uncle his heir because his son's too young and Myron doesn't want to be Rho, so he'll be glad when his great-nephew is old enough for the position. Everyone's wink-wink, nudge-nudge about it. Does everyone wink at Tony being Lu Nuncio, then?"

"More or less. We've assumed Leo would remove Tony before long."

She nodded again. "Okay, so there's an issue of territory and rights with Isen telling Leo to step down. I get that, but how does letting Leo live change the way the boundaries are drawn?"

"It was Leo who was responsible, you see. Not the mantle."

Lily chewed on that a moment. "In a weird, lupi sort of way that makes sense. Leo took responsibility for his actions, so he's personally culpable, which lets his clan off the hook. But Isen's decision was about the mantle, which makes it about Laban."

"Some will see it that way."

"Is my head spinning? It feels like it's spinning. And all that doesn't explain why this new Rho is ordered to join us. Or why we should let him."

"You and Cullen and I are exposed to risk because of

Laban's actions. Laban's Rho will therefore be exposed to risk, too—and given a chance to help recover what his clan caused to be taken from Nokolai."

"Grandmother says that if you make an enemy lose face, you have to either kill them or give them a way to regain face."

"Laban is not our enemy, but otherwise . . . yes."

Lily fell silent, thinking that over. Or maybe she'd reverted to worrying about him.

His fault. He hadn't found time to have a word with her alone. He took her hand. She looked at him once, a slanted glance from under her lashes. She wanted to ask him questions, but she wouldn't, not here. He looked away, stroking his thumb over the fleshy base of her thumb. He didn't want her questions. Shame clung to him, vague and sticky as a spiderweb. He saw no reason for it.

It had been a shock to learn he had otherkin. He hadn't reacted well. No doubt some of that was due to the timing, falling as it had on Mick's birthday. But he wasn't shamed by his reaction.

How did he feel now? That's what Lily would ask if they were alone. Or perhaps not. Much as she loved questions, she did understand that some answers arrived more fully without tacking words to them. He was . . . curious. Yes, now that the shock was past, he wanted to know more about Machek. He didn't want the man in prison, if it could be avoided—a goal Lily might help or hinder, and there was a question he needed to ask when they were private. But there was no real bond between him and this newly discovered kin, even if Machek had called him brother on the phone last night.

But Jasper Machek was fifty-three years old. Rule knew this because Lily had asked Isen while Rule was still reacting. And while Rule might have been utterly unaware of Jasper Machek's existence, Machek had known about Rule. So Isen had said just before Rule left the room last night. The man had had ample opportunity to call Rule brother before now.

Easy enough to see what had changed. He wanted something.

Rule roused from his thoughts, feeling Lily's gaze on him. "Yes?"

"I think we should be sure we're all on the same page here," she said. "Cullen wants his prototype back. I do, too, but even more I want to find out who has it and why. What's your priority, Rule?"

"Determining if Friar has any connection to the theft, of course. Which puts us very much on the same page." He added very softly, "I'm okay, Lily."

She nodded, but not as if she believed him. More like she was willing to let him say that. "We don't have any reason right now to think there's a connection. This could be good, old-fashioned corporate theft."

"You said Ruben had a hunch you should be there."

"His hunch didn't include why, though. It doesn't mean Friar's involved." She drummed the fingers of her free hand on her thigh. "I've got two good witnesses, or will have. Your brother and what's-his-name . . . the new Laban Rho."

"Tony Romano."

"Right. Tony and Jasper both had contact with whoever commissioned this theft." She gave him a quick glance. "I'm assuming that information is part of this deal your brother wants to make."

"I think of him as my *alius* kin."

"Okay. I think of him as your brother."

He didn't respond. Eventually Lily would understand, but she didn't now, and he wasn't inclined to explain while they had an audience.

After a brief pause she went on. "But whatever label we give Jasper, he knows things we need to know. Talking has to be part of whatever deal we make."

"Obviously. Information is all he has to offer, if what he said about the device being stolen from him is true. I don't know what he wants in return, but I'd guess that staying out of prison is involved." He paused. "I would prefer that he not go to prison."

"I'll bear that in mind. I think I should do the dealing."

His eyebrows lifted. "I'm quite capable of—"

"Yes, but it gets you two off to a difficult start if you have to be a hard-ass."

"Considering that our relationship began with him stealing from the clan, I'd say we're already well into 'difficult.'"

"Then let's not make it worse. Besides, you can't agree to grant him immunity from prosecution, which he'll likely insist on."

He suspected that technically she couldn't, either, but she could neglect to arrest Machek. She must think she could keep this under the table. He considered a moment longer, then nodded. "Am I supposed to be the good cop, then?"

"You can stand there looking mysterious and vaguely scary. You said he wouldn't talk about what he wants until we get there."

He nodded, toying with the ring on her finger. His ring.

"Can you give me your impression of him?"

"He knows what he wants, even if he wasn't willing to tell me. He was calm, in control, when he might have been panicky or angry about losing something he'd gone to great trouble to obtain." He thought a bit more and added, "He's educated, or knows how to sound like it."

"He's got a degree in art history and owns a small gallery."

Art history. Why did that surprise him? He'd known about the man's existence for less than twenty-four hours. Surely that wasn't enough time to develop preconceptions. "Last night I wasn't ready to learn about him. I am now."

She cocked her head. "I've got the FBI's file on him, plus some recent stuff Arjenie dug up. You want to see it?"

The FBI didn't keep files on everyone. "Do you mean a file or a rap sheet?"

"No rap sheet. He's never been arrested, but several years ago he was a person of interest in a theft at the National Gallery in D.C. That made it an FBI matter, see—

National Gallery, federal law. They never had enough evidence to make an arrest, but it's clear the lead agent had him picked for the perp. He put together the file."

"He is a pro, then. As you suspected."

"Looks like it, though there's—"

Cullen interrupted. "What was stolen?"

She looked at him. "That was odd. Only one item went missing—a thirteenth-century chalice, solid gold with precious gems. No one could figure out why he targeted that one item. It was worth plenty, sure, but there were other things he could have grabbed that were worth more."

"No, there weren't," Cullen said.

"What do you know about this?"

"That chalice was an artifact."

"An artifact?" Rule said, startled. Artifacts were major magic—so major no one on Earth knew how to make them. It took an adept to make an artifact, and the knowledge had been lost even before the Purge. "What did it do?"

"No one knows. At least I never heard a whisper that anyone had figured it out, and I sure as hell couldn't. I studied the damn thing for days, but all that showed was the trigger—and that was locked."

"Locked," Lily repeated.

"*Locked* as in keyed to someone who has probably been dead for a few hundred years, so no one could use it. Resetting the key would take knowledge we just don't have."

"And you studied it for days?"

"That was about three months before it was stolen. And no," Cullen added with preemptive irritation, "I didn't have anything to do with that. Not from any moral objection on my part, but I couldn't afford Umbra."

"Umbra."

"That's the name your thief goes by. Or used to. Kind of pretentious, isn't it?'

"I don't know," she said dryly. "What does it mean?"

"It's the scientific name for one part of a shadow. Anyway, everyone assumed Umbra was the one who took the chalice because it was such a slick, high-dollar job. There was a lot of speculation about who his client might have been, but it was bullshit. No one really knew anything."

"Who's 'everyone'?"

Cullen waved vaguely. "People. You know."

"No, actually, I don't. But I'd like to."

"I'm not going to tell you about them. First, it was seven years ago, and I don't remember exactly who I talked to. Second, if any of them had an inkling I mentioned them to someone official, they'd never talk to me again. And that would be bad."

"Are they other sorcerers?"

"Did you hear me say I wouldn't tell you about them? I could've sworn I heard those words come out of my mouth." Cullen sighed. "I feel a bit better knowing it was Umbra who got through my wards. Not a lot, but some. He was supposed to be the best."

Rule's eyebrows lifted. "Was?"

"Two or three years ago word went out that he wasn't taking jobs anymore. Rumor was divided about why. Some said he'd retired. Some said he'd died. Looks like he was just on sabbatical."

Lily made a note. "Huh. Guess we'll have the chance to ask him. How did people reach Umbra to hire him?"

Cullen considered the question a moment. "I can tell you that much. Here in the States he used an agent, a big fat guy named Hugo. I met him once on an unrelated matter. Back then—this was maybe five years ago—he hung out at a dive called Rats in San Francisco. He's Gifted—can't tell you which one because I don't remember. Maybe one of the Air Gifts. Caucasian, around fifty, bald or else he shaved his head. Tattoo of a lightning bolt on his forehead. Looked like prison work."

"Last name?"

"No idea. He went by Hugo."

"How big was he?"

"About Rule's height and maybe three hundred pounds."

"Okay, I'll see if Arjenie can do anything with that." She

turned to Rule. "I need to ask Cullen some more questions before we get to the airport. Want to read that file now?"

No. "Yes."

She bent and dug a folder out of the case that held her laptop. It would have been easier to send the material to his iPad, but that left an electronic trail. Technically Lily had the authority to share information with a consultant; technically Rule could be called a consultant. But there was always the chance that someone would decide to make an issue of it.

He accepted the folder and opened it. The first page was a brief bio.

Jasper Frederick Machek
Born: San Francisco, California

Two years and nine months after she handed me to my father and walked away and never looked back . . .

Father: Frederick Alan Machek; b. 12/7/1929
Mother: Celeste Marie Machek, nee Babineaux; b. 9/27/1928 d. 3/11/ 2006

Rule stared at the page, his eyes dry and unseeing, his mind blank save for one thought.

Dead. She was dead.

SIXTEEN

LILY did not watch Rule read the file she'd handed him. She wanted to, but she was pretty sure that was a bad idea. When you're raw you don't want people studying your reactions, even if you've convinced yourself you're just fine.

Maybe especially then. She leaned forward and pulled her notebook and pen out of her purse. "Okay, Cullen, I need you to tell me more about the prototype. You're not the only one working on the problem—everyone from megacorporations to individual practitioners are giving it a shot. But this is the first really promising device for shielding tech from magic, right?"

"Wrong."

"You said it worked. You said that several times. That isn't promising?"

"I mean that it's not a shield."

"But it's supposed to protect tech from magic."

He nodded. "Naturally you think 'protect' equals 'shield.' I did, too, at first. So has everyone else. The problem is, the only way to absolutely, positively shield against every type of magic is to be you."

She blinked. "Ah—be a touch sensitive, you mean?" Able to feel magic, but impervious to it.

"Right. The first thing you need to know is that no substance shields really well against raw magic. Earth comes closer than most, but it's too varied to shield predictably. And it takes a lot of dirt to do much good."

"Raw magic is what comes from nodes."

"Right. Ambient magic is at least ninety percent raw. A small percentage is elemental, but the vast majority is raw—unless you're in an old forest, of course, but that's a special case, and there's not much tech deep in the Sequoia National Forest, so it doesn't matter. Now, some substances do offer minimal shielding, like the silk case you use for your phone, but they're ineffective near a node, a ley line, or even the ocean. Or if there's even a small surge. We don't get the kind of power blasts we did when the Turning hit," he added, "but there are frequent small surges, and the level of ambient magic continues to rise."

Rule looked up from the folder. He was on the second page, she noted. "A company came up with a polymer that showed promise initially, but they can't make it work longer than . . . what was it, thirty minutes?"

"Thirty max," Cullen agreed. "Theory suggests that no substance can shield well against raw magic for long because matter is, by definition, not magically inert."

Lily's eyebrows went up. "By definition? No, wait—don't explain that." Once Cullen got going on theory it was hard to shut him up.

His grin flashed. "I'll spare you. Mind, not everyone agrees with that theory, but most do, which is why most everyone is looking to combine some type of natural shielding with shaped magic. Charms, in other words. I won't go into all the reasons that's so hard to do, but one big problem is that tech isn't very useful if it lacks input and output. You can build an underground bunker and shield the hell out of it and be pretty sure the computer inside is protected, but as soon as you hook that computer up to something else—

even if it's a wireless connection—you've breached the shield."

"But you're not going to go into that." Her hand moved automatically, jotting down notes that would help her remember later: *even wireless = shield breach.*

"Right. Because the real drawback to creating a shield isn't the difficulty, though that's huge. It's that even if you succeed, all you've done is deflect the magic. Say you're Delta Airlines and the shielding on your big 747 deflected the hell out of a magic surge, but that deflected power hit the cell tower you were flying over and now the phone company's suing you. Or maybe it hit a small plane that couldn't afford fancy shielding, and that plane crashed." He shook his head. "Shields are not the answer."

"You found another answer." *Shields = deflected magic = collateral damage.*

"Damn straight. Based on you and dragons."

Her forehead wrinkled. Dragons were magical sponges. So was she, to a much lesser degree. "You want to soak up the magic instead of deflecting it?"

"Soak it up and store it . . . that's the way to go. We do know something about storing magic. Not as much as the sidhe, but something. Enough to get me started, but I wasn't making much headway until I started playing around with truth charms. You know that Arjenie burns them out?"

"That's what you said, yeah. Something about her Gift overloads them." Benedict's new Chosen had a rare Gift, a variant of the sidhe ability to cast illusions that let her go undetected. It wasn't true invisibility. It was better, because it also baffled hearing, scent, and most wards.

"I was curious about that, and so was she, so we experimented a bit. We figured it out, too. Her Gift is essentially the ability to lie to the mind. Even when she isn't actively lying, the kind of magic she uses overloads any truth charm touching her."

"That makes sense." *Arj. magic mental lie—overloads trth charms,* her pen noted. She snuck a glance at Rule. He was on the last page, but she wasn't sure he was reading it.

He seemed to be off in some private world, staring at the words without seeing them.

"But the cool part is what that meant. It meant the charms were soaking up some of her magic. They had to be, or they wouldn't burn out. Only a teensy trace, sure, but when I looked into it, I found that truth charms sample a trace of whatever magic is around—including raw magic."

Trth charms sampl magic. "No one knew this?"

He shrugged. "No reason to. They're designed to work on nulls as well as Gifted, so why would they sample magic? Plus the amount of power they sample is so tiny . . . it took a lot of tinkering with my magnify spell before I could see it, but I did see it. That was the first time I'd seen any formed magic work at all the way your Gift does—by sampling a smidge of magic—so I knew I was onto something. After a godawful amount of trial and error, I made a charm that does more than sample. It acts as a funnel, sending all the magic it comes in contact with into an array of lemon quartz crystals."

"Why lemon quartz?"

"Trees are too big and diamonds cost too damn much."

"Okaaaay."

"If I explained about trees, you'd yell at me for getting sidetracked. As for diamonds, they are the best portable way to store raw magic, no question about it. But they don't provide a great matrix for elemental magic, and the power the charm funnels is . . . you might say it's predisposed toward becoming mind-magic. It's not there yet, but the potentialities have been changed by the charm, giving it an affinity for Air, which is the element for mind-magic. Mind, all this classifying by element type is as imprecise as most generalizations. We're really talking about how the magic gets shaped by whatever absorbs then releases it, so—"

"Cullen."

"Too much? Okay. I used lemon quartz because Air magic can't be stored, but mind-magic can, and lemon quartz is generally the best matrix for mind-magic. But in this case, the power settles easily into lemon quartz." He stopped. His expression shifted to gloom. "And that's the problem."

"I thought the problem was that the device makes the unGifted have false memories. Memories of weird stuff."

"It does that when the array discharges suddenly, and it does that because the magic is unstable when it enters the array. It finishes transforming into mind-magic while it's in there, but the initial instability messes up the matrix." He brooded on that a moment before adding, "At least I think that's what's happening."

"Why does the discharge only affect nulls?"

He shrugged. "I've told you what I know. I need the damn prototype back to run more tests."

"You can make another if you have to, right?"

"It's not that simple."

"Tell her," Rule said.

Okay, he had been listening, after all.

"But . . ." Cullen's gaze went significantly toward the front seat.

Rule closed the folder. "Oh, very well. Scott, you will not speak of or otherwise reveal what Cullen says about his prototype to anyone who is not present in this car now. José, the same instruction for you, with the exception of your Rho. That was unnecessary," he added to Cullen, "but I trust you feel better now."

Cullen scowled and looked at Lily. "No notes. This does not go into your report. It doesn't get written down."

"I'll agree to keep it off the record for now. I can't agree it will never go in the record."

His scowl didn't ease. "Rule—"

"You mistake my authority if you think I can tell Lily what to do."

"I just thought . . . never mind." He looked directly at Lily. "No notes."

She clicked her pen and set it down.

"I made the prototype over five weeks ago. It's still working."

"Okay."

He made an impatient sound. "Five weeks, and I haven't renewed the charm."

"But you told me charms couldn't last beyond one moon cycle without being renewed. Only artifacts can. . . . shit. You mean—"

"It's not an artifact. Not really. It has about as much in common with real artifacts as Alexander Volta's 'voltaic pile' would with a modern lithium battery. But it is the first self-renewing charm created in our world since the last adept died, and it is possibly a first step toward creating a genuine artifact."

"But that means . . ." Her fingers twitched. Writing things down helped her think, dammit. "That means that whoever took it may not be interested in how it protects tech, or in creating weird fake memories. They may have had it stolen because it's a . . . a quasi-artifact. Who else knows about this?" she demanded.

"Three more people than did a minute ago," he said dryly. "The only ones I've told until now were Cynna, Rule, and Isen. But it's possible the wrong person saw the prototype. I'm no adept. I don't know how to hide the guts of a spell or charm the way they did. If a sorcerer saw my prototype, he or she might be able to figure out what it was. What it could do, if not exactly how it worked."

"So now we've got sorcerers as well as several major corporations for suspects." Not that this expanded their pool enormously. Sorcerers were extremely rare. But they were also extremely secretive, which meant they'd have a helluva time figuring out who, exactly, went on the suspect list. "And you're just now mentioning this?"

He sighed. "We probably have to add one more group to your list."

"Who?"

"You know that trade delegation that arrived in D.C. via the Edge gate about two weeks ago? First inter-realm trade in hundreds of years."

"Of course." The news had been full of it.

"The delegates include three elves, several humans who seem to be servants, and a halfling of some kind."

"Yeah, I've seen the pictures. She's kind of . . . shit. You don't mean—"

"I'm afraid so. Last week, I heard from some flunky in the State Department. Benessarai An'Cholai expressed an interest in seeing a demonstration of my prototype. We're supposed to meet on January second."

Shit, shit, shit. "Don't tell me this Beness-whatever is a sidhe lord."

"Ben-ESS-er-aye. Accent on the second syllable."

"Benessarai," she repeated impatiently. "Is he a sidhe lord?"

"He's certainly sidhe—an elf—but not a lord. Or so the flunky said."

"Would he be able to see magic the way you do? Some sidhe do, right? And how did he even hear about your prototype?'

"Excellent questions, and when you find the answers I hope you'll share them with me."

SEVENTEEN

THE addition of the sidhe—any sidhe—to the mix changed things considerably. Lily called Ruben with the news on the way to the airport. She put her phone on speaker. No point in pretending it was a private conversation. Not with lupi hearing.

Ruben made an *ah* sound of satisfaction. "There's a connection," he said definitely. "I don't know what, but one or more of our visiting sidhe are connected to this theft. Your investigation is suddenly more important, Lily, but also a good deal trickier. There are political ramifications—you'll let me worry about those—and the trade delegation has been granted temporary diplomatic immunity."

Lily grimaced. "So I can't arrest them even if they are guilty as hell."

"The connection might be innocent. I don't at the moment see how, but that doesn't negate the possibility. For now, focus on finding out who's involved and why they wanted the prototype and let me worry about how to make an arrest, if one is warranted. I have a feeling the 'why' will prove important. Oh, and ask Mr. Seabourne to please keep that appointment. I'd very much like to know why Benessarai is interested enough in the prototype to fly across the country."

Cullen twisted around in his seat—his was sitting up front—and snorted. "So would I. The sidhe know how to make *real* artifacts. I'd also like to know how he heard about the prototype in the first place. Learning anything will be a real trick, of course, given the way the sidhe are about information. They consider secrecy an art form. Literally." Cullen sighed. "Of course, Benessarai may not show up now, especially if he was just wanting a chuckle at the barbarian's crude little device."

Lily asked Ruben if he'd heard all that. Assured that he'd caught most of it, she said, "I can't see this elf guy crossing the country just to laugh at your prototype."

Cullen shook his head. "Elves are not human. They don't organize life the way we do—and by 'we' I mean lupi as well as humans, because we both sort the world into good and evil. Elves don't. On a fundamental level, they just don't. Their highest value is *dtha*, which roughly translated means knowledge and beauty, which they don't consider separate constructs, but more like two shades of the same color, or two lenses in a pair of glasses. Amusement is part of *dtha*. And no, I don't understand why, but it is, and it matters to them in ways that seem frivolous or absurd to us. You know that sidhe lord I met when he came here on walkabout?"

"You've told me about him."

"He violated an important ban to come to our realm. He left his land, his people, and sundered himself from a vast amount of power—he was a sidhe lord, remember, with the land-tie and all that implies. And he did all that because he thought it would be amusing."

"If elves are so secretive, how did you learn so much from him?"

"We made a deal. I can't tell you about what. That's part of the terms of the deal."

Lily thought about that a moment. "And was he amused by his visit?"

Cullen looked surprised, then grinned. "I asked him that myself. He said he was."

Lily glanced at Rule, sitting beside her. He hadn't said one word since she punched in Ruben's number. He seemed to be listening, but in an abstracted way. "I need to know whatever you've got about Benessarai and the other delegates," she told Ruben.

"I'll have Ida send you the file. It's quite slim, unfortunately. We do know that none of them are from Rethna's realm—at least, the realm they claim to represent isn't the one he came from. Arjenie tentatively confirms that, based on conversations with three of them. I'll call both her and State and see what they can tell me that isn't in the file."

"Okay." She hesitated, then, watching Rule, said, "About Jasper Machek . . . do I have the authority to make a deal with him if it leads us to whoever hired him to steal the device?" She'd told Ruben who Jasper Machek was. She'd had to. Rule hadn't objected. He hadn't really reacted at all.

"Are you certain you can separate your connection to him from the needs of the investigation?"

Lily considered several answers. She settled for a simple "no."

"That's honest, at any rate. I think you'd best tell him you can offer only a provisional agreement, which I'll have to approve."

That was better than she'd feared. She thanked Ruben and disconnected. "Are you okay with that?" she asked Rule.

He smiled. It didn't touch his eyes. "Fine. I'd rather Machek isn't arrested. Imprisonment wouldn't affect him the way it would one of my people, but I'm unable to see it as a decent sort of deterrent or punishment."

But Machek is one of your people, she wanted to say. *From the human side of your family.* Instead she took his hand and kept silent and wondered if she was being wise or really, deeply foolish.

*   *   *

LILY hadn't visited San Francisco in years. The city hadn't had any major magic-related crimes since she switched from local law enforcement to the federal variety, and before that . . . well, she and Cody used to come up here when they could both get time off. She figured it was normal to avoid a place loaded with memories after a bad breakup.

She did wonder, as their plane circled SFO, what kind of memories the city held for Rule. If she asked, he'd tell her, but then he'd get to ask her the same thing. She thought about that and decided it was okay. He knew about Cody, after all. But she'd ask later, when they were alone. Surely they'd be alone again sometime.

They did not leave the airport in Rule's usual choice of cars. His brother had told him to stop being so damn predictable, so he'd been tricky instead. He'd reserved a Mercedes, but changed it to a BMW at the rental desk. Scott drove. Hungry lupi were not focused lupi, so they picked up hamburgers and ate them as they wound up and down, through and around.

They were stopped at a light on Market Street when Rule got a call from Mike, who was holding down the fort at the hotel where they'd stay. "Already? But he hasn't had time to go to Clanhome, much less . . ." A longish pause. "Hmm. Welcome him for me, then, and feed him. Tell him it will be at least an hour before I can be there to accept and could be longer, but the delay is one of necessity, not disrespect." He disconnected and looked at Lily. "Isen is being unconventional again. The new Laban Rho just arrived at the hotel looking for us. He brought one of the Laban counselors to act as witness."

"Witness for what?"

"Isen told him I would accept his submission on Nokolai's behalf."

"Is that kosher?"

"Oh, yes. It's been done in the past, when circumstances didn't permit the usual ceremony and witnesses." He glanced at the back of Scott's head.

Lily understood that she wasn't supposed to ask what in the world Isen was up to, not within Scott's hearing. She didn't, but she wondered really hard.

They ended up on a horizontally challenged street in a neighborhood that was nothing like the kind of places where she'd hung out with Cody. It was an older area, but older in the pricey way, the kind of street where people sacrificed parking for charm and period details. Parked cars lined the curbs. Scott was lucky to find a spot two and a half blocks from their goal.

It was at least ten degrees colder here than back in San Diego. Lily was glad for her jacket and the brisk walk to keep her blood moving. She suspected Rule didn't notice. *Preoccupied* was one way to describe him. *Silent* was another. *Scared*, she suspected, would also fit, though he might not know it.

At the corner nearest Machek's home, they stopped. Tall, narrow Victorians with shared walls crowded the sidewalk on one side of the street. On this side the houses were a different style, identical aside from paint and whatever landscaping their owners had chosen for the pocket-size front yards. Each had a single-car garage at street level flanked by a long staircase leading to the second-floor entry; the stairs would make a claustrophobe uncomfortable, she thought with a glance at Rule, being closed in by walls on both sides. Wide bow windows arced out over the garages. "It's the blue one in the middle of the block, right?"

"Yes." Rule glanced at Scott. "Disposition?"

"Chris on the roof," Scott said. "Alan and Todd are on the adjoining roofs. The rest are patrolling."

That much Lily could see for herself. Barnaby and Steve were chatting across the street from Jasper Machek's house. Joe was with them, investigating a lamppost. Joe wore a harness and a leash and wagged his tail at a passing Pomeranian yapping at the end of its leash, but Joe did not look like a dog. He looked like a wolf trying to impersonate a dog. "You really think no one will guess what he is?"

"We've taken Joe for walks all over the place," Scott said. "No one raises an eyebrow. People see what they expect to see. It helps that Joe's wolf is smaller than most."

Small for a lupus, yeah. Or for a Great Dane. Outsize for pretty much anything else, but Scott seemed to be right. The woman at the other end of the Pomeranian's leash was more interested in checking out Barnaby and Steve than in their large but well-behaved dog.

Okay, time to call on the other member of their little force, if she was going to do it. Lily took a deep breath and did. "Drummond."

"What the hell—is he here?" Rule scowled.

"He is now." The misty form in front of her gradually coalesced into a lanky man with a receding hairline and a smirk. "What have you heard? What do you know?"

"Don't know much." Drummond's mouth moved as if he was pushing words out the usual way. She tried to spot some difference between this and regular speech, but couldn't. "I heard what you said at the airport and on the plane. You're going to make a deal with someone named Machek, but it could be a trap."

She nodded. "That's enough for now. You still want to help?"

"Lily," Rule said, "this is not a good idea."

She glanced at him. "If Drummond's still playing for the other team and this is an ambush, he'll either encourage us to walk into a trap or he'll try to buy our trust by giving up the bad guys. In the first case, we're going in anyway. In the second, we get a warning. How do we lose?"

"You forgot the third possibility," Drummond said sourly. "The one where I'm doing the right thing."

"I covered that with the first 'if.' "

Rule did not look as if he agreed, but he didn't object out loud. Cullen was looking from Lily to the place where Drummond stood. Or hovered. Whatever. He muttered something and made a gesture.

Drummond turned to glare at him. "Shit! Tell your spooky friend not to do that. It itches."

"You're calling *him* spooky?" Lily looked at Cullen. "What did you do? Drummond said it made him itch."

"Variant on a Find spell. Checking for ghosts." He grinned. "It worked."

"You couldn't just take my word for it?" Lily shook her head. "Never mind." She looked at Drummond. "You willing to check out that blue house in the middle of the block? Number 1129. Jasper Machek should be inside. He's fifty-three, six-one, around one-fifty-five, dark hair and eyes. We need to know if anyone else is with him."

"Should be within my range, but just barely. Don't go wandering off." With that he evaporated, or mostly. A wispy trace zipped off down the sidewalk.

"It's so weird that you can't see or hear him," Lily said.

"Maybe I can make it so I can," Cullen said. "It will take some tweaking, but if my Find spell works for him, I should be able to make him visible. At least briefly, and to me," he added. "And it won't help with hearing."

"Aren't ghosts connected to spirit?" Wiccan doctrine claimed there were five elements—air, earth, fire, water, and spirit. Spirit was different from the other four. Fire, earth, air, and water were types of magic, but spirit was something else or other or more. Lily didn't know what, and no one had been able to define it for her, but that "something else" quality was why she could see and hear Drummond. Her Gift didn't block spirit. "I thought your kind of magic didn't work on spirit."

"It doesn't, but if I . . . do you really want me to explain?"

"Now that you mention it—no."

"Lily."

She looked at Rule, who was staring down the sidewalk, an odd expression on his face. "What?"

"I saw it. Him. For a minute it looked like a bit of fog moving down the sidewalk."

"That's almost weirder than you not seeing him."

"It has to be the mate bond, doesn't it? Somehow it let me share what you see, in a limited way. It hasn't done anything like that in a long time."

Not since they were captured by the Great Bitch's agents, in fact. "The bond was new then. I thought that was why our abilities sort of slopped over onto each other for a while."

"The newness made it possible. The Lady made it happen. Why would the Lady want me able to see Drummond?" He frowned. "I think you need to talk with the Etorri Rhej again."

"I just did. What could I ask her that I haven't already?"

"It's more what you'd tell her. Drummond says he can't manifest at Clanhome. That's what you told me, isn't it? It makes me wonder if he's contaminated by *her.* If he's the Great Bitch's agent, being at Clanhome might inhibit what he can do."

"Wouldn't your father know if he were?" If someone contaminated by *her* power crossed onto Clanhome, the mantle would alert Isen. At least that was how it was supposed to work.

"Does that apply to a ghost? I don't know. Do you?"

If he didn't, she sure as hell had no clue. "I guess I should call her. But not," she said with a glance up the street, "right now." A pale mist wafted quickly back down the sidewalk toward them. She waited until it reached them to say, "That was quick."

The fog shaped itself into Drummond's too-familiar form. "Doesn't take long if I'm just counting live bodies. You glow."

"Who does? What do you mean?"

"All you embodied types. From this side, you've got a glow. I don't have to manifest to see it."

"Huh."

"Machek's there, or someone who matches his description. No one else, except for the cats. Two of them."

"They glow, too?"

He grimaced. "They've got bodies, so . . . yeah."

She glanced at Rule. "He says Machek's inside with two cats. No one else."

Rule cast a hard look in Drummond's general direction. "Guess we'll find out."

RULE didn't feel sick. Maybe his stomach felt like he'd swallowed rocks, but that was not the same as feeling sick. He was tense, yes. His muscles were tight in a way that would interfere with quick action, if such were needed, so as he climbed the stairs he went through a quick relaxation routine . . . again.

Why was he reacting this way? He didn't understand. He wished he would stop.

There was a narrow porch at the top of the stairs, over-hung by the roof. The door was stained rather than painted, the wood mellow with age and sheened by a recent cleaning with mineral oil, judging by the faint scent. Lily stood to his right, Cullen to his left and slightly behind. Scott had his back. Lily had her weapon out.

Rule pressed the doorbell.

Footsteps on a wooden floor. The door opened. Rule looked into his own eyes.

"Rule Turner," the man with his eyes said. His gaze drifted to Lily, snagged for a second on her gun. First his eyebrows shot up, then his mouth kicked up . . . a mouth not shaped like Rule's. It was wider, with a mobile flex that spoke of easy smiles. "And company. More company than I was expecting, but come in, all of you." He opened the door wide, then wandered away, apparently trusting them to follow.

Rule did, with Lily right behind him. Then Cullen, then Scott, who closed the door their host had apparently lost interest in.

The entry hall was small, dominated by a huge abstract painting—mostly orange, with geometric shapes dancing across it in a way that suggested fire. Beside the bit of wall that held the painting was a staircase; otherwise the entry was open to the living room on the left. That was eclectically furnished, with tables in both old wood and polished steel; African masks, ink drawings, and framed posters on taupe walls; an old church pew and two wing chairs grouped with a cream-colored contemporary sofa.

Jasper plopped down in one of the wing chairs and gestured at the sofa. His hair was the same color as Rule's, but curly. And graying. "Come in and sit, and perhaps you'd like to put that gun away?" The last was accompanied by a roguish waggle of his eyebrows, as if he invited Lily to some faintly wicked act.

"We'll see," she said pleasantly as she and Rule entered the room trailing Cullen and Scott. "You're Jasper Machek?"

"And you're Lily Yu." That wide mouth stretched in an attractive smile. "I've seen you interviewed. You're even lovelier in person, I must say, than on TV. But I don't know the two gentlemen with you who are not Rule Turner."

"Cullen Seabourne and Scott White."

"Seabourne." Machek's eyebrows lifted. "How awkward, yet how convenient."

Cullen answered him coolly. "Is it, now?"

Machek didn't respond, apparently fascinated by the sight of Cullen. Rule glanced around the large room. Someone had poured quite a bit of money into the house, gutting this floor to create the kind of open floor plan beloved of designers these days. At one end, the big bay window held a cluttered roll-top desk, its top open. A pile of fur slept on top of an assortment of papers there . . . a cat, actually, but Rule wouldn't have known that if not for his nose. Couch, church pew, and chairs in the middle. Dining at the far end, with the kitchen around the corner.

The room smelled of cats, people, peppers, and ginger. Chinese takeout, he guessed, glancing at the square dining table, where a foam container held what remained of today's lunch.

With his immediate territory charted, he took Machek up

on his invitation to sit, choosing one end of the couch. The end nearest his newfound kin. He drew in a slow breath and learned that Machek was a good deal more anxious than he looked. And guilty about something.

Machek met his gaze. Blinked. "This is disconcerting, isn't it? Especially when you look like my much-younger brother, not older. If you'll tell me who does your work, I know any number of people who'd love to make him rich."

Work? Oh—plastic surgery. Rule smiled a trifle grimly. "Clean living."

Machek snorted.

Cullen sat while they were talking, taking the other wing chair. Scott fell back to the wall sheltering the stairway, where he could keep an eye on most of the room. Lily holstered her weapon, advanced toward Jasper, and held out her hand. "It's good to meet you."

His eyebrows flew up. "Is it?" But he rose automatically and accepted her outstretched hand.

"Well," she said after they shook, "that's a surprise." She glanced at Cullen. "It's a very slight Gift, but it feels like yours."

Cullen leaned forward, studying Machek intently.

Machek frowned at her. "I don't know what you're talking about."

"You must have seen the wrong news clips, or you'd know that I'm a touch sensitive."

"Son of a bitch," Cullen said. "You're right. He's a sorcerer."

Machek stiffened. "Don't be ridiculous."

"I'm frequently ridiculous. You're still a sorcerer."

"But—" Machek drew a breath, exhaled, and waved one hand. "Never mind. I have a touch of the Sight. It doesn't make me a sorcerer, but if you—"

Cullen didn't let him finish. "What do you think a sorcerer is, anyway?"

"The legal definition is someone who sources their spells outside themselves. Since I don't have any spells—"

"The legal definition is bullshit. You must know that. You've stolen enough texts to understand—"

"I steal them. I don't read them."

Cullen looked astonished. "You must."

"Why?"

"Never mind," Lily said, finally sitting down herself next to Rule. "Whatever you call your Gift, it must come in handy in your profession. No one can pass a dummy magical item off as the real thing when you can see the magic, or lack of it."

He cast her a wary glance. "Yes, well, I'm retired, actually. Or was. Is he"—a nod at Scott—"just going to stand there?"

"Yes," Rule said.

Machek's eyebrows lifted. "What is he—a bodyguard? Do you trail bodyguards everywhere?"

"Yes," Rule said again. "Every so often, someone tries to kill me or Lily. I'd like to hear about the deal you wanted to make."

"We should get to it, shouldn't we?" But instead of launching into explanation, he leaned forward, head down, rubbing his hands together as if they ached. "I want," he began. Stopped, and muttered, "No, I'm making this too complicated. Keep it simple." He drew a ragged breath and raised his head. "This would have been easier if you'd brought Cynna Weaver. She could have found . . . they took something of mine, you see. Something I want back. But you wouldn't bring your Finder, so I have to ask for my side of the deal first. After that, I'll tell you everything. Do whatever you ask."

Rule's lips twisted. "We're supposed to give you what you want and trust that you'll honor your end of the deal afterward?"

"I'm afraid so." He glanced at Lily. "You did insist on bringing the authorities along, in the person of your fiancée. Once I'm all officially confessed, I may not be free to retrieve what's mine."

"Speaking of which—" Lily began.

"No. We won't speak of it. Not at all."

Very softly she asked, "Where's Adam?"

His eyes widened. Just for a second, so briefly she would have missed it if she hadn't been watching closely. "Out of town."

"They've got him, don't they? Whoever 'they' may be, they've got your partner, Adam King."

EIGHTEEN

JASPER Machek shook his head. "You're wrong."

Lily studied him. He had good control, but he didn't do stone-face as well as his brother. He couldn't keep the fear out of his eyes . . . eyes so much like Rule's, except for the crow's-feet, the subtle toughening of skin that comes with age. "Easy enough to prove. A phone call would do the trick."

"I don't have to prove anything."

"You might want to rethink that. Kidnapping's a felony. Failure to disclose a felony is a felony."

"There's nothing to disclose. Adam likes to get away from everything sometimes, doesn't even take his cell phone. I won't tell you where he is because, well, I don't want him to know about this. Any of this."

"I suspect he'll notice when you go to jail."

"I'm hoping you won't arrest me." He rubbed both hands along his thighs and essayed a smile, directing it at Cullen. "That would be in part up to you, I imagine. If you get your item back—with damages," he added quickly. "Payment for the, uh, insult and inconvenience—maybe you won't feel the need to press charges."

Cullen responded to that with a scornful curl of his lip. Machek just smiled. "Money's useful. Think about it."

He didn't really care, Lily thought. Staying out of jail wasn't what mattered at the moment. Later it might, but not now. "Okay," she said, mildly. "We won't talk about Adam. How long has your stolen whatever-it-is been missing?"

"You've got things switched." He leaned back in his chair, crossing one leg at the knee. He had long legs, much like his brother's, to go with a similar build—tall and lean, with wide shoulders and slim hips. He was lighter than Rule, though—less muscular, with elbows and shoulder blades and knees providing an emphatic punctuation where bone met bone. He slid a glance Rule's way. "I won't discuss my stolen property, but I love to talk about Adam. That would be a distraction, though, wouldn't it? A waste of time, and I have a deadline. I have to give them what they want or they'll destroy my property."

"And you don't have the prototype anymore. Or so you told Rule."

"We should make that deal before I say more."

"My boss will have to approve any deal I make. At this point you haven't given me much reason to push him for any kind of deal."

He frowned. Fidgeted with his hands—long fingers, a little longer than Rule's—rubbing them on his legs again. "I need to stay free until my property is recovered. After that I can talk about all kinds of things, and we can renegotiate. If you can agree—or get your boss to agree—to that much, we have a deal."

"The timing of an arrest is up to me. I can agree to delay it until you have your property back."

"Good." His breath gusted out. "That's good. We have a deal."

"You need the prototype to get your property back, but you told Rule you don't have it anymore."

"That's right."

"Who took it? How? Where were you?"

He shook his head. "I'll answer all that gladly, but not yet."

"We can't recover it if you won't tell us anything."

"Oh, I don't expect you to. I had to tell them the prototype was missing. These aren't people you can lie to."

"They?"

"Their identities will be up for discussion later, not now. Fortunately, they agreed to a substitution. Instead of the prototype, they'll take the man who made it."

Cullen barked out a laugh. "First you steal from me, then you want me to exchange myself for your lover? With balls that big, I don't see how you get your jeans zipped in the morning."

"It's a wonder," Machek said agreeably. "But I thought . . . I may be all wrong about this, but I thought this wasn't entirely up to you. If Rule orders you to do something, you have to do it, don't you?"

Rule's eyebrows lifted. "And you thought I'd exchange Cullen for what you insist is an object, not a person?"

"Well . . ." He spread his hands. "I thought you'd come up with a way to make the exchange, then reclaim him. I leave it to you to figure out how to do that. As to why you'd go to all that trouble—"

"And a certain amount of risk," Rule said dryly.

"And risk," Machek agreed. "Judging by your actions in Washington in October, I'd say you're willing to risk quite a lot to protect others. But perhaps there has to be some self-interest involved, too. Something of importance to you or your people, such as the man you claim was behind the attacks in October. You'd want to find him if you could."

"Robert Friar?" Lily said sharply. "You know where he is?"

"Not precisely. Not his exact location. But he's in California, and I have information that may lead you to him."

"Is he behind all this? Did he hire you?"

Machek slid her a glance as opaque as Rule at his most closed down. "I won't answer questions until I have my property back."

He meant it. Lily was convinced of that. How much of the rest did he mean? He'd stepped around certain statements meticulously, as a man might who preferred to speak truth, but was constrained from real honesty. Or as a clever and expert liar might. He didn't claim to know where Friar was. He didn't say Friar was behind this. He implied the possibility, but he wouldn't say who had kidnapped his partner. He wouldn't admit King had been taken.

If Lily weren't here, he might have told Rule that much of the truth, instead of talking about "property." Even with Lily here he might have taken that risk if they'd brought Cynna along, hoping she could find King before his captors realized the FBI was involved. Instead, they'd brought Cullen. *How convenient,* he'd said. "How is the exchange—" Her phone chimed the opening to "Boy" by Ra Ra Riot . . . Beth's ring tone. Lily grimaced and reached into her purse to turn the ringer off. "How will the exchange be handled?"

"I don't know. I'll get a call sometime today or tonight with the details."

Rule spoke. "You had us meet you here at your home. I take it this mysterious *they* know you're talking to us. What do they think you're telling us?"

His eyes flashed with what might be amusement. "Why, right now I'm telling you that I'm acting as a go-between for the real thief, who is now willing to sell it back to you in order to avoid those violent types who attacked him and tried—unsuccessfully—to steal it from him last night."

Lily's eyebrows lifted. "They assumed I wouldn't see through that and arrest you?"

"They expressed confidence in my ability to talk you out of that until you had the prototype back. To keep you busy, I'm to feed you misinformation about the attempted snatch so you'll look in the wrong places until it's time for the exchange. Then I lure Seabourne to the place named."

"Just Cullen?" Lily asked.

He shrugged. "I'm to bring him alone if I can, but they accept that you might not agree to that. Once we're all in

place, ah . . ." He cast Cullen an apologetic look. "Seabourne will be incapacitated with wolfbane."

Rule said, "Do you know how, exactly, they plan to do
that? It's not as easy to do as it might seem, given your success with the stuff on Big Sister."

"They didn't say. I assumed they'd burn it, but assumptions aren't the best guide. Should I try to find out when
they call?"

Rule shook his head. "Too easy to make them suspicious. They'll expect you to be focused on getting King . . .
on getting your property back, not on what they do with
Cullen."

"They know I've some concern about his welfare. That's
how I pried out of them that they'd be using wolfbane. They
assured me he'd be treated gently, that he's no use to them
dead."

Cullen snorted his opinion of that.

"Don't get fancy," Lily said to Machek. "Find out anything you can about the location and means of the proposed
exchange, but don't go beyond that." She looked at Rule,
wondering where he wanted this to go. He met her gaze, but
his was shuttered, telling her nothing.

When in doubt, ask questions. Lily did, coming back to
the same ones in multiple ways, until Machek politely suggested she could either arrest him or leave, but he hoped
they'd agree to the exchange. And at last Rule spoke again.

"We can't agree to anything without more information,"
he said, standing. "When you know the where, when, and
how for this proposed exchange, call me and we'll discuss it."

"I have your number," Machek said calmly, rising like a
good host whose guests were departing.

He hid differently than Rule did, Lily thought. He used
lightheartedness for a shield. "And mine," she added, taking
out one of her cards and setting it on the cluttered coffee
table. "Just in case."

NINETEEN

THEY were gone. At last they were gone. Thank God.

Jasper closed the door and scrubbed his face with both hands as if he could erase some of the lies he'd told. No point in dwelling on it. He'd done what he had to do.

No, that was lying to himself, a sin at least as bad as lying to others and often far more destructive. He'd chosen to put Adam's life above these strangers' welfare. However terrible a choice it might be, it had been his to make, and he had to admit that. If one of those strangers was his half brother, did that matter?

Not enough, he thought as he headed back to the couch where he'd snatched a few hours of sleep last night. He'd cleared away the pillow and blanket before Rule Turner and his entourage arrived. It was the first time they'd been put away since that bastard took Adam. Funny how his innate tidiness had fled ever since he got that phone call. He'd been deliberately leaving clutter around as if that would create a homing beacon for his messy partner. Adam would laugh when he saw . . .

God, he hoped Adam would still be able to laugh.

He sank onto the couch and picked up the card that

Rule's fiancée had left. Lily Yu. He turned it over as if he might find a clue on its blank back. She sure didn't look like an FBI agent . . . she had the serious part down, but she was so little. Pretty, too, though somehow that word didn't seem to fit. Flowers were pretty. She was . . . compact, he decided. As if something much larger had been crammed into a deceptively small size.

Odd choice for his brother to make. He couldn't picture Lily Yu putting up with a partner's roving eye, but what did he know? Nothing, really, about the lady, and not much more about the man who shared half Jasper's genetic inheritance. No more than however many zillion others who occasionally read a gossip mag. Jasper didn't pick them up ordinarily, but he'd been curious. Now and then he'd toyed with the idea of meeting Rule Turner. Like when his mom was dying and he learned how much Isen Turner had paid for over the years. Or when he first came out. He'd come boiling out of the damn closet, pissed at the world, and that had seemed like a great target for his anger—the overwhelmingly hetero half brother who was sure to be disgusted.

If he'd been disgusted today, he'd hidden it well. But he'd hidden everything well, hadn't he? Jasper had seen a certain intensity, but he had no idea what the man was feeling intense about. Maybe Rule wasn't the heedless tomcat he'd been made out to be. Maybe he used to be, but had changed. Now and then people did.

The resemblance had startled Jasper. It had never seemed that strong in photos or on TV, but when he looked into his brother's eyes . . . and just why did Rule look so damn young? He was six years older than Jasper, but he looked fifteen years younger. The best surgeon in the world didn't give you back young skin. Could it be a lupi thing? Maybe in addition to being preternaturally strong and sexy, they didn't age.

That was an unsettling thought. But what about this day wasn't unsettling, grim, terrifying—

His phone buzzed. His heart jumped in his chest, loathing

and longing coupling promiscuously with fear, shame, and more—a veritable orgy of feelings that had him snatching the phone up quickly, then hesitating. He didn't recognize the number, but Adam's kidnapper never called from the same number twice. "Yes?"

"You did well, Jasper." It was a warm voice, friendly, with just the right touch of sympathy, the kind of voice that could coax a smile from a sullen child.

Fresh diarrhea was warm, too. And just about as welcome. This wasn't the voice Jasper longed for. "I'll speak with Adam now."

"Will you?" The amusement was light, not without that tracery of sympathy.

"That's our deal. You want me to remain confident that you'll honor your end, don't you? You want me to go on believing that Adam is alive and that I'll get him back."

"I do enjoy dealing with an intelligent man," his nemesis said in an approving way. "And yet I suspect that hope would work as well as certainty. Maybe better. It might be helpful for me to find out."

Fear broke out the razor blades and sawed at Jasper's gut. "I'm not a very optimistic person. I need certainty to keep me motivated. I'll speak with Adam now, or I'll speak to Lily Yu."

"The laborer is worthy of his hire, I suppose. The Bible is wrong about a great deal," he added, "but there are nuggets of wisdom among the debris. You've done as you were told, and you will receive your agreed-upon pay . . . since Adam is in fact quite well, though not particularly happy at the moment. First, however, I have instructions about tonight."

"Wait while I get a pen." He did that, collecting his notebook at the same time, then listened, jotting the pertinent facts down in his personal shorthand. Jasper had long since established the habit of putting any notes about a job down in a form no one could use against him in court.

"I'm surprised by your concern," the warm voice said when Jasper questioned one point. "Have you changed your mind about Rule Turner now that you two have met? You told me you didn't know much about him, but what you did know, you didn't like."

"Oh," he breathed, "but I dislike you so much more."

"Do you not think it impolitic to say so?"

"Who can we be truly frank with, if not our enemies?"

A chuckle, rich with amusement. "Oh, Jasper, don't fool yourself. You're bought and paid for. You'll do as you're told, and that's hardly the behavior of an enemy, is it?"

TWENTY

⟿

RULE headed down the outdoor stairs, so baffled by emotion he barely noticed the closed-in feeling piling on top of the rest. He was only too aware of how poorly he'd handled himself in there, but at least he'd realized that and let Lily take the lead.

She'd done that efficiently, asking plenty of questions. Not the ones he'd wanted answered, such as: *How did your mother die?* Or *Did she look like you? Like me?* Or *Did you ever think about contacting me?* No, she'd asked the ones that should have mattered . . . and would, once he pulled himself together.

Time to make a start on that. At the base of the stairs, Rule began, "If Friar—"

"Let's talk about it when we get to the car," Lily said.

He grimaced. If Friar was involved, he'd been about to say, it changed the possibilities considerably . . . including the chance that someone was pointing a directional microphone their way right now. That was unlikely but possible, and he should have thought of it. "Point taken." Then, to Scott: "Keep Chris and Alan here to keep an eye on Jasper. The others will follow us to the hotel. Send Barnaby and

Joe ahead to check the car." As he started down the sidewalk he asked Lily, "Is Drummond around?"

"Not visibly."

Which was supposed to mean he couldn't listen in,
but . . . "Would you mind putting on your necklace?"

For answer she reached in her purse and pulled it out,
closing her hand around the stones. "It works when it's in
contact with my skin. Or it's supposed to."

She didn't tell him it was understandable that he was
shaken. She didn't ask what he thought of Jasper Machek
or how he felt. She held the ghost-repelling necklace in one
hand and took his hand with the other one, then walked
beside him in silence. Bless her for that, as for so much
else. He didn't know what he felt or what he thought, and
he couldn't afford to be shaken. Not if Friar had his finger
in this pot.

They moved briskly down the street. Rule tried to empty
his mind. It didn't work. He was still a jumble when they
crossed the first street and Lily broke the silence.

"I liked Jasper."

"I did, too." He hadn't expected to. He hadn't
expected . . . any of this. He wasn't going to be able to put
it aside, was he? He wouldn't be able to concentrate on the
things that ought to matter until he'd dealt with what, inex-
plicably, did. He stopped and glanced back at Scott. "I need
to walk a bit and clear my head. If the car's clean, have
them drive it around the block until I signal." He made the
quick gesture that told Scott to drop back several yards.

"You want me to take a hike?" Cullen asked.

"Or a ride. I'd rather you didn't wander around where
someone could grab you or attempt to. Either stay with
Scott or get in the car with the others."

Rule resumed walking. Scott and Cullen fell behind. If
he kept his voice low, they wouldn't hear more than the oc-
casional word. And now that he had this much privacy, he
didn't know what to say.

Lily didn't prompt him. For once, she didn't ask questions. She just kept pace with him for another two blocks.

But now, for whatever reason, he could at least turn his attention away from the noise in his head, listening to the city sounds . . . cars, voices from some of the houses they passed, a dog in the last block, a cat in this one. The soft sound of Lily's footsteps beside him. Her hand was warm in his. He watched as a woman in workout clothes pushed a jogging stroller along on the other side of the street. Its occupant looked sound asleep. And he heard himself say, "It never occurred to me that she was dead."

Lily stopped, so he did, too. She looked at him. "Oh, Rule."

"It should have occurred to me. She'd be over eighty by now if she'd lived, so it was an obvious possibility. But as long as I didn't think of her . . ." He shoved his free hand through his hair. "She wasn't real. She wasn't a person to me, yet as long as I didn't think about her, she was still alive somewhere." Frustrated, he added, "I don't know why it matters."

"Death cuts off possibilities. Even if they were possibilities you never meant to act on, it feels different when they're gone."

Possibilities he never meant to act on, never thought he wanted. And now he ached from their loss. "She wasn't a mother to me, but she was a person. I'll never know that person. I never thought I'd want to."

"She was bipolar."

"What?" He stared. "I mean—I know what that is, of course, but how do you know that?"

"Isen told me last night. She was in treatment for it several times, on his dime. I thought he should have told you years ago. He and I argued about that."

A dozen thoughts and memories tumbled around in his head. The past was supposed to be fixed, unalterable, but it was shifting on him. Finally he said, "It takes determination to argue with Isen."

"The Rho thing doesn't work on me."

"Even so." He started walking again. After half a block he said, "I want to get to know Jasper."

"That would be good. We've got some heavy shit to get through first."

Too damn true. "Speaking of which . . ." Rule stopped again and looked behind them. Scott and Cullen were half a block back. He gave the signal for them to approach.

"Jasper thought you'd be upset about Adam."

He quirked a surprised brow at her. "I am, of course. Assuming that our assumption about his kidnapping is true."

"Not that kind of upset. Upset because his lover is a man. Once he got past the shock of me figuring out what property had been taken from him, he watched you. He was waiting for you to go all ick on him."

"How did you see that? I didn't."

"Not so much baggage. No," she corrected herself. "Different baggage. Mine doesn't involve Jasper."

He felt better. Not good, but not as jumbled. He smiled to tell Lily that. "Why do you suppose he never contacted me?"

"He was raised by a bipolar mother who didn't get adequate treatment for years. He grew up gay in a society that made him a target for every kind of hate and bullying. Chances are he has his own baggage, don't you think?"

The rented BMW reached them quickly. Rule and Lily took the backseat; Cullen sat up front with Scott. Lily, he noticed, put her necklace back in her purse. Why didn't she just keep it on? She had some kind of crazy tolerance for Drummond's ghost that he couldn't fathom and didn't like.

"All right," Rule said once they were moving. Short of planting a bug—which the guards had checked for—it was almost impossible to target a moving vehicle either electronically or magically. "I'd like to hear your impressions. How much of Jasper's story was true, do you think?"

Lily shrugged. "All, some . . . impossible to say." She reached for her laptop and popped it open.

"He smelled anxious and guilty," Cullen put in, "but the anxiety could be about his lover. So could the guilt. Nothing gets the guilt gland pumping like thinking you've endangered someone you love."

"That part I'd put money on," Lily said. She was typing something on her laptop as she spoke. "The part he didn't admit—that they're threatening his partner to force him to do what they want. Not that I'm taking his word that it's 'they' rather than 'he' or 'she.'"

Rule hadn't noticed Jasper's use of the plural pronoun to refer to whoever had Adam, but now that Lily brought it up . . . "If Friar's involved, 'they' is appropriate. Especially on this coast." Friar's East Coast lieutenant was in jail awaiting trial, having been refused bail as a flight risk. But his West Coast lieutenant was still free and active.

"Friar must be part of it," Cullen said. "How would Machek know to mention him otherwise? The official story is that Robert Friar died when the mountain came down in September."

Lily looked up. "But Machek didn't mention Friar by name, did he? I did. He said something about us wanting to find the one behind the October attacks. I filled in the blank for him."

Cullen looked over his shoulder at her, startled. "Son of a bitch. You're right. Did he do that on purpose?"

"I don't know."

"How did you guess that he was talking about his partner, anyway?"

"That's right, you didn't see his file, did you?"

Rule, on the other hand, had pretty much memorized it. "Arjenie dug up a fair amount about Adam King," he said. "He showed up in one of her databases because he and Jasper purchased the house together three years ago. King is an architect who was laid off during state cutbacks a couple of years ago. He's put out his own shingle and is enjoying some success, but he works from home. He wasn't there today. He might have left the house for any number of reasons, but there was only one takeout lunch at the table. Only one mug on the coffee table, too."

Lily nodded, tapping away on her laptop. "Add to that Machek's attitude. He wasn't worried about getting arrested. He made the right noises, but he didn't really care.

What else would cause that kind of funneling of priorities? Odds were he was frantic about a person, not an object."

"Okay," Cullen said, "I can see that. What are you working on, anyway?"

"A request for a phone tap."

Rule's head jerked. "A tap? On Jasper? But if he isn't reporting a kidnapping—"

She gave him a look he couldn't read. "I'm not going to charge your brother with failure to disclose. That doesn't mean I have to pretend Adam King's really gone off for some downtime without his phone. First step is a tap on Jasper's phones—at his store, his house, on his mobile. He could have a throwaway given him by his employer especially for contact, but we can't do anything about that."

Cullen grinned. "You're sneaky. Isen would approve. Where are we going, anyway?"

Sometimes Cullen was unnervingly observant. Sometimes he failed to notice the proverbial brass band. "To the hotel," Rule said. "Assuming Lily still wants to put off checking in with her local office?" She nodded, and Rule went on, "Tony Romano is at the hotel."

"What, already?"

"Per Isen's instructions, he didn't go to Nokolai Clanhome. I'm to accept his submission on behalf of Nokolai."

"Huh. What's on the list after that?"

Lily raised her brows. "You have something else you need to do?"

"I could be working a Find spell for the prototype. Cynna stayed up damn near all night working up a more detailed pattern for it, and she gave me a copy of the pattern. Integrating that pattern into a spell takes longer than using it the way she would," he added, "and I'll need privacy for that."

"Oh. Right. You should be able to work on your spell at the hotel. What comes next for me and Rule depends on what Romano tells us. Also on if we hear from Machek, or if Arjenie has learned more about that Hugo character you told me about. If she . . . shit, I forgot to turn my ringer back on." She glanced at Rule as she reached in her purse. "Have you got someone who knows the city well, or should I supply someone like that? If we end up faking an exchange, that could be important."

"There's Murray, but I don't like to pull him away from Beth." Rule considered briefly. "Tony Romano knows San Francisco. He's lived here for . . . what is it?"

She was frowning at her phone. "Beth called two more times, and there's a text from her, too. She wants me to call. She put 'urgent' in all caps. It probably isn't, but I'd better call."

Rule knew what she meant. Beth wasn't the fashion-obsessed airhead she liked to impersonate, but Lily's family had a blind spot about her job. They tended to think it was a great deal more interruptible than it was.

Lily tapped the screen. Rule heard the phone ring, then: "Lily!"

"Beth?" Lily said. "What did you—"

"Thank God you called. He's missing. The police don't want to hear about it," she said bitterly. "They gave me this bullshit about waiting forty-eight hours. They think he's forgetful or drunk or just doesn't want to see me, but Sean's as dependable as sunrise. We had an appointment today at ten—a business appointment—but he wasn't there, and that's so not like him. And I can't find anyone who's seen him since our Bojuka class last night."

"Who are you talking about?"

"Sean. I thought I said that. Sean's missing. Sean Friar."

BETH'S tiny walk-up wasn't far from Machek's house geographically, but it was light-years away economically. The living room—which was also the dining room and kitchen—was colorful, cluttered, and cramped. After one glance inside, Rule had told Scott to wait in the hall. Lily wasn't sure where the other guards were.

By the time she shoved pillows aside to sit on the shabby but comfortable couch, Lily had counted five elephants, including the framed print she'd given Beth for Christmas this year. Beth loved elephants. The large, square coffee table was Beth's contribution, too, though it hadn't been painted neon pink back when it sat in their mother's living room. The apartment smelled funny. Not pot, but some kind of incense, she thought.

Rule sat beside her on the couch. Cullen parked his rear on the lone barstool that served as additional seating. Beth paced and talked, clutching her phone in one hand like a security blanket. Hoping he'd call, Lily thought. Hoping it was all a silly mistake. Not believing that, but not willing to put down the phone, either.

"His bike and his car were there, so I checked the windows, but they were all locked. The ones on the ground floor, anyway. I couldn't get to the upper story." Beth whirled to face Lily. "What if he's lying in there, too hurt to answer?" Tears sparkled in her eyes. "The stupid police won't check!"

She'd cut her hair again just before Christmas, so Lily had seen the current crop already, but the blue streak was new. The spikes were more due to distraction than to make a fashion statement. Beth kept running her hands through it. "They aren't supposed to break into people's homes unless the need is immediate and urgent. It's a house, not an apartment?"

"Yes. Does that matter?"

"Sometimes an apartment manager will open a unit for the police without a warrant. Sean works from home, you said. Does he have a housekeeper?"

"She only comes in twice a week. Today isn't her day."

"And he doesn't have any other employees."

"I told you I called Carly and John!"

"You didn't tell me they were his employees. What did they do when they came in to work and Sean wasn't there?"

"Oh. They didn't. They're contract, like me, though they're more full-time than I am, but they still work from home. See, Sean designs a program's basic architecture and handles the trickier parts—he's brilliant, really—and they work on some of the components. He calls me in for the graphics, if they're needed. That's what we were to talk about today. I've roughed in some possibilities, and we were going to talk about them."

"I need their phone numbers and full names. Also the names and numbers of anyone else you called or can think of, his address, and the make and model of his car and bike."

"But his car and motorcycle are still there."

"Humor me."

The car was an older Lexus; Beth didn't know the year, but thought it was at least ten years old. The motorcycle was newer, a black BMW with lots of chrome. Beth didn't have a clue about the license numbers, but that would be easy to find. She sent Lily Carly's and John's contact information, as well as that of the other two people she'd called. She'd also called the hospitals, who hadn't admitted to having a Sean Friar on their premises. Ditto for the morgue. "You said he referred to your appointment when you saw him last night."

"Yes, yes. 'See you tomorrow,' he said. Shouldn't you be doing something?"

"I am. Do you know if he's seeing anyone?" Beth had insisted she and Sean were not a couple.

"He's not."

"You're sure."

"We're friends. He would have told me."

Lily didn't doubt Beth believed that. "Do you have a picture of him?"

"Sure." Beth lifted her phone, touched the screen a few times, and held it out. "This one's pretty good."

It was a close-up of a forty-something man with sun-streaked hair and dark eyes. Caucasian, clean-shaven. His nose and his grin were both slightly crooked, lending an appealing asymmetry to otherwise regular features. Lily's heart sank right down to the pit of her stomach, where it thudded around uncomfortably.

Rule leaned in to look at the small screen. He and Lily exchanged a glance. There'd been a chance, however faint, that Beth's Sean Friar wasn't the one Lily had a file on. The photo took away that small hope. "Send it to me, okay?" she said, handing Beth back her phone.

"What are you going to do?"

"I'm here on a case, so I can't—no, wait, don't explode. I'm taking you seriously, but I can't drop everything and personally look for him. I'll put someone on it."

Beth looked dubious. "You've got people you can put on things?"

"Yeah." Lily pulled out her own phone. "Local FBI, in this case. There's a chance this is connected to, ah . . . a Unit matter. I'll explain that in a minute." She looked up the number, touched the call button, then glanced at Rule. "One of your people, maybe, for the house?"

He nodded. "We do want to be sure he isn't there and injured."

Or dead, but neither of them would mention that possibility in front of Beth.

Cullen spoke for the first time since sitting down. "I'm good with locks."

Rule stood. "You're too appealing a target. I'll talk to Scott. He'll know who else can handle the lock."

"I'm faster. Besides, there could be a connection."

"Target?" Beth said, looking between them. "What do you mean, he's a target?"

Meanwhile, Lily had identified herself and asked to speak to Special Agent Bergman. She'd already talked to the woman once today, on the flight in. That wasn't the first time they'd spoken. It was Bergman's office that'd run the original check on Sean Friar when Lily first crossed paths with his brother, Robert Friar.

Bergman agreed to have someone look into Sean Friar's apparent disappearance right away. Lily gave her Beth's number and address verbally; the rest of the info could be sent electronically . . . in a minute. First she had to do something she dreaded.

Rule stood at the door, talking to Scott. Cullen was still on his stool. Beth was standing bolt still, staring at Cullen.

"What do you mean, someone wants to kidnap you?"

"Or kill me," Cullen said cheerfully. "We aren't sure which, but taking me hostage seems more likely."

"But—but—" She spun to face Lily. "Someone wants to kidnap Cullen and someone already has kidnapped Sean, so—"

"Whoa." Lily held up both hands. "We don't know what's happened with your friend. It's a huge jump from 'I don't know where he is' to 'he's been kidnapped.'"

"Did someone try to kidnap Cullen? Is that why you're here?" She shook her head. "That doesn't make sense. Why would you come here if someone tried to kidnap him back in San Diego?"

"It's connected to the case." Lily felt the slow, dull throb of a headache begin. She rubbed her neck. "Beth, I need to tell you some things you won't like hearing. There's other stuff I won't be able to tell you. You won't like that, either." She patted the couch. "Sit down and let's talk."

Beth didn't move. "Is this an I've-got-bad-news sit down?"

"It's an I-don't-want-to-crane-my-neck-watching-you-pace sit down. Come on. Sit."

Beth scowled, took three steps, and dropped onto the couch. "So talk."

Lily took a deep breath. "Sean Friar is the brother of a very bad guy named Robert Friar."

Beth rolled her eyes. "Like I didn't know that."

Lily couldn't think of one thing to say.

"Sean and I are *friends*. Maybe I'd like to be more, but the friend part is for real. Of course he's told me about his brother. Half brother, really—same mother, different fathers. Robert was adopted by Sean's father, who was Robert's stepfather, which is how come they have the same last name."

"You knew. You knew, and you didn't say a word to me." Lily grabbed onto her temper and yanked it back. It was not good technique to yell at a witness . . . even when that witness was your own stupid, thinks-she's-at-the-center-of-the-world little sister who . . . *deep breath*, she told herself. "What do you know about Robert Friar?" Beth had to know some of it. The news had been full of the story for a week.

"You're pissed."

"Yes. Yes, I am."

"I knew you'd react like this! I knew it! That's why I didn't tell you about Sean, because you'd leap to all kinds of conclusions before you even met him!"

Lily leaned forward. "Did you stop to think for even one moment that this might be about more than your feelings? That maybe, just maybe, I might have more on my mind where Friar is concerned than interfering in your—oh, but it isn't a romance, is it? Your *friendship* with the brother of a man who tried to kill thousands, including Toby, and—"

A warm hand landed on her shoulder. "Lily." Rule squeezed gently. "May I take this for now?"

Sure. Yes. Because if she said another word, she was going to speak it while shaking Beth so hard whatever passed for brains in her sister's head spilled out.

Rule took her silence for assent. "Beth, Robert Friar is the man who took me and Cullen and several others captive. He attempted to set explosives off at Clanhome, which would have killed Toby and many others in my clan."

Beth nodded seriously. "I heard about all that, of course—on the TV, since Lily refused to discuss it, but it was all over the news. Friar was with that elf, right? I can't think of the elf guy's name, but they were killed when the elf did some kind of big magic and brought the mountain down on them. You and Lily and Cullen escaped in the nick of time with—was it Benedict?"

"And a few others, yes."

"That's horrible, it's really, deeply horrible, but"—she gave Lily a dirty look—"it had nothing to do with Sean."

"It wouldn't, perhaps," Rule said, "except that we don't think Robert Friar died."

"What? But that—the news said—Sean thinks his brother is dead!" She bounced to her feet to glare at Lily. "You let him think his brother was dead!"

Lily kept her voice steady. "We have no concrete evidence that he survived, but no body was found, and we do know . . . have you heard of patterning?"

Beth shook her head impatiently. "I haven't, and what does that have to do with Sean?"

"Patterning is the ability to manipulate possibilities. It's a rare Gift and usually shows up in its weak form, but it's known in some circles as the Gift of the gods. A really strong patterner can make even highly unlikely events occur—such as surviving the collapse of a mountain."

Beth followed her meaning well enough. "Except that Sean's brother wasn't Gifted."

"He didn't start out that way, but Robert Friar is now a listener and a patterner. He received his second Gift just before the node imploded and brought down the cave system."

"No one can give someone else a Gift."

"Old Ones do the damnedest things," Lily said dryly.

Beth opened her mouth. Closed it. After a moment she said quietly, "I think I need to hear a lot more than I have about what happened."

"I think maybe you do." Lily looked at Rule, a frown pleating her forehead. "I know you don't like to split up."

"I don't, no. Tony can wait a little longer. You're worried about leaving your sister alone." He raised one brow slightly.

She knew what he was asking. And he was right, dammit. She couldn't make any sense of Sean Friar's apparent disappearance, but just because she couldn't see what Friar was up to didn't mean he wasn't knee-deep in whatever was happening here. He had to be. Her sister hadn't just happened to meet Friar's brother, not without a push from someone who could manipulate possibilities.

Of course, Beth wasn't entirely alone and hadn't been since she moved here. The time had come for her to meet Murray and the others who'd been watching over her. Guarding her from a distance wasn't a good option anymore.

Lily sighed, sure she knew how her sister was going to take that news.

TWENTY-ONE

~~

"**THAT** didn't go well," she said, clicking her seat belt in place.

"It could have been worse."

"I suppose." It had helped some that it was so abundantly obvious that the guards Rule had assigned to Beth hadn't been spying on her, reporting on her. If they had, Rule would have known about Sean Friar months ago.

Rule squeezed her hand. "At least she's letting Murray stay in the apartment with her for now."

"Not because she sees the need. Murray gave her puppy dog eyes, and she caved." Lily hadn't met Murray before, so he'd been almost as much of a surprise to her as he was to Beth, though for different reasons. She had this theory that lupi were genetically incapable of ugly. It made sense—the continuation of their species depended on them charming, seducing, and otherwise trying to impregnate as many women as possible.

Murray turned out to be the exception. Sort of. He was short and squat and looked like he'd grabbed his features at random from the bargain bin, yet somehow he was five feet, five inches of adorable. Maybe it was the so-ugly-they're-cute deal some creatures had going, like that breed of dog that seemed to be made entirely out of wrinkles.

"Whatever works."

"I guess." Bergman's agent had arrived just as they were leaving—Richard Snow, a studious-looking fellow with a competent manner. Cullen was already gone by then; he'd left with Marcus and Steve to check out Sean Friar's house. Well, Marcus would check out the house. Cullen would let Marcus in, then wait outside with Steve, who would be keeping an eye out for trouble.

Lily drummed her fingers on her thigh. Nothing was adding up. Rule's brother's partner was missing, held hostage. Friar seemed to be involved. Lily's sister's not-a-boyfriend—who was also Friar's brother—was missing. Fate unknown.

That had to be more than coincidence. Didn't it?

"I see three possibilities," she said abruptly. "One, Sean is genuinely missing—dead, injured, or held hostage by person or persons unknown for reasons unknown. Two, he's dancing to his brother's tune, and his absence is part of some plot. Three, he isn't Mr. Reliability the way Beth thinks. He fell off the wagon and is on a binge or sleeping one off."

"Alcoholism is an insidious disease," Rule agreed in the mild way that meant he didn't really agree. "But Beth has good people instincts."

"She's only known him for three months."

Rule reached for her hand. "It didn't take us three months."

"We were different." Oh, that sounded lame. "We had the mate bond."

"Mmm. That did force us to pay attention. Perhaps Beth doesn't need as much of a prod as we did."

That made her grin in spite of herself. "The women in my family are pretty stubborn. The question is, where does Beth have her stubbornness dial turned? If it's set to 'Sean is my soul mate,' she'd miss seeing all the signs that he isn't."

"How much of your attitude is professional skepticism, do you think? And how much is because you don't want your sister involved in any way with Robert Friar's brother?"

"I have no idea. But it's way too much of a coincidence for Beth even to meet Friar's brother, much less fall for him."

"Friar is a patterner with too much power. He wouldn't have needed his brother's active cooperation to bring about a meeting."

"But why?" Lily spread her hands. "What is he after? If he wants to grab Beth and use her against me, he doesn't need this complicated setup. Why such complexity?"

"Ruben says patterners work in complex weavings. It's the natural outgrowth of their Gift."

Lily drummed her fingers again. When in doubt, look at outcomes. "What does this give him that he couldn't get another way?"

"Hmm. Well, if the theft of the prototype hadn't brought us to San Francisco, Beth's cry for help when Sean disappeared would have."

Was that it? Did Friar have some reason he needed them in San Francisco? Maybe he intended to blow the city up. She shivered. That sounded like something he'd try, but he had to have a reason. There were easier ways to kill her and Rule than by destroying a city. "Maybe he doesn't need us here. Maybe he just wants us to not be at Clanhome."

"Perhaps." Rule tipped his head as if listening to his own thoughts. "But I can't fit that in with the demand made by Adam King's kidnapper."

"Yeah." If Friar wanted Cullen, kidnapping his own brother would be an odd way to go about getting him. She sighed. "I feel like I'm swimming in glue."

"What if," Rule said slowly, "he needs Cullen for some reason and wants to eliminate the two of us at the same time?"

Lily's stomach tightened the way it did when something clicked. "*And* get his hands on the prototype? Because that's part of it. There are simpler ways to get our attention, but . . . that feels right. Or like it's on the right track, anyway."

She reached for her phone. She was late in briefing Ruben—and she had a lot to tell him.

RULE had booked them into a posh downtown hotel. He hadn't had time to research less expensive spots, and he'd stayed there before so he knew the Childer had decent security. Hardly impregnable, he said, but the hotel sometimes hosted visiting heads of state and others with security concerns and bodyguards, so they paid more attention to it than the average chain.

The guards who'd gone with them to Jasper's house had followed in two vehicles. They waited for the first one to arrive before letting the attendant have their BMW so they could make an entrance worthy of a mafia don, surrounded by men with wary eyes. Lily didn't argue with the necessity. Anyone setting up a hit would consider this point a prime opportunity. Once they were inside the danger went down considerably, due both to the Childer's security and to the guard Scott had posted in the lobby. Gun oil had a distinctive scent. Rick would have known it if anyone in the lobby were armed.

The lobby was small, the antiques real, the carpet a magnificent Oriental. They were met by the manager, who handed them their keys personally and introduced them to the security chief, a burly man whose appearance matched his name—Connor Murphy. Murphy had a good handshake and a trace of a Find Gift. When he released Lily's hand he said conversationally, "Twenty years with the SFPD."

She nodded back, pleased. "Good to know."

Rule introduced Scott and asked if Murphy would mind discussing security with him. That, of course, was why the manager had arranged the meeting, so Scott peeled off after sending two of the guards up ahead of them to make sure their floor was secure. And she and Rule rode up in the elevator alone. It was the most privacy they'd had since she'd sat on his lap last night.

Lily watched the number lights gradually change. It was a slow elevator. "I hate this."

Rule cast her a glance, his brows pulled down over eyes gone anxious. "Lily—"

"I don't expect you to fix things. I understand the need for guards. I just wanted to point out that I hate it. You said you booked us a suite?"

His eyes stayed on her face, searching for something. She wasn't sure what. "Two bedrooms and a sitting room. Scott and three of the others will bunk in the second bedroom. Cullen will have to put up with the couch in the sitting room. The rest will be in a similar suite next to ours. They'll be crowded, but the hotel brought in extra beds. There's a door between the two suites."

All of which made good sense from a security standpoint. You didn't split your forces if you didn't have to. Lily hadn't had the FBI's advanced training in protecting a witness or other targets, but she knew the basics. "Is there anything I should know about . . ."

"What?"

She sighed. "Drummond's back." When Rule glanced around—an automatic reaction, however useless—she nodded at the white mist hovering in one corner. "He's behind you, up near the ceiling. All misty at the moment, so I guess he doesn't have anything to say."

Rule's mouth thinned. "I don't like the way he can pop in without me knowing. I know you'll tell me, but I don't like it."

She nodded. "We've got little enough privacy these days, and knowing he can show up at any moment. . . . shit. I just thought of something."

"Nothing pleasant, I take it."

"Major creep-out. Drummond's the only ghost I've ever seen, but that doesn't mean there haven't been others hanging around, watching. And I never knew."

The elevator eased to a halt, the doors sliding open. "You're right," Rule said. "That's a major creep-out."

Lily didn't have to ask which door led to their suite. The pair of young men standing guard outside it tipped her off. She raised her eyebrows at the identity of one of them. "Joe, you were still in the lobby when we got on the elevator. How'd you get up here ahead of us?"

"Awesome lupi superpowers."

"He took the stairs," Rule said dryly.

Which actually was awesome lupi superpowers. The elevator might be slow, but he still had to have run up all ten floors. He wasn't winded. "Barnaby's in the stairwell," Joe went on. "Steve and Todd are in your suite with Mike and the new Rho and his witness. Man." He shook his head. "That must be why you wanted Mike to hold down the fort here."

Lily glanced at Rule, puzzled. Mike knew how to sweep for bugs. That's the reason Rule had sent him to the hotel. "Is there something I should know?"

"Tony is a physically impressive young man," Rule said blandly. "Shall we go meet him?"

He clearly wasn't going to say more at the moment, so she nodded. The other guard—Todd—let them in.

It was a typical hotel entry. Short hall, bathroom to the left, closet to the right, but it opened onto a not-so-typical sitting room. Lily hoped the antiques weren't real. Lupi could be hard on their surroundings at times. There was plenty of room and seating available for the five men waiting there. One of them rose from the plush red couch the moment he saw them—and made the room and everyone else shrink.

Tony Romano was huge. Mike was a big guy, and Tony topped him by at least half a foot, making him maybe sixten. And every inch of him was beautifully proportioned, like a larger-than-life-size statue of some god or ancient hero. He had the dark hair and olive complexion his name suggested and a face saved from outright prettiness by a strong nose. He was also absurdly young, or looked young.

That didn't mean much with a lupus, but something about him made her think his apparent age wasn't that far off from his calendar age. Maybe it was his eyes—big, brown, and innocent. And a little dull, as if not much went on in that beautifully shaped head.

The gorgeous young behemoth looked at Rule gravely. "Laban would speak with Nokolai."

"V'eius ven," Rule said. "Nokolai receives Laban."

Tony flushed. *"V'eius ven,"* he repeated, and reached for the hem of his polo shirt and pulled it off over his head, tossing it on the floor. When his hands went to the snap on his jeans, Lily's eyebrows rose. Sure enough, he chucked them off, too.

Turned out he'd come to the meeting commando-style. And he was proportional everywhere.

He sank to his knees, then prostrated himself fully on the floor. His buttocks were a work of art. Michelangelo's *David* would weep with envy. He spoke slowly and gravely, his voice slightly muffled by the carpet. *"Laban subiciit Nokolai, plene et simpliciter."*

Rule's eyebrows flew up. "Tony—it is acceptable to Nokolai to renew our previous pledges—"

The dark head moved once in a negative. *"Plene et simpliciter."*

"As you will, then. *Nokolai accipit Laban subiiciuntur."*

Tony sighed deeply as if relieved it was done and rose to his feet in one smooth motion. "Thank you. Fred?" He glanced to his right, and Lily finally noticed the other man new to her—a short, dark guy with a thick mustache. Both his hair and the mustache were grizzled more gray than black.

Fred sighed. "I witnessed my Rho's submission *plene et simpliciter* and will so state to any who ask." He bent and retrieved the discarded jeans. "Here."

"Thank you," Tony said again. He stood on one leg to begin pulling his jeans back on.

"What just happened?" Lily asked. "I know he submitted, but something about it surprised you."

"Laban submitted *plene et simplicite*—that means fully and completely, nothing held back. Such language is unusual. It's sometimes used when one clan defeats another in battle, but even then there are often terms applied to the submission."

"Like how long it will last?"

"Among others, yes. Tony, this is my Chosen, Lily Yu. Lily, this is Tony Romano."

He was back on both feet now and zipping his jeans. "Miss Yu." He gave her a nod, but his attention returned to Rule immediately. "I submitted fully. It was the right thing to do. Laban lost honor through my father's actions. I needed to acknowledge that wrong. He meant well, but he was wrong." His brows drew down. "I told him so, but he doesn't listen to me."

"He'll have to now, won't he?" Rule said.

"It will take time for him to learn how to do that. Isen didn't let my father change his heir back to my brother before passing the mantle. He must have wanted me to be Rho. Why me instead of James?"

"He didn't tell me. It may be that he trusts you more than he does James."

The young man thought that over, then nodded. "James thought Father's scheme to sell information was clever. I thought it was wrong. Maybe Isen guessed that. Or maybe Fred is right. Fred thinks that Isen preferred me because I would be easy to manipulate because I'm not very smart."

"Tony!" the short man exclaimed. "I didn't say—"

"No." For the first time he smiled, a singularly sweet expression turned briefly on his counselor. "You didn't call me stupid. You never do. But I am slow in my thinking. I'm an odd choice for Rho. My father never meant me to be Rho. I was his way of telling James to shape up. But now I am Rho, and so I submitted *plene et simplicit*. Now Isen won't feel he has to manipulate me because he has all the control, and we can be comfortable together."

A single sharp crack of laughter burst from Rule. "And so you prove that thinking slowly is not the same as being stupid. You may have just gotten the best of my father, Tony, and there are very few who can say that."

Lily was confused. Her expression must have shown that, because Rule turned to her with a half smile. "This makes Isen more fully involved in Laban's welfare, you see. Increasing his authority increases his responsibility to them."

"Isen is sneaky," Tony said, "and very clever, so it would do me no good to try to outthink him. He is also very much a Rho. He will deal honorably with us."

Fred didn't seem as sure of that as his new Rho. He sighed faintly. Lily thought Tony was right, though. Isen was both clever and sneaky, but he was also as dominant as they came . . . the lupi version of dominant, that is, which was as much about taking care of those in your charge as it was about taking charge.

"Who did you name Lu Nuncio for Laban?" Rule asked.

"My cousin Charlie."

Rule's eyebrows rose. "I'd expected you to name your father."

Tony's sigh was long and windy. "So did he. He'd be a safe choice, but he was Rho too long to make a good Lu Nuncio, and he doesn't listen to me. Charlie is very dominant and thinks he'd make a better Rho than I will, but he listens. He's not jumpy the way James is. He won't try to kill me. Not right away, anyway. He'll give me a chance."

"You have much to do within your clan," Rule said. "I stand ready to help, if I can."

"Thank you. First, though, I must do as Isen said. He wants me to help you investigate the theft. How can I help?"

"For now, by answering some questions," Lily said.

"Okay," he said, but barely glanced at her before looking back at Rule with doubt writ large on his face.

"Lily is in charge of the investigation," Rule said. "She's an FBI agent."

"I think I knew that, but I'd forgotten." For the first time he really looked at her . . . and kept looking for a disconcertingly long time. Finally he nodded. "I'm not used to women being in charge. I know they are sometimes, but not in the clans, and I don't see many women on my job."

"What do you do?"

"Underwater and hyperbaric welding."

"Ah . . . that's a very specialized skill."

"I like it. I'm good at it, too, and the pay's good, but I won't be able to do it anymore. There's a lot of travel involved."

Rule spoke. "Tony works for an underwater fabrication and repair firm. They work on ships, drilling platforms, and underwater installations of all kinds. He's been all over the world."

Lily exchanged a glance with Rule. There was more to this slow-speaking new Rho than met the eye. "I need to ask you some questions. Do you have a problem with a woman having authority?" she asked Tony.

He thought that over a moment. "I don't think so. I'll need to study on it awhile, I expect, since I'm not used to it. If your questions are about who paid my father to betray Nokolai, I know some things that may help."

"Good. Have a seat," she said, gesturing at the round table and chairs near the window. She glanced at Rule. "Maybe we could have a few less bodies in the room . . . and some coffee?"

TWENTY-TWO

~

LILY, Rule noted with amusement, was sublimely unaware that she'd shocked some of their company. Those who hadn't been around her much weren't used to seeing someone casually ask a Rho to get her some coffee, and these were Leidolf. Leidolf tended to cherish women in the abstract while devaluing them as individuals.

It was good for them to see that Lily was his partner, not his subordinate, and that she possessed her own authority that didn't devolve from his, even if they didn't really understand. Yet. Rule emphasized the point by ordering the coffee himself, then asked her, "Do you need me?"

"Always, but not immediately. Why?"

He gave her a quick kiss to show how much her response pleased him and told her he needed to tend to a few security matters. While she questioned Tony, Rule conferred with Scott. They needed to rotate the guards, with some sleeping, some present but in the other suite, and some in the second-floor gym. Confining a number of lupi in a relatively small space for long periods of time created problems. Burning off some of their energy would help. He also wanted to change the guard rotation on Beth. They'd been handling it with three guards—Murray, who was in charge, plus two Laban men—with each taking an eight-hour shift. Rule wanted two men on her at all times, starting immediately. For now they'd have to take twelve-hour shifts. After a brief discussion with Scott, he sent Patrick McCausey. Patrick was a steady sort with excellent control, unlikely to offend the notoriously prickly Laban.

He was probably locking the barn door after the fact, but they didn't have any idea why Sean Friar was missing. In the absence of data, Rule preferred to add a belt to the suspenders. If the belt proved unnecessary, good.

After that he talked to Scott about a contingency he wanted covered—if they did end up faking a trade of Cullen for Adam, he didn't want some sniper doing away with Cullen before they could act. Then he called Isen and brought him up-to-date, learning in turn that Lily's crime-scene people had come and gone and that Benedict and Arjenie would be stuck in D.C. for a while. Some of the sidhe delegation were staying holed up in their suite due to an unspecified indisposition, and the administration wanted Arjenie around when they emerged.

That struck Rule as suspicious. Elves' ability to heal varied, but it seemed unlikely they'd caught a bug. Perhaps "indisposition" was diplomatic code for "we're sick of talking to you." Still, he called Benedict and, after some discussion, they agreed on a plan.

Then he called an old acquaintance who had lived in San Francisco a long time and had contacts in some less-than-legal venues. He might know about this Hugo they wanted to find.

He didn't, but he promised to ask around. Just as Rule disconnected, Cullen arrived with Marcus and Steve. They hadn't found a body or signs of a fight, so Rule called Beth to let her know, then directed Cullen to the small conference room he'd booked on the second floor, where he could work on his Find spell. Marcus and Steve would remain Cullen's personal guards, so they went with him.

At last Rule was able to pour himself a cup of coffee from

one of the insulated carafes room service had delivered and sit beside Lily, who was just getting off the phone. Good coffee, he noted, savoring the aroma. "What do I need to know?"

She glanced at her notebook. "This part is secondhand. An individual calling himself Ahab contacted Leo Romano on December second."

"Just after the demo Cullen gave for the T-Corp people."

She nodded. "Ahab is a male with a voice described as a 'resonant tenor.' Accent and diction suggest a native Californian, educated, no perceptible ethnicity. Contact was by phone only, with Ahab calling Leo from a series of numbers—probably throwaways, but we'll check. Ahab claimed to work for a large multinational corporation, though he refused to say which one."

Ahab certainly could be Friar. Rule looked at Tony. "You know quite a lot, considering you never spoke to this Ahab."

"I thought you'd want to know things like that, so I asked my father once I was Rho."

"Good thinking."

"I don't think fast," Tony said with a hint of humor, "but I do think."

"I'll speak with Leo to confirm, of course," Lily said. "Ah . . . I'll skip some of the details to get to the interesting part. Payment was in cash, with the first installment left at the Golden Gate Park on December twenty-first. Tony persuaded his father that it would be good to know more about their mysterious Ahab, so they'd staked out the drop hours before it occurred. Successfully." She flashed him a grin. "A Laban guard saw the drop made and followed the woman who did it to her car—an older model Toyota, license number 2LBZ112. Which is registered," she finished smugly, "to a Ms. Carrie Ann Rucker. Special Agent Bergman is sending someone out now to pick her up for questioning."

BETH hit *send* and leaned back with a sigh of relief. It was not her best work, but it was what the client wanted, and it was finished. Which was something of a miracle considering she didn't really give a damn, not with Sean missing, but working was better than pacing. So she'd worked.

When she wasn't Googling Humans First, that is. And the October massacres and Robert Friar and sociopaths. She hadn't expected to find anything about this war the lupi thought they were fighting, and she'd been right about that. She'd turned up plenty about the Azá and their attempt to open a hellgate a year ago last November, but very little about the goddess they were said to worship. The one Lily called the Great Bitch. Who they didn't name because *she* was attracted to her name. Who was apparently behind everything—Harlowe and the staff he'd used on Beth. The demons who'd killed so many at the Humans First rallies. The sniper who'd shot Lily last September and the plastic explosives planted at Nokolai Clanhome that they'd found barely in time.

There was a good chance *she* was behind Sean's disappearance, too. Lily said Robert Friar was *her* agent and acolyte. Beth didn't know why Robert would kidnap his own brother, but she didn't have to understand to think he was involved.

Kidnap, Beth repeated silently, giving the word a mental underline. Sean had been kidnapped, not killed. He was alive. She believed that fiercely, knowing she was being irrational and not caring. He was alive, and they'd find him.

On the rational side, they did know now that he wasn't lying dead or dying in his house. That was something, she told herself as she powered down her laptop.

Not enough, shouted the anger simmering inside her. Not nearly enough, and if Lily had only told her more about what was going on—at least that Sean's brother was still alive! If Lily had told her that, she would have warned Sean, and he'd have been on his guard, and maybe he wouldn't be missing now.

She hadn't wanted to know.

Grimly Beth acknowledged that truth. She'd avoided learning more about all the bad things that had happened in the past year. She hadn't wanted to know how scary things really were for her sister and for anyone connected to her. How dangerous it had become to be lupi or Gifted, and how many people purely hated them. How much crap was out there masquerading as fact, and how many people believed it. She really hadn't wanted to know there was an Old One auditioning for the role of Baddest Megalomaniac I-Will-Take-Over-The-World Villain Ever. She hadn't wanted to know, so she hadn't asked Lily the questions that were now burning up her brain. After she'd been enspelled by Harlowe, held prisoner by a gang, and nearly killed, she'd just wanted her life back, wanted to choose her own course, not get sent careening off on some crazy trajectory like a badly struck cue ball.

No. Lily was the cue ball. Beth was just one of the random balls sent crashing around the pool table, hoping to find a safe pocket to hide in. That's what San Francisco was supposed to be—her safe pocket.

Beth snorted in disgust. She'd played ostrich, and that was on her. Lily still should have told her way more than she had. Now Beth was pissed. And scared. Scared for Sean and scared for herself, and there didn't seem to be anything she could *do*. Beth shoved away from her desk and grabbed her sneakers. "Murray!"

He appeared in her doorway. "Yo."

She glanced up at him, annoyed. That probably had more to do with his presence than his word choice, but still, he was here and she didn't like it. "No one actually says 'yo.'"

"I do."

Murray had such pretty eyes. They reminded her of the half-starved puppy she'd snuck into her room when she was eight. She'd named him Samson. Lily hadn't told on her. Even Susan had kept mum, but there was no way to keep a puppy a secret, and their mother thought dogs were dirty and full of germs. Beth had cried and cried when Samson's new owners came to take him away. "Are you an army wannabe or something?"

"I was with the Rangers for six years. Are we going somewhere? It's not time for your Bojuka class."

Which he would know because he'd been following her to the damn class all along. "I'm not going to Bojuka." Not with Sean missing. It would hurt too much. She tugged on one shoe. "I didn't think lupi could be in the military."

His mouth crooked up. "Legally, you mean? The jury's still out on that. But there's always been some of us who joined anyway, especially during World War II. Not so many these days, but a few."

"How did you pull it off? I mean, I know you don't absolutely have to Change at full moon, but still. That had to be hard."

"It can be. You have to be okay living away from clan, and you have to have really good control. It's not just keeping your wolf from showing up at a bad time. You have to be able to fake human-level responses and strength pretty much all the time, and not everyone can do that."

"This was back before it was okay to go public about being lupi?"

"Some would say it isn't okay now," he said dryly. "I ask again. Are we going somewhere?"

"Out." She tied the second shoe and stood. "Maybe we'll pick up something for supper. You like pad Thai? There's a place six blocks over that makes incredible pad Thai."

"We could order in."

"You can do what you like. I need to get out. I need to move." And she needed to figure some things out before her roommates showed up. Susan wouldn't be home for at least an hour, but Deirdre might turn up any minute. Deirdre knew that Sean was missing—Beth had called her about that this morning—but not about any of the rest of it . . . such as the homely man with the gorgeous build watching her warily now with those pretty brown eyes.

What was Beth supposed to tell her roommates?

The truth, she supposed glumly. She couldn't yell at Lily for hiding stuff then hide stuff herself. Beth pulled her favorite hoodie, the one with the fake fur trim, from her over-stuffed closet. "Come on, if you're coming."

He was, of course. Not only that, but he insisted on going first when they reached the stairs. She frowned at the top of his shoulders as they started down. Great shoulders. "Haven't you ever heard of ladies first?"

"Ladies first is for idiots. Or for people who don't care if the lady takes a bullet."

"Don't talk about bullets."

"Okay."

"It's not like I can't take care of myself, you know."

That amused him, damn him. "The Bojuka."

"I'm just starting, but I do pretty well."

"Rule has guards, and he's probably a tiny bit better at taking care of himself than you are."

"Oooh, sarcasm. Those puppy-dog eyes are such a lie. How did you stand it, not being able to issue orders to me while you were sneaking around following me?"

"It was rough."

He was still amused. She wanted to hit him. "Not that you were all that good at sneaking. I saw you sometimes, you know, and—"

"You thought I was a neighbor."

"Yeah, but aren't you supposed to—hey!"

He'd stopped so abruptly she almost smacked into him. "Back!"

"What?"

"Go back up. Quick."

But he didn't wait for her to obey, grabbing her and turning her physically, which pissed her off and got her heart scared. He shoved. Her feet obeyed him even as her heartbeat went crazy. "What is it? What's happening?"

"Patrick sounded the alert. Move faster."

Patrick? Who was Patrick? What alert? She hadn't heard anything—but she didn't have lupi hearing, and his hand was urging her to move, move faster, and she took the stairs as fast as she could so that all she heard were her own feet, her own breath coming hard and rough.

She reached the third-floor landing. His hand left her back for her shoulder, and he pushed down and gave a piercing whistle. She went to her knees, dazed and frightened and wondering what—

"Get flat!" he ordered, but he didn't pause to see if she obeyed. He spun back around and leaped. Leaped down the stairs, his arms spread so that one brushed the wall, as if he wanted to make himself the biggest target possible. Leaped right at the man racing up the stairs with a gun pointed up at him.

The sound of the shots was deafeningly loud in the closed-in space.

TWENTY-THREE

~

CARRIE Ann Rucker was fifty-nine, a placid woman with graying blond hair and a crooked front tooth that lent a certain charm to her smile. She owned a small handcrafted jewelry store and was wearing a sample of her merchandise with her neatly pressed jeans and white blouse—a pretty pair of chandelier earrings.

She also worked as a mule for a drug cartel. Her only arrest had never made it to the grand jury, thanks to some clumsiness on the part of the arresting officer and a very expensive lawyer. One who also worked for said cartel.

"And you never looked inside the bag," Lily said.

"He asked me not to, and I agreed. I do believe in keeping my word, don't you?"

One of the interesting things about Carrie Ann was the way her attention stayed with Lily. Sure, Rule wasn't saying much, but people always noticed him. Especially women. Even if Carrie Ann was wired for women, Lily would expect her to take more interest in a guy who occasionally turns into a wolf. "That seems like an odd thing to ask. Even odder that you agreed."

Carrie Ann smiled comfortably. "I'm not a very curious person."

"Remarkably incurious, considering you've been arrested for transporting illegal substances in the past. Substances you had no idea someone had planted in your car," Lily said dryly. "Hard to believe you wouldn't want to make sure this man you'd never met before wasn't taking advantage of your helpful nature."

"He had such a good vibe. I'm sure it was all perfectly innocent."

"Are you, now? And yet the FBI takes very little interest in scavenger hunts."

Carrie Ann just smiled.

Lily looked down at her notes, wondering how much longer to push. Carrie Ann was a pro. She knew what to say and when to shut up, and she was enjoying herself way too much. She knew damn well Lily didn't have a lever to pry loose any actual facts. Sure, she'd given them a description of the "nice older man" she met at the park, but that only meant that whoever really had her make the drop looked nothing like the guy she'd described.

Lily looked up from her notes. "That's what he said he was doing, right? Setting up a scavenger hunt for the grandkids. He asked you to leave a Macy's shopping bag at the base of the Dutch windmill. He specifically asked you not to look inside."

"That's right."

"He was a white male, about seventy. He had white hair, thick for a man his age. You don't remember what he was wearing, but you're sure you would have noticed if he'd been in a suit."

"No one wears suits on Saturday at the park, do they?"

"You think he may have been wearing glasses, but you aren't sure about that, either. And you don't know his name."

"He must have told me," she said apologetically, "but I don't remember it. And I think the bag was from Macy's, but it might have been Nordstrom's. I shop at both places, and I'm sure it was from one of them."

Rule touched Lily's arm lightly and stood. She glanced up. He'd taken out his phone and was heading for the door of the office they'd borrowed from one of the local agents. She looked back at Carrie Ann. "How much do you think the bag weighed?"

"Oh, not too much. Perhaps as much as two or three books?"

"It's curious that you would think of comparing it to objects made of paper. It did, in fact, hold paper."

"Oh?" She said that politely, as if she felt a certain social obligation to express interest.

"Mmm. Ms. Rucker—"

"Please make it Carrie Ann," she said warmly.

Lily bared her teeth in something not meant to be mistaken for a smile. "Carrie Ann, I hope you'll search your memory carefully. Amazing as it seems, that nice old man was not arranging a scavenger hunt. As I said, the Bureau takes very little interest in such things. We do, however, really perk up and pay attention when kidnapping's involved."

The slight widening of her eyes was Carrie Ann's first unscripted response. She didn't like that word, not at all. Whoever told her to make the drop hadn't given her any hint it might be ransom money. She recovered quickly, lifting one hand to her throat and allowing herself to look uncertain. "Kidnapping. Oh, surely not. If one of that nice old man's grandchildren was—"

The door opened. "Lily," Rule said. "They tried for Beth. She's okay. Murray isn't. I need to get there quick."

Lily shoved her chair back and fixed Rucker with a look. "Stay here."

One second later, she was out the door and flinging orders at the first face she saw. "Get me a driver and a car with a siren. Black-and-white or Bureau—whichever's faster. I need the car waiting on the street by the time the elevator gets me down there."

"What—"

"Do it. Now. Bergman!"

The door at the end of the hall opened. The woman's face creased with annoyance. "You yelled?"

"They attacked my sister. One of Rule's people is badly hurt. I'm leaving. Keep someone on Rucker. Use this attack to shake her loose, if you can." She flung the last over her shoulder as she headed for the elevator bank, Rule beside her. "Who called you," she asked him, her voice low, "if Murray's badly hurt?"

"Patrick."

"Patrick? But—"

"I added him to Beth's detail while you were questioning Tony. The attackers came at her in the stairwell of her building—four men, two from above, two from below. Beth is unharmed. Murray took at least one bullet in the chest. I told Patrick to call an ambulance. I need to be there. Murray's not conscious now, but if he survives long enough for the EMTs to load him, he could wake up."

"Right." Badly hurt lupi were dangerous. Murray might Change; he might see any attempt at help as an attack. Rule could control him. She jabbed the elevator button and thought about the stairs, but they were on the thirteenth floor. Rule might beat the elevator down, but she couldn't. The car she'd ordered probably wouldn't be there yet, anyway.

Bergman caught up with them. "Is your sister all right?"

"I think so. Four men came for her. Could have been an attempted hit or a snatch, but my money's on the latter. Who sends four men to kill a single young woman?" She looked at Rule. "What happened to the attackers? Was Patrick able to hold on to any of them?"

"Who's Patrick?' Bergman said.

Rule answered Lily, not the other woman. "Two are dead. One escaped. One is alive, but badly injured."

Bergman scowled. "Sounds like one hell of a mess. Your sister didn't repel four men on her own. Who's this Patrick?"

"One of Rule's men." Lily stabbed the stupid damn elevator button again and looked at Rule. "Are the locals on the scene yet?"

He looked blank. Rule tended not to think about calling the cops.

"Someone's probably called it in," Lily told Bergman as the elevator finally opened. "At least one shot was fired. Get in touch with the locals. Make sure they're expecting me and Rule." She and Rule stepped into the elevator.

"Wait. What do you mean, he's one of Rule's men? Were you expecting something like this?"

"Not like this, no." The doors shut on Special Agent Bergman's frustrated face. Lily looked at Rule. "You were, though. You sent Patrick."

"Belt and suspenders," he said obscurely as the elevator started down. "Lily, the two dead—Murray took out one, and Patrick got the other. The badly injured one, though, that was Beth's doing. Do you want Patrick to take responsibility for him? I need to let him know."

"Shit."

TWENTY-FOUR

"**SURE,**" Lily said. "I'll call you later. No, I'm here and . . . I know you do. I'll give her your love, and . . ." Lily listened patiently to another list of things she must be sure to do. It wasn't that hard. She knew the list was her mother's way of saying she loved Beth, and this time, at least, her mother wasn't blaming Lily for what had happened to her sister. This time, her mother seemed to trust her. "Uh-huh. No, don't worry about that—she'll be staying with me and Rule."

Beth paused in her pacing to glare at her. "No, I won't."

Lily gave her a look. "I need to go. I don't like to leave Beth alone with that detective and . . . of course I will. 'Bye."

"She's not coming here, is she?" Beth demanded.

Lily slipped her phone in her pocket. "No, and you owe me big-time for telling her you were still talking to the local police. You'll call her yourself later. And you *are* staying with me and Rule."

"No, I'm not." Beth resumed her furious circuit of the surgical waiting room. "Haven't I proved how damn good I am at taking care of myself? Sent him sailing—*splat*!" She slapped her hands together. "Took him right out."

"Uh-huh. You figure you can protect your roommates, too, if the bad guys try for you again?"

Beth's mouth opened. Closed. She turned away and started pacing again, up and down the room, like she'd been doing since they got here.

There was only one person other than Lily to watch. Tony Romano sat in the corner pretending to read an old issue of *Better Homes and Gardens*. Maybe he really was reading it—who knew? He'd insisted on coming to the hospital, claiming he had no problem with the setting. Most lupi didn't do well in hospitals, but Tony was a Rho. He was supposed to be aces at control. He said he hoped to be useful to Rule, but of course Rule didn't stay where Tony could hang around being helpful. He went into surgery with Murray. That's when Tony attached himself to Lily like an enormous barnacle. She thought he must be "studying on" her, getting used to the idea of a woman with authority. She wasn't sure why she was letting him.

Scott and Todd were just outside in the hall, glaring at anyone who looked like they might come in. Either the glares worked or the hospital was having a slow surgical day, because they'd had the room to themselves for the past twenty minutes. Lily knew that was temporary. If nothing, else; the press would find them eventually.

Somewhere nearby was the man Beth had sent sailing over a railing to plummet three stories down. He was still in surgery. Lily had told Rule it was Beth's choice about whether to ask Patrick to claim responsibility for that. Beth had reacted just as Lily had expected—she'd been horrified by the idea.

Murray had come around at the scene, but Rule had kept him calm, and Cullen had met them at the hospital. Murray had taken two bullets; one wasn't much of a problem, being in his shoulder, but the other had hit his heart. He had to have surgery, but anesthesia didn't work on lupi. Fortunately, sleep spells did, and Cullen was good at them, so he and Rule had scrubbed and gone into surgery with Murray. They were with him now in post-op.

Lily was not needed for any of this. She'd rather have taken Beth to the hotel once they could leave the scene of the attack. Beth could be guarded better there—and Lily had so much to *do*. The locals were handling the immediate investigation of Beth's attackers, but that wasn't exactly the only thing on her plate. She'd ended up video conferencing from the damn ladies' room—the one spot at the hospital with some privacy—when the judge insisted on a personal discussion of her need for taps on Jasper Machek's phones.

At least the woman had ended up granting permission, so . . . her phone buzzed.

It was the detective Lily had maligned to her mother, a perfectly courteous woman named Rachel Jones. They'd confirmed the ID on the three perps whose bodies—living or dead—were in their hands. They had a line to follow on who they'd worked for, too. Did Lily want to sit in when they picked the man up?

She did. Lily thanked Detective Jones and disconnected.

"Who was that?" Beth said brightly. "One of your police buddies? Have they decided for sure they won't arrest me?"

"They're not going to arrest you." Lily had told her that several times. "They've got names for all of the perps but the one who escaped. The guy in surgery is—"

"You're right. Why would they arrest me? I didn't do anything wrong. He deserved it, right?"

Beth didn't want to hear the man's name. Having a name made him real, made it a person she'd tossed over that railing, not a lump of meat. Lily understood, but dehumanizing your opponents was bad for the soul . . . and it was weird for her to think in terms of the soul, but things had changed a lot in the last year. The good news was that her sister wasn't very good at that particular form of denial. Beth had insisted on coming here to wait until the guy got out of surgery. You didn't do that for a lump of meat. The bad news was that Beth insisted she was fine, just fine, while her movements grew more frantic and her eyes brittle with everything she was determined not to feel.

After a too-long pause Lily said, "Maybe it doesn't matter what he deserved."

"I guess you think it should bother me," Beth said. "It doesn't. I defended myself. That's why I went to Bojuka—so I'd be able to defend myself. And it worked, didn't it? So I'm not upset."

"You're doing a pretty good job of acting upset."

"I'm not acting. And I'm not . . . it's the adrenaline. I was attacked, and all that adrenalin has me kind of wired. But not upset."

"The adrenaline's worn off by now." Lily stood. "His name is Robert Clampett."

"Why do I need to know that? I didn't need to know that."

"I don't know if Clampett deserved his fate, but I don't have to know that. You did the right thing, Beth. You did what needed to be done."

"Aren't you listening? That's what I've been saying." Beth stopped moving. Her eyes were too big, too bright.

"Is it what you're feeling?"

"I don't know. I don't know what I feel. It's not guilt, but I don't know what it is. I'm glad you're here."

"Me, too." Lily moved closer and slid an arm around Beth's waist. "Maybe you can just feel whatever-it-is without naming it."

"But it has to have a name. Something so large—other people must have felt it, too. There must be a word for it."

The word was *change*. Lily didn't think Beth would know what she meant if she suggested it, though. People didn't use *change* as an emotion word, but as a little-*c* verb—change the oil, the channel, your hair color or your address or your diet. Even the phrase "change your life" referred to an act of volition, taking charge of something and making it better, or at least different. They weren't talking about the kind of volcanic upheaval Beth was caught up in where ash covered the landscape and lava spewed up into the air and the ground shook and shook, and nothing looked right or normal.

Of course, another word for what Beth felt would be *trauma*. Lily didn't think her sister wanted to hear that one, either. "Are you glad you're alive?"

Beth nodded firmly. "Of course."

"It looks like Murray's going to be okay. Are you glad about that?"

"I—he—Lily, he jumped at that man with the gun so he would take the bullet instead of me. I'm sure of it. He— he—" Her breath hitched. Her eyes filled. And at last she started to cry.

Once the sobs hit, they hit hard. Lily wrapped her arms around Beth and held on while Beth cried out some of the confusion. For a long time she didn't say anything, not until Beth stirred. "Tissue?" She disengaged enough to reach for the box on a nearby table.

"Oh, God, yes," Beth took the box and pulled one out and blew her nose. "I'm sorry for falling apart like that."

"Why?"

"You don't."

"Just because you haven't been around for any of my collapses doesn't mean they don't happen. Murray's going to be okay, Beth. What he did—"

"He could have died."

"He could have, yeah. But that's the sort of thing lupi do, especially if a woman's in danger. They heal so much faster than we can, so they go flinging themselves in front of bullets or knives or demons or whatever as if that were a *good* idea."

Beth's laugh was damp and shaky. "That's it. That's it. I didn't want him there, and I was giving him a hard time, and he—he still threw himself in front of that gun!"

The shooter had carried a .22, and Murray had been trained by Benedict. He knew rounds from a .22 weren't likely to go through him and hit Beth, so he'd jumped the perp. The two of them had tumbled down a flight of stairs, coming to a stop with one of them passed out, the other one dead.

The official version might say that the perp had probably

broken his neck falling down those stairs, but Lily knew better. Lupi didn't like to leave threats cluttering up the landscape if they expected to be dead or unconscious shortly, and they were ungodly fast. Murray had broken the man's neck the instant they collided. "And in a week or so Murray will be strutting around—"

"A week?" Beth said, eyes widening. "I know they heal fast, but—a week?"

"He might not be back to normal, but he'll certainly be up and around and thinking he's pretty hot stuff. And we'll let him, because he is. He saved you. But Beth . . ." Lily smoothed her sister's hair. "You saved him, too. Probably yourself as well, but definitely Murray. When you repelled the second attacker it gave Patrick the seconds he needed to take out the third guy before he could put more bullets in Murray."

Patrick had been outside. He'd given a sharp whistle to warn Murray of suspicious strangers entering the building, but procedure was for him to remain on post unless summoned—which Murray had done, but Patrick wouldn't have gotten there in time to save Murray if Beth hadn't been able to stop the man who'd grabbed her.

"I didn't repel him," Beth said flatly. "I flipped him, and he went sailing over the railing. He fell straight down. Lily, he made the most horrible noise when he hit. It wasn't loud, but it . . . I keep hearing it."

Lily nodded. Beth would remember that sound all her life.

"I feel horrible when I think about it, and I can't stop thinking about it, and I'm not at all sorry I did it, and that doesn't make sense! And even though I hope that man doesn't die, that's really all about me. I don't want to have killed someone. So I hope he doesn't die, but not because I really want him to live."

"Do you think you're supposed to?"

"I don't know. I don't know anything."

"You do. You think you're all uprooted, but plenty of you is still rooted nice and deep. You just can't see that for all the debris." And that clearly had sailed right past Beth, judging by the confusion on her face. "You think we could sit down for a few minutes?"

"Sit down? Okay, but that doesn't . . . okay."

"Come on." Lily tugged her over to the chairs and they both sat. "Now. You know that I've killed."

Beth nodded solemnly. "But you're a cop. That . . . it was a line-of-duty thing, right?"

"Do you think cops get a moral pass on killing?" Lily shook her head. "Never mind. I'm not good at putting words to this, but the way it seems to me, everyone is born capable of killing others. That's hardwired in us the same as loving babies and craving sugary foods. But killing is more dangerous than a sweet tooth, isn't it? So it gets a pretty universal thumbs-down in human cultures everywhere. That's necessary and important, but it's also true that we need for some people to be able to kill, under some circumstances. Cops, once in a while. Soldiers. People like you who get caught in a kill-or-be-killed situation. Problem is, we don't give them much to go on except stupid shoot 'em up movies where the good guys blast away at the bad guys and everyone cheers. If you think the bad guys aren't really people, you don't have to worry about the whole thou-shalt-not-kill bit, do you? So you call them by some name that sets them outside the realm of real people— they're gooks or weers or whores and . . . and I just gave you way too much philosophical shit when that isn't what you need at all, is it?"

"Probably I'll want the philosophical shit later," Beth said apologetically.

A muffled sound that might have been a chuckle came from the chair across the room, reminding Lily they weren't alone. When she glanced over her shoulder, Tony looked apologetic, too. "I'm sorry. I don't mean to overhear. Beth, is it okay if I talk to you about this?"

Beth shrugged. "Sure. Why not?"

Lily could think of a couple of reasons—he was male and lupi, and he didn't know Beth at all. She doubted he could understand, much less help, but she held her peace. He probably wouldn't do any harm.

Tony crossed to them and went down on one knee, putting his eyes more or less level with Beth. He held out both hands. Hesitantly she put hers in them. He squeezed and looked her in the eyes and spoke in his slow, measured way. "Someone tried to hurt or kill you. Maybe you killed him instead. Maybe you hurt him very badly. You are having a hard time with this." He paused.

Beth nodded.

"That's okay. Killing is not supposed to be easy."

Beth's mouth rounded in a silent "oh." Tension eased out of her shoulders. "You mean I'm supposed to be confused."

"You are."

"And I should quit thinking I need to figure everything out right away."

He chuckled, a rumble so low Lily barely heard it. "*Pequita*, no one ever gets everything figured out."

She smiled back and looked more like herself. Flirty. "Hey, who are you calling 'little one'?"

"Almost everyone."

Beth laughed. It was a good laugh, and it looked like it surprised her as much as it did Lily.

Out in the hall someone said, " . . . give me that look. I don't know what your problem is, but I'm perfectly entitled to go in the—"

"Deirdre!" Beth sprang up. "That's Deirdre. I'm in here," she called hurrying to the door, and a tall skinny blond with enormous hoop earrings and a small butterfly tat on her collarbone sailed into the room. "Beth! I just checked my messages, and I'm so sorry I didn't check earlier! Are you all right? You look—"

"I'm good except—"

"—like you've been through the wringer, and I—"

"—that I'm awful, too, and I'm so glad to see you!"

The two collided in a hug and just kept talking over, under, and around each other.

Lily sighed and smiled and stood, suddenly tired. She

looked at Tony, who was unwinding his not-quite-seven feet back to standing. She cocked her head and said quietly, "What would you have said to her if she'd said she felt anger or regret instead of confusion?"

Deep in those brown, bovine eyes a spark of humor glinted. "Same thing. You asked her good questions," he added in an encouraging way.

"Then tried to give her my answers instead of waiting for her to find her own."

"We always want to fix things for the people who matter. Can't, mostly, but we want to."

"I think you're going to make a good Rho."

"Do you?" He slid her a glance as opaque as any Isen might use. "Even though I don't think so quick?"

"The thing Isen does best, the thing the clan needs him for the most, is people. You don't handle people his way, but your way—" Her phone vibrated. She took it out. "Your way works, too."

Her caller was Arjenie. She asked about Beth first. Lily wasn't sure how she'd heard, but Rule had of course told his Rho, so maybe Isen had called Benedict, who would have told Arjenie. Lily assured her Beth was okay, then they got to the business of the call. Which was basically that Arjenie hadn't been able to turn up a Hugo in San Francisco that fit Cullen's description, or a Hugo who'd been through the prison system anywhere in the country who was a good match, and she was out of options to check. Lily grimaced and thanked her and disconnected.

"This Hugo you're looking for," Tony said. "He is here in San Francisco?"

"He was. We think he still is. Why?"

"I know people. Those in my clan will know people I don't. Tell me about him."

"He's a big man—big as in fat, weighs around three hundred, or did five years ago when he hung out at a bar called Rats. At that time he was either bald or shaved his head. He's white, maybe fifty-five years old, and has a tattoo of a lightning bolt on his forehead. He's got an Air Gift and contacts in the magical community. At one time he was the go-to guy for people who wanted magical items stolen."

Tony nodded slowly. "I'll find him for you."

Just like that? Well, Rule had said Tony had lived here a long time. Maybe he wasn't as young as he looked, after all. Why not let him have a try? "Thank you. He's one of the few leads we—"

"Lily," Beth said, having detangled from her friend, and tugged Deirdre forward. "You know Deirdre, right? And Deirdre, this in Tony, whose last name I've forgotten—sorry. Tony, Deirdre Marks."

"My pleasure," Tony said gravely.

Deirdre's eyes went big as she looked him up and down. "Wow. I mean . . . wow."

"Lily, I've told Deirdre most of it, but I couldn't remember his name. You know—the sorry son of a bitch who tried to get me who I don't really want to die, even if he is a sorry son of a bitch. I've forgotten his name."

Lily didn't smile except inside, where relief broke out in a grin. "Robert. His name is Robert Clampett, but on the street he goes by Little Mo."

TWENTY-FIVE

THREE-PLUS hours later, Little Mo had made it through surgery. The doctors put his chances at around fifty percent, but they'd go up if he made it through the night. Beth was at the hotel in a small but luxurious room on their floor. Her friend Deirdre had opted to stay there with her tonight, which sort of negated the don't-put-your-friends-in-danger argument, but at least they were guarded.

Murray was at Laban Clanhome. It was on a small ranch outside the city, much closer than Nokolai Clanhome—the ranch where the black dragon picked up his payment for overflying San Francisco once a week, in fact. This was one of the ways Laban had benefited from its association with Nokolai. The government paid them handsomely for providing Sam a cow or three. Housing Murray gave Laban another opportunity to regain face.

Tony was somewhere in San Francisco, presumably looking for Hugo. Rule was back at the hotel, and Lily was headed there.

"Did you eat?" Rule asked.

"I ordered in for everyone. Bad enough I kept them late. Didn't have to keep them hungry, too. You ate, too, right?"

"It's nine thirty-five." Meaning of course he'd eaten. Rule never let himself get too hungry, and his metabolism insisted on plenty of fuel. "Pizza or hamburgers?"

"Hamburgers."

"Extra pickles for yours."

She smiled. "Right. See you in ten." She disconnected.

"More like fifteen, in this traffic," Scott said. He was driving. Lily sat up front with him; Mike and Todd were in the back. As squad leader, Scott probably should have been at the hotel, but she hadn't argued when Rule wanted to send him and the others with her. She knew he trusted Scott the most. Rule had a real problem with the two of them splitting up when she might be targeted.

But he'd needed to stay at the hospital until Murray could be moved, and Lily couldn't wait there with him. In the hours since she dropped her sister off at the hotel she'd talked to her father, Ruben, Grandmother, and the agent monitoring the taps on Jasper Machek's various phone lines. Nothing of note there. Next she'd sat in on the SFPD interview with the man who'd probably given Little Mo and the rest their orders—Robert "Peep" Holland. The nickname was a reference to his first arrest. At the downy age of fifteen he'd been booked as a Peeping Tom, but he'd probably been planning a robbery, judging by his subsequent career. After that, she'd needed to brief Bergman and her people, and that had turned into a brainstorming session.

The interview with Peep had been brief and unproductive. Not Detective Jones's fault. Peep had been around the block so many times he'd mapped out each crack in the sidewalk. He had no idea what they were talking about and he wanted his lawyer.

The session with Bergman and her people had gone better. Lily had needed to tell them about Jasper Machek's unofficially missing lover, the theft of the prototype, and Robert Friar's possible connection to both. She followed that with a rundown on Robert Friar—what was known, what was suspected, how his Gifts worked. Of course, they should have known that already. Friar might be officially presumed dead, but there were "watch for" bulletins out on him all over the country. But unGifted cops sometimes glazed over about magical shit. They didn't understand it, wanted it to go away, and so they tuned out.

They would be treating the attack on Beth as an attempted kidnapping, and the disappearances of Sean Friar and Adam King as suspected kidnappings.

Why kidnappings? That was the ten-thousand-dollar question, and they didn't come up with any answers. Murder was a hell of a lot easier. Even with a good team to handle the snatch itself—and Little Mo's bunch were competent; they'd have succeeded if they hadn't been up against lupi—you had to keep your hostage alive, locked up, and hidden. Holding multiple people hostage for several days compounded the difficulty. Why would Friar do that?

Lily didn't think he was. Neither did Bergman. Chances were that Sean Friar and Adam King were already dead, but maybe not. They had no idea what Friar's game plan was, so maybe he needed them alive. In any event, they had to proceed as if the hostages were still around to be rescued.

At the end of the briefing Lily had turned to Special Agent Bergman and said, "This is a Unit case, both because of Friar's probable involvement and because of the prototype. But we've got two kidnappings and one attempt, and you've got ten times my experience with that sort of thing. You know your people and you know the city. What do you want to do?"

Bergman had taken off like a racehorse given its head. She was quick, she was precise, and she knew her stuff. In five minutes she'd outlined a course of action that included liaising with the locals on the attempt on Beth—one of Bergman's men had worked with Detective Jones and had a good relationship with her; bringing Carrie Ann Rucker back for a second round of questions; putting more people on Sean Friar's disappearance to find out when, where, and how he'd been snatched; and finding out what Peep was afraid of. "We can't sweat him with threats of prosecution," she said. "Prison's his home away from home. We need to know what scares him and use that."

She also wanted to look for matches to the attempt on Beth because "those assholes knew what they were doing. This wasn't their first tango, but nothing in their priors suggests that kind of expertise. I think they had help." And she wanted to put a tap on Jasper Machek's phone.

"Help . . . as in training?" Lily nodded thoughtfully. "Well worth checking out. The tap's in place as of two hours ago. I'll see that you get transcripts. You're in charge of investigating the kidnappings."

"What the hell are you doing?" Drummond demanded.

He'd faded in to join them in a misty-white-cloud sort of way when Lily began the briefing. Now he was fully formed, floating, and fuming.

It was really hard not to react.

Bergman spoke levelly. "It's a Unit case."

"Yes, it is, and you'll report to me, but you don't need me to tell you how to tie your shoes."

Drummond glared down at her. "No, I can do that! Dammit, Yu, with me to help, you can handle this just fine."

"Set things up," Lily went on briskly to Bergman, "keep things moving, keep me informed. If your people get anything—anything at all—that gives a tug on Robert Friar's whereabouts, call me that instant. Do not attempt him yourself."

Drummond announced that she was a goddamned idiot.

Bergman nodded, still wary. "That's standing orders for Friar. 'Contact Unit Twelve immediately. Do not attempt to apprehend.'"

"I'm underlining it. This is not about territory or who gets the collar."

"I'm not territorial."

Sure she was, but Lily didn't have a problem with that. "Robert Friar can't be handled without magical protections that your people don't have, and I can't give them." She paused to glance around the small conference table at the four agents other than Bergman . . .

Drummond sank to floor level and stomped silently up to Lily. "Dammit, you need to listen to me! Investigations like this are what I do, and I'm damn good at what I do. If you can't handle an investigation this big, let me help so—"

Shut up!

He looked startled—and did. That disconcerted her as much as his yelling had. Lily hoped her reaction didn't show as she finished her visual circuit of everyone present— everyone but Drummond. "Everyone clear on that? Okay. What do you need that you don't have?"

Bergman snorted. "A dozen senior agents, a car that doesn't stall out when I try to go over fifty, and a vacation in the Bahamas."

"Can't help with the vacation. Do you have an immediate need for a dozen senior agents, or was that number just for ha-ha?"

Bergman's eyes narrowed. "You can get me a dozen senior agents?"

"To get Robert Friar? Damn straight. I can pull in the army if I need them, but I'd better really, deeply need them. How many senior agents do you really, deeply need?"

Bergman went silent, her eyes unfocused. She was taking time to come up with a real number. Lily appreciated that. "Three seniors, three juniors," she said at last. "I can put the three seniors to work right away, and the juniors can handle some of the grunt work."

"How fast do you need them?" Lily glanced at her watch. It was after ten in D.C. "I don't want to wake Ida up if I don't have to." Lily could make the calls herself, but in a nonemergency situation it was better to let Ruben's secretary handle things. She'd pull in agents in a way that didn't disrupt their current workload too badly.

Bergman smiled slowly. "How about by noon tomorrow?"

"Works." Lily made a few notes, talking as she wrote. "While you handle the heavy load, I'm going to be coming at this from another angle—the prototype. If we knew who wanted it so damn bad and why, we'd have a better idea who the players are." She looked up. "If no one here's going to miss their kid's birthday or an anniversary or something, I'd like to order in some food and bat this around while we eat."

That's what they'd done. Drummond had reverted to his misty, untalking shape for most of the session, though he had formed up enough to comment now and then. They were useful comments, so Lily had passed them on. And maybe no one came up with any breakthrough ideas, but brainstorming got them farther along. And more invested. It put them on her team. Lily had felt satisfied as she rode down to the ground floor.

Drummond joined her as she stepped out of the elevator in his fully formed version, his usual scowl in place. "What you did—that was creepy as hell."

Lily glanced around. The lobby was empty except for the security guard, but her back was to him as she walked away, and he was plugged into his iPod, listening to something with lots of bass. That made for lousy security, but came in handy at the moment. If she whispered . . . "A ghost is telling me something's creepy?"

"You yelled right in my mind!"

"That's how mindspeech is supposed to work." Lily felt a bit smug. Mostly she couldn't make the mindspeech thing work. She'd been practicing for months now with Sam, but her ability remained so erratic as to be useless. Maybe this was a breakthrough? *Can you hear me now?*

He winced. "Don't do that."

Get used to it. I don't want people to wonder why I keep talking to myself.

He sighed. "I can see that. I handled it wrong up there, but I was so . . . why did you hand it off to Bergman? I could have helped. I'm supposed to help, dammit."

The lobby had revolving glass doors. She could see Scott waiting right out front, as arranged. She glanced at Drummond and shoved on the glass. *Because she's good, and this frees me up to do what I'm good at. Unless you know something against her*, she added as she stepped out into a chilly San Francisco night. Maybe Drummond had worked with Bergman and had some reason to object. They were roughly the same age. The age he'd been when he died, anyway.

"No," he said grudgingly. "Bergman's competent. But you don't get anywhere by handing the juicy cases off to someone else."

"Depends on where you want to go, doesn't it?" Whoops—she'd forgotten and spoken out loud. She glanced over her shoulder—no one nearby, so maybe no one noticed.

Not even Drummond. He'd stopped dead and was staring at the car with loathing. "I *hate* it when you go in the car," he'd said—and winked out.

He hadn't come back when she called him. Lily was beginning to understand why responsible mediums rolled their eyes when asked about getting supernatural aid from the dead. Ghosts—coherent or not—just weren't much help.

She didn't see him at the hotel, either. Marcus and Steve were on duty in the hall when Lily approached the suite trailing her own contingent of guards. She greeted them absently, used the key card, and opened the door.

Joe sailed down the short entry hall to land on his back with a grunt, right at her feet.

TWENTY-SIX

~

LILY'S gun was in her hand before she even thought about it. Joe grinned up at her. "Whoops. No alarm needed. Rule's been showing me a few tricks."

Joe was wearing boxers. Period. Rule was in shirt and dress slacks when he appeared at the end of the short hall. The shirt was unfastened. "Sorry." He ran a hand through his hair, which was already pretty messed up. Sweat gleamed on his chest. "I should have warned you."

Lily holstered her weapon. "Or at least thrown Joe the other direction."

Steve was shamefaced. "It's my fault. I knew they were working out. I should have told you before you went in. It didn't occur to me you'd . . . sorry."

"No one got shot, so I'll accept the apologies." Steve hadn't been around her much, and he was Leidolf. He wasn't used to women who reacted the way she did. "Next time you'll know."

Rule, however, had been around her plenty, and while she hadn't shot anyone, she might have. It wasn't as if he never made mistakes, but this . . . this had been stupid in the didn't-bother-to-think sense. That wasn't his kind of mistake. Lily closed the door and moved on into the room, studying him while trying to look like she wasn't. "I don't see any damage to the furnishings."

"We moved things around to make room." Absently he began buttoning his shirt.

"Where's Cullen?"

"Casting his Find spell. Again."

"It didn't work?"

"Oh, he claims it worked. He said the spell located the prototype, but it doesn't know where that location is. Apparently that makes sense to him." Rule ran a hand through his hair a second time, but this time with fingers spread to smooth it down. He glanced around. "It was a good bout, Joe. Thanks. Everyone on duty, take your posts. Off duty, get some food or sleep or head for the hotel gym."

The sitting room emptied quickly. She and Rule were as alone as they'd been since she climbed in his lap last night . . . God, yes, that was only a little over twenty-four hours ago, wasn't it? As alone as they ever got lately. She walked up to him and put her arms around his waist, leaned her head against his chest, and hugged.

He sighed and hugged back, rubbing his cheek along the top of her head. For a long moment they just stood there, neither of them speaking. He smelled of fresh sweat and the faint, underlying scent that was his alone. Even her poor human nose could identify him from this close. "What do you smell like?"

"Hmm?" He raised his head. He was smiling slightly.

"If I could smell you the way your men can, I mean. What were they smelling when you and Joe were working out?"

His smile fled. "Tension," he said at last. "I hope they didn't smell the anxiety. If they'd been in wolf form, they would have."

"Hence the sudden need to throw Joe around."

"Hence that." His smile returned, but didn't make it to his eyes. "Hence turning suddenly stupid. I thought I was dealing with this better."

"This" being his unexpected acquisition of a brother?

His worry about her? The war? All of the above, she thought, and stretched up and kissed him lightly on the mouth. "You're dealing okay. You sent Patrick to look out for Beth. If you hadn't, they'd have gotten her."

"I didn't claim to be stupid all the time, but I can't afford even brief bouts of it."

"I didn't shoot."

"And thank God for that, but—"

"Point being that you aren't perfect, you aren't going to turn perfect just because you feel like it's all up to you, and sometimes you have to rely on other people to do the right thing. What did Scott do when I drew?"

"Shifted to the side so he could leap past you if needed. Todd turned enough to keep both you and the hall in view. Mike . . . his posture suggested he was ready to take you to the floor if there was a threat. I need to talk to him about that. Standing orders are that they never block your shot. And yes, I take your point, which I gather is something about teamwork."

He sounded irritated about the whole concept of teamwork, which she gathered had something to do with being a Rho and, therefore, a control freak. The latter condition she understood only too well, so she gave him another quick kiss to tell him that, then simply lingered, held close, and thought about all the questions she'd been saving up for when they were alone. And didn't want to ask any of them. She didn't want to talk at all, not with her body stirring and beginning to yearn.

She sighed. "We need to talk."

"Why do those words always sound so ominous?" he murmured. But he was more relaxed now, more himself. "You want to discuss the venue for the wedding?"

Their wedding had been so far from her thinking the last twenty-four hours that his question took her aback. She shook her head. "This is about the case. The cases."

He squeezed her waist and let go. "All right. Would you like some wine to go with our words? I had a pleasant Syrah with dinner. There's some of that left, or I could open the Riesling the wine steward recommended."

"Some Riesling would be good." As he moved to the room service cart she took off her jacket, draped it over the back of a chair, and began unfastening her shoulder harness. "Why Leidolf?"

"Hmm?" He inserted the corkscrew and began twisting.

"I wondered why you brought an all-Leidolf squad with us."

"Oh." With a soft sound like a sigh the cork came out. He reached for a wineglass. "Call it a gut impulse, but my head agreed."

She set her shoulder harness on the table and toed off first one shoe, then the other. It felt good to wiggle her toes, dig them into the plush carpet. "What did your head say?"

"That it's hard on my Leidolf guards at Nokolai Clanhome. They're surrounded by Nokolai and constantly see me in my role as the other clan's Lu Nuncio. They need time with me as their Rho."

He wasn't making any effort to lower his voice, which meant any guards in the other bedroom who were awake could hear him easily. Which meant he was okay with that. Maybe he wanted them to. Lily picked up her jacket, shoulder harness, and shoes and carried them into the bedroom that was hers and Rule's. "It's kind of weird to hear you call Nokolai the other clan. I know what you meant, but . . . do you think you'll become more Leidolf than Nokolai?"

Glass clinked. "The balance has shifted, but I've been Nokolai all my life. I won't lose that. It's too much a part of me."

She set her shoulder harness on the bedside table where she could get it in a hurry, if needed. Shoes and jacket went in the closet. "And your gut said?"

He came into the bedroom carrying two glasses. "I wanted Leidolf around me. I wanted them to feel the change. They may not consciously notice, but they'll feel it. Leidolf is truly mine now."

"That's a very dominant way of seeing it."

His grin flashed. He held out one brimming glass. "I'm a dominant kind of a guy."

In the lupi sense of the word, she reminded herself as she

accepted the wine. He knew he was in charge—but of the clan, not her. Which was sort of the problem, considering what she needed to tell him. Lily took a sip of wine. "Hey. That's really good." Good enough to burst through her pre-occupation and make her notice. "It tastes kind of like the sky looks up high in the mountains. You know—really saturated, but crisp."

He took a sip, too, his eyes steady on hers. "I agree. I'll have to tell the wine steward we approve. What is it you wanted to talk about that you can't bring yourself to talk about?"

He was too damn perceptive at times. She sighed. "Before we left Clanhome, Cynna asked me to promise I'd let her know if we needed her. You said Cullen can't make his Find spell work. We have two people missing that we're pretty sure are hostages. We need Cynna."

"No."

He said that coolly and with complete assurance. It was exactly the reaction she'd expected. In his mind this was a clan matter—Nokolai clan, not Leidolf this time, but either way, his territory. "You don't get to make that decision."

"Lily, stop and think," he said impatiently. "Bringing Cynna here could be the reason for all of this. Why is Friar kidnapping people? That's what you keep asking, isn't it? Maybe because he wants the best Finder in the country to show up and try to find them. Stealing the prototype might get her here, but if not, grab some people, too, because that's exactly the sort of thing we'd need her for. Exactly the sort of thing she'd *want* to come here for. Cynna has no apprentice. If she were killed, the clan's memories would be lost." He shook his head. "It's unthinkable."

"And it's still not your decision. Look." She set her wine down on the bureau and went to him. "You lupi have been around for over three thousand years. In all that time, has a Rhej ever died before she could pass on the memories?"

His eyebrows went up. "It hasn't happened, therefore it won't? You usually argue better than that."

She laid her hands on his chest, wanting the contact. "It

hasn't happened, and maybe there's a reason. You protect your Rhejes in every way possible, and that's got to be part of it. What if the Lady protects them, too? By warning them, maybe, in certain special circumstances. Like if a Rhej who hasn't passed on the memories is about to do something that's apt to get her killed."

He was silent for a moment. "I've never heard of such a thing."

"I'm pretty sure the Rhejes know a lot of stuff they don't talk about."

"The Lady doesn't speak to her Rhejes often. I know that much."

"Speech isn't the only way she communicates with them, though. Hannah talked about having dreams or feelings about stuff. And the Lady is a patterner. Like Friar, only with aeons more experience and knowledge. She'd be able to read patterns really well. She'd have a good sense of when one of her Rhejes needs to stay home."

He didn't say anything. She felt the tension thrumming through him.

"When Cynna asked me to promise I'd call if we needed her, she said she might not be able to come. She wanted me to call, but she couldn't say if she would come or not. I didn't think much about it then, but later I got to wondering . . . was she just keeping her options open? Or did she think she'd get some kind of mystical thumbs-down if coming here was a bad idea? Either way," she finished gently, "Cynna gets to decide. Not you or me."

His breath gusted out. One corner of his mouth turned up. "Nice of you to include yourself in the we-don't-get-to-decide-for-her ultimatum."

"Yeah, well, I was tempted to find a loophole in my promise. Don't think I wasn't."

"You're going to call her."

"I am. But not right this second." She drifted her hands up to his shoulders. "I'm all talked out at the moment. You?"

He lowered his hands to cup her hips. Then he just

looked at her, his gaze intent, as if he needed to find something in her eyes. Uncertainty pinched at her. "What? What is it?"

He smiled slightly and shook his head. "Nothing. Or nothing important, and I find I, too, am not in the mood to talk." He bent his head and nibbled at her lips. "Especially not of unimportant things."

She leaned into the kiss. He reciprocated for a moment, then pulled back, tending to the side of her neck instead of her mouth. Delicious little thrills raced over her skin, a goose-bumpy delight that made her smile as she reached for the buttons he'd just refastened on his shirt.

He smiled at her with lazy, hooded eyes and covered her hand with his. "Not yet," he whispered, and turned her hand up and kissed her palm.

He wanted slow. He wanted lingering and teasing, and she was not in a patient mood. As with so much in a relationship, compromise was key.

She compromised by cupping his balls. And squeezing exactly the way he liked.

He gasped. When he smiled this time his eyes were still hooded, but not lazy. Not at all. "So that's how it is, is it?" And he launched his counterattack.

Lupi move really fast when they want to.

She didn't notice any buttons go flying, so maybe he'd unfastened her pants before sliding his hand inside. But then, she didn't notice much at all except his fingers sliding, parting, moving. She forgot what she'd meant to do to him and grabbed onto his shoulders for balance—then, because her hands were right there, grabbed his head and pulled it down.

No more nibbling. This kiss was hot and deep, and she twisted against him, reveling in the flood of feeling. Wanting him to be flooded, too—to turn loose, pop the clutch, let go of that fearsome control he used and needed everywhere else in his life and go flying with her.

The flying buttons came from his shirt. It took her two

tugs because he bought quality, and the thread didn't break easily.

He laughed. His eyes were on fire and he laughed, full and delighted, and he jerked her tank up over her head and lowered his head and . . .

And she remembered something. "The door," she said, as he traced a hot, wet path with his mouth along her collarbone and down.

"What door?" He hadn't removed her bra. He didn't let that stop him.

"The . . . ah, ah . . ." She had to pause and gulp in a breath. "The door to the bedroom. It's open."

He paused ever so briefly to glance that way. "But so very far away." He resumed what he'd been doing.

Which was incredibly distracting, but she choked on a laugh and grabbed his head and said as firmly as she could, "Rule. The door."

He flashed her a grin as impish and delighted as that of any little boy with a frog he meant to present to the girliest girl in class. He was thinking about making her forget the damn door, she knew it, and she wasn't sure she'd be able to stop him, but the guards—they could hear too much. Even if they didn't come out of their bedroom—and they wouldn't. He'd sent them there and they wouldn't come out until shift change, but even so—

"The door," he agreed, and straightened and drew her hand to his lips again, but this kiss was placed softly on the back of her hand—a knight's salute to his lady, not a seduction.

She used those few seconds to get rid of the bra and everything else, too. She might not be as fast as a lupus, but she was motivated.

He closed the damn door and turned and stopped, looking at her. "Sometimes," he said softly, and stopped, then started again, "I often wonder why human men are so fixated on how a woman looks when there's so much more to explore, and so many kinds of beauty—why obsess over one particular version? But sometimes, when I look at you, I understand."

And sometimes, when he looked at her the way he was now, she was beautiful. Not just okay. Not even really pretty. Beautiful.

"And you're mine." He sounded smug as he slipped off the shirt she'd ripped open and reached for the zipper on his slacks. "Not theirs. Mine."

That smugness made her want to laugh because it was so innocent. Possessiveness was a forbidden delight for lupi, not one Rule was used to, and most of the time he was wary about indulging in it.

"And you're mine," she agreed when he came to her, and she put her hands on his wonderfully bare shoulders while down lower another part of his body said hello to her stomach. "The Lady says so."

"As do I." He kissed her lightly . . . then again . . . and again . . . and they were gasping and clutching and stroking all the delicious bare skin they could find, and stumbling in mutual haste to the bed, and when he slid inside her she felt jolted by reality—felt suddenly twice as real as usual, brimming with more than sensation. Full. So full.

He started to move and reality shimmered, breaking up into shards of need and demand. *Rule!*

Here. He moved smooth and fast. *I'm here, right here with you,* nadia, *my love, my Lily . . .*

It may have been pure startlement that broke the connection—his or hers or both. Certainly it broke their rhythm. She stared up into his astonished face. "Well," she said, and gripped his waist and pushed up against him. "Well, that's interesting, but so's this."

He grinned and followed her lead.

LILY lay sprawled on her back amid a tangle of bedclothes and Rule, breathing hard and frowning at the lovely but too-bright chandelier. "That's stupid."

Rule turned his face on the pillow—how had he ended

up with a pillow, and where was hers?—to smile at her.
"What is?"

"Most hotels don't have ceiling lights. Why does this
one? And the switch is all the way over there by the door.
Why didn't they put a switch by the bed? Stupid."

Rule looked up at the light. After a moment he nodded.
"You're right. It shows a sad lack of planning." He paused.
"I can wiggle my toes again, however, so I'm sure I'll soon
be up to the challenge of sitting. No doubt walking will be
possible soon after that."

She smiled and snuggled closer. No matter how enthusi-
astic the sex, Rule recovered quickly, and in every way. It
was nice to think she'd wrecked him for a little while,
though. "You heard me. Earlier, I mean."

"And you heard me."

He didn't sound sure. She nodded. "Does that freak you
out?"

"A little. And yet . . . it was lovely, too."

She propped herself up on an elbow so she could see
him. "I didn't do it on purpose."

He smiled and toyed with a strand of her hair. "That
much I knew."

Since Lily had discovered her capability for mindspeech
and began the sessions with Sam, she'd accidentally mindspoken Rule a few times. The first time was right after she
nearly died. The others had been more random, in perfectly
ordinary situations, like when she'd been trying to reach a
bowl he'd put on the top shelf in the kitchen and was annoyed because it was supposed to be on the second shelf,
where she could get it. That time, she remembered, the
communication had been along the lines of, "Why can't
you remember to put things where they belong?"

It had never happened during sex, and she'd never
"heard" Rule in return.

Eavesdropping on him that way him was intrusive and
freaky and just as he'd said. Quite lovely. "I forgot to tell
you, but earlier this evening I thought I had a breakthrough.
Drummond was talking at me during the briefing with

Bergman, and I told him to shut up. I mindspoke it," she added, to be clear. "And he heard me, and I did it again later."

Rule's brows pulled together. He didn't speak.

That made her frown, too. "What?"

"It bothers me, that's all. You and Drummond seem to be getting downright chummy."

Disconcerted, she swallowed her first retort. "You're jealous. Of Al Drummond."

"Don't be ridiculous."

Someone here was being ridiculous. She didn't think it was her. "I don't even like him, Rule."

"You never wear the necklace. You could keep him away, and you don't. It's not a matter of him being potentially useful. There's something else going on. I don't understand."

"I don't know if I do, either, except that he has nothing. Literally nothing and no one, not even a body. It's not just that he can't move so much as a paper clip. He can't *touch* the paper clip. When I make it so he can't manifest, he can't even see it."

"You feel sorry for him."

Yeah, she did, and that was kind of weird, considering what Drummond had done. But it wasn't the whole story. "Maybe it's some random roll of the dice that got him tied to me. Maybe there's actually someone in charge who did this on purpose. I don't know, but either way, it's up to me to do the right thing. I'm not sure what that is, but making it so he can't see the damn paper clip can't be right."

Rule sifted a hand through her hair. "You're trying to do the right thing. That I understand. But I can't help thinking he's using this tie. Using you. In life, Drummond was a betrayer. He betrayed you and the Bureau. Do you really think dying changed him that much?"

"I don't know, but—shit!" She rolled off him and grabbed for the sheet.

White, misty, and right there at the foot of the bed, Al Drummond sang out, "Incoming!"

TWENTY-SEVEN

～

AL Drummond really enjoyed the look on Yu's face as she leaped out of bed. She probably figured he'd been hanging around while she made whoopee with her wolf man. He wasn't that kind of creep, but that's what she'd think. She'd probably come up with some way to make him pay for his grand entrance, but it would be worth it.

"It's Drummond," Yu said as she grabbed a fistful of clothes off the floor. "Who or what is incoming?" she demanded, stepping into her pants.

Al considered commenting on her lack of underwear. What could she do—hit him? Maybe later. He did have a warning to deliver. "I can't tell," he said. "It's dark where the intruder is. He's paying a visit via the ductwork."

"The ductwork?" she repeated. Her lover—who'd sprung from the bed in that fluid, too-fast way lupi moved sometimes, which Drummond didn't like at all—looked up and around. They both spotted the vent. "It isn't big enough," Lily said.

"The one in the other room is. That's where he's headed."

"He says the intruder's heading for the one in the sitting room," she told Turner as she pulled her shirt over her head.

She tugged it down and glared at Al. "So why the hell did you pop up in here? You could have materialized on the other side of the damn door."

He smirked. "More fun this way."

A low growl rose in the chest of her wolf man. Turner must have figured out where Al was by watching where Lily looked, because he seemed to look right at him. "Been hanging around watching, have you?"

He spoke to Al. Right to him. No one but Yu had done that since he died, and it shook him, how good that felt. *Keep talking to me. Please. Please keep talking to me.* "Maybe that's how you get your jollies. Not my thing."

Yu rolled her eyes. "Rule may see you now and then, but he can't hear you. Come on."

"See me?" He tried to grab her as she reached for her shoulder harness. Didn't work, of course. It made him want to growl like the wolf man, or maybe howl like one.

The worst thing about being a ghost wasn't when she went in the damn car. Even being alone, bad as it was, wasn't the worst. It was the sheer, unrelenting uselessness of his existence. Hell was being unable to do one damned thing, and maybe he'd earned a stint in hell. Maybe he deserved it. But God, what he'd give to be able to affect *something*. If Turner could see him . . . "What do you mean, he sees me sometimes?"

"Just what I said, and this isn't the time to talk about it."

Turner opened the door and moved silently into the other room. Drummond followed Yu through the door. He could go through walls, but he liked to use doors. Made him feel more real. She had her rig fastened by the time she stopped beside Turner. She drew her weapon and held it down at her side.

The two of them glowed. He'd told Yu that all the embodied had a glow, but these two lit up brighter than most . . . and brighter still when they stood close like that. Drummond thought he knew why. It was that weird, glowy cord stretched between them.

No one else had one. None of the people he'd seen since

he died, anyway, and with nothing to do but watch, he'd
been paying attention. He didn't know what the cord-thing
was, but it glowed like the living did. As if it was alive. It
freaked him out. He stepped back, not wanting to touch the
eerie thing.

Turner stood in front of the vent, studying it. Yu started
to say something, but Turner tapped her arm and laid a finger to his lips.

"You hear something?" she whispered so softly that
Drummond wasn't sure he heard it with his ears. Well,
whatever passed for ears with him like this. It wasn't like
when she'd talked in his head at the branch office, so it
probably had to do with their goddamn mystical connection.

Turner nodded and tipped his head to one side. Yu
glanced that way and nodded back as if she knew exactly
what he meant.

Maybe she did. She went to the door to the other bedroom and opened it. She didn't step inside, though, but
whispered real softly again. "Get up. Be quiet. Someone's
coming."

In total silence, three men went from what looked like
sound sleep to standing. Then they stood there, naked and
motionless. Waiting.

Yu jerked her head at them—come on—and went back
in the sitting room, where Turner looked at them and wiggled his hands around as if it meant something, pointing
now and then. Two of the naked guys stood with him in
front of the vent. One went to the door to the suite and
opened it.

"Did he tell them to do all that?" Drummond said.

Yu glanced at him, opened her mouth, then closed it.
And put words right into his damn mind again. *Yes. It's
ASL, mostly. He wants the guards at the door to know
what's happening.*

The guy who'd gone to the door came back. Drummond
hadn't heard him say anything to the two guys guarding the
door. Maybe he'd used ASL, too. Turner made some more

hand-talk at him, and he loped silently into the bedroom he'd emerged from, returning with a wood-gripped 9 mm in one hand—a Smith and Wesson 952, he thought. An expensive piece, if so. He was still buck naked.

Turner pointed at the other two, made a circle in the air . . . and the two guys without guns turned into wolves.

Al had been around when lupi turned into wolves once, but he hadn't really watched. He'd been busy at the time, what with being freshly dead and trying to stop a bunch of demons shaped like wolves from killing a few hundred people. This time, he paid attention. It gave him the creeps to think of a man morphing into a beast, but it was better to know your enemy, right? So he watched, but he didn't see much. It was like they flowed somewhere else, somewhere he couldn't go, then flowed back, reformed.

He hadn't expected to hear anything. "Did you . . ." He had to stop and clear his throat. "Does that music happen every time they do that?"

Yu looked at him sharply. *You heard music?*

He nodded. Clear and distant, so distant he shouldn't have heard it . . . and pure. Pure like a baby's laugh or the way stars look, spattering the darkness. Pure like nothing he'd ever heard or imagined. "Real faint," he said. "It was . . ." He shook his head, out of words.

Yu had a funny look on her face, like he'd made her sad. Wistful, maybe. *Moonsong*, she said in the way he didn't like but was getting used to. *You heard moonsong.*

A faint scraping came from the vent. Drummond shook off his preoccupation with something he'd barely heard and paid attention to what was happening now. So did Yu and her wolf man and the two wolves.

The vent cover wiggled, started to fall. A man's hand shot out and grabbed it. A man's head emerged. "Oh," Jasper Machek said, blinking like an owl at the odd group assembled below him. And, "Shit."

TWENTY-EIGHT

~

"I guess you heard me coming," Jasper Machek said. He shook his head. "I'm rusty, that's what. Getting old and rusty."

"Rule's hearing is better than ours," Lily said. "A lot better."

"So I'm told." The thought didn't cheer him up. His face was tight, his expression abstracted. If he was bothered by the two very large wolves sitting in front of him, watching his every muscle twitch, it didn't show.

Drummond was leaning against the wall, his arms crossed, watching and listening. Or that's what he seemed to be doing. Could a ghost be supported by a wall?

Rule had assured Machek that the suite had been swept for bugs and Friar couldn't eavesdrop here magically. Machek hadn't believed him, but it was clear that either Rule was correct or it was too late to worry about it. Once he'd wriggled out of his hole in the wall, Rule had had Todd pat him down. Not that he could conceal much with all the Lycra in his clothes—they were skin-tight, even the handy-dandy vest he wore with its interesting pockets. All the better for crawling through very tight spaces, Lily assumed.

In the vest's pockets Todd had found two phones, a set of lockpicks, and a small, top-of-the-line bug detector. There was also a wallet with five hundred in cash and an ID that claimed he was Richard Spallings. No weapons. Rule gave everything back to Jasper, then invited him to have a seat while he called Scott. He filled Scott in quickly, told him to alert the other guards—those with Cullen and the two Laban with Beth—and return to the suite. He said he'd call the guards at Machek's house himself.

Machek sat bolt upright. "Don't pull them off my house! If Friar knows you've pulled them, he'll—"

"I need to know they're alive and well," Rule said.

Machek smiled bitterly. "Did you think I could overcome werewolves? I suppose I should be flattered. They're fine. They didn't see me leave because I used an alternative exit."

"Did you, now? Perhaps you'll tell me about that in a moment." Rule tapped on the screen of his phone.

Lily was standing beneath the hole Machek had crawled out of, studying it. "I can't believe you fit. It's wide enough, but it's not even a foot high."

"Twelve point two inches," Machek said absently. "Tight but doable."

"You measured?"

"I did a job here once. That was years ago, but I took a chance they hadn't refitted their ducts. People don't, mostly. Costs too much."

The hotel hadn't cleaned their ducts, either. Jasper Machek's black, stretchy clothes were covered in dust. Lily had hurriedly tossed a blanket on the couch before he sat down. They'd managed not to break any furniture so far. Why add a big cleaning bill to their tab?

Rule finished talking to whichever guard he'd called and disconnected. "Chris and Alan are fine, if chagrinned that you evaded them. They'll continue to watch the house.

What can I offer you to eat or drink? The bar here is reasonably well stocked."

"Nothing." After a moment he remembered to add, "Thank you."

Rule looked at Patrick, who'd hastily pulled on a pair of jeans. "Have room service send up four pots of coffee and an assortment of—"

"Don't call room service! They can't know I'm here. If they—"

"Jasper," Rule said, "There are eight adults registered to this suite, seven of whom are lupi. It's barely past ten o'clock. Room service will not be amazed by an order for refreshments."

"Of course." Machek rubbed his face. "I'm panicking. I don't usually, but this is . . . I need to tell you why I'm here."

"You do, yes," Rule said, and moved to sit in the chair facing his brother. "Has Friar called?"

Machek shook his head.

"Sandwiches and fruit okay?" Patrick asked, picking up the hotel phone.

"That would be fine. Jasper, am I to assume you came through the ductwork to avoid being seen, rather than from some hope of surprising and slaughtering us?"

"Absolutely."

"It's usually a bad idea to surprise lupi," Lily said. "It can be a bad idea to surprise me, too."

Machek glanced at her shoulder holster. She'd put her gun up when Todd didn't find any weapons on him. "I didn't have many options. I had to talk to you. The prototype is missing."

Dead silence. Rule broke it to say dryly, "Does that mean it wasn't missing before?"

"Yes. I mean no, it wasn't." He rubbed his face again. "Maybe I do need some coffee. I haven't been sleeping well. I'll start over. Most of what I told you was true, but even the true parts were carefully selected. I was given a script to follow. I did as I was told, and I'm not apologizing for it. He has Adam. You were right about that. He . . . they hurt him once, while I was on the phone. Friar wanted me to hear."

Lily exchanged a glance with Rule. He nodded, meaning she could take it for now. "You've talked with Adam."

He nodded. "Every day. I refused to do anything unless I spoke to him every day. I made sure they weren't using a recording. I asked questions they couldn't have anticipated."

"When was Adam taken?"

"Nine days ago. That's a hellishly short time to plan and execute the kind of job he wanted me to do, but it's hellishly long in every other way."

"How did Friar know you could do that kind of job?"

"I've got an idea about that, but—look, can I just tell you what happened without questions for a minute?"

"Go ahead."

"There was an attempt to get the prototype from me last night. That part was true. Three men, one armed—at least I only saw one gun. It loomed large in my sight at the time, but I think it was a smallish 9 mm. They were waiting for me when I got home. The one with the gun was on the stairs between me and the door. The other two came up behind me, blocking me. They demanded the prototype. I'd allowed for the possibility that Friar would double-cross me, so I'd stashed it elsewhere. They assured themselves I was telling the truth about that, then demanded I tell them where it was. I refused. They made the obligatory threats. I refused again. They weren't going to kill me, not when I was the only person who knew where the damn thing was, and we were on a public street. It was late, but we were too public for them to hurt me badly. Or so I hoped." He paused. "I got lucky. Mr. Peterson's dog had gotten out again. He's a Great Dane with a low boredom threshold, thinks he's a puppy. He came racing up, all excited at these new playmates, and jumped up on one of the men. It was enough of a distraction for me to get away."

Lily had quietly retrieved her notebook while he was talking. "Where did you go?"

"At first I just ran. Once I was sure I'd lost them . . . there's a little coffee shop on Bradbury that stays open all night. I was close enough, so I went there. They'd searched me, but they hadn't taken anything. I still had both phones—"

"Both?" The door to the hall opened. A quick glance told her it was Scott; Rule asked him something using hand-talk, and he left again. Lily focused on Jasper.

"My phone and the throwaway Friar sent me. I contacted Friar."

"You have his number."

"No, he calls me. To contact him, I log on to a chat board and leave a message. I was told what name to use. They look for posts from handydog12 and for certain key words. That's how I let him know I had the prototype—I used 'success' in a post. To get him to call me I posted 'disregard my last message.' Thirty minutes later he called me. I told him about the attempt."

"Did you tell him the thieves weren't successful?"

"Yes." He leaned forward, looking at the hands he clasped between his knees. "I thought about lying, but if those were his men, he'd know, wouldn't he? I couldn't take the chance. If I lie, he punishes Adam. That's why they hurt Adam before. Friar caught me in a lie."

Drummond stirred. "I've got a couple questions for him."

In a few minutes, she told him, *if I haven't asked your questions already, you'll get a shot.* It was getting easier all the time to talk to him this way. Out loud she said, "You told Friar what happened, but you didn't go get the proto-type and give it to him."

"No." He looked up. "Once I do that, he doesn't need Adam anymore, does he? He . . . we were supposed to make the exchange that night, but I didn't trust him. I told him so. I said he'd need to prove they weren't his men. He laughed at me. He didn't have to prove anything, but if I wanted to hang on to the device for a few days, why, he had plenty for me to do. That's when he told me to call Rule and what to say when he got here."

"He expected Rule to bring Cullen?"

Jasper nodded. "And you. And he wanted Rule to bring the Finder, but I couldn't talk him into that." Bitterly he added, "*I* wanted him to bring the Finder, too. If he had, I would have taken a chance. I could have passed one of you a note. Friar has my house most thoroughly bugged, so I had to follow his script when you were there, but I could have passed a note. If your Finder could have found Adam . . . but you didn't bring her."

"If your house is bugged, he must know you left it to-night."

The twist of his mouth was meant to be a smile. "Now you're impugning my professional abilities. I left record-ings, of course. Several of them, because there are bugs in almost every room. No visual, but audio is damn near as tricky if it's done well, and his people did a good job. But I'm better."

"How long before your recordings end?"

He glanced at his watch. "I can stay another three hours, tops. The recordings will run out in four hours and seven minutes. Right about now," he added, "I'm in the kitchen getting some nibbles from the refrigerator."

"If he has someone watching—"

"The lights are on timers."

A high-end thief would need to be good at fooling sur-veillance, she supposed.

"I don't think there are watchers 24/7," Rule said. "Chris and Allan haven't spotted any. How did you leave your house without my men seeing you?"

"There's a way to go from my basement to my neigh-bor's. I go to the third floor in his house, out a window, and into that huge oak in his backyard. From that tree I connect with another one in the yard behind him, then down, out the gate, and away."

"Your neighbor doesn't mind you wandering through his house to get to his tree?"

"My goal is for him to remain unaware of it. Mr. Peterson is eighty-two, deaf, and goes to bed at nine every night, so this isn't challenging. His dog has excellent hearing, but we're buds, so he doesn't object to me visiting."

Rule's eyebrows lifted. "Surely this is not the Mr. Peterson with the Great Dane."

Jasper smiled faintly. "In fact, it is. Mr. Peterson is a remarkably fit eighty-two, and while Ajax has a bad habit of hopping over the fence when he's bored, he behaves well on their daily walks."

Drummond spoke from his spot near the wall. "Machek doesn't sound all that retired to me."

He didn't to Lily, either. Jasper still had all the gadgets he needed to fool surveillance. He'd worked out a route to leave his house unseen and had apparently used it before tonight. "How long did it take you to make the recordings you're using tonight?"

Jasper's lips thinned. "I've had plenty of time. Nine days. When he first took Adam I suspected he'd bugged the house. Never mind why for now—I suppose you'll want to hear all about that, but later. I didn't know about him being a listener, not then, so I looked for less arcane ways of eavesdropping. Once I was sure I'd found all the bugs, I started making the recordings. It seemed likely I'd want to leave without him knowing at some point."

"Okay. How do you know the prototype is missing?"

"Because it isn't where I left it."

"But you weren't going to make the exchange for the next few days. Why would you check on or move it? Isn't there a chance you'd lead Friar to it?"

"Oh. Right. I see why you wondered." He grimaced. "It's hard to overcome the habit of secrecy. I'd followed my usual procedure, you see, so I needed to move it to a better hiding place."

"Your usual procedure being—?"

"FedEx, in this case."

"If you FedEx'ed it to yourself last night, it wouldn't arrive until tomorrow."

"No, I use their delivery trucks, but not that way. UPS vehicles work, too, but FedEx was closer."

The front door opened. "—said I'd take it. Isn't there someone else with vital and sensitive work you need to interrupt? No? Then you can guard my ass while I . . . oh. Hello."

Cullen had entered pushing a room service cart, trailing his two guards. He stopped short when he saw Jasper. "Now that's interesting. Not interesting enough to justify interrupting me, but I suppose you have questions you want to ask."

"Something like that," Rule said dryly. "I'm guessing the Find spell still isn't working."

"Not worth a damn. Weirdest thing I ever saw." Cullen lifted the lid of one of the dishes. "That looks good. Did I eat supper?"

"Yes, but don't let that stop you. Perhaps you'd get something for my guest as well."

"If you mean me, I don't want anything," Jasper said.

"I'll take a cup of coffee," Lily said. "Jasper—"

"Oh, good, interrupt my spellcasting so I can play waiter." Cullen did sarcasm so well. But he did pour a cup for her and drift in her direction while biting into the half sandwich he'd picked up.

"Are you going to keep interrupting me as some sort of payback?" she asked as she took the cup.

"Maybe. What am I interrupting?"

"Your prototype wasn't really missing before. It is now. Jasper dropped by to tell us about it. He went to get it today, and it was gone. He was about to explain what that has to do with FedEx."

"Um. Yes." Jasper cast a wary glance at Cullen. "I prefer to avoid confrontation with those whose property I've appropriated. Some of them have nasty tempers and even nastier spells. My first goal is always to put as much distance as possible between me and the object's previous owner. If I can hand it off to the person who ordered the job right away, fine. If not, I affix the item to a delivery truck. FedEx is my first choice. The trucks stay in motion and they—"

Cullen broke in. "Tell me you didn't just duct tape the skull to the axle."

"I did use duct tape. That takes a few minutes to cut through at retrieval, but it's worth it to make the object secure. But don't worry. The skull is in a bowling ball bag with plenty of padding. That did limit my options for where to tape it. I prefer to put objects near the engine, but a dry run showed that wouldn't work this time."

Cullen nodded. "Makes sense."

Lily rolled her eyes. First Cullen bitches about having his spellcasting interrupted, then he compliments the thief who made it necessary. "Explain."

"If you're using a spell, it's harder to find something that's moving, and some Find spells—not mine, but some— are dispersed by large chunks of metal, like an engine. Doesn't work against a good Finder, though."

"True," Jasper said, "but last night I needed to hide it from people other than your Finder. I was out of her range—or so I'd been told. Her limit is a hundred miles, right?"

Cullen scowled. "Told by who?"

"Robert Friar."

"And you believe a *vesceris corpi* whose word is as rotten and rancid as that which he consumes?"

Jasper spoke admiringly. "That was a master-level insult. I agree about Friar, but in this case I think he spoke accurately. He wanted me to succeed."

Lily yanked them back on track. "Tell me when you went to get the prototype, why you went at that time, and how you found the right truck."

"To answer your last question first—GPS. I went to get it tonight at eight forty because it had been stationary for thirty minutes, suggesting the driver was done for the day." He sighed. "Unfortunately, it was at a garage, up on a rack.

The GPS tracker was still in place, but the prototype was gone."

"You didn't just look at the truck. You searched elsewhere."

"In the trash, the Dumpster—everywhere I could think of." He leaned forward intently. "That's why I'm here. I don't think Friar has it. Either one of the other people looking for it—"

"There's more than Friar after it?" Cullen asked sharply.

"Yes, yes—I'll get to that in a minute. Either one of the others somehow tracked it down, or one of the mechanics took it home with him. Either way . . ." He looked directly at Rule. "Seabourne can't find it. He's tried. We *need* your Finder now. You have to send for her."

Rule's face was tight. "Two things you need to know. First, she isn't under my authority. Second, she's a young mother with a new baby, and Friar wants to kill her."

Hope drained from Jasper's face as visibly as water swirling down the drain. "Then you won't—you can't—"

"I can't send for her. I can ask her to come." Rule looked at Lily for a long moment and sighed. "I will call her."

"Like hell you will!" And Cullen sprang at him.

TWENTY-NINE

~

LILY transferred quickly to the couch to get out of the way. Rule parried Cullen's charge with a variation on a hip lift—and sure enough, Cullen crashed into the chair she'd just vacated. It toppled. Lily sighed. "So much for the undamaged furniture."

"What—" Jasper turned wide eyes on her. "Aren't they going to stop it? I thought those men were Rule's guards, and he's the big leader. The Rho. Why are they just standing around?"

"Cullen is Rule's friend. He's got certain privileges." She winced. The next exchange of blows had been so quick she didn't see who got hit where, but when they separated Rule's nose was bleeding. "Plus Cullen is Nokolai, not Leidolf, so Rule is his Lu Nuncio, not his Rho. The rules are different for a Lu Nuncio, and Rule hasn't ordered Cullen to stop."

"Being friends means it's okay for Cullen to beat the hell out of Rule?"

"Not that different from human men, are they? Don't worry. He can't hurt Rule too much. Cullen's fast, but Rule's a much better fighter. He—shit!"

Rule had gone sailing this time, skidding on his back into a table—which nearly went over, but Scott darted forward and steadied it at the last minute. Lily sent him a pleased smile. "Rule wants to let Cullen burn off some steam. The Finder you want so badly is Cullen's wife."

"His . . . but lupi don't marry."

Lily looked down at her ring. "Cullen's unusual in many ways. And your assumptions are out of date."

"I know. Sorry." He waved a hand. "But I thought you and Rule were the first to decide to tie the knot."

"You can't believe everything you read. Cullen and Cynna kept their wedding quieter than we are keeping ours."

"Cullen—" Rule ducked a roundhouse kick. "I'm trying not to break any of your body parts," he said, exasperated, "but you need to start calming down."

Cullen crouched. "When you tell me you aren't going to drag Cynna into this—"

Enough. "He won't have to." Lily stood. "I'd already decided to call her."

Cullen spun to face her, anger and incredulity vying for control of his ridiculously beautiful face, which was bleeding where one of Rule's blows had connected with his cheekbone. "You would do that?"

"Before we left, she asked me to promise I'd let her know if we needed her. I did. She wants to be sure it's her decision, not yours or mine or Rule's." She glanced down at Jasper and added gently, "It doesn't mean she'll come. She may not be able to. But I will ask."

Cullen stared at her, turned, and stalked into the bedroom. He was limping slightly. A few seconds later she heard the water come on. He must have noticed the blood and decided to wash it off.

She went to Rule. In the few seconds since the fight stopped, both his eyes were turning black and his nose had swollen. Lupi healed fast, but they went through all the stages first. He was breathing through his mouth. "Ouch. Your poor nose."

He touched it gingerly. "He's a quick son of a bitch. It's displaced. Mike, you put Samuel's nose back when it got knocked out of—"

"I'll do it," Cullen called from the bathroom.

He sounded peevish rather than furious, but Lily raised skeptical eyebrows at Rule. Cullen had the training—if he'd bothered to finish, he could have gotten his medical degree—but how careful would he be at the moment?

"He messed it up. He can put it back." Rule looked around the room. "Not too bad, considering." He took a couple of steps and righted the chair. "The leg's a bit loose, but it isn't broken."

"Scott saved the table." Lily retrieved her notebook and coffee cup from the rescued table. In spite of Scott's care, most of the coffee had slopped out, so she went to refill it. Whether through chance or instinct, the combatants had avoided the room service cart. Good. "You ready for a cup?" she asked Jasper.

"I guess I am."

He looked a bit dazed. Well, it took awhile to get used to lupi ways. She poured hers and Jasper's cups and said, "Rule?"

"After my nose is back in place."

Cullen emerged from the bedroom with a sopping hand towel. His limp was worse. "Here." He tossed the towel to Patrick. "Put that in the freezer. Rule will appreciate it being nice and cold after I put his nose back where it belongs."

"Couldn't you just suck the heat away?" Lily asked as she carried Jasper's coffee to him.

"The towel won't have to concentrate to stay cold the way I would. Okay." Cullen stopped in front of Rule and nodded once, pleased. "Got you pretty good, didn't I? I'm going to use the pain block spell just long enough to set it," he said, raising both hands to Rule's face.

"Thank you," Rule said dryly.

"Hold still."

Lily handed Jasper his cup and sat beside him. She took a sip of hers. Good and hot still.

"If he has a pain blocking spell, why use a cold towel?" Jasper asked.

"The spell blocks healing along with pain, so they don't leave it running." Lily flipped to the right page in her notebook. "We've got less than three hours left and a lot to cover. I was about to ask you about the garage where the FedEx truck ended up. The address?"

He gave it to her, adding, "Maybe we'll luck out. One of the mechanics could have taken it home. He might have thought it was a decoration or just wanted the stones. Even if you can't see the glow, they're—"

"Glow?" Cullen had finished with Rule's nose. He stiffened all over, like a bird dog on point. "Describe this glow."

Jasper gave him a puzzled look. "You ought to know. It's subtle, like I said—makes the stones look like they've got a bit of sunshine trapped inside."

"It only glows to those who can see magic. And only when it's turned on."

"I didn't turn it on. I don't know how to turn it on, and I'm not an idiot. I didn't try."

"It's easy to turn on if you're a sorcerer."

"I told you, I'm not—"

"You see magic. You're a sorcerer. And you turned the damn thing on. Son of a bitch." Cullen paced a few steps. Turned. Pointed at a small vase on one table. "Pick that up."

"What?"

"Humor him," Rule said, "if you don't mind."

"Pick it up," Cullen repeated, "paying careful attention to your hands. As if you were handling something important and fragile."

Looking mystified and annoyed, Jasper went to the table and slowly picked up the vase.

"You don't even know you're leaking, do you?"

"I don't even know what you're talking about."

"You don't leak much. Probably not enough for you to see, given how slight your Gift is. But when you focus on your hands, you shoot out small streams of magic. Enough," Cullen finished gloomily, "to turn on my damn prototype."

"Wait a minute," Lily said. "You made it so any stray bit of magic could turn it on?"

"Not stray magic. Focused magic. The kind a sorcerer uses without aid from props likes spells. It was supposed to be a safety precaution. I wouldn't have thought an untrained, denies-he's-a-sorcerer, barely Gifted neophyte could focus power he can't even bloody see, not tightly enough to be a problem. It seems I was wrong."

"So the prototype isn't just missing—it's broadcasting," Lily said grimly. "Which means any nulls in the vicinity could be having some real strange memories." She pulled out her phone. "Damn. It's after one in D.C. I hate to wake Ruben."

"He may not be asleep," Rule said. "He doesn't need as much sleep these days. But perhaps we should decide first how much of this to believe."

She met his gaze. Nodded. "Even if it's all true, he could still be omitting things. Maybe he's still acting on Friar's instructions, and the goal is to get Cynna here."

"Or to get us to that garage."

"Or both. Most of what he's told us confirms what we already suspected."

"I understand why you would doubt me," Jasper said, "but there's one thing I can tell you that you haven't suspected. Friar's working with one of the sidhe."

"I knew it!" Cullen exclaimed. "Damned elves."

Jasper's eyebrows shot up. "You already knew?"

"He didn't, actually," Lily said, "but we did suspect they were involved somehow. Why do you say Friar's working with them?"

"With them or for them. Or one of them. I heard her talking once when Friar called to chat, and it sounded like she was telling him what to do. Not that I know what she said, but she sounded in charge. And that voice . . . it had to be an elf. No one else could sound like that."

Some of the sidhe delegation had given interviews on TV. The translation device they used relied on a form of mind-magic, which only worked in person, so the gnome had translated for the television audience. But everyone had heard their voices as they answered in their own language, and Jasper was right. No one and nothing sounded like an elf.

Except maybe a halfling? One of the elves was female, but so was the halfling. She didn't look elfin, but halfling meant mixed blood and she was sidhe, which meant some of that mix was elf. The halfling hadn't given any interviews, though—at least none Lily had seen. Lily didn't know if she sounded like a fountain or a flute or something else impossibly musical the way the elves did. "You're sure it was a female voice?"

He nodded.

She looked at Rule and tried something. *You buying this?*

A flicker of surprise on his face told her it had worked. She felt ridiculously pleased, kind of like when, in the second grade, she'd suddenly grasped the mystery of fractions. He gave a small nod, but she didn't "hear" him reply.

Apparently sending and receiving mindspeech were two distinct skills. *Me, too,* she sent, or thought she did. Impossible to be sure, since his face didn't give her a clue this time.

She'd have to chance waking Ruben up. The trade delegation was almost certainly involved. The prototype was not just missing, but active—and therefore actively altering memories in weird and unpredictable ways.

"Hold on a minute," Drummond said. "I've got an idea. If I'm right, you'll want to hear it before you call Brooks."

Lily had almost forgotten he was here. What did it mean that she could get so used to a see-through guy that she stopped noticing him? "What?" she said—and realized she'd spoken out loud, and glanced at Jasper. Should she tell him? Did it matter if he knew she was a mite haunted?

Reluctantly she decided it might. If spilling his guts to Friar would buy Adam's life—or if he thought it would—Friar would know all about Drummond, too. She wasn't sure that mattered, but any information they kept from Friar might give them an advantage.

Drummond had straightened away from his spot against

the wall and walked closer. He went around Scott just as if he'd been solid. "I've got a couple questions for the sorcerer."

Okay. She glanced at Rule and tried to do it again with him. It felt different when she mindspoke Rule. She couldn't define the difference, but it was as obvious as the difference between her right hand and her left. *I'm going to wait so Drummond can ask some questions first. He thinks it's important.*

His eyebrows lifted.

Drummond looked at Cullen. "This gizmo of his—it puts out some kind of mind-magic, right? And it's turned on."

Lily spoke to Cullen. "Your prototype is turned on. That means it's putting out mind-magic."

Cullen looked impatient. "Good to know you paid attention when I told you about it this time."

"What about his Find spell?" Drummond asked. "Is that mind-magic, too?"

She repeated it: "Is your Find spell mind-magic?"

"Not exactly. It—wait. Shit. That's it. That's why I can't make the bloody spell work! Lily, you're a bloody genius!" He took two long strides—right through Drummond, who scowled fiercely—grabbed her by the shoulders, and kissed her smack on the mouth. "Find spells aren't mind-magic, but they're Air, and so is mind-magic, and when you look at the congruencies—never mind. You don't want to hear all that. The prototype itself is screwing up my spell!"

"And you're delighted about this because . . . ?"

"Because now I *know.*"

Drummond answered at the same time. "Because now we know why they want it so damn bad."

Lily looked quickly at him. "What . . ." *What do you mean?*

He rolled his eyes. "Isn't it obvious? The prototype keeps the woo-woo types from Finding things. These perps have kidnapped two people, and if they have the prototype, you aren't going to Find them."

THIRTY

RULE knew by the look on Lily's face that Drummond had said something important. When she passed it on, Cullen's eyes went wide. "That's it. Could that be it? Hard to believe I made something the elves don't have twice as good already, when they could—no, wait, what if that bit from Kålidåsa's *Siddhanta* is new to them? They don't borrow much from human traditions. Hell, they don't think much of humans, period, so if they never—I need to go."

"Go where?" Rule asked.

Cullen started for the entry. "Go *think*. I can't think with everyone yammering."

At the moment, he was the only one speaking. "The conference room?" Rule said to Cullen's back. He gestured for Marcus and Steve to follow.

"Yes," Cullen said on his way out the door.

"I don't know," Lily said slowly, "if Cullen's a hundred percent on target, but close. Only why is Friar involved? I don't think we can assume the main purpose he has for the device is to hide his captives from Find spells."

She said that to empty air. At least it looked empty to Rule at first, but something was there, a paleness blurring the air . . . and a glow. A soft, golden glow in one spot. Abruptly that paleness sharpened into clarity. He saw Al Drummond standing there—the combed-back hair, the sardonic expression, and the gold wedding ring on his left hand.

Rule jerked in shock.

"What?" Lily said.

"Nothing." And that's what he saw now. Nothing. He needed to tell Lily he'd actually seen the ghost. The mate bond was still bleeding something of her ability into him— was maybe turning up the power on that—and she needed to know.

But later. When they were alone. "Friar wants to sell it," Rule said. "The sidhe realms run heavily on magic. It's their tech. They might have dozens of uses for such a device that we can't imagine."

"And they could pay for it with more of the kind of stuff he got from Rethna. God. That's bad news. I need to call Ruben right now. If he—" Her eyebrows went up as her hand went to her pocket. She took out her phone, snorted, and answered. "Hello, Ruben."

Rule heard Ruben Brook's reply. "I had a hunch I should call. Is my timing a problem?"

"No, you're being your usual uncanny precog self. I need to bring you up-to-date." Lily began pacing as she briefed her boss.

Rule went to the spot on the couch she'd vacated and sat beside the man Lily insisted on calling his brother. He looked at Jasper. "You haven't laid down any terms this time."

"Tonight I come as a supplicant. One without power can't set terms."

Lily had been right. Jasper didn't care if he went to jail, not as long as Adam was safe. "Did you consider just asking for help before?"

Jasper looked down. His hands were clasped between his knees, and his face was still. "I didn't know you. I had some preconceptions, mostly negative. I was just bright

enough to know that's what they were—glimpses caught
through a distorted lens—but I was used to them. They
were all I had to go on."

"I didn't have any preconceptions. I didn't know about
you. Until last night, I didn't know you existed."

Jasper nodded. "So Isen told me."

"You've talked to him."

"The last time my mother went in for treatment. Until
then, I didn't know Isen had paid for Mom's treatments all
along. I knew Dad hadn't—he never made that kind of
money—but he'd told me it was a relative of hers, someone
with plenty of money and a guilty conscience, who covered
the cost." Jasper's smile flickered. "True enough in a sense."

"Isen didn't feel guilty about Celeste."

Jasper's eyebrows climbed. "No? My father . . . but his
perspective could be skewed, I suppose. He's a good man,
a fair man, but it was hard on him, accepting help from the
man who'd abandoned her."

"Abandoned her?" Rule heard the sharpness in his voice.
Carefully he smoothed it out. "I don't think we've heard the
same story."

To his surprise, Jasper laughed briefly. "I'm sure we
haven't. I've heard dozens of stories. Mom was . . . I'm not
sure she knew which version was real. But Dad's head is
screwed on straight. He says that Isen wanted nothing more
to do with her once she gave birth to you. He'd gotten what
he wanted."

Isen would never abandon a woman, and certainly not
the mother of his child. Hadn't he proved that, paying for
Celeste's treatment over the years? But . . . Rule forced
himself to stop mentally defending his father. He didn't
know what had gone on between Isen and Celeste Babineaux. If Isen had stopped wanting to be her lover, she
might have experienced that as abandonment. Back then,
when human mores were very different from now, it was no
light thing for an unmarried woman to take a lover. To bear
his child.

Had Celeste been desperately in love with Isen? Had she

felt betrayed when she realized he wanted the child she bore more than he wanted her?

She'd been fragile. He knew that now, and he remembered his father cautioning him more than once about fragile women, women too damaged or needy to take as lovers. *They might seem to hear you*, he'd said, *when you tell them it's not forever, but they need so much. Sometimes all they can hear is their own need. You can be completely honest with them and still hurt them terribly.*

Had Isen hurt Celeste terribly?

Such a woman might resent the baby Isen loved and wanted so much. Such a woman might find the sight of that baby impossible to bear. He looked at his mother's other son, who looked so much like him. "You love Adam very much."

Surprise flickered across Jasper's face. That was one way they were different—Jasper's emotions tended to be writ large and clear for all to see. "He's funny and tender and tough and a huge pain in the ass sometimes. He's more than I can say. He's the light of my life."

Lily had finished talking to Ruben and was making a second call. Her hair was loose, still tousled from their loving. She kept tucking it behind her ears, and it kept slipping free. She was giving instructions this time, her voice crisp as she told someone why they were to check out a particular FedEx garage and those who worked there.

She was funny and tender and tough and, yes, sometimes a pain in the ass. She was the light of his life, and he knew all too well what it was to fear for the one you loved. He spoke to Jasper. "I can't promise we'll get Adam back safely, but you have my word that we'll do everything we can to make that happen."

Jasper studied him for a moment, maybe trying to see what his word meant. He nodded. "Thank you."

Rule took out his own phone. This was his responsibility, after all. He had no good reason for pushing it off on Lily. He was about to select Cynna's mobile number when the phone in his hand vibrated.

It was his brother. His brother Benedict, that is, whom he'd thought was his only brother after Mick died . . . and that was a confusing thought. Rule answered.

AN hour later, it looked like Jasper would run out of time before Lily ran out of questions. Jasper glanced at his watch. "I need to leave soon."

"We've still got forty-five minutes." Lily flipped to a fresh page in her notebook.

Cynna had said she would come if she could. She hadn't said what the qualifier meant—just that she'd let him know tonight. It might be late tonight, but she'd call and let him know.

It was an odd response. Maybe Lily was right. Maybe the Lady did have the habit and the means of warning her Rhejes away from too-dangerous actions.

Rule hadn't been able to pass on Benedict's news yet. It involved Arjenie, and her Gift and heritage was not a secret he could pass on to others.

"We've been trying to find the agent you used to use," Lily began.

Jasper snorted. "You, too?"

"Are other people looking for him?"

"Me. I suspect he's where Friar learned about my professional abilities, mainly because no one else knows."

"The Bureau did turn up a police file on you."

"Agent Adamson. Dogged fellow. He couldn't tie me to anything, but he had good instincts. But he didn't know about my specialty or my nom de guerre."

"Umbra."

Jasper's eyebrows climbed. "That wasn't in your police file."

"No, I got that from another source. Your former agent's name was Hugo, right? Over fifty, overweight, unusual tat on his forehead."

"You have good sources."

"Tell me about Hugo. What's his last name?"

Jasper shrugged. "Variable. He's got at least three identities that I know. Or he used to. He doesn't seem to be using any of them these days. He's a big guy, like you said. Doesn't talk much. He's greedy, fit beneath the flab, hates drugs but likes bourbon, and he's crooked as they come. So why did I use him, you ask? Because his handshake meant something to him. Once you struck a deal and shook on it, that was it. He'd hold to that. He did time once to protect a client's name. More practically, I was worth a pretty penny to him—he got five percent of any deal he brokered, and why would he give that up?"

"Yet you think he gave up your name to Friar."

Jasper smiled wryly. "I did say he's my former agent. A couple of years ago, I caught him in a lie. Now, that wasn't unusual—Hugo likes lying—but this was a stupid lie. It only netted him a couple grand, and for that he broke his word?" Jasper shook his head. "I severed our relationship."

"My source says you retired a few years ago, or at least stopped taking jobs."

"Ah. Yes. The loss of my agent played into my decision."

"You've tried to find him recently?"

"And failed."

"Do you have a photo of him?"

"No, he's camera shy."

"Describe him, then."

"He's, uh. . . . at least three hundred pounds and maybe an inch taller than me. That would make him six-three. He's bald—lost the hair on top years ago and shaves the rest. The tattoo you know about. Brown eyes. His nose is kind of squashed—I think it got broken when he was in prison, but it might have happened earlier. I don't know his age, but it's not far from mine."

"Has his weight changed much since you met him?"

"He's always been heavy. Maybe fifty of those pounds were added over the last sixteen years."

"That's how long you've known him?"

Jasper nodded and looked at his watch again. "Listen, I . . ."

Rule heard Jasper's phone vibrate. Lily probably didn't, but she must have seen the way he jumped. "It's him," Jasper said. "Friar. That's the phone he gave me." He reached for one of the pockets in his vest.

"Wait a minute," Lily said. "Could that have a GPS in it?"

Jasper shook his head. "I checked. Quiet. For God's sake, everyone needs to be real quiet."

"He won't hear your conversation on the house mics."

"I know. *Shh.*" Jasper thumbed the phone, held it to his mouth with his hand cupped over it, and whispered, "Yes."

Rule heard a much-hated voice: "Are we playing a whisper game, Jasper?"

Jasper replied so softly Rule wondered how well Lily could hear him. "They've got some of their people watching me. One's on my roof. You want them listening to us talk?"

Friar was amused. "And do you think this watcher could hear a phone conversation two floors beneath him over that music you play every night in your ongoing effort to baffle my listening devices?"

"I don't know. Do you?"

"It's an excess of caution, but never mind. It's almost time for you and dear Adam to be reunited. You have twenty-five minutes to reach Hammond Middle School. Set your timer now. You are to call your brother in fifteen minutes—do be precise, you will be graded on this—and tell him to meet you there at eleven forty-five. He's to leave his bodyguards at the hotel. Make sure he brings Seabourne. Say whatever you have to. Just make sure he brings Seabourne."

"A middle school? You want to meet at—I don't even know where that is!" Jasper's eyes were wild, but he kept his voice to a whisper.

"Look it up. And don't be late. Every minute you're late, something unpleasant will happen to poor Adam."

"Twenty-five minutes isn't enough! And you have to let me talk to Adam first. I need proof—"

"Twenty-five minutes," Friar repeated. And hung up.

Jasper looked up, his knuckles white on the phone he clutched in one hand. "The recordings. They've got over an hour to go. He won't hear me leave the house. He'll know. He'll know, and—"

"Leave that to me," Rule said, taking out his phone. "Chris is fairly tech savvy. I'm sure he can follow your instructions."

"But how—"

"He'll enter your house secretly through one of the windows and, under your direction, shut off your recordings and the timers on the lights. He'll leave out the back where it's dark so any watchers don't see his face. Then he'll vanish." He set the timer on his phone, then tapped the screen again, calling Chris.

"You can vanish?" Jasper said, befuddled.

"Lupi don't disappear," Lily said. "It just seems like it. They're good at concealment. Tell me what Friar said."

Jasper did that while Rule gave Chris his instructions. Rule listened to see if Jasper altered anything or left it out— he didn't, until he added that Hammond Middle School was close to the hotel, much closer than his house, so he had a few minutes. Not many, but a few. Rule disconnected and signaled to Scott: *Bring Cullen here.* Scott grimaced, no doubt anticipating more complaint. But Cullen wouldn't bitch about this. He never did when the emergency was real.

"He didn't tell me to bring the prototype," Jasper was saying to Lily. "Does that mean he's got it?"

"Maybe," she said. "Or maybe . . . tell me something. If you still had the prototype, would you have brought it to this meeting if Friar told you to?"

"No. Not like this, with no guarantees. Too easy to kill me and Adam both and take the damn thing."

"He probably knows that."

Jasper scrubbed his face. "He does. Of course he does. I've been clear about that. I wish to hell I'd quit panicking. It plays hell with thinking. So the next question is, how do I leave here without being seen? There's no time to leave the way I came in, so I'll have to exit as someone else."

"If you're in the center of my men when I leave," Rule said, "you won't be clearly visible."

"I need to get there ahead of you, and you're supposed to leave your men here."

"Friar knows I won't do that. He wants something to hold over you—you didn't do the impossible, so he won't honor his end of the deal. Which he has no intention of doing anyway, but he wants you to keep thinking he will if you jump through his hoops just right."

"Right. Right. That sounds like him. I still need to leave before you do." He looked at Lily. "Do you have some makeup I could use?"

"Makeup? Uh—sorry, but I don't think any amount of makeup will make you look like a woman. And I don't have anything that would fit you."

"No, I won't cross-dress. But another shirt, yes, the more expensive the better, given where you're staying. Not black. Black points up the resemblance between me and Rule. And mascara, shadow, lipstick, liner—I don't suppose you have any glitter? No? What about cotton balls?"

"LILY was right," Rule said from the doorway to the bathroom. "You don't look like a woman. You do look different, but not like a woman."

"Different but charming, yes?" Jasper met his eyes in the mirror and blew him a mocking kiss. "You don't approve."

"It's disconcerting, like looking in the mirror and seeing someone else there. Was Chris able to shut down your recordings?"

"I think so. He seemed to follow instructions well." Jasper's voice was clear in spite of the scraps of washcloth he'd stuffed in his cheeks in lieu of cotton balls to change their contour. In six minutes he'd transformed himself— removed his shirt, gelled his hair into spikes, and applied liner, mascara, and shadow with a lavish hand. He was now brushing on blush. He met Rule's eyes in the mirror again. "It's my SFGS disguise."

"Will this do?" Lily said, pushing past Rule and holding out a white cashmere scarf he'd given her recently.

"Perfect, if I had a shirt to—ah, you've got something."

She handed him the silk shirt that had been draped over her arm. "Todd donated it to the cause."

Todd liked color. The shirt was lime green with a paisley pattern picked out in royal blue. It was slightly too small, but Jasper dealt with it efficiently, rolling up the sleeves and leaving it unbuttoned. He draped the scarf around his neck, twitching it until it fell to his satisfaction.

"SFGS?"

"Stereotypical Flaming Gay Slut." He put down the blush brush, picked up the lip gloss Lily had contributed, and his voice changed, turning light and merry. "Works a treat, sweetie. Everyone notices me. No one sees me. Ask for a description later and you'll hear about the shirt, the pants, the makeup. Hotel staff do pay some attention to prostitutes their customers bring here in case they cause trouble—either the prostitutes or their customers. But they won't give much more of a description than the man I annoy by my mere presence in the elevator. They just won't sputter as much."

"You've used this disguise before," Lily said.

"La, dear, of course! This isn't the first time I've needed to leave a place openly, yet without being properly seen." He gave her a roguish wink, then dropped back into his own voice. He grabbed a washcloth and the tube of facial cleanser Lily used every night. He'd need that to get out of character once he left the hotel. "Time to go. I'll need to head up a flight or two before getting in the elevator, just be sure I'm not connected with this floor."

Rule nodded and moved out of the doorway. "You'll see Barnaby in the stairwell—tall, dark skin, plain white shirt. He's expecting you."

"You have people everywhere?"

"We keep track of entrances and exits. You don't need to worry about surveillance on this floor. The hotel's hallway cams are disabled, and we've checked thoroughly for others. There's a hotel cam in the stairwell, but Barnaby will have it knocked out by the time you get there. He'll brief you on how to avoid the hallway cam on the floor above this one."

Jasper's eyebrows climbed. "You're thorough. If—ah. Thank you. Much better than a shopping bag."

Cullen had met them in the bedroom and handed Jasper the shoulder bag he used to carry some of his spellcasting supplies. "I put one of Rule's shirts in it."

"Excellent."

Rule glanced at his watch as they reached the sitting room. "You have nine minutes to call me. Will he know when you do?"

"Yes. He can't listen in, but he's installed something on my phone that tracks what numbers I call and when."

"And where?" Lily said, suddenly worried.

"The GPS on my phone has never worked right. That's intentional, but Friar doesn't know it. Do you know what you're going to do? Do you have a plan?"

"We have various plans," Rule said, as they reached the entry, "depending on what we find when we get there. Jasper."

Jasper reached for the door. "Yes?"

Rule didn't know what he needed to say, but his throat was suddenly tight. He settled for "Be careful."

Something flickered in Jasper's dark eyes, but he answered in character. "Always. Ta, love." And he left.

Rule shut the door behind him, turned, and said, "All right. Scott, you've located Hammond Middle School?"

Scott nodded.

"Take Joe and get in place. Cullen, your vest."

"In a minute." Cullen was handing out necklaces. That's what they looked like, anyway. They were charms made by the previous Nokolai Rhej to protect against a Chimei, a foe far more powerful and adept at mind-magic than anything they were likely to encounter tonight. The charms worked . . . when hung on Nokolai necks. The problem was that they were tied to the clan's mantle. Rule carried enough of that to activate them, but there was no way of knowing if they'd protect a Leidolf clansman who wore one.

Tonight they might find out.

"Why those charms?" Lily asked. "Friar's the only one with big magical mojo, and his deal is patterning and listening, not mind-magic. And he won't be there. He's close. He has to be, to direct things, but he won't risk being present tonight."

Rule nodded. "So I thought, too. You haven't called your Bureau compatriots."

"Because Adam won't be there, either. This is a trap, pure and simple, and I don't think having a lot of unGifted agents around will help. Why those charms?"

"We're not just using these," Cullen said, shrugging into the bulletproof vest Scott had located for him. "I already activated the sleep charms."

"But other than the odd side effect of the prototype, we haven't seen any evidence of mind-magic."

"No," Rule said, "but these are in case someone other than Friar is present. Earlier I asked Benedict to see if he could find out if the sidhe delegation's claim of indisposition was genuine. After some discussion, he and Arjenie decided she was best suited to the job. She's passed unnoticed by a sidhe lord, after all. Other sidhe shouldn't be a problem." Which Arjenie had no doubt pointed out to Benedict more than once before he agreed. "The delegation is sharing a single large suite with several bedrooms. She was able to enter it without much difficulty, and she learned that some of them are missing. One of the elves, the halfling, and all of the humans. It's possible they're here."

"How?" Mike said. "I guess they could take a plane the same as anyone else, but they'd be spotted immediately."

Cullen rolled his eyes. "You've heard of illusion? Since elves are the only ones who can do that—"

"Never mind. I get it."

"—they can look as human as they want. At least the elf can. We have no idea what the halfling's capable of. And since illusion is a form of mind-magic—"

"I get it," Mike repeated loudly.

"—you'll wear that charm and hope it works."

Lily was looking at Rule with narrowed eyes. "And why am I just now hearing about this?"

She was angry. But why? "Benedict called while Jasper was here. I didn't feel free to speak about Arjenie's Gift in front of him."

"No—why am I just now hearing that you asked Benedict to investigate the sidhe's apparent indisposition?"

He matched her frown with his own. "It's been a busy day. I forgot to tell you."

"I think that mantle helped you forget. It defaults to secrecy even worse than—damn." Her phone had chimed. "Later," she muttered as she took it out. "We are going to talk about this, but later. Hello?"

"Scott," Rule said curtly, and gave a jerk of his head to tell him to get moving. Scott gestured to Joe, and the two headed out.

Why was Lily so hung up on the idea that the Leidolf mantle was changing him? He'd told her many times it didn't work that way, but she seemed to think she knew more about it than he did. "Cullen?" he said. "You're comfortable with your role?"

"More comfortable with that than with this damn vest. It weighs a ton."

"Bear up beneath your burden," Rule said dryly. "Everyone, make sure your phones are on silent." The vibration was as audible as a ringtone to lupi ears, but humans wouldn't hear it unless they were very close.

He checked his watch. Scott and Joe would leave through a hidden exit the hotel's security chief had shown Scott. It was possible Friar knew about that, but unlikely enough that Rule would take that chance in order to have them in place ahead of time. The rest of them would leave openly as soon as Jasper called . . . which he should be doing in three and a half minutes.

Rule wanted to pace. He had a bad feeling about tonight, and not just because of the mate bond's behavior. Friar had

had too much time to set things up, and they'd had too little time and too little information to plan effective counters. They'd simply have to outthink him on the ground . . . but Rule kept thinking of all the times the Great Bitch had targeted Lily. She wanted Lily badly. Rule was sure that hadn't changed, even if sometimes *she* preferred to take Lily alive and others seemed willing to settle for her death. If only there was some way to leave his *nadia* out of . . .

". . . but the timing sucks," Lily was saying. "Can you get to him and . . . No, you're right, it's not worth the risk. Damn. Well, stay with him and see if he does board. It's always possible the booking is a red herring."

"That's Tony?" Rule said, suddenly paying attention.

"Yeah. He found Hugo."

THIRTY-ONE

~~

"I'M not easy about this," Lily said as she shrugged into her jacket.

Rule cocked one eyebrow at her. "Wanting to stay close to protect me?"

"No—yes, I guess I am. But if that elf's around and pulling mind-magic crap, I'm the only one guaranteed not to be affected."

"The charms will protect Cullen and me and possibly the others."

"Yes, but—"

"You can change your mind. I'm not sure why you think Hugo is so important, not now that we've got Jasper's input. But if you do—"

"I don't know why, either. It's a hunch." Clearly frustrated, she grabbed his face in her hands, pulled it to hers, and gave him a quick kiss. She kept her hands on his face to say fiercely, "There's a *reason* Friar set this up at a middle school."

Yes. Friar didn't care if children were harmed. They did. "It's approaching midnight. There won't be any children at the school."

"Don't assume." With that last instruction, she turned and left.

Mike and Todd were already in the hall. They'd go with her, so Rule was reasonably satisfied with her protection. Jeffrey and Patrick would stay here—Patrick with the two Laban guarding Beth, Jeffrey to watch the suite. Jeffrey wasn't happy about that, but he was the youngest, barely trained and still unblooded. The rest of the men would go with Rule and Cullen.

"Kudos," Cullen said. "That was as masterful a bit of manipulation as any I've seen your father pull off. I especially liked the part where you encouraged her to reconsider."

Rule's mouth crooked up. If anyone actually noticed his father manipulating others, Isen was having an off day. "I don't know what you're talking about."

"Keep telling yourself that if you like, but don't try telling it to Lily once she realizes what you did."

True. "I hope Hugo turns out to be as important as she thinks. She'll forgive me faster."

Somehow Tony had tracked Hugo to a bar in the port area. The window for getting their hands on him was closing fast, though—he'd booked passage on a ship that left port in just over an hour. Lily had briefly considered sending Bureau people to pick Hugo up, but that might be problematic, given that he had some kind of Gift. And due to intuition or sheer stubbornness, she was determined to get hold of him.

It made sense to split up. Rule was pleased by how logically it all worked out . . . and gave him what he wanted. What most of him wanted, anyway. His wolf didn't like it. The wolf wanted Lily close by, and never mind that *close by* meant *heading into extreme danger*. As far as the wolf was concerned, they should always act as a team, and Lily was always safer if they did.

But the man was in charge this time, and the man was relieved. About Lily, anyway. Jasper hadn't called, and the alarm he'd set would go off in—

His phone vibrated. It was Jasper. Rule listened, responded briefly, and disconnected. "Let's go."

THE Joyce K. Hammond Middle School was one of those staunch redbrick buildings erected soon after the great earthquake. Three stories rose in impeccable symmetry above the street, their multipaned windows designed to admit both light and breezes. The school's gymnasium was more recent, though they'd done a good job of blending it visually with the existing structure. On the inside, that gym looked like thousands of others—a glossy wooden floor, bleachers, basketball hoops.

Jasper sat on a folding metal chair in the middle of that shiny floor with his hands tied behind his back. He'd come here knowing it was a trap. He'd expected to see Friar holding a gun at Adam's head to force Jasper to obey, and he'd been ready to do just that. Ready to trust—however desperately—that his newly found brother would somehow save them both.

Adam wasn't here. Five young girls were.

The girls hadn't been given chairs. They sat motionless on the floor a few feet from him. Two movie-extra thugs complete with black ski masks held automatic weapons on them. The thugs were both white. The girls they aimed at were more varied—one black, two white, two Hispanic. An admirably diverse assortment of hostages, Friar had pointed out, save for the uniformity of gender. They were dressed alike, too, or mostly so. Their tops varied, but they all wore jeans and athletic shoes and duct tape on their wrists and mouths. Above the duct tape their eyes were glassy.

The girls were alike in one more way. They glowed.

Not very much, and only when Jasper concentrated hard on using that kind of seeing. Robert Friar was a lot brighter, bright enough that Jasper didn't have to work much to see the magic that wrapped him. Spells are always dimmer than the one who casts them.

This spell supposedly lodged them in the immediate moment. They had less short-term memory at the moment than an ant, Friar had told him cheerfully. They wouldn't remember a thing about tonight. Death would provide the same result, he'd added, but they were all trying to avoid that particular outcome, weren't they? For different reasons, but that was the point. The spell would encourage Jasper and his brother and his brother's lovely fiancée to have confidence in Friar's word. Once Friar had what he wanted, he promised that the girls would be set free, unharmed. The spell would wear off, and they wouldn't remember anything, so turning them loose was easier than killing them. No bodies to dispose of, no police involvement.

Jasper didn't take anything Friar said at face value, but the spell did keep them calm—almost comatose, in fact, but surely that was better than terrified. Maybe the rest of what Friar said about it was true, too. Jasper had to act as if it was. He had to act as if the girls could be saved. Somehow.

Friar stood beside Jasper's chair. He was a middle-size, middle-aged man, slim and healthy, so deeply tanned he looked Hispanic, though he wasn't. He was a good-looking man who had aged well, even to the silver streaks in his dark hair. His clothes—pressed khakis, loafers, a royal blue cotton shirt—were expensive but not ostentatious. He wore a Rolex on one wrist and an earbud in one ear. He would blend in most places, dressed like that.

Had he come to Hammond Middle School in those clothes to choose his victims? The school was in a prosperous neighborhood. He would have looked like any other parent. Older than some, but not enough to stand out.

Jasper searched the gym with his eyes yet again. It was two stories high with a bank of windows set along one wall just under the roof. The bottom of those windows was about eight feet from the top of the bleachers—a distance he could leap. He could get out that way . . . if he broke the window first. If he weren't tied up. If the gun-wielding thugs would both decide to go take a piss at the same time.

Aside from the less-than-useful windows, there were

three exits. Two led to locker rooms—one for boys, one for girls. One led to the rest of the school. All three were impossibly distant from where Jasper and the girls sat in their respective spots in the middle of the shiny wooden floor.

Lupi were fast. Jasper had some idea of how fast. He'd barely gotten away from them last night in spite of everything he could do to stop or slow them. For several terrible seconds he'd thought they were going to catch up with his damn motorcycle. But no one was fast enough. No one could cross that floor faster than the thugs could spray those girls with bullets.

This was not going to end well.

Friar glanced at the Rolex on his wrist. "Your brother is ten minutes late."

"He'll be here."

"He agreed to come at eleven forty-five." When Jasper didn't respond, Friar gave him a sharp glance. "He did agree, didn't he, Jasper?"

"He agreed."

"Then it appears I need to teach him the value of punctuality. Which of these pretty little darlings should I use for that lesson, do you think?" Friar smiled his shark's smile. "You choose. Shall I use the little redhead or one of the pretty señoritas?"

"Rule will be here," Jasper said forcefully.

"Oh, I'm sure, I'm sure. But he isn't here on time. He's violated our agreement already. Choose one for my little lesson."

"I'm not playing your games."

"Of course you will. If you don't, I'll hurt all five of them."

Jasper swallowed. There was no answer, no possible response, he could give.

"Choices, choices," Friar said amiably. "I'll just get started now to encourage you to make up your mind. We'll call your brother in a moment and let him listen in." He knelt beside the nearest girl. The redhead. She wore a thin gold charm bracelet on one wrist. Her hair was short and curly. One of her shoes had come untied. She looked about ten.

The spell might keep her from remembering what had been done to her. It wouldn't keep her from hurting.

"Hurt me instead," Jasper said quickly. "I'll scream, if you like. Sob. Make all kinds of noise and beg Rule to hurry. That's better because he'll know it's happening right now. He might think that—that whatever sounds the girl makes is from a movie or something."

"That's clever," Friar said approvingly. "I like to reward cleverness, so I'll let you have it your way this time. I think you should use your own phone to call him." Friar took Jasper's phone out of his pocket.

"I'm kind of tied up at the moment."

"Do you enjoy those action shows where the hero wise-cracks while the villain does dreadful things to him? I can't say I do. So unrealistic. Not just the fight scenes—one makes exceptions for that sort of thing—but those ridiculous heroes. No one behaves that way in such situations. You can trust me on that," he added. "I've had experience with would-be heroes. They don't make jokes for long."

"The villains aren't realistic, either, are they?" Jasper said. "Always so one-dimensional. Greedy bastards with small minds and large delusions, given to fits of rage when things don't go their way."

Friar smiled. "You make me glad I decided to do this your way. I'll dial for you, shall I?" He pulled a knife out of his other pocket. A switchblade. A single touch and the blade snapped out. He stood and started toward Jasper.

Maybe Friar was right. Jasper's throat was suddenly way too dry for witty repartee.

"I won't do anything too permanent." Friar looked so sane when he said that. He looked like a dentist reassuring a nervous patient. "Not your eyes, then. Did you know that the soles of the feet are one of the most nerve-rich places on the body? I think we'll start with . . ." He tipped his head. "Ah. This is your lucky day, Jasper. Or night. Your brother is here."

Jasper's mouth was suddenly as full of spit as it had been dry a second ago. He swallowed. "Glad to hear it. And you know this how?" Did Friar have others stationed around the school that Jasper hadn't seen?

"A ward. A very simple one. I'm quite the novice with them, so simple is best."

"Is that how you knew—"

"I'd like you to be quiet now. Absolutely silent, in fact."

LILY got out and slammed the car door. They'd gotten bloody damned lost on the way here. GPS could only do so much, and San Francisco streets were crazy.

Never mind. They were here now, and she'd just texted Tony, who'd replied that Hugo was still at the bar. It was two blocks away, but they'd driven past it while hunting for a place to park. There weren't any. The streets were lined solid and the nearest lot was full, so Lily had Todd park illegally next to a hydrant. The bar Hugo has chosen was small but with a large neon sign that screamed TOPLESS! in red. Below that, in smaller letters, it said DINGOS. No apostrophe, so it was hard to say if the owner wanted to welcome wild dogs but didn't know how to pluralize *dingo*, or if he was claiming to be one.

Mike and Todd closed in on either side of her. It was not a great neighborhood, but hardly the worst she'd been in. At this hour it was lively. Men outnumbered woman at least two-to-one, and Lily did not blend in with those women she saw. They probably weren't all hookers, but you couldn't tell by looking.

"You see Tony?" she asked. "Or smell him?"

"My nose isn't that good in this form," Todd said apologetically.

"I can't see much in this crowd," Mike said. "Why isn't he waiting for us inside?"

"He's banned from Dingos. Got in a fight there once, and they remember him."

"He's a memorable guy."

"Is that why he couldn't nab Hugo for you?"

She nodded. "That, and the fact that Hugo's probably got some spellcraft, which makes dealing with him tricky. He definitely has a Gift, but we don't know what kind. Something connected to Air."

"I don't know what that—"

Between one word and the next, Todd's eyes rolled up in his head as a wall of magic rolled over Lily. Todd collapsed like a puppet with its strings cut.

So did Mike.

So did every damn person around her . . . save one.

The woman was short—around Lily's height—but a lot more muscular. Also a lot furrier. Tawny fur covered every exposed inch from the toes of her bare feet to the tips of her catlike ears. A slightly darker ruff stood up between those ears. She stood twelve feet away from Lily with one hand pressed to the windshield of a parked car.

Aside from the fur, her face looked quite human as she smiled. "Miss Yu. My compliments on the strength of your Gift." Her voice was lovely and lilting. Her English was West Coast American. "Or would you more properly be addressed as Agent Yu?"

Lily drew her gun and aimed. "You're under—"

Something stung her cheek. "Under arrest," she finished, automatically reaching up. She touched a feather. There was a feather stuck in her cheek. It burned, and her mind wasn't working right. Neither was her hand, which felt clumsy gripping her weapon. She tightened those fingers as hard as she could, but her weapon was heavy. Way too heavy. It was pulling her down . . . all the way down . . .

THIRTY-TWO

~

THEY came through the double doors in twos—four men in dark jeans and dark shirts with expressions to match. They were fit and dangerous and beautiful.

"Stop," Friar said, and they did.

Jasper's not-quite-human brother wasn't the tallest or the most beautiful. The dark-skinned man on his left was six-five, and Cullen Seabourne had probably been the most beautiful person in the room all his life. But Rule was the center. He held the others in place with one quick gesture while his eyes swept the room—pausing on Friar, then on Jasper, lingering briefly on each of the girls.

Jasper saw his throat move. Maybe he was swallowing the same terrible frustration and horror Jasper felt.

Too far. He was too far away.

The girl nearest the lupi—nearest, yet yards and yards too distant—whimpered. One of the thugs had her by her hair, holding her head up to expose her throat. He held a knife to it.

"I'm disappointed," Friar said in his silkiest voice. "Where's the lovely Lily?"

"She couldn't make it." Rule looked at the man on his

left, then the two on his right. He didn't speak or signal with his hands, but the glance must have meant something. The tallest one's eyes widened. He returned his gaze to Friar, his expression giving away nothing. "What did you have in mind, Robert?"

"Why, an exchange, just as I said."

"Adam King isn't here."

"No, he'll remain my guest awhile longer. Jasper will join him. They've been pining for each other—I'm quite looking forward to reuniting them. But you'll still make the exchange, I'm sure, given the terms. You'll give me Cullen Seabourne. In return, I won't kill any of the pretty girls here."

Rule was silent for several heartbeats. Then he smiled slowly, a smile as hard and pure and cold as Arctic ice. "What pretty girls?" he said. And shouted, *"Go!"*

A great many things happened in the first two seconds.

The lupi charged, flowing forward across that shiny floor absurdly fast. Glass shattered up high. The thug with the knife dropped it and reached for his gun. The one with the gun swung it toward the racing lupi and deafening sound crashed and ricocheted through the gymnasium. Four enormous wolves leaped off the bleachers—the windows, they must have come through the windows!—and if Jasper had thought the men were fast, the wolves were unbelievable. In the next second they would—

Beside him, Friar shouted something over the bestial roar of the guns.

All six girls sprang to their feet brandishing wicked-long knives—and flung their free arms over their eyes.

The sun exploded right there in Hammond Middle School's gymnasium.

Jasper's eyes squeezed closed, but he still saw light—searing, intolerable brightness. His eyes streamed. He gulped and gasped and realized there was no heat. No heat, only that terrible brightness.

He heard screams. Screams, not gunfire, and the meaty thud of fighting. He forced his eyelids to lift, but he couldn't see anything. Blind. He'd been blinded, and oh God—

"Hold still," Rule's voice said right next to his ear. He felt Rule's hand on his, still bound behind his back. A second later his hands parted. They tingled and stung and he brought them to his face with the duct tape still tight on his wrists, but severed. "I can't see."

"Nor can I," his brother said, and shoved him out of the chair.

He landed heavily on his side, and now there was heat—the fiery breath of a furnace.

"Goddamn elves!" someone shouted.

"Cullen!" Rule roared. "Your fire's too damn close!"

"That wasn't mine!"

"Shit," Rule said, and rolled on top of Jasper, covering him with his body.

"They're getting away," Seabourne cried. "Out the window, I think—take that, you slimy, pointy-eared bastards!"

Then it was silent. Almost silent. Jasper heard breathing—his, Rule's, and was that the panting of a wolf nearby? He felt Rule shift. "My vision's coming back," Rule said.

"Mine's not," Cullen said sourly.

"What were you throwing fire at if you couldn't see?"

"Elves. Goddamn elves glow plenty bright to my other sight. They're gone," he added.

"Yes," Rule said, and rolled off Jasper. "They left their two gunmen behind, however. Or their bodies. Can anyone else see yet?"

"I can, a little," someone said.

"Good. See if the gunmen are dead. Jasper, I have to check on Ian. He's down."

Jasper blinked his streaming eyes, still seeing only the afterimage of that intolerable brightness, and sat up. He heard movement from several directions. "This one's dead," a voice said. Then there was the low whine of an animal in pain.

A moment later Rule spoke. "Ian's alive, but they took his front left leg off. I've tied it off. Cullen, I need you."

A voice announced that the "other one" was still alive,

and did Rule want him to stay that way? Rule told him yes. More sounds of movement. Cullen said, "Damn elves. No, I can see well enough now. I'm going to cauterize the stump. I'll put the no-pain spell on first, but I can't leave it on, Ian. You know that. It's going to hurt like a mother in a minute."

Someone came over to Jasper. "Is that your blood or Rule's?"

"I . . ." Jasper touched the front of his shirt, just now realizing it was damp. "It's not mine. Is Rule hurt?"

"Took a bullet in the shoulder, looks like," the voice said cheerfully. "That's not too bad," he added a moment later, maybe in reaction to Jasper's expression. "If the bullet didn't go through he'll have to have it dug out, but there're a lot worse places to get shot."

"I guess so." Rule had been wounded when he covered Jasper with his body, shielding him. Jasper passed a shaky hand over his face.

"You still can't see?"

He shook his head. "I don't know who I'm talking to. Maybe I should know your voice, but I don't."

"Oh, sure. You only heard me that once in the stairwell, and you can't identify us by smell. I'm Barnaby."

"Barnaby, what in the hell just happened? Those girls—"

"They weren't girls. At least not human ones. Some of them might have been female—I mostly saw what you did, so I can't say for sure. But they were elves. So was Friar. The one who looked like him, I mean."

"Elves."

"Yeah. Rule had an idea we might run into one elf. He wasn't expecting a whole fistful, but he had us wear these charms, just in case. They're Nokolai work, though, so they didn't work great for us. They did help some. The elves looked like girls to me, but in a wavery way, like they weren't quite in focus. It's hard to attack someone who looks like a young girl," he added, "even if you know she isn't. Even if the image is kind of wavery, it's hard."

"I guess it would be."

"They didn't smell quite right, though. They smelled human, but like they were all the same human, so that helped. Plus the charms worked like they should for Rule and Cullen, so they told us we were looking at elves, not kids."

Jasper frowned, puzzled. "When did they tell you?"

"Oh, before we came in. Scott got here ahead of time and he reported to Rule, who wanted to see for himself. Scott and Joe were on the roof, see, with a rope to let them look in the window. Rule saw elves, not girls, so he had Chris and Ian stay with Scott. He wanted wolves coming at them through the windows, see, and Chris and Ian can Change really fast, almost as quick as Rule." Regret entered his voice. "We were maybe a little slow on the attack because of how they looked to us, but we'd have had them. If they hadn't had that big flash-bang, we'd have had them."

Jasper digested that. Friar hadn't been here at all. Some unknown elf had been talking to him, wanting him to choose which girl got hurt. Only they weren't girls. The glow he'd seen hadn't been a spell. They'd glowed because they were elves, and the not-Friar elf hadn't intended to harm them. He'd manipulated Jasper into offering to be hurt.

After a moment he said, "You call that a little slow?"

"Any hesitation in a fight can be deadly." That was Rule. "Barnaby, can you walk on that leg?"

"Not really," Barnaby said apologetically. "I can hop on my other one, though."

"Go see Cullen."

Barnaby sighed and, from the sound of it, got up. Jasper realized the whiteout of his vision wasn't quite complete. At the edges it was turning gray and fuzzy. His heart jumped. Maybe he wasn't permanently blind. "Barnaby said the girls weren't girls. They were elves, but they all smelled the same."

"Ah. Now that is interesting."

"He also said you were shot."

"So was he. Very few people can hit a rapidly moving

target, but with automatic weapons little aiming is required."

"Especially if you run straight at them."

"Which is why I had some of my men Change and come through the window. Wolves have a way of commanding the attention of most people. Jasper, I'm trying to decide if I should call this in."

"Call it in?" Jasper blinked rapidly. The fuzziness at the edge of his vision was spreading. Everything in the middle was blank, but he could see dim shapes at the edges.

Amusement warmed Rule's voice. "Lily's jargon is contagious. Call the cops, I mean. Probably her people, though it might be better to call Ruben and . . ." His voice trailed off.

Funny how Jasper could feel the sudden tension in Rule even though he still couldn't see him. "What is it?"

"I can't find her." Rule's voice was utterly flat. "I can feel Lily, but I don't know where she is."

Cautiously Jasper asked, "Should you?"

Rule didn't answer.

Jasper turned his head slightly so he wasn't looking straight at Rule. It worked. He saw Rule take out his phone. Dimly, fuzzily, but he could see his brother. Relief swamped him so hugely that for a second he was afraid he'd cry.

Rule held his phone to his ear. Waited. Waited some more. Then snarled, clutching the phone as if he wanted to throw it. "Scott!" His voice cracked out like a whip. "Take those who aren't mobile to the hotel. The rest of you, with me. Now."

"Your shoulder—"

Rule growled. It was not a human sound. He turned and started for the door. *"Now."*

"**IT'S** like with my Find spell, then," Cullen said. "You know she's somewhere. You just can't tell where."

"So I assumed." The mate bond hadn't broken. Rule kept repeating that mantra. The bond hadn't broken, so Lily was

still alive. Still alive *somewhere* . . . but he had no sense at
all of where. The directional sense he'd grown so used to
was completely screwy.

He reached for his phone.

"No, dammit, hold still. Unless you think bleeding out
will improve matters?"

Rule forced stillness on himself. It was not easy. His
friend was driving a hot poker into his shoulder.

And Lily was missing. And it was his fault.

They were in the backseat of the rented BMW. Joe was
driving. Jasper sat beside him. He'd insisted he was mobile,
his vision was returning, and he would damn well go with
them. If nothing else, he could give directions. He knew the
city, knew where Dingos was. Chris and Alan followed in
another car.

Cullen jabbed. Pain shot off the scale, a white-hot burst
so acute it had to mean he'd finally found the bullet. Rule
hissed through his teeth. Sweat sprang up on his face, his
chest . . . and finally, finally, Cullen stopped.

"Got it."

Rule took a moment to regain his breath. He'd told Cullen to skip the pain-blocking spell, which drained both the
caster and the recipient. Rule wanted nothing to slow his
healing, and he wanted Cullen to hang on to as much juice
as possible. He might need it. "Good. I need to call Ruben."
Rule used his left hand to reach for his phone. His right
would be useless for a while yet. His shoulder throbbed in
blazing pulses.

"You need a sling."

"Got one?" First Rule checked for calls or texts. He
knew Lily hadn't called him back. He knew that, but he
checked anyway. He'd called her twice. He'd also called
Tony and Todd and Mike. None of them had answered.

Cullen pulled his T-shirt off over his head. "I'll impro-
vise."

"If—" The phone in Rule's hand vibrated. He answered
quickly. "Cynna—"

"I can't do it." She sounded weary and frustrated. "I'm sorry, Rule. I can't come there."

If anyone could find Lily, it was Cynna. He needed her to come. Needed her to at least try. She didn't know Lily was missing. If he told her—

If he told her, she might well come anyway. Rule squeezed his eyes closed. He gave up guarding his expression, his body, so he could make sure he had his voice under control. "I see. I was wondering. . . . is it possible that your decision is based on information I don't have? Information, perhaps, you aren't able to share with me?"

A long pulse of silence, then she said, "That's an interesting idea."

If the answer had been no, she would have said so.

He could change her mind. He was sure of it. He could tell her about Lily, and loyalty and friendship would bring her here. Cynna would tell herself that whatever omen or communication the Lady had given her wasn't 100 percent. She'd come, determined to Find Lily.

Rule would have rather had Cullen digging in his shoulder again than say what he said next. "I see. Well, there's an excellent chance you wouldn't be able to find anything, anyway. Cullen's prototype is doing an excellent job of blocking that sort of thing. We're having a rather busy night, so I'm going to go now, but give Ryder a kiss for me."

"Will do. Rule, you know I'd have come if I could."

"I know." He disconnected before he could change his mind and beg her to come.

Cullen was watching him. "Thank you," he said softly, so softly Jasper probably didn't hear. Then, more briskly, "What you told her might well be true. If the prototype can screw up the, uh, thing that lets you know where Lily is, Cynna's Gift might be just as screwed. Here. Let's get this on you." He'd twisted his T-shirt into a sort of rope that he tied behind Rule's head. "I'm thinking it was too easy."

"I haven't noticed anything easy about tonight." Rule used his left hand to ease his right arm through the loop.

"How's the length?" Cullen said.

"Forget the damn sling and explain what you mean."

"After that damn elf tossed the magical flash-bang—"

"That was magic?" Jasper said.

Cullen nodded. "A-grade magic. Not that the bastard is on Rethna's level, for which I thank every god present and past, but he's pretty damn good. What, did you think they used a regular flash-bang?"

"I stopped thinking about the time the lot of you raced into that hail of bullets. I thought everyone was dead—you, the girls, everyone."

Rule had set his phone down to get the makeshift sling on. He picked it up again. "You think the elves should have hung around to try to finish us off while we were blinded?"

"Wouldn't you?' Cullen said. "But it seemed they only wanted to confuse us long enough for them to get away. Which they did, dammit. Though I may have singed two or three of them on their way out the window."

"That's the way a good thief reacts," Jasper said. "If a job goes south, you don't hang around and duke it out."

Rule selected Ruben's number. "But Friar doesn't think like a thief, does he? If that had been Friar instead of an elf wearing his seeming, I suspect some of us would be dead. So would several of them, but Friar has no objection to using up his people to kill some of us."

Cullen nodded. "So maybe the elf and Friar don't have the same goal."

"Or else the elf isn't as cavalier as Friar about getting his people killed."

"Or Friar isn't part of this at all," Cullen said slowly. "The elf could have been using his seeming, his voice, all along."

"No," Jasper said. "That much I'm sure of. The person I met here tonight may not have been Friar, but the guy who's been calling me is."

"How can you be sure?' Cullen asked.

"Because I know Robert Friar. Or knew him—it's been

awhile. But the man who called me when Adam first went missing knew things only Friar would have known."

Ruben wasn't answering. The call went to voice mail. Rule scowled. It was the wee hours of the night in D.C., but Ruben always answered this line. Always. Except tonight he wasn't . . . just like everyone else Rule called. He texted a terse message: *Lily is missing, probably taken. Magic involved. Call me.* And forced his attention back to what Jasper had said. "You already knew Friar? When was this?"

"About three years ago," Jasper said. "He and I met at a party given by a mutual friend, and . . . this was before I met Adam, understand."

Rule stared. "Are you saying that you and Robert Friar were lovers?"

"That's not the best word for it. *Affair* doesn't fit, either, because that implies a real connection."

Cullen looked as dumfounded as Rule felt. "You hooked up with Robert Friar at a party."

"It lasted about three weeks. I was coming off a difficult breakup and ripe for a fling, but I sure as hell chose badly. I'm afraid," Jasper added apologetically, "that's when he learned that you were my brother, Rule. I don't remember how the subject came up, but it did."

Rule was turning this new puzzle piece over and over in his mind, trying to make it fit. He'd done a great deal of research on Robert Friar. Nothing he'd learned suggested this. Friar seemed to have a contempt for women, but he'd been enthusiastically hetero all his life. And yet . . . "You're saying that Friar is gay."

"Bi, I think. There used to be a bit of controversy in the gay community about that, and a few still don't consider bisexuality authentic. They believe you're either gay or straight, and those who call themselves bisexual are fooling themselves. To me that sounds too much like what the right-wingers think about homosexuality—that we're all fooling ourselves about being born this way, and they know better. If someone identifies himself or herself as bi, that's good enough for me."

"Did Friar tell you that?' Cullen demanded. "He said he was bisexual?"

"I don't think he used the word. Does it matter?'

"It might." Rule was getting a glimmering of an idea. "This was three years ago, you said."

"Roughly. Um . . . let's see. He said he'd always preferred women, but had recently decided—or maybe he said he'd been persuaded—to explore things 'on the other side of the fence.' I'm pretty sure that was the phrase he used. Now, I know what you're thinking. Friar is a liar from the soles of his feet to the tips of his hair, but that much may have been true. There's a certain . . . call it a beginner's enthusiasm, only it has less to do with experience than acceptance. When you first truly believe it's okay to want who you want, you get giddy, extravagant, excessive. It's like falling in love, only you're in love with an entire sex. That's hard to fake."

"Rethna," Cullen said.

Rule nodded slowly. Friar had been recruited by *her* just over three years ago. As part of his recruitment, he'd spent time in Rethna's realm. "Elves are often bisexual, you told me."

"They're bisexual, period. Whether that's innate or a cultural norm to which they all give lip service—pun intended—I can't say, but they consider monosexuality downright deviant."

Rule felt a tingle of excitement, as if he'd found tracks left by his prey. Old tracks, but they led somewhere. A bisexual Robert Friar was no more evil than the heterosexual version, but Rule's understanding of his enemy had shifted. "I told Lily once," he began. And stopped. Saying her name opened up the terror and rage, the primal need that was ready to explode inside him.

His wolf wanted out. He wanted out *now*.

For the space of three slow, careful breaths Rule rode the razor's edge of Change. Cullen—who would know, who would smell it on him—didn't speak. Out of lucky instinct or preoccupation, Jasper didn't, either.

That was just as well, for where he was in that moment, words couldn't reach.

Eventually the wolf subsided enough for him to find words useful again. He picked up where he'd left off. "I told Lily once that I think sex is Friar's weak point. It is, of course, an avid interest for many and a twisted interest for some. With Friar, I think sex is both of those, and more. I think sex defines and controls him. Knowing that he's bisexual matters. I don't yet know how, but it matters."

"If I helped, then good." Jasper's face was shadowed, lights from outside the car playing across it. "Your eyes turned black a minute ago."

"I was resisting the urge to Change."

"Not your clothes."

"No."

Another car's headlights played over Jasper's face, which for once wasn't giving anything away. But he smelled ever so faintly of fear. "Does Friar know you intend to rip his throat out?"

"Oh, yes," Rule breathed. "Yes, he knows."

In the brief silence that fell, the buzz of Rule's phone seemed very loud. He grabbed it. That wasn't Lily's ringtone, and he didn't recognize the number, but maybe she'd gotten hold of someone else's phone. Maybe— "Yes."

"Rule, it's Tony. I have failed you. I failed Lily. She's gone, and there is one fucking big mess here."

THIRTY-THREE

~

THREE ambulances and half-a-dozen patrol cars with their uniformed occupants were attending the fucking big mess when Rule reached the scene. There had been no getting here in the car; the streets near Dingos were jammed. Jasper had offered to stay with the car so Rule's men could go with him. Chris and Allan would follow when they could.

The reason for the stalled-out traffic was obvious. Police had cordoned off the street where the attack took place. At least two cars had crashed when their drivers suddenly passed out, according to Tony, but Rule couldn't see them right away. He pushed his way through the inevitable crowd until he could.

There were people everywhere. And bodies. No blood. EMTs, police officers, and what Lily would call civilians were tending the fallen, some of whom were stirring . . . the ones at the edges, he thought. The ones who'd been farthest from whatever magical attack took place.

Lily would not have been knocked out by magic. Something else had happened to her.

He didn't see Todd or Mike. Too many people blocked his view. He did, however, see Tony, who stood a head and more above everyone else—including the two cops with him. "I need Mike and Todd," Rule said. "Joe, I want up on your shoulders. Brace. Cullen, give me a stirrup."

Joe planted his feet, Cullen cupped his hands and bent, and Rule used those cupped hands to launch onto Joe's shoulders. He'd needed the assist because of his shoulder, which complained fiercely about being jostled. He ignored that. Crouched, he looked over the crowd until he spotted Todd. He straightened so that he stood upright; Joe automatically grabbed his feet to steady him. He put his fingers in his mouth and whistled.

Todd turned and started loping toward them. Everyone else heard him, too. He gathered a lot of startled looks before he jumped down.

The cops didn't stop Todd. Sloppy. If they let one bystander leave, others would, or already had.

"Where's Mike?" Rule said as soon as Todd reached him.

"I woke up while Tony was talking to you. Then Mike did. Tony told us you wanted him to find Hugo. Mike went with him. I stayed out here to look for Lily or some sign of what happened to her. Rule, we—"

Rule chopped one hand, cutting him off. "She's alive. I don't know where. Tell me what happened, but keep it short."

Todd's story was short and told him little. He'd passed out instantly, without warning. When he woke up, the humans around him were all unconscious and there was no sign of Lily. Tony, however, had been awake and, as Todd had said, talking to Rule on his phone. Todd hadn't found any sign of Lily—no blood, thank God—but he had found a scent. One he couldn't identify. He didn't have a very good nose in this form, however.

Rule looked at Cullen. "You would recognize the scent of an elf."

"Damn right I would."

"Todd, take Cullen to the place you found the scent. Joe, with me. I need to see to Tony."

"Your shirt," Cullen said.

He looked down. "Damn." He'd bled freely. It didn't show as much on the black cotton as it would have on something else, but it showed. He should have thought of that earlier.

"Take mine," Todd said, already unbuttoning it. "We wear the same size."

The delay made Rule want to howl, but he gritted his teeth and put up with it. He disposed of the old shirt by having Cullen rip it off, then had to thread his bad arm through the sleeve of Todd's shirt. "No," he said tersely when Cullen started to replace the makeshift sling. "It's got blood all over it, too."

At last he strode forward—only to be stopped by the officer who'd ignored Todd leaving the scene. "Stay back, now." The man put a hand on Rule's shoulder.

It *hurt*. Rule snarled.

The officer's eyes rounded. He fell back a step, his hand dropping to the gun holstered at his waist.

"Rule." Cullen touched Rule's other arm, then went on too softly for human ears. "As soothing as it would be to rip off his arm and beat him with it, it would really slow things down."

True. Rule took a slow breath. Somewhere he found a smile. "Sorry, Officer. I'm worried about my fiancée, who I believe was abducted from this scene. I'm an FBI consultant with Unit Twelve. I'm going to reach into my pocket for my ID now."

The cop's eyes flickered to Rule's hand and back to his face. "Reach nice and slow."

"Of course." As if he'd be more of a threat with a gun. Rule didn't explain the officer's mistake, however, but slowly took out his wallet and flipped it open. The ID Ruben had arranged for Rule to carry was not a badge. Rule wasn't a law enforcement officer. But it did proclaim his security clearance and his connection to the Bureau, most notably to Unit Twelve.

It wasn't enough for the cop to let them pass, but he did call his superior—who may have misunderstood Rule's credentials slightly. Rule heard his response in the cop's headphones: "Fucking yes, you let him through. He's fucking Unit Twelve. Unless the fucking terrorists have decided it's nicer to knock people out than blow them up, we're ass deep in some kind of fucking magical shit here."

The cop directed Rule to go to a Sergeant Bellows, pointing him out—a short, bald guy who was one of the officers with Tony. How convenient. Rule thanked him and moved forward, carefully restraining himself to a speed that wouldn't alarm the humans around him. Carefully cradling his bad arm, too, because a show of strength wasn't as important as shepherding his strength so he would heal faster. Halfway there, he nodded at Cullen. Cullen and Todd split off to check out the strange scent.

The sergeant turned as Rule got close. "What the fuck? You're not a fucking FBI agent. You're that damn lupus guy. The prince one."

"I'm Rule Turner, yes. I'm also a consultant with Unit Twelve of the FBI, and I've reason to believe a federal agent was abducted from this scene." Now he looked directly at Tony, whose arms were fastened behind his back. Tony looked like a big, sleepy bear. He smelled furious. "Why is this man in restraints?"

"Violent altercation inside the bar. He won't talk to us. Thinks he's a POW or something—gave his name, then wouldn't say one fucking word. I want to see your ID."

Rule took it out again and handed it over. The sergeant passed it to an older officer. "Call it in. Make sure it's legit."

"Romano will talk to me," Rule said.

"Yeah? Well, he sure as shit better, or—hey!" His gaze swung to the left. "What the fuck are you doing?" He was looking at Cullen, who was down on his hands and knees, sniffing the sidewalk. "Goddamn loonies. Turner, get Romano talking." He stalked off.

Rule sacrificed Cullen to the sergeant's wrath and started for Tony, who stood a few feet away.

"Not too close." A much younger officer stepped in front of him. "This man is dangerous. He's lupus."

"So am I." Rule allowed himself to move quickly, tired of the way everyone kept blocking him. He stopped about a foot from Tony—a distance too close for comfort. Challenging distance.

"Sir, you need to move back."

"Let him be," the older officer said. "Sergeant's orders."

Rule looked up and met Tony's eyes. "There are only three ways I can see that they could have known where to find Lily. One, our enemies have some new magical trick we don't know about. Two, my men were sloppy and allowed themselves to be trailed. But it's the third option that seems most likely. She was set up."

Tony still looked calm. His control was excellent . . . but not perfect. Rule caught the quick spike of *seru* in his scent.

Seru was sometimes the scent of anger, but more, it was the scent of challenge. Of dominance. It was an olfactory *How dare you.* Tony was able to submit when he needed to. He could obey. He looked and sometimes spoke like an oversize child. But he was a man, he was Rho, and he was dominant. He didn't like Rule's stance or his implicit accusation. "I did not set her up."

Rule continued to hold his gaze. "Will you pledge on Laban?"

After a moment Tony nodded. Rule felt it when Tony drew on his mantle. Or rather, the mantles he carried felt it and responded in a way Rule had no words for, but recognized. "I did not set up Lily," Tony said slowly. "I did not know what would happen. I don't know what did happen. I pledge this on Laban."

Rule stepped back. "Thank you. If not you, then Hugo. Damn, I wish I knew where Mike was."

"Following Hugo. He was still in Dingos when I got there, but he made a commotion so he could get away. I distracted the humans so Mike could follow him."

"Did you break much?"

"None of the people. Some furniture."

"You haven't been answering the officers' questions."

"I didn't know what was okay to tell them." He bunched

his shoulders. "I don't like this plastic thing. Can you get them to take it off?"

"I'll see what I can do. Officer Pearson." He looked at the older man. "How can we get the restraints removed?"

"You'll have to talk to the sergeant about that."

Who was, Rule saw, marching Cullen this way. At least that's what the sergeant thought he was doing. Cullen's expression told Rule he wanted to come here anyway and was putting up with the sergeant's hand on his arm to speed things up.

"This bastard says he's one of yours," the sergeant said.

"He is. What—"

Rule got a finger jabbed in his direction. "You tell him to quit fucking with my scene."

"Don't fuck with the man's scene, Cullen. What did you learn?"

"Pretty sure there are two scents. One's definitely elf. I'd have to Change to be sure about the other one. Lily's scent is there, too. It stops where it meets theirs."

"She was carried off, then."

The sergeant scowled. "Elves? You're fucking crazy." Without waiting for a response he swung to speak to the older officer. "What do they say about his fucking ID?"

"He's legit."

The sergeant shook his head morosely. "Elves. Shit."

Rule had to agree. "We need to find Hugo. He may be boarding a ship about now." Though Rule suspected that had been part of the bait—make it look as if Hugo was about to vanish to draw Lily out here. "What was . . . ah. These people should be able to help."

Rule had called Special Agent Bergman on his way here. She'd just badged her way past the officer at the end of the street and was headed for him, trailing two of her agents. Rule started for her.

"What's this about Special Agent Yu being missing?" she demanded as she drew close.

"I believe she was taken from here after her guards—and about four dozen other people—were incapacitated magi-

cally. Special Agent, a ship is about to depart that may have
our prime suspect aboard. I need you to stop it."

"Yeah? Well, I need you to tell me what you were doing
at Hammond Middle School tonight that broke several windows, burned some of the bleachers, and left bloodstains on
the floor."

Rule wanted to howl. "Let me guess. You received an
anonymous tip."

"Right now I'm talking to you, and I want a really good
explanation, or you're going to be wearing restraints like
that oversize Adonis who's following you."

"Lily has been *taken* and you're playing right into—"
Rule's phone sounded. This ringtone he knew. He snatched
it from his pocket, and maybe he moved too fast, because
one of Bergman's agents drew on him. He snarled at the
man and thumbed the phone's screen. "Yes."

"Sorry I couldn't call sooner," Ruben said. "There was a
bad situation in Baltimore. People died. What's happened?"

"Lily's been kidnapped. I need a ship stopped."

"All right. Which one?"

CONGRESS kept talking about rescinding or lessening the
strength of the emergency provisions that gave Unit Twelve
agents an unprecedented level of authority. As usual, they
couldn't agree on how to go about it. Until they did, when
the head of Unit Twelve said jump, authorities both local
and federal had to start hopping.

Ruben had the *Valkyrie* held in port so it could be
searched. Odds were that Hugo wasn't on it, but they
couldn't afford to assume that.

Special Agent Bergman was temporarily seconded to the
Unit. Ruben had no Unit agents available for the case, and
this would, he said, keep the chain of command tidy. She
took Rule's statement about the events at Hammond Middle
School, but she stopped talking about restraints.

Jasper, Chris, and Alan arrived. Then Mike showed up,
four-footed. Once he was back on two legs, he told Rule

that Hugo had had a car parked in the alley—a beat-up 1990 Jetta—and Mike had Changed so he could try to follow. He'd kept up at first, but cars are faster than wolves if they don't bog down in traffic. Hugo had lucked out on the traffic, which hadn't yet backed up, and he didn't mind breaking the speed limit. Mike had lost him, but he did have the license plate number.

The cops put out an APB on the Volkswagen, but Rule didn't expect much from that. The man would have ditched it by now.

As all this happened, more and more people woke up. A few were transported—two of those who'd been in vehicles when they passed out, a woman who'd cut her leg somehow, and a man who'd hit his head on a table. He'd been in the bar next to Dingos. The effect, whatever it was, hadn't been stopped by walls, so some of those inside nearby buildings had been affected. Most, however, were unhurt.

Throughout all this, the pressure inside Rule kept building. None of it was helping. None of it got him one inch closer to finding Lily. He paced. He wanted to run, to Change and run. He could focus for a few minutes on something else, could start to plan, but then his brain hiccupped and he was thinking about Lily. About her in Robert Friar's hands, and what he might be doing to her right this minute.

Tony hadn't set Lily up. Rule had. He'd oh-so-cleverly manipulated her into taking what he thought would be the safer path. Friar had Lily, and it was his fault.

Cullen stepped in front of him. Rule jerked to a stop. "What?"

"You aren't Lily."

Rule's fists clenched tight—and his shoulder sent a burst of pain to remind him he was not healed. "What the hell is that supposed to mean?"

"You're hanging around the crime scene, trying to do the things she'd do. But those aren't your things. That special agent with the great legs and lousy attitude is a pain in the ass, but she's competent. Let her handle things here. You need to go do your thing."

For a long moment Rule said nothing. Finally, quietly, he said to Cullen what he couldn't have said to anyone else, save Lily. "I don't know what to do."

"Do something the others here can't. You're Rho. Do something Rho."

"I am doing something Rho. I'm exercising incredible control and not knocking you on your ass."

Cullen's mouth smiled. His eyes didn't. "Hold on to that control, because I'm about to really piss you off. You can't figure out what to do because you're too busy feeling guilty. Later, when you've got her back, you can wallow in guilt like a dog rolling around on a nice, stinky pile of dead fish. You can't afford guilt now. Lily can't afford it, so stop." Cullen turned and walked away.

For a long moment Rule stood there, not moving. Cullen was right. He was 100 percent right. And Rule still didn't know what to do.

Do something Rho? What did a Rho do? Stay in control, take care of his people, plan ahead, give orders . . . Rule's control wasn't what it should be, but he was holding on. He didn't have a plan, and the only order he could think to give was to send his men searching the city block by block, looking for Lily. Which was about as useless an activity as the proverbial needle hunt, only this haystack covered roughly forty-six square miles, which just proved how poorly his brain was . . .

No. No, they shouldn't look for Lily. And it wasn't a Rho he needed to be, but a Lu Nuncio. The Nokolai Lu Nuncio.

He looked around, spotted the person he wanted. "Tony," he called sharply. "I need you."

Several minutes later, Rule was telling Ruben what he needed while Tony was on his own phone, summoning his clan. The lupi portion of it, that is.

Elves' ability to cast illusions only affected those around them. They left scent trails like anyone else, and they smelled like nothing in this realm. The Laban lupi would go to Hammond Middle School—more elves had been there, and they'd thoughtfully lain on the floor, leaving plenty of scent behind. After Changing and getting a fix on the scent, each lupus would leave for his assigned area accompanied by a police officer, park ranger, or member of the military. People in uniform, that is, so humans wouldn't be alarmed by the enormous wolves who were suddenly all over their city. Enlisting those authorities had required Ruben's authority, but he'd agreed it was worth trying.

It was still one damn huge haystack, but he was sending ninety-four Laban noses out to sniff it, and they would be looking for multiple needles, not just one.

Tony had his head down with Special Agent Bergman over a map of the city, deciding how best to divvy up search areas. Rule wasn't needed for that. They knew the territory. He didn't. He looked around for his men and saw someone who wasn't his.

Or was he?

Jasper sat slumped on the curb. Overlooked by the cops, forgotten by Rule and everyone else. Rule wasn't the only person with a loved one in Robert Friar's hands, was he? And Jasper didn't have clan around him. He didn't have Cullen to bitch-slap him with a few hard truths. He didn't have a task, a function.

Rule went to sit beside his brother.

Jasper didn't look up. For a long moment neither of them spoke. Rule was thinking again, and he was thinking about Hugo. Lily's instinct about Jasper's former agent had proved all too accurate. If Hugo was actively working with Friar. . . . and he must be. He'd helped set up Lily.

Maybe Rule knew who had the prototype now.

But Rule didn't ask the questions that were beginning to burn in him. Instead he asked, "How did you do it? How did you hold yourself together for nine bloody long days with Adam missing?"

Now Jasper looked at him. At first he didn't speak. His face said plenty, though. It spoke of despair. "What in the world gave you the impression I've held myself together?"

"You planned and executed a remarkable theft. You

didn't fall apart when you were tied to a chair and bullets started flying. You complained about not being able to think, but you kept doing it anyway."

"I've screwed up every step of the way." Jasper looked at the hands he'd clasped between his knees. "I've finally gotten around to really thinking, you see. You say you're supposed to know where Lily is, but you don't. Cullen's supposed to be able to find things with his spells, but he can't. It's the same thing blocking you both, isn't it? The prototype."

Rule kept his breathing even. He could fake calm, even if he couldn't feel it. "I think so, yes."

"Then Friar's got them both. Lily and the prototype. Which means I've nothing left to negotiate with. Nothing I can use to buy Adam's life. Which means . . ." He drew a long, shuddering breath. "He may already be dead."

"We don't know that. Friar wants Cullen, too."

"But does he need me to get him? I don't see why."

"Listen to me." Rule gripped his arm. "Adam is alive. Until we see his dead body, he's alive, and we're going to get him back. Just like I'm going to get Lily back, and quickly. To hell with what logic says. Logic hasn't served us all that well, has it?"

Jasper blinked. Took a shuddery breath, and straightened. "Right. He's alive. Of course he's alive. And we're going to get him back."

"We'll get both of them." A quiet electronic gong sounded in Rule's pocket. It was a ringtone he seldom heard, and it startled him enough that it took him a moment to say, "I have to take this call. That's Lily's grandmother."

"Oh, Jesus."

He'd have to tell Beth, too. And soon. Perhaps Madame Yu would take on the task of telling Lily's parents. Rule steeled himself and answered. "Madame Yu—"

"When were you going to tell me that something has happened to my granddaughter?" an imperious voice demanded.

"You know? But—how?"

She made a small, dignified snort. "Sam, of course. How would her teacher not know when she—bah, this language lacks words. She is hidden from him. He says she did not do this, and so we know that someone else did. What did they do?"

"She's been taken. I think . . ." It was hard to say. "I think by Friar's people. I can't find her. I can't sense where she is."

"But she is alive."

"Yes. That much I'm sure of." The rest came out without him having a clue he was going to say it. "It's my fault. I tricked her, manipulated her into doing what I thought would be safer than going with me. I was wrong. It was a setup."

"Bah."

What?

"You take too much on yourself. *I* can trick Lily. Your father maybe can. You? No. You are sneaky sometimes, but not so good as that. You think you fooled Lily? I think she got what she wanted. Now, I will be there as soon as possible. I do not know when. Planes are fast, but airports are not."

"You're—Madame Yu—"

"Sam cannot do this. He has foreseen certain events. He says it is not foreseeing, but I lack another word to describe his knowledge. He will be very busy today. I do not tell you more about this. Do not ask. He is busy, but I will come." She hung up.

Rule sat there looking at the phone in his hand.

"She didn't take it well, I guess," Jasper said. "Hard to give that kind of news."

"No . . . no, you don't understand. But then, you haven't met her." Slowly Rule looked up, relief blooming inside. He felt like he had as a small child, waking from some terrible nightmare to find his father's hand on his shoulder. The sudden bone-deep reassurance wasn't logical, wasn't reasonable. But it was real. "It's okay. It's good. Grandmother is coming."

THIRTY-FOUR

LILY woke to the soothing lilt of Brahms's "Lullaby." Her head throbbed and ached the way it had the time a three-hundred-pound perp threw her against a wall. Or like it had on one miserable morning of her freshman year, when she'd decided that nothing, absolutely nothing, was worth getting a hangover that bad.

But she hadn't been drinking or playing arrest-the-perp, had she? What . . . wait, there had been a perp, and Lily had told her she was under arrest, and then she'd been . . . shit. *Captured.* That was the word.

The quick spurt of panic cleared the fog from her brain. She made herself lie still and take stock with her eyes closed. She lay on something soft that sure felt like a bed. Good news: she wasn't naked and the only injury seemed to be to her head. Her arms rested at her sides, unbound. She didn't hear anything but the Brahms, nor did she smell anything in particular. Rule would have, but . . .

The panic this time was an ocean, not a spurt. Her eyes flew open and the light made her headache worse, but the pain in her head was drowned by the cold fear racing through her. After an endless, drenched moment, she realized the mate bond was screwy, not severed. Rule wasn't dead. He wasn't dead, but she couldn't tell where he was. When she tried to use the mate-sense, it felt like he was everywhere, in every direction, and she had no idea how far away he was. When she tried harder she felt queasy. Motion sick, like when she'd seen that *On Motion* film at the IMAX and the crazy 3-D zooming around had forced her to shut her eyes so she wouldn't puke.

Lily lay very still and waited for her stomach and heartbeat to settle. Her mouth was dry. Her head hurt. If she couldn't find Rule, she had to assume he couldn't find her, either. She'd been captured by a furry woman, and Rule couldn't find her.

Couldn't find her that way. He'd still be trying.

Unless he'd been captured, too, and was in the room next to hers. She didn't know. With the mate-sense wonky, he could be on the other side of the wall and she wouldn't know it. Or he might have been hurt at the middle school. Badly hurt.

Keep taking stock, she told herself firmly.

Okay, point number one: her head hurt, but it wasn't the kind of crippling pain that suggested serious injury. It was an all-over ache, too, not localized like it would be with a concussion. Number two: she was dressed, she was not tied up—in fact, someone had tossed a blanket over her, as if they cared if she got cold while she was out cold. Number three: the whiteness overhead was an ordinary ceiling, not an underground cavern, which was encouraging. The last sidhe she'd tangled with had stashed his captives underground where he . . .

A small ball of light bobbed into her field of view. A mage light. Common in sidhe realms, not so common here. She'd seen a lot of mage lights in that underground cavern.

She frowned at the glowing ball. Rethna hadn't been able to block the mate-sense, and he hadn't just been sidhe—he'd been a sidhe lord. And when Rule had been dragged to the hell realm, she'd still *known* his direction. When an ancient being had locked Lily and Cynna in an underground bunker warded so tightly Cynna's Gift couldn't tell up from down, the mate bond had still worked.

And somehow Cullen's prototype could do what Rethna, hell, and the Chimei couldn't? It didn't make sense.

Enough taking stock. She needed to see where the hell she was. Expecting it to make her head worse, she sat up.

It did.

"You're awake." The voice was male and sounded pleased. "How do you feel?"

"Like crap." The room didn't spin, and her head didn't fall off. It might have felt like that, but then it would have stopped hurting, wouldn't it? Carefully she looked around.

She was in a bedroom. An ordinary enough bedroom with blue drapes at the only window and two chairs at the other end of the room. There was a tall stack of books next to one of the chairs. A bowl of fruit rested atop it. Two doors, both closed. All very ordinary, if impersonal, except that the light didn't come from something as prosaic as a lamp. It came from those mage lights bobbing up near the ceiling.

Being a bedroom, it had beds. Twin beds. She was sitting on one. The man sitting on the other bed was taller than her. Hard to say how much taller with him sitting all yoga-like with his feet tucked up on his thighs, but maybe five-ten, and built solid. One seventy, maybe. He wore jeans and a plain gray tee. Socks but no shoes. His hair was longish and streaky, with a dozen shades of brown and blond all mixed up. Dark eyes were framed by crow's-feet; deeper creases bracketed his mouth.

She knew him. Knew who he was, anyway. "Sean Friar."

His eyebrows lifted. "Right the first time. And you're Lily. Beth's sister. Is your head hurting?"

"Yes." She pushed the blanket back and saw that she was barefoot, too. She wore the clothes she'd had on before, but without shoes. Also without her weapon, shoulder harness, watch, and phone . . . and the ring with the *toltoi* charm. They'd taken the *toltoi*, but not her engagement ring.

The loss of the *toltoi* infuriated her. Anger made her head pound. "You have some ibuprofen?"

"No, but she left something for you." He unwound his legs and stood. "I'll get it."

"She?"

"Our captor. Alycithin. I'm probably not saying it correctly, but that's close." He went to one of the doors and opened it. She saw a sink in an ordinary vanity. He vanished briefly from her line of sight, then emerged with a clear plastic cup in one hand. The cup held about two inches of a dark liquid. "It's supposed to be a painkiller that works for humans."

"Do you honestly expect me to drink that?"

He shrugged. "They haven't poisoned me yet. Haven't hurt me at all, save for the little detail of taking me prisoner. Harming us would be against the rules, a violation of honor. She's big on honor."

"Is Alycithin about my height and covered in fur?"

His eyebrows shot up. "You know who she is?"

"We met briefly. Then someone shot me with a dart." Lily remembered the feather sticking out of her cheek and reached up and found a small scab.

"She used a sleep spell on me. That wouldn't work on you, I guess."

"You know about my Gift."

"Beth talks about you. Alycithin told me you'd be waking up with a sore head because of whatever they used to knock you out. Want to give this a try?" He held out the cup. "She gave her word it would help with the pain and wouldn't harm you."

Lily's head hurt enough that she was tempted. Tempted, but not stupid. "No, thanks."

He looked at her a moment, then turned and set the cup on the floor near the wall. "You may be right."

No tables. That's what was missing. No bedside table, no table by the two chairs—which were heavy upholstered things, not the sort you could smash to make a club from one of the legs. No chest of drawers. Also no television or radio or anything electronic. "Where is the music coming from?"

"The walls. They seem to be stuck on a classical station."

Lily looked at the wall next to her bed. It was painted white, like the ceiling. It looked like any other wall. She leaned closer and laid her palm flat on it.

Magic. Lots of it, and it vibrated. She'd never touched magic that vibrated before. She pulled her hand back. "I saw Alycithin, but I didn't see your brother."

"He's not here. He's the reason I'm here, but I'm a mistake. If you don't want to drink her whatever-it-is, would you like some water? It's from the tap, and it hasn't poisoned me yet."

"Not yet." Though she was thirsty. She also needed to use the bathroom, and with an urgency that suggested a fair amount of time had passed. "Do you know how long I was out?"

"Not really. I'm pretty sure it's morning, and they brought you here sometime last night, so you were out several hours, but I can't say how many."

Still, it helped to know it was morning. It oriented her some. Lily swung her legs off the bed and stood. And shut her eyes for a moment at what the motion did to her head.

"Are you okay?" Sean Friar's voice was closer.

She opened her eyes and stepped back. "It's just a headache."

He'd stretched out one hand as if about to steady her. He let it fall to his side. "You don't trust me. No reason you should, I suppose."

"I'm a cop. I don't trust anyone right away." The door that didn't lead to the bathroom was the obvious first thing to check out. She headed there. Her head didn't like the motion, but it was settling into a steady ache. Annoying, but not incapacitating.

"Especially people with the last name *Friar*."

He didn't sound upset. More like resigned with a whiff of wry. "That's a factor," she agreed, and touched the door. More magic, but this wasn't vibrating. It felt slick, slightly oily. She tried the knob and was unsurprised to find that it was locked. Then she pressed her ear to the door. Nothing.

"They're probably out there," Sean said. "They did something to soundproof this room. She says that's for my privacy. Our privacy now, I guess. But clearly it's also so we can't listen in on them or get the attention of anyone outside here. Wherever 'here' is."

She straightened. "They, not she?"

"I've seen three of them. Alycithin and two others—uh, Dinaron or something like that. I don't remember the other one's name. The one whose name starts with a *D* is male. I'm not sure about the other one."

"Elves, halfling, or human?" She headed for the window between the twin beds. "The two who aren't Alycithin, I mean."

"Elves, I think. At least they look like it. Alycithin is in charge."

"And she's a halfling." Lily pulled back the drapes.

A shiny silver rectangle looked back at her. Not silvery, like a mirror. Silver. And shiny in a literal way. Light leaked through the silvery surface, but no images. She pressed her fingers to it. What should have been a window felt like glass, cool and slick, but it was heavily coated with magic. A slippery sort of magic similar to that on the door. It made her think of cheap lotion, the kind you can rub and rub and it doesn't soak in.

"Weird, isn't it? It lets in light in the daytime, goes dark at night," Sean said. "Which is how I know it's early morning. The light's not bright yet. And it doesn't break. I tried."

"With what?"

"I'm pretty good with a flying kick. I connected solidly three times. It didn't break."

She glanced at his bare feet.

"I still had my boots then," he said dryly. "After I kicked their window they decided I could get by without footwear. Maybe that means I had a chance of breaking it, or maybe they were annoyed that I tried."

She ran her fingers along the place where the glass—if

that's what it was—met the frame. The magic coating the frame vibrated like that on the walls . . . which were now broadcasting something by Mozart. "If they aren't listening to us in here, how did they know you were kicking their window of weirdness?'

"Window of weirdness. Huh. I like that. It's the walls. When I kicked the window, the vibration created something like static in the walls' sound system. They act like a magical intercom."

She turned to face him. "A what?"

"If I want to talk to them, I press my palm to a wall. Any wall. The music fades and sooner or later someone answers. That's how they invite me to lunch or whatever—through their magic intercom."

Cullen would kill to study whatever spells were laid on those walls. Unfortunately for both of them, she was the one that had been grabbed, not him. But she and Sean weren't the only ones who'd been taken prisoner. "Are those three the only people you've seen since you were snatched? Alycithin and the two elves?"

"That's all."

"Someone else was kidnapped. At least one other person." Adam King and maybe Rule. Maybe more.

"Maybe the others did that."

"Others?" she said sharply.

"Alycithin is in some kind of competition with another of the sidhe, or maybe a group of them. I don't know what they're all after, but apparently Robert has agreed to do something for the other group, and Alycithin wants him to do it for her instead." He shook his head. "It was a shock to find out he was alive."

"This other group takes hostages, too?"

He spread his hands. "I'm guessing about that, but hostage-taking is how her people do business. It's SOP, like a contract would be here. Alycithin wanted to use me as a bargaining chip with Robert. She didn't expect him to laugh at the idea. Robert and I," he added wryly, "are not close. I got the impression she thinks you'll make a better bargaining chip."

If he was telling the truth and Friar wasn't here . . . if the halfling woman intended to sell Lily to Friar . . . then she had time. She didn't know how much, but some. She really wanted to believe Robert Friar's brother was as sincere as he seemed, and that was about as bizarre as the shiny silver window. "You've learned a lot in the short time you've been here."

"We dine together and chat. It's all very civilized. I know," he said ruefully, maybe reacting to her expression. "It's strange. They're strange. You're taking all this very calmly."

"You seem pretty calm yourself."

"I wasn't when I first woke up. Freaked out all over the place. I've had time to accept what I can't change. It helps that she promised that her people don't dispose of mistakes."

"You believe her?"

"Oddly enough, I do."

Not so odd. A smart kidnapper wanted his or her hostage calm, convinced he would live if he obeyed. It sounded like Alycithin was a smart kidnapper. Persuasive, too. "You said you dine with them. In here?"

"No, if I accept their invitation I'm escorted into the other room. If I don't behave, they freeze me."

"Freeze you?"

"I can't move." His jaw clenched tight enough to make a muscle jump. "I hate it. My body stops being mine. I . . . but they can't do that to you."

"No." It sounded like a spell Rethna had used. The sidhe lord had pointed a finger, and *zap*! His target couldn't move. His flunkies hadn't seemed able to that. Other really nasty things, but not the freezing. "You said 'they.' Do they all have the ability to freeze you?"

"I . . . assumed so, but it was the orange-haired elf who froze me. Does it matter?"

"It might. Elves all have some body magic and some illusion magic, but they specialize in one or the other. One
who's aces at body magic won't be that strong at illusion,
and vice versa. That freeze spell—I think it's something
only a body magic expert can do. What does the other room
look like?"

"It's maybe twenty-five feet by fifteen. Chairs and a
couch at one end, dining table at the other. Two doors on the
wall opposite this bedroom, but I don't know what's beyond them. The kitchen's on this side. I think this is an
apartment or a condo—something about the layout makes
it seem like one."

"You haven't seen outside?"

"The windows are weird in there, too."

Lily looked around the room again. Nothing jumped out
at her as a potential weapon. Nothing suggested a means of
escape. She might as well deal with what her bladder insisted was a pressing situation. "I need to use the restroom."

"Sure. The shower works, there's shampoo, and you've
got your own toothbrush. I told them humans did not share
some things, so they brought another one. There's a closet
off the bathroom. No hangers we might use to poke their
eyes out, but there's a closet, and they brought some
changes of clothes for you."

"Considerate kidnappers."

"All part of their code. From what Alycithin said, I think
it's like the Geneva Conventions. We have to be fed,
clothed, and housed decently. I gather there are a lot of
rules about that."

"The Geneva Conventions outlaw the beating or torture
of prisoners."

"They're not allowed to do that. They can freeze me or
take my boots, but they can't hit me unless I attack one of
them."

Had Jasper lied about Adam being hurt? About him being taken in the first place? Or was the "other group" not
following their version of the Geneva Conventions?

Friar, of course, wouldn't follow any codes that didn't

suit him. Lily nodded thoughtfully and headed for the bathroom.

The bathroom door locked. It was the push-button kind, easy enough to jimmy or bust, but it locked. That was a surprise. Mozart was playing in there, too. Otherwise it was as ordinary as the bedroom, if lacking the sort of detritus that accumulates in a lived-in space. On the narrow strip of counter next to the sink she found a small stack of washcloths, Ivory soap, and Colgate toothpaste. Two toothbrushes, one slightly damp from recent use, the other still in its plastic wrapper. Ordinary towels were draped on a towel bar. Suave shampoo in the tub enclosure. The closet was a small walk-in and empty except for two small, neat stacks of clothes—Sean's things on the left and hers on the right. They'd provided her two pairs of jeans, two pairs of panties, two T-shirts, and two bras, all in her size, which was creepy. No shoes or socks.

She emptied her bladder, splashed water on her face— her headache was easing off some—and turned on the shower. She did not strip and get in, though. She stood next to it and said very quietly, "Drummond."

THIRTY-FIVE

~

AT the very tag end of December, the sun didn't make it over the horizon until after seven. Rule stood at the window looking out at a city still wrapped in predawn twilight. That was plenty of light for his eyes, but there was nothing worth seeing.

He wanted coffee. He'd started to make some, but thoughts of Lily crashed down, and he'd left the little kitchenette to stare out the window. He hadn't thrown anything, though he'd wanted to do that, too. It would worry his men and wake up Jasper, who was asleep on the couch that had been intended for Cullen. He wouldn't be using it. He was in a helicopter.

"Why," Grandmother had announced, "is your sorcerer down here? He should be overhead, looking for the magic these bad elves are using."

Rule had explained that Cullen had been charging the charms they might need.

Madame Yu had raised her eyebrows. "Are they charged now?"

"Yes," Cullen snapped, "but they aren't enough. We're going up against magical heavy hitters. We need—"

"More than you will have. You have power and some skill in using it. You do not have the decades or centuries of training and knowledge these elves have. You will not make up that lack in the next few hours. Instead you will search for evidence of their magic."

"Do you have any idea how much magic there is in a city this size?" Cullen had demanded. "There's two major nodes here and two minor ones, and all the ley lines pouring out from them. Plus there's the randomized magic pouring in from the ocean, the power puddles that collect everywhere—"

"You are telling me all magic looks the same?"

"Of course not, but . . ." Cullen had stopped. Rubbed his head. "Maybe, if I wasn't too high off the ground and if they were doing some powerful spellcasting . . . but they won't be casting major spells every minute."

She had sniffed. "Elves use magic as we use electricity. Constantly."

Madame Yu's journey here hadn't been quite as simple as she'd seemed to expect. Commercial flights didn't depart that late. In the end, Rule had called Ruben, telling him they needed Madame Yu here because she was in touch with Sam. Which was true, if incomplete. Even Ruben didn't know everything about Lily's grandmother . . . but then, who did? Ruben had arranged for military transport, which turned out to be an Air Force C21-A—a Learjet, in other words, the kind reserved for VIPs. Rule didn't know how Ruben was going to justify that in his budget, but he was grateful. Li Lei Yu had arrived at San Francisco International Airport about two this morning, as erect and indomitable as ever.

By three o'clock, Rule had brought her up-to-date. He told her everything, ending with what they'd learned about Hugo—which now included the name he'd been born under. Given a little more information, Arjenie had come through. Anson "Hugo" Bierman was a naturalized citizen. Born in Germany fifty-five years ago, he'd immigrated to the United States with his parents. He'd never officially changed his name to Hugo, but had begun calling himself that about the time he was kicked out of high school for fighting, truancy, and theft. He'd used a multiplicity of surnames since then, but always with Hugo for his first name.

The next bit of information had come from Special Agent Bergman. Hugo had managed to pile up some very large debts to some very bad people. Gambling debts.

Jasper had confirmed Rule's hunch. Hugo knew about Jasper's habit of using FedEx trucks to stash a stolen item until it was convenient to reclaim it. He could have followed Jasper on the night of the theft, seen where he put the prototype, and gone back for it.

The question was, had Hugo already passed the prototype on to Friar? Or was he holding on to it, trying to jack up the price? Jasper suspected the latter. "If he's given up on keeping his word, there's nothing left but greed."

Cullen had received his assignment first. Rule chartered a helicopter for him to use to look for sidhe-type magic—which meant, Cullen said, formed magic of unusual power, clarity, and intricacy. Unless he got really lucky, that would be a long, slow business. Maybe impossible, he'd grumbled. But worth trying.

Then Madame Yu sorted out the rest of them.

Tony was to allow his Lu Nuncio to coordinate the scent hunt and look for the person who'd tipped Tony to Hugo's location, since the police seemed sadly incapable of finding him. Rule was to contact Ruben, who was to do whatever was necessary to expose the absence of some of the sidhe from Washington. Beth was to stay here, in this suite—it was unforgivably foolish for her to be anywhere else. Jasper was to get some sleep.

Jasper had protested politely—people were polite to Grandmother; something about her forced it on you—that he could not possibly fall asleep yet. She'd looked at him sternly, though Rule had glimpsed the pity the sternness was intended to hide. "You are Rule's human brother."

"Uh . . . yes."

"You are not lupi. You cannot be up all night and be any

good tomorrow. Sit," she told him, pointing at the couch. He had, though it looked like he'd barely refrained from rolling his eyes like a resentful teenager. She'd sat beside him, nodded once, and touched his face.

He'd dozed right off.

Rule's eyebrows had climbed. "I didn't know you could do that."

"Shh. I put him to sleep. I do not keep him asleep." She'd studied Rule a moment. "You, I think, will not sleep. Instead you will go run. As wolf."

He'd told her that was unforgivably foolish. He needed to be here, coordinating the search. Besides, he was a target, and perhaps she hadn't noticed, but his shoulder had a hole in it. "Then run on three legs, and do not be seen," she'd snapped. "You do not help Lily by staying on this edge. It is cutting you. *I* will coordinate. You go run."

He had. After he talked to Ruben one last time, he'd slipped out the secret exit with Scott and Mike. The three of them had run in a nearby park. When he got back, Madame Yu and Beth were asleep in his bed, Jasper was sleeping on the couch—someone had found a blanket to toss over him—and Rule's head was clearer. His shoulder ached like crazy but his mind was working better.

The wolf didn't like waiting any more than the man did, but he was better at it.

Rule abandoned the gray window and went to the tiny kitchenette—more of a closet with appliances, really. He'd Changed twice. With or without coffee, he needed to eat. There was little to choose from; those who stayed at this hotel expected others to cook for them. He grabbed three energy bars, downed one in three bites, and was contemplating the coffeepot when he heard footsteps.

Beth stood in the doorway blinking sleepily and hugging herself. She wore a pair of flannel pj pants with a pink T-shirt that read HYPERBOLE IS THE BEST THING EVER! The sight of her clutched at his heart. She looked so like Lily, yet so different. Beth's face was rounder. She had her mother's mouth, while Lily's was a feminine version of their father's. But her nose was the same as Lily's, and her ears, and her neck. She and Lily were exactly the same height.

Her eyes were dark and shadowed and lost. "I guess there's no word," she said.

"Nothing yet." She had two missing—her sister and the man who, for better or worse, she was in love with. "We've got a lot of people working on getting them back, Beth. Both of them."

"I just wish there was something I could do!" She rubbed her arms as if they were cold. "I don't have anything to contribute. We don't need a kick-ass graphic about evil elves. We need to find the real evil elves and kick their ass, and I'm no good for that."

Rule was supposed to be good for that. So far he was batting zero. "You could have a cup of coffee with me."

"Yeah, that's a big help."

"It won't help Lily. It's . . . she loves coffee, you know that. I couldn't make any this morning because she isn't here. I started to, but I . . . have a cup of coffee with me."

Beth's eyes filled. She came to him and hugged him and put her head on his chest and sniffed. He hugged her back, and it helped.

A MISTY shape materialized in the bathroom the moment Lily said his name, but it took several seconds to form into a man. Then Drummond was scowling his usual scowl at her. "I thought you were never going to call me."

"You—" She stopped and tried again, this time silently. *You couldn't show up until I did?*

"Not all the way. There's something weird about the walls. It's like Clanhome in here. Not as bad, but a real pain."

Wards, probably. If they can make the walls act like a combination intercom and iPod, they can probably set really strong wards. Can you find out where "here" is?

"What do you think I've been doing while you napped? We're on the third floor of a seven-story building. It's stucco, an older building, well maintained, in a residential area. The address isn't anywhere I can go to see it, and we're in the middle of the block. I can't go far enough away to read the street sign. We're not close to the water. I don't see any landmarks I recognized, but I don't know San Francisco."

It wasn't enough, but it was something. *Good. That's good. What about when they brought me here? Did you see which way—*

"No. When you go in cars, I can't . . ." He looked embarrassed, as if she were making him admit to something vaguely shameful. "I tatter. I can't hold together at all. So I don't know how the hell you got here. Not the route. They loaded you in the back of a gray 2007 Honda CR-V, California license 5FLT230."

You got the license plate! Lily itched to write it down. Nothing to write on or with, so she wrote it with one finger in her palm to help her remember. "Did you see who was driving?"

"Sure. Pointy-ears drove, furface rode shotgun."

Lily jerked, startled. One of the elves could drive a car? But the sidhe delegation had only been here for two weeks. How . . . but Alycithin had spoken English to Lily, hadn't she? American English, and that hadn't come from her translation charm because those didn't work on Lily. Lily reached out absently and touched one of the walls that were currently playing Mozart's Piano Sonata in C Major. *They've been here a lot longer than two weeks, haven't they? Long enough to learn the language, learn to drive, and set this place up.*

"Looks like it. Listen, if you want to . . ." He gestured at the shower, which was filling the little room with steam. "Go ahead. I'll wait in the other room, keep an eye on that guy. Friar's brother, right? I caught some of what the two of you said. Snatches. I, uh . . ." His scowl tightened a couple of notches. "I was just yanking your chain before about watching. I don't do that shit."

She hadn't intended to shower, but maybe she would. It

might clear the last of the drug-induced headache. Might help her think. *Okay. That would be good. No, wait. You said 'they' loaded me into the Honda. Did you see her clearly? The halfling, I mean.*

"The furry woman? Yeah, of course I saw her. You want to be careful if you go up against her. She's strong. Lifted you up like you didn't weigh anything."

Now that was interesting. Lily was pretty sure no one but her and Drummond had noticed Alycithin at all. *Okay. Thanks. I'm going to take a shower while I've got the chance.*

Drummond faded back to mist, which made him blend in with the steam from the shower. Well, either he'd left like he said he would or he hadn't. Being seen naked was not the biggest problem on her plate. Lily stripped quickly and stepped into the tub.

It felt ungodly good. For several moments she just stood beneath the stream of hot water, blessing plumbers everywhere. Who needed magic when you had indoor plumbing and plenty of hot water? Then she let her hands go through the automatic stuff with the shampoo while her mind got busy.

When Mike and Todd and everyone else went tumbling down, Lily had felt a wall of magic smack into her. The thing was, she'd felt that kind of magic once before. Not as strong, but the same kind. That time it had been Arjenie Fox standing with her hand on a car's windshield while everyone around her passed out.

Glass, Arjenie said, did weird things to her Gift. One of those things was the way it knocked out everyone within twenty feet if she pulled strongly on her Gift while touching glass. That "everyone" included Arjenie herself, but the halfling had probably had training not available to a part-sidhe woman raised here on Earth. Training that let her shield herself from the effect.

It didn't make sense that Cullen's prototype could block the mate-sense . . . because it wasn't the prototype doing it. It was her. Alycithin. The halfling. Who had a Gift like Arjenie's, only a lot stronger. A Gift that allowed her to go

unnoticed by everyone but ghosts and touch sensitives—
and which could baffle wards, too. And, apparently, confuse
the mate bond.

The mate bond was magic, after all. Not wholly magic—
there seemed to be a spiritual component—but Cullen
could see it, and he didn't see the spiritual stuff, so part of
it was built from magic. That would be the part the halfling's Gift messed with.

Gifts were always stronger than formed magic, Lily had
been told. Still, the mate bond came from the Lady. Who
was an Old One.

Alycithin must have one hell of a strong Gift.

Lily finished rinsing her hair, turned the shower off, and
grabbed a towel. She frowned as she dried herself off,
frowned harder when she realized she'd forgotten to get
some of the clothes the sidhe had provided. She padded
over to the closet.

If the halfling was baffling the mate bond with her Gift,
what was blocking Cullen's Find spells?

That had to be the prototype itself, she decided as she
fastened the bra that was such a creepy perfect fit. Alycithin
didn't have the prototype, or why bother grabbing Lily?
Either Friar had it, or there was yet another group or individual in this mix who did.

Say Friar did have it. Lily simply didn't believe the prototype could confuse the mate bond the way Alycithin's
Gift did. So if Sean was right and the halfling did intend to
trade Lily to Friar, then once Lily was in Friar's hands, her
mate-sense should start working again. So should Rule's.

Lily stood stock-still in her underwear as a really stupid
idea seized hold of her. Stupid and crazy. Sure, she wanted
Robert Friar, wanted him badly. But aside from the risk
she'd be taking, she had a civilian here. Sean Friar wasn't
likely to escape on his own, and she didn't buy whatever
soothing platitudes the halfling had fed him about her code.
Sean was too big a liability.

But there was another civilian. Another hostage, one
held by "the other group." The easiest way to find Adam

King was to find Robert Friar. And Lily had someone who wanted to take her to him.

She pulled on her clothes slowly, thinking hard. Then stood and thought some more. At last she moved in front of the sink, where she stared at the fogged-up mirror without seeing it. She reached for that place in her mind . . .

It was like a dial. The default setting on her personal dial was set to the frequency where she talked to Drummond, and that was downright annoying. Why would her personal dial be set to him? But maybe it had nothing to do with him, being more about whatever weird thing tied them together. That was why she could mindspeak him so easily now that she'd gotten the knack of it, she'd decided.

But she'd mindspoken Rule on purpose a couple of times now. She had a sense for where he was on her dial. Changing that dial was tricky, and she didn't always get it right. It was probably pointless to try. She had no idea how far away he was, but distance mattered. She'd never tried to mindspeak anyone who wasn't with her. And she was behind warded walls, her mate-sense baffled by the halfling's Gift—which might not affect mindspeech, but still. There was no reason to think this would work.

And no reason not to try. Lily took a slow breath and hunted for Rule on her dial. *Rule, I'm okay. I'm being held by the halfling, who has a Gift like Arjenie's, but stronger. She brought me here in a Honda CR-V, license plate 5FLT230. I'm on the third floor of a seven-story building in a residential area that's not near the water. Sean Friar is here, apparently a hostage. I haven't seen Adam King or Robert Friar. I'm told they're not here. I think there's another group of elves. I think the halfling intends to trade me to Friar, who may be with the other elves, who may have Adam King. I think I should let her. The mate bond will work again when I'm not around the halfling, and you can find me. And Robert Friar and Adam King.*

Lily took a deep breath. That was tiring. She had no idea if she'd done it right, but if it tired her out, she'd done something. She told herself she'd have no way of knowing if she was reaching Rule. She hadn't learned how to receive, just how to send, and that only a little bit. But her gut was clenched and unhappy. Her gut was sure she hadn't reached him at all.

Better try it again. She ran through the whole spiel a second time. Then she stared at the slowly clearing mirror, frustrated, wondering if her gut had a clue about what was going on that her mind wasn't able to tap in to, because it insisted she was getting nowhere.

On impulse, she reached up and drew on the foggy mirror with her finger. Drew a simple, stylized bee—a crude representation of the *toltoi* charm. Which wasn't exactly magic, but the halfling had taken it, hadn't she? Maybe she had a reason. Lily stared at that silly outline the way Sam always had her stare at a candle flame. *Find me here,* he'd say. She stared at it and tried to find Rule.

"**MORE** eggs?" Rule said.

"No, thanks." Beth pushed the eggs still on her plate around with her fork.

Beth hadn't eaten much, but Rule let it go. Lily was always telling him he tried to stuff her as if she were lupi.

He'd ordered enough for everyone. Madame Yu was still asleep, but several of his men had woken as soon as the smell of sausage and bacon reached them. As he'd known they would. He was doing Rho things. Taking care of his people. He wasn't sure how much longer he could . . .

LT230 . . . stucco building, not near the water . . . hostage . . . trade me to Robert Friar.

Rule's fork fell from his hand. His head swung to the left. To the east. "That way," he breathed. "She's that way."

LILY swayed, suddenly so dizzy she could scarcely stand. She gripped the sink with one hand and waited for it to pass. Her head swung to the west.

That way. Rule was that way.

Not that she felt him now, but she had. She had. For a few seconds while she was focused on the *toltoi*, the mate-sense had broken through. Rule was *that* way, and about ten miles away. Maybe a little less.

When the music faded, she scarcely noticed. Then a lovely, musical voice replaced the Mozart. "Lily Yu. We never did settle the matter of your correct title, did we? I would like it if you would join me for breakfast. Sean, I regret the discourtesy of not including you this time, but hope you will join me for lunch later. Lily Yu, to respond you must press your palm to the wall."

Lily straightened, swallowed, and shoved her wet hair behind her ears. Her hands were shaky. She didn't know if that was because she'd spent a lot of power, or if she was just scared spitless. Or so relieved she couldn't think straight.

All of the above, maybe. She took a deep breath and did as she'd been told. The magic in the wall still vibrated, even though it wasn't making music at the moment. "I appreciate and accept your invitation."

THIRTY-SIX

~

"**But** what the hell's LT230?" Scott said.

"I don't know." Rule scrubbed his face with both hands. "Maybe that isn't all of it. She was fading in and out—more out than in, I think."

Everyone was gathered around the table, looking at a map of the city. Rule had called Cullen to let him know: Lily was somewhere east of the hotel, and she wasn't near water. She was possibly in a stucco building. He needed to call Tony, tell him to concentrate on the east side of the city, but they'd hoped to narrow it even further with that mysterious number.

"If that's only part of it," Jasper said slowly, "maybe it's from a license plate. California plates are usually a number, three letters, then three numbers."

"Maybe." Rule stared at the letters and numbers he'd scribbled down as if the scrap of paper could yield some certainty. "I'll call it in as a possibility." He reached for his phone. Ruben first, to get the ball rolling on what might be a partial license plate. Or might not. Then he'd call Tony.

THIRTY-SEVEN

⌐⌐

THE main room was much as Sean had described it. The sidhe might be using mage lights for their hostages, but out here the lighting was electric. One elf sat on the couch, doing something with his fingers. It reminded Lily of the way Cullen drew spell diagrams in the air, only she didn't see the lines of light Cullen doodled with. He—she thought it was a *he*—wore the kind of clothes Rethna's elves had, a soft blue tunic with darker blue pants and green boots. His hair was white and long and pulled back in a single braid.

There was a big-screen TV across from the couch, tuned to a station that played pretty pastoral scenes and classical music. Mozart's sonata was just ending as she walked across the room with the other elf at her back.

Her stomach hurt. That was nerves . . . oh, use the right word. That was *fear*, and to be expected, maybe, but she didn't like feeling this way.

Her hostess and captor was already seated at the table. She wore a yellow tunic that looked like silk and would probably hit her knees when she stood. It was belted at her waist with a narrow leather band that held a sheath. The hilt of a knife protruded from that sheath. Her legs and feet were bare.

At the table, Lily pulled out a chair at the place that was obviously meant for her. The elf who'd walked behind her went to stand behind the halfling woman. He had long hair the color of a Creamsicle and wore jeans and a T-shirt, which looked strange as hell on an elf. He was armed with a SIG Sauer, not a knife. He held the weapon in his hand, not pointing it at Lily, but ready to.

A drift of white mist hovered over the table. Lily's gaze flicked up to it once, then away. It was surprisingly reassuring to know Drummond was here. He couldn't do anything, but he was here, and on her side.

She believed that, she realized with a small jolt. Her gut did, anyway. Seeing his ghostly self nearby settled her stomach.

"You may call me Alycithin," the halfling said politely. She pronounced it much as Sean had, accent on the second syllable, only with more lilt. "I'm unsure of your preferences, and we have no servitors here, so I must ask you to serve yourself." Her eyes were a bright, clear green. Like a cat's.

"I'm used to serving myself." The table was set with plates for her and the halfling. Cloth napkins, but no silverware, Lily noted. No fork or butter knife to stab her hostess with. The food was all finger food—bacon, fruit someone had cut and arranged attractively on a platter, and a second platter with slices of bread. No butter, but it smelled good, like it wasn't long out of the oven.

There were also pitchers of water and what looked like orange juice with glasses for both. Also a delicate china cup and saucer at each place. And a teapot. No coffee. Lily grieved briefly, then took a slice of bacon and some strawberries. "Does your culture encourage or allow business to be discussed during a meal?"

"It is thoughtful of you to ask. Normally we do not, but it is possible to make an exception to usual practice, if we both wish this."

"I wish it." Tea was not, in Lily's opinion, a substitute for coffee, but it was better than nothing. "Do you think the tea has finished steeping?"

"I believe so." Alycithin poured herself some water, smiled, and drank deeply before setting her glass down. Letting Lily know it wasn't drugged—though a substance that affected Lily might not do a thing to one of the sidhe. "Would you care for some water?"

"Thank you, yes." No point in continuing to refuse to drink. If they wanted to drug her again, they would.

The halfling poured for her. Lily drank thirstily, then poured herself a cup of tea. She was doing her best to channel Grandmother. Grandmother absolutely killed at the polite game when she wanted to—which, admittedly, wasn't often, but she'd had three centuries to practice. Lily took a sip of tea. Not up to Grandmother's standards, but it wasn't bad. "Very nice. May I pour a cup for you?"

"That would be kind."

Lily did so in the manner Grandmother had taught her. "Are we agreed that we can skip to some of the business we need to discuss?"

"It is always a shame to curtail the more pleasant aspects of conversation, but you have a saying—'needs must when the devil drives.' I agree to this."

"I have two points of immediate concern. The first is the other two hostages. Sean Friar believes you are going to free him, unharmed."

"I have given him my word that I will do so, or, if I should die, my people are in turn bound to see it done."

"I hope you will forgive a question asked out of ignorance. Under what circumstances would you consider breaking your word?"

"None."

Lily lifted her eyebrows. "None whatsoever? Not to save your life, your world, a roomful of tiny babies?"

"I suppose if I were tortured long and artfully enough that my mind broke, the creature who remained might do any number of things I would not." She picked up her cup and sipped. "A piquant aroma. Short of a death, which destroys the person if not the body, I honor my word."

"I'm happy to hear that. Did you give your word about Adam King, also?"

"Adam King is held by Benessarai, not me, but he will act according to the code. What was your other concern?"

"I must ask you to return my ring."

"Oh, surely not." The halfling smiled at her over the rim of her teacup. "That is, surely you don't expect me to hand you a totem containing . . . but your language doesn't have a word for this. We call it *arguai*."

"Grandmother is often vexed by the limitations of English." Lily set her cup down in the precise manner she would have used had this been a proper tea ceremony. "I called it my ring. This was misleading. The band itself is mine, but the charm on it was entrusted to me by my clan. My honor—the lupi would say *du*—is involved."

"I can assure you the ring is safe. It will not, however, be returned to you. Do try the berries. We don't have their like in our realm, and I am quite infatuated with them."

Lily had learned what she needed to. The *toltoi* did possess some kind of power, one the elves recognized. One they thought she could use. She ate some strawberries, commented on their sweetness, and asked if Alycithin planned to include strawberries in whatever trade deal she was negotiating.

"Perhaps, though I am not sure the plants would thrive in our climate. We are very interested in obtaining a good supply of duct tape. A remarkable substance, and one that will not be affected by the higher levels of magic in my realm the way your technology would be."

Duct tape? Really? Lily dragged her thoughts back on target. "Excuse me for saying this, but you seem to be going about your negotiations rather awkwardly. Sean told me that your people consider hostage-taking an integral part of doing business. You've been here long enough to know that we don't do things that way. In fact, part of my job is to arrest people who do things that way."

That amused her. "And how long have I been here?"

"A lot longer than two weeks, obviously. Are you able to shift between realms without a gate the way some sidhe do?"

"You will find that my people take a long view. In the short term, your people will not appreciate some of our practices. In the long term, you will discover the value of doing business our way. Already your corporations are gratifyingly eager to import some of our wares." Alycithin held out the plate of bread. "Won't you try some? It's from a bakery Dinalaran found, and is quite good."

Lily accepted a slice. "Is Dinalaran the one with the SIG or the one practicing spellcasting over by the TV?"

Alycithin had eyebrows. They weren't obvious, blending in as they did with the short, golden fur on her face, but she had eyebrows. She raised them now. "He stands behind my chair. Aroglian practices runic writing. You are familiar with such practice?"

"I have a friend who fiddles with spells that way."

"Ah. Cullen Seabourne. The . . . your word is *sorcerer*."

"The guy who made the device everyone is so eager to get their hands on, yes. Though I admit I'm puzzled about why *you* would want it. Your Gift works a lot better than any device could."

Silence. One heartbeat, two . . . just long enough for Lily to be sure that arrow had hit home. "Whatever do you mean?"

Lily tore a piece off the bread and popped it in her mouth. Alycithin was right—it was good bread. She washed it down with tea. "Your Gift is really good at hiding things. You can't do outright illusion the way the elves can—that's why Dinalaran or the other guy does the driving, isn't it? Going unnoticed works great unless you're in the driver's seat of a car. It upsets people if they don't notice a driver in a car. But in many ways, your Gift is better than straight illusion. It's not just that you can knock everyone out, though that came in handy last night. You can baffle wards and Find spells. You can hide whatever needs to be hidden. Coming like you do from a place where magic is used for all kinds of things, that must be a very valuable talent. A very rare one, too, I'm told."

Alycithin tipped her head to one side. "You have been told things I did not expect anyone in this realm to know."

"And you have not been told some things you need to know. Like about Robert Friar and the war you've landed yourself in the middle of."

"Oh, that." She brushed it off with a graceful gesture. "I am aware that he and your lupi consider yourselves at war. This is why he will trade what I want for you."

Lily took another sip of tea and prepared to roll the dice. "Your realm must be subject to Queens' Law." The sidhe realms had many rulers but only two queens: Winter and Summer. The queens had great power and only a fistful of laws, but when they said "thou shalt not," they meant it.

Those subtle eyebrows lifted subtly. "You know of Queens' Law?"

"Some. There's one that says no one is allowed to invoke a certain Name." Lily ripped off another bite of bread, but didn't eat it. She looked squarely at the halfling. "Do people in your realm know about Rethna? What he did, what he tried to do, and what happened to him?"

"Stop." Alycithin turned to the elf standing behind her, who'd watched Lily closely the entire time. The one with the gun. She said something short and musical to him, then to the other elf. They didn't like it. They argued—at least Lily assumed that's what they did, because although they sounded terribly polite, Alycithin responded in a voice cold enough that their balls should've shriveled on the spot.

The two elves bowed and left. Not the apartment—they went into another room. A bedroom, Lily thought, though she only caught a glimpse before the door closed on them.

Alycithin turned back to Lily. "They do not speak your language, but they understand some of it. I would protect them from hearing that which can be dangerous to know. Why do you bring up Lord Rethna?"

"Because you haven't landed in the middle of a war between Robert Friar and the lupi. The war is between the lupi and the one we don't name. Ever. *She* is who Rethna invoked, and *she* is who Robert Friar serves. You may not be invoking *her* name yourself, but if you're helping Friar, you've signed up on the wrong side."

Silence stretched out between them. Alycithin didn't speak. Didn't move. Didn't even blink. Lily's heart pounded. She was gambling big-time now. Alycithin might not give a tinker's damn who Rethna had served. She might be on the same side as Friar, already recruited into the Great Bitch's service. She might simply not believe Lily.

"And why," the halfling said at last, "should I believe you?"

"Why did you send your people out of the room? Why did you leave Sean out of our little tête-à-tête? Why have you allowed me to steer the conversation so far? Something's already bugging you. Something's not right. That's why you wanted this chat."

"It is customary to dine with one's captives or see that they have other company for meals. The code calls for captives to be treated civilly. This includes providing opportunities for pleasant conversation."

She sounded abstracted, however, as if she were speaking automatically while her mind was busy with some other subject. Lily decided to take a step back. T.J., her mentor in homicide, used to say that once a fish takes the bait, you let him run out the line. Grandmother put it another way: it's best if your enemy persuades himself to do what you want. "You were right about the bread," Lily said politely. "It's delicious."

"We were pleased to find a good bakery, as none of us possess that skill. Tell me, Lily Yu . . . but we never did settle on what I am to call you, did we?" Her smile was a work of art, warm and lovely. "We use few titles, and I am not familiar with the nuances of those you use. What title do you prefer?"

"Special Agent is correct. But why don't you call me Lily?"

"Lily. A pretty name. It sounds similar to our word for a

certain type of happiness. Your English does not have an equivalent. It is the happiness one feels at a pleasant surprise."

"Given your remarkable command of English, you probably know that here in America *lily* means a type of flower. But I was named for my grandmother, who is Chinese."

"I do not have any Chinese, I'm afraid. Is it permitted to ask what it means in that tongue?"

"Oddly enough, it has no precise meaning. This is uncommon with Chinese names." Should she ask what Alycithin's name meant? Cullen said names were a big deal to elves, but what kind of big deal?

"Languages are interesting, are they not? My language has many more names for some things than English does. For example, we have sixteen words that would translate, if rather poorly, as *enemy*."

"Does that mean you see sixteen types of enemies?"

"It does." Alycithin took a moment to select a slice of fresh pineapple. "We have only seven words for *friend*. It is . . . what is your phrase? Ah, yes. It is a sad commentary on us that we have so many more words for enemy than for friend, yet we find these distinctions useful. Of course, three of our words for *enemy* also denote a friend, so the imbalance is not so great as it seems."

"We call that sort friendly enemies."

"Yes, that is one type—enemies for whom one feels some cordiality. There are also enemies who seem to be friends, aren't there? Hidden enemies. And those with whom one would be friends if not for other circumstances. Such as, for example, having given one's word."

"Circumstances can be a bitch."

Amusement gleamed in those bright green eyes. "*Bitch* is a rude word in your culture, I believe. Yes, sometimes one regrets that someone who is *so'elriath*—ah, that is an enemy for whom one feels no hostility, one who is simply on the other side—cannot become a friend, perhaps of the fifth degree. But once one's word is given, it must be adhered to."

"Of course. But what was that other word? The one for

someone who would be a friend, under other circumstances."

"*So'amellree.* That is the word in the feminine. My language is somewhat like your Latinate tongues, but it is not the adjectives we change to suit the gender of the noun. When appropriate, we make the nouns themselves either masculine or feminine to suit their referent. *So'amellree,*" she said, looking Lily directly in the eye, "refers to a woman who would have been a friend, perhaps of the fifth degree, had circumstances been different."

"*So-amel-ree,*" Lily repeated. And smiled. Bait taken. Alycithin might be going the long way around, but she was swimming in the right direction. "Do you have a word that means the enemy of my enemy is my friend?"

THIRTY-EIGHT

~~

THE conversation with Ruben took longer than Rule expected. Ruben had persuaded the president to order the secretary of commerce to visit the sidhe delegation at their hotel under some diplomatic pretext or another. In an hour or two the secretary would arrive and be amazed to discover that some of the delegates were missing. When Rule got off that call, he started to touch Tony's number when his phone vibrated.

It was Tony. One of his wolves had found the scent, but at a location north and slightly west of the hotel. Did Rule want to check it out?

He did, once he learned where it was. He called Special Agent Bergman and asked her to meet him there. Rule got there first and congratulated young Ed, who was extremely proud of himself and wiggled all over in delight, his tail wagging madly. Ed's escort—a tall, morose city cop—watched with disbelief. "If that's not the damnedest thing," he said. "Damnedest thing I ever did see. I could swear he understood everything I said to him."

"He's not a dog, officer. Most of the time he's a man."

"Still." The cop shook his head. "Damnedest thing I ever did see."

Bergman had one of her people drop her off. She'd had a long night, and it showed in the dark circles under her eyes, but those eyes were bright with anticipation. She knew what this meant as well as Rule did.

Ed had found the scent at a bank.

Follow the money. Lily had said that often enough, and this was something Rule knew. Something he understood. Something the Bureau understood, too. They had excellent forensic accountants.

"I'll do the talking," Bergman told him.

"Of course."

"Yeah, that's why you called me. You want my badge."

"Of course," he said again, this time with the hint of a smile.

She almost smiled back. "Let's go—and pray one of those tellers remembers something or someone who was a little odd."

"We won't be relying on memory alone," Rule said, pushing open the door and holding it for her. "We'll want the bank's records of every transaction at this branch in the past two days, whether through a teller or at the ATM. The scent is probably from yesterday, but it might be as much as two days old. We'll need names, addresses, everything the bank has."

She snorted. "You've got funny ideas about banks if you think they'll hand all that over just because we say pretty please."

"Ruben is getting you a warrant." Rule glanced at his watch. "It should arrive in about thirty minutes."

She stopped and frowned. "What does he do, wiggle his nose and poof, I've got a warrant?"

"That wouldn't take thirty minutes. He's having someone deliver it here."

"Huh. I'm starting to like working with Unit Twelve." They'd paused just inside the doors. Bergman reached into her purse and took out a leather folder much like the one Lily used for her ID. "Even if it's just two days' worth of names, it's going to be a long list. These elves could look like anyone, young or old, male or female, right?"

"Right." Rule slanted her a smile. "We'll be able to trim the list by eliminating those who've had accounts here for several years, but it will still require a lot of resources to check out whoever is left. Which is why I like working with your Bureau. You have resources."

That time she did smile—the quick, hard grin of a hunter with a fresh trail to follow.

"I think I like you, Special Agent."

She snorted and strode over to the nearest desk. "I need to talk to the manager." She slapped her ID down. "Now."

They'd follow the money, see where it went . . . maybe to the third floor of a stucco building on the east side of the city.

THIRTY-NINE

~

"So this Benessarai is the one who wants the prototype."
Lily had long since finished eating, and she'd sipped all
the tea she could stand. She pushed the cup and saucer
away.

"She said so, didn't she?" Drummond snapped. "This is
no way to question a witness. Make her get to the point."

Drummond had pulled himself into his talkative shape a
few minutes ago and was pacing like a man whose patience
was used up.

She's not ready yet, Lily told him. *Don't distract me.*

She and Alycithin were getting along like gangbusters . . .
if gangbusters meant being terribly polite and careful with
each word. They had cautiously exchanged some information. Alycithin had been embarrassed when Lily told her
that Cullen had not refused to sell the prototype—that he
had never even received an offer. Benessarai had lied to her
about that. For some reason he wanted to obtain it the hard
way, using theft and hostages and a complicated plot. Lily
thought Alycithin knew very well why he'd taken that
route, but she'd waved Lily's question away with a vague
comment about it making him look more skilled. But Al-

ycithin had not known about the confrontation at the middle
school, so she couldn't tell Lily what had happened there.

Lily still didn't understand what the halfling woman
wanted from her. Or what she was offering in return. "Benessarai is responsible for holding Adam King, although
Friar's the one actually doing the job. He's supposed to be
on your side, but he's lied to you, kept information from
you, and undermined your mission. And yet you don't think
he'll violate your code."

Alycithin grimaced. "Lies, however crude, are not dishonorable."

"Just bad form." In sidhe eyes, it seemed, you kept your
word even if it killed you and all your family, but deception
and trickery were fine. Expected, even. Yet to lie outright
was on a par with farting loudly in church. "He'll lose a lot
of points back home for lying."

"That does not mean he will kill a hostage."

"Friar would. In a snap."

"Too damn right," Drummond said.

Alycithin shrugged. "Robert Friar wishes for many
things from Benessarai. He will not anger him. However, if
Jasper Machek did violate his agreement with Friar, who is
Benessarai's agent in this, he has forfeited Adam King's
freedom. I will make sure Benessarai does not leave him in
Robert Friar's custody, but the best I can do is see that
Adam King returns with us to our realm, where he will
spend the rest of his life as a hostage."

"Even if Friar violated his end of their deal?"

"Do you believe Robert Friar will admit to Benessarai
that he broke oath?"

Put that way, no. "Will Benessarai believe Friar over
you?"

She spoke very dryly. "He has so far."

"Because you two are rivals." And a hair away from being enemies outright, Lily thought. Benessarai did not trust
Alycithin, or claimed he didn't. He'd set up his own
hostage-keeping spot elsewhere in the city, though this
apartment had originally been intended for any hostages

either of them acquired. Lily had the idea that he and Alycithin were barely speaking to each other.

"It is not so simple as that word suggests, but perhaps you do not need to understand the nuances. It may be helpful to know that my position on the delegation is both punishment and opportunity."

"A punishment?"

"If the delegation does poorly, the blame will go to me."

"Even though he's in charge?"

A touch of impatience flickered in her green eyes. "We are coleaders. Did I not tell you that?"

"You said you were both, *ah* . . . I've forgotten the word."

"I failed to explain. Benessarai and I were given joint leadership of the delegation's goals, but he has far more authority than do I. You may confirm this with your own eyes. He has six people. I have two. They are capable and loyal, but they are two to his six."

"Listen," Drummond said. "I'm not doing you any good here. I'm going to see what else I can learn, but you'll have to call me again to get me through those walls."

Lily drummed her fingers, careful to look at her hand, not the ghost. She didn't want him to go, but he was right. He wasn't helping here . . . except for making her feel less alone. *Go on, then.*

"Call me in thirty minutes." He evaporated.

Lily looked up at the halfling again. "I think I understand. On paper, you and Benessarai are coleaders. In reality, he's running the show."

Alycithin nodded. "If I understand your idiom, that is the case. His father is Lord Thierath; his mother is Lord Sessena. My own breeding is . . ." Her smile flashed, quick and charming. Very nearly a grin. "You may have noticed, Lily, that I am not elfin."

"I had noticed that, yes."

"There is some overt prejudice in my realm and a good deal of stereotyping. A most useful word, that," she added with a lazy smile. "For all its limitations in some areas,

English provides an excellent framework for certain concepts. My father is Rekklat. His people are honored as worthy and excellent warriors, but they are not considered capable of the subtleties of *dtha* through which one may rise in . . . but now I arrive at those limitations. The closest English word I can think of is *society*, yet that does not convey my meaning well."

"Status?" Lily suggested. "Or caste?"

She tipped her head, considering. "Perhaps caste is closer, as it partakes of elements of status as well as power. I am ambitious, you see. Some do not believe ambition is fitting in a halfling. Lord Thierath is one such. Lord Sessena, however, is my sponsor."

Lily's eyebrows rose. "Benessarai's father doesn't approve of you, but his mother is your sponsor? What does that mean?"

"You have not an equivalent status. I am life-sworn to her. She arranged for me to be coleader with her son. I will speak now with a degree of bluntness that would be considered stupid and absurd by my mother's people." She paused as if waiting for Lily to give her permission to be blunt.

"Okay."

"Benessarai is a fool. His mother knows this. She wished to have one with him who owes her much. One who is, perhaps, not a fool."

Carefully Lily asked, "Is that the opportunity part of the deal?"

Again a quick smile. "Very good. If the delegation is sufficiently successful that Benessarai is not disgraced, I will receive little public credit, but Lord Sessena will have reason to be very pleased with me."

"And Lord Sessena has the whole package—authority, power, breeding."

"She is very high caste." She selected a grape. "Perhaps you are wondering why I tell you so much about myself."

"If you were one of my people, I'd say you were trying to enlist me. Convince me we were on the same side in some ways so that I'll do something you want."

Alycithin peeled the grape slowly. Her nails were a little longer than Lily's, well-shaped, but just a bit off. Narrow, as if they'd considered being claws at one point, but changed their minds. "I would say we are negotiating. I wish you to understand why I would negotiate with one who seems to be without power in this situation." She contemplated the grape she'd peeled, put it in her mouth, and bit. "I must tell you something more, I believe. Lord Rethna's realm is in chaos. Not simply his land, but the entire realm. The Queens are there. Both of them. You do not know how . . . astounding . . . this is. The Queens have not left Thalinol together in over three thousand years."

"Since the Great War?"

The eyebrows lifted. "Yes." She paused. "I do not know what your word, your promise, means to you. You seemed surprised I would consider mine binding."

"Not surprised, exactly. Lupi consider their word binding in an absolute sense like you do. They're very careful what they promise. Ah . . . my culture places a high value on honoring one's word, but it is not absolute. We believe there can be mitigating circumstances. If breaking my word was the only way to save lives, I would do that. But it would truly have to be the only way."

Alycithin looked at her hands. She smoothed an invisible crease from the yellow silk of her gown then looked up and met Lily's eyes. "Will you give me your word you will not repeat what I tell you now?"

"No."

"No? You give me that single, naked response?"

"I'm careful where I give my promises, too. First, I don't withhold information from Rule. That's firm. I very seldom withhold things from my boss, and only when there's . . . you might call it a conflict of honor. When I think honor is better served by my silence. You asked for too broad a promise."

A smile tucked itself into the corners of Alycithin's lips, making her look more catlike than ever. "Will you promise not to repeat what I tell you to any sidhe, and to withhold it as much as you honorably may from your own people?"

Lily thought that over, looked for trouble spots, and found one. "I will promise not to reveal it to any out-realm sidhe, and to withhold it as much as I honorably can from my own people."

"Out-realm sidhe? But Earth has no . . . I see that you do not intend to explain."

Lily shook her head. Arjenie's secret wasn't hers to reveal.

"Very well. I accept those terms. Do you so promise?"

"I do."

"Benessarai and Lord Rethna were friends of the third degree. This is not known in my realm. This is not known by his father, Lord Thierath. Benessarai is known to have been friends with Lord Rethna, but all think it was of the fifth degree. He is not the only one now tainted in this way, for Rethna entertained widely among the lords of many realms, but there is no real danger from such an association. Fifth-degree friends have liking for each other, but very limited bonds of obligation. Third degree is quite different." She took a slow breath. "That is the real reason Lord Sessena ensured I was coleader of this delegation. Benessarai needs a success to redeem himself, yes, but he also needs to be watched. Above all, it cannot be known that he had such close ties to Lord Rethna."

Lily tried to think herself into Alycithin's shoes. Her big fear was the Queens, Lily thought. Her people were scared that whatever was happening in Rethna's realm would spill over into theirs. "It must have come as a shock when I told you that Friar, who is allied with or working for Benessarai, is the Great Bitch's creature."

"The . . . oh." Amusement flashed in her eyes. "This is how you refer to the one we do not name? How charmingly irreverent. Also clever. Even a casual use-name may acquire resonance with sufficient repetition, but I think *she* will not recognize any resonance with that appellation. It was a shock, yes, but it did allow me to make sense of some things that have been bothering me. I have reworked my plans considerably while we talked. And so I have given you the knowledge to destroy me utterly, should you disregard your word. Just as I could destroy you, did I choose to dishonor mine. I have made us equal in power, Lily Yu. Do you see why?"

"You needed me to believe you," she started. Stopped, and went in a slightly different direction. "And this is a negotiation. You can't truly negotiate with someone who lacks power, can you?"

"Precisely! I like you, Lily. You are so grave, but quick and flexible. Those qualities do not often march together. I cannot violate my agreement with Robert Friar."

"Even if he violates it first? Robert Friar places no value on his word. The Binai who killed Rethna was freed from her contract with him because he'd already broken it."

"With all respect to the Binai, a vow is far more binding than a contract. If Robert Friar proves dishonorable, I have erred by entering into an agreement with him. My error does not affect what I have bound myself to do. And yet I must find a way to keep such a one from succeeding, for reasons both moral and personal. You were correct that I have been uneasy. I had . . . suspicions about Benessarai's goals, but he and I are, to use your word, rivals. I thought he meant simply to damage my standing. I thought he did not understand why it would be disastrous to bring the masking device back to our realm."

"The masking device? Is that what you call—wait. You mean you don't want to take it back to your realm. You want to destroy it."

She nodded. "Such a device would destabilize our realm. Hostages are fundamental to both our economic and our civic life, and the masking device would drastically alter the way power is balanced between hostage-holder and those with whom they would negotiate. Centuries-old agreements would turn unsteady. Imagine what would happen in your world if only one side in a contract had the

means to enforce it. I took pains to explain this to Benessarai. He understood only that making such a device
available would weaken my position, for my Gift is, indeed, both rare and valuable. He does not see the
repercussions . . . or so I thought. Hoped. This is why I
took the risk of making my own deal with Robert Friar. It
took some time to learn what he wanted enough to . . . I
believe your word is *double-cross*? An interesting word. I
wanted him to double-cross Benessarai. You were the
price he asked. As part of our agreement," she added, "he
is bound to observe the code."

Lily snorted. "And you believed him?"

"If he does not, I must in all honor kill him. He knows
this."

"He may not be as afraid of you as he ought to be."

She shrugged. "I arose from the warrior caste. If he did
not know what that means, he should have asked."

"That won't be much consolation to me if he's already
fed me to his goddess."

Alycithin's lip curled in distaste. "Death magic?"

"That's what I think he's got in mind, yeah. He may
want to do some really unpleasant things to me first, but
apparently I'd make a tasty snack for *her*. Death magic violates one of those Queens' Laws, doesn't it?"

"This is not one of the Queens' realms, however."

"Bummer." Lily decided she'd gone as far as she could
without having a clue what they were negotiating. "Alycithin, I am puzzled. You want something from me, and you
are unwilling or unable to say what. Nor have you offered
me anything or hinted at what you might offer. Negotiations
among your people may be conducted this way, but it's not
what I understand."

"That is plain speaking." The halfling woman spread her
hands. "I cannot tell you. To do so would violate my word."

Even bigger bummer. Lily drummed her fingers on the
table. Alycithin hadn't told her all this without a reason.
There was a hint, a clue, hidden in what she'd been told, but
damned if she could spot it. Maybe she hadn't asked the

right question yet. "Can you tell me what you promised Friar?"

This smile spread slowly. "That I can do. I agreed to take you hostage, if possible, and then hold you until Robert Friar notifies me that he is ready to exchange you for the masking device. While I hold you, I must make sure you have no weapons and no means of contacting your people. I am to let you know that you are going to pass into his hands."

"Wanted me to worry about that, did he?"

"I believe so. Lily, Robert Friar is your *dielgraf*. Your soul-enemy."

"That sounds about right. Is that all of the agreement?"

"Oh, no. Robert Friar was meticulous in his terms. Neither I nor my people can in any way reveal your situation, either while you are my hostage or after you become his, to anyone who is not sidhe. When Robert Friar tells me he is ready to take possession of you, I must make the exchange promptly and without attempting to alter or add to the terms of our agreement. At that point, if we have both honored the terms of our agreement, we are mutually bound not to act against each other, or allow our agents to so act, for twenty-four hours."

"Is that the exact wording? You can't reveal my situation to anyone who is not sidhe?"

"That is the wording. However—" She held up a hand, stopping Lily before she spoke. "You have hinted that someone in your realm is sidhe. While speaking to such a one would be allowed under one of the terms, it violates another. I vowed to hold you. Were I to reveal your presence while you are in my custody, I would be acting against that vow."

"After I'm not in your custody anymore . . . ?"

Alycithin smiled. She all but purred. "I did not agree to see that you remained in Robert Friar's custody. Only that neither I nor my agents would act against him for twenty-four hours."

Lily wasn't purring. This, she wanted to say, is your solution? Your deal?

From the halfling's perspective, maybe it looked like a good deal. Maybe Alycithin would have gone happily to torture and death if she knew she would be avenged. Maybe Lily would think so, too, if killing Robert Friar were her only goal.

Problem was, she really wanted to be alive and at least mostly intact when Rule came racing to her . . . which he would do long before the twenty-four hours were up. Once Lily was away from Alycithin's Gift, the mate bond should work fine.

Alycithin didn't know about the mate bond. That was the important takeaway from her offer. She didn't know about the bond, so she wasn't honor-bound to keep Lily from using it. Lily spoke slowly, as if reluctant. "You have my phone."

"Yes."

"You know how to use it?"

"Of course. I do not understand how the device works, but from what I have seen, most people in your realm do not understand it, either, yet they operate phones without this understanding."

"One of the contacts on my phone is for a sidhe who passes as human. Will you take my word for this?"

"Do you give me your word?"

"I do."

"Then yes, I accept that this is true."

"Will you call this person and reveal what you can, in honor, speak of concerning my situation?"

"Twenty-four hours after the exchange, yes, I will. But you have not yet told me this person's name."

Lily looked up at the ceiling. Drummond was still all misty. She looked down at her hands. "I have a question about your code. Does it allow you to give me aid in pursuing my spiritual needs?"

It was Alycithin's turn to be puzzled. "It would depend on the type of aid, but if it does not violate the terms of my agreement, then yes."

"I am facing either death or torture or both. I need to

meditate to strengthen myself for the coming ordeal. It would be a great aid to my meditation if I had my ring."

She shook her head. Her sadness seemed genuine. "I am sorry, Lily. The charm on your ring holds *arguai*—which, by definition, means I cannot measure or judge the nature of the power it holds. I cannot be certain you will not somehow use it to escape."

"If by *arguai* you mean that something's there, but it isn't exactly magic, then that's what I've sensed about the charm. I don't know how to use the whatever-it-is, or even if I could. I'm a sensitive. I can't use magic. I simply want the ring as a focus for my meditation." If she'd broken through briefly to Rule using a crude drawing of the *toltoi* . . . and she had. She was sure of that, even if she didn't know if he'd "heard" a single word. If a crude drawing helped enough for that, having the real thing on her hand ought to let her do a lot more.

Alycithin's eyebrows lifted in polite skepticism. "Most objects containing *arguai* are used as foci, and usually in spiritual practices. You . . . oh. You truly do not know what you were entrusted with, do you?" She sighed. "I am sorry. I still cannot allow you to have it. *Arguai* acts unpredictably. It might choose to reveal its nature to you, or act through you even if you do not consciously will such action."

Strike three and you're out. Good thing she wasn't playing baseball. "In that case, may I have privacy and a candle?"

"Of course." Alycithin seemed glad Lily had asked for something she could agree to. "My people, too, sometimes use a candle as a focus. This is specifically allowed in the code. I will have to enspell the flame, of course. It will burn long if you do not move the candle or attempt to use it to burn anything else."

That sounded like tricky spellwork. Cullen could do it, Lily felt sure, but not casually. Alycithin seemed to consider it a minor task. "Thank you."

"And if I may know the name of the person you wish me to call when it is time?"

"Arjenie. Arjenie Fox."

Several minutes later, Sean had been invited to join Alycithin in the main room. Lily sat on a pillow on the floor of the bedroom where she'd awoken. The walls were playing chamber music, a piece Lily didn't recognize. Alycithin brought the candle in herself while the armed elf—Dinalaran—kept his SIG trained on Lily. She chanted softly with her hand hovering over the candle's wick. A flame popped into being there.

The elf and the halfling left, closing and no doubt locking the door behind them. Lily tried to settle. Her heart was racing. She felt halfway nauseous. *Drummond,* she said.

Nothing happened. No white mist. No annoying yet reassuring ghostly shape.

She swallowed. If she couldn't even reach Drummond, how was she going to . . . *Try again*, she told herself. This time she spoke his name. "Drummond."

And this time it worked. He shaped up pretty quickly. And he was grinning. Actually grinning. "We're at 1132 North Bretton. The neighbors ordered pizza and gave the address. 1132 North Bretton."

Hot damn. She sent him that along with a quick, fierce grin. *Now I have to make use of what you learned. You need to go in the other room or something so I can concentrate.*

He seemed to notice the candle for the first time. "What the hell are you doing?"

Trying to mindspeak someone else. Someone who can send help to 1132 North Bretton.

He hesitated, then jerked a quick nod and went misty. He didn't go in the other room, though, but drifted up to the ceiling.

She'd just have to pretend he wasn't there, watching. Or whatever he did when he was misty.

Look into the flame, Sam always said. *Find me there.*

One more thing Alycithin didn't know about Lily. Her teacher, her grandfather-in-magic, was the black dragon . . . who was currently about five hundred miles away. Who approached teaching in a toss-the-kid-in-the-water-and-see-if-she-drowns sort of way. And Lily was really bad at mindspeech and had little to no chance of reaching that far . . .

Don't think about that.

She might suck at mindspeech, but Sam was very, very good at it. He mindspoke across the entire damn continent—five hundred miles was no problem for him. But it might not be five hundred miles. He overflew San Francisco regularly; it was part of his territory, one of the cities he'd agreed to patrol to sop up excess magic. He didn't keep to a strict schedule, but this was the right part of the week for his overflight. He might be at Laban Clanhome right now, chowing down on a couple cows.

If not, well, she'd had a breakthrough, hadn't she? She was a little better than totally sucky now.

She might be able to reach Rule again. Without the *toltoi* she wasn't confident she could, but she might. But she couldn't hold the connection long enough to be sure he "heard" the address, much less who held her, what their capabilities were, what part Robert Friar played, or why the elves wanted the prototype. With Sam, all she had to do was get the merest whisper of a message to him and he'd do the heavy lifting. At minimum, he could pass what she told him to Rule. At maximum . . . she didn't know what Sam's maximum was, and she wouldn't find out today. He wouldn't exert himself that much. But all he really had to do was tell Rule where she was. And Rule would take it from there.

Lily looked into the candle flame.

FORTY

~

THE conference room at the FBI's San Francisco office was small and crowded. The room smelled of clan—Scott, Mike, and Alan were among those at the table—but also of stale coffee, humans, and all the various scents they were so fond of. In addition to cologne, aftershave, and shampoo, Rule smelled six different brands of deodorant. One of them wasn't working as well as it might.

His wolf did not like it here. It didn't help that humans were forever closing doors. It was a damn fetish with them. Rule told his wolf to settle, that they were hunting Lily and everyone here was helping and he needed to focus, dammit.

"Stop that," Madame Yu snapped.

Everyone looked up at her. The man who'd just come in—Agent Smith or something similarly bland—stopped in midstride.

"Stop closing the door," Madame Yu said. "The air is stale in here."

"Sure," Agent Smith said. "No problem." He swung the door wide open. Everyone else went back to studying their printouts.

Rule made a mental note to buy Madame Yu something

foolishly extravagant. He gave her a grateful nod and looked back at his own set of lists.

The California Department of Public Safety had coughed up a list of the owners of cars with license plates ending in LT250, along with their addresses of record and driver's license numbers. That was on a database. Upon being served with the warrant, the bank had produced a list of every transaction in the last two days. *That* was a paper list. A very long paper list. It was a busy branch. Rule had gotten a second list from the bank, too—also on paper, but much shorter. That one contained only those transactions involving accounts that had been opened since the sidhe delegation arrived two weeks ago.

They'd been able to eliminate those account holders quickly. No matches. Not even any near misses.

Rule was operating on the assumption the elves had had help acquiring false identities, bank accounts, and renting a condo or house or apartment under their fake IDs. That help had probably come from Friar. They might have been in touch with him well ahead of their arrival. It was also possible one or more of them had been here much longer than two weeks. A few sidhe could cross between realms without a gate. Most of those with that skill were lords, according to Cullen. Most, but not all. Arjenie's father was able to cross realms.

So they would check older accounts as well. Robert Friar had been recruited by *her* six years ago, so Rule eliminated accounts more than six years old. That still left them with a very long list.

The data from DPS had been easy enough to import into the Bureau's computers. They'd tried scanning in the bank's list, then importing the scanned data. It hadn't worked. Scanning introduced too many errors. So they were doing it the old-fashioned way, comparing the two lists visually, looking for matches on the names, addresses, or driver's license numbers.

Cullen was still searching. His copter had refueled twice—and had been detained at the airport the second time. The pilot had to fly so low for Cullen to see the kind of detail he needed that they were breaking some law or another. Rule had applied to Ruben for help, and the airport had released pilot, copter, and Cullen. They were back up again.

Laban was still searching, too, on the ground. They hadn't found any more traces of elves. It was a big damn haystack.

If "LT250" wasn't a partial license plate number, they were wasting an enormous amount of time. Time Lily couldn't afford. Dammit, dammit, dammit . . . carefully Rule relaxed the hand he'd tightened into a fist atop his copy of the LT250 license plates. He realized he'd scanned most of the current page on autopilot. He could have missed something.

Damn it to hell. He didn't want to look at lists. Man and wolf, he wanted to *act*.

He made himself take a slow breath, rolled his shoulders to loosen them—and winced. His wounded shoulder was not finished healing. Had he been able to sleep to speed the process, it would be almost whole again, but—

"Found something," Mike said.

Rule beat Bergman to Mike's side, but only by a hair. She'd been closer, but still, she was fast for a human. "Show me."

"Here." Mike pointed at a line halfway down one sheet, then at another sheet. "Abraham Brown. Got it on both sheets. Driver's license number matches, too."

Jasper sat up eagerly. "What is it? What's the address?"

"44191 West Crescent," Bergman said. "Bill, check the map."

Jasper slumped. "That's damn near in the bay."

"He's right." A dark-haired man—Bill, presumably—had jumped up to look at a large map of the city pinned to one wall. "44191 would be right around here." He tapped on the map with one finger.

Bergman gave Rule a sharp look. "You said she wasn't near the water."

Rule moved up to look at the map. The spot Bill had his finger on was very near the bay. It was also west of the hotel. Not all that far from the area where Lily had gone looking for Hugo, in fact.

"A lot of warehouses there," Bill said. "Good place to stash a hostage. I can find out if that address is a warehouse pretty quick."

"All right. Yes. Do it." Rule scrubbed a hand through his hair. Was the match a coincidence? It could be. The list of plates ending in LT250 was long, and they were only guessing it was a partial plate number.

Bill did not jump to do what Rule said. He hesitated, looking at his boss.

"It's west, not east," Bergman said. "Either your tip was bad, or we're looking in the wrong direction."

Rule had told Bergman the truth—that Lily had contacted him through mindspeech, the kind the dragons used, though he'd only received a few words. Much to his surprise, she'd believed him. She had not, however, told her agents that. As far as they were concerned, Rule had received a mysterious tip they were supposed to treat as golden.

"If this isn't where they're holding Lily," he said slowly, "it could still be connected. Maybe Friar used that identity himself before he gave it to one of the elves. It could lead us to him, if not them. We have to check it out."

She nodded. "Good point. Come on, Bill—you and I will check out Abraham Brown and 44191 West Crescent. The rest of you keep checking your lists."

"Oh, yes," he said, looking at his share of those lists with loathing. "We'll keep checking."

THERE was nothing but fire. Fire in the tiny flame flickering at the end of a candlewick. Fire stretching from flame to flame, to the heart of flame. . . . fire, and Lily's voice.

Am at 1132 North Bretton. There are two groups of sidhe who are both competing and working together. The halfling has taken me and Sean Friar hostage. She will trade me to

Robert Friar. She has two elves with her, capabilities un-
known. Robert Friar is with the other group, led by Benes-
sarai. He has Adam King. Location unknown. Capabilities
unknown. I am at 1132—

Another voice sliced into her monologue, quick and cutting and as cold as the fire was hot: *Not now! Send the*
ghost.

A door slammed shut.

Lily jolted. Blinked in disbelief.

"What?" Drummond said urgently. "Did you connect?
Did he hear you?"

Drummond had fully materialized again. When had he
done that? She'd stopped seeing anything but the candle
flame some time ago . . . how long? The chamber music
was long since over. She heard Debussy now, the prelude to
his *Afternoon of a Faun*, and she ached all over. She was
exhausted. Limp and drained and exhausted. "I reached
him. He shut me out."

Drummond's scowl came quickly. "He wouldn't do that.
Maybe I don't like him, but he'd do anything to get to you.
There's no way he'd shut you out."

"He . . . oh." She realized she was speaking out loud and
switched. *I wasn't trying to reach Rule. I did manage that*
once, but it was so short and I couldn't tell if anything I sent
got through. She wouldn't let me have the toltoi. *I needed*
the toltoi *to contact Rule, so I was trying to reach Sam, the*
black dragon. And I did. And he shut me out. Lily blinked
back tears of exhaustion. Not despair, no. It was just that
she was so tired. But she wouldn't cry because the dragon
had been her last hope and he wouldn't listen. Wouldn't
even listen to her.

Drummond came and crouched in front of her. "You
can't give up."

"I'm not." She heard how flat her voice sounded, though,
and realized she'd forgotten again and spoken out loud.

"Turns out all those assholes who said 'where there's
life, there's hope' were right. Because on this side of the
line, you can't do anything. Not one damn thing. You're still

on the other side of that line. You can do something. Even if it doesn't work, you can do something. You just have to keep doing something."

Keep doing something. Yeah, sure, that sounded fine— but what?

She straightened, wincing at how sore her back was. *He told me to send the ghost. That would be you. I guess he doesn't know as much as he thinks he does. You can't go to Rule. You can't get more than a couple hundred feet from me.*

Drummond didn't answer.

I can try to reach Rule again. But even "talking" to Drummond felt draining. She'd about used up whatever resource she drew on for mindspeech.

"You said Turner could see me."

Yeah, some. But you can't get to him, so how does that—

The walls quit playing Debussy. Alycithin's lilting voice replaced the music. "Lily, I regret that I must interrupt your mediation. I have heard from Robert Friar. It is time to make the exchange."

THEY came for Lily with a gun, the SIG Sauer Al had seen earlier. The elf in jeans carried it. Al wanted to punch him so bad his clenched fists were shaking.

"I wish we had had longer to talk," the halfling said in her beautiful voice. She held an object very familiar to Al— a set of police-issue restraints. "I enjoyed your company. Please put your hands behind your back so I may secure them."

"What have you done to Sean?"

The other elf—who looked barely strong enough to carry a large sack of dog food—was toting Sean Friar back into the bedroom they'd just left.

"Only a sleep spell. He will be fine."

She didn't deserve this. Lily Yu was bright and brave and resourceful. She was a good cop. One of the best, and he had the years on the job to know what the best looked like. She was what he had been . . . once.

"Put your hands behind your back, please, Lily."

"Are you out of drugged darts?"

"Robert Friar does not want you drugged."

"I guess it would take all the fun out of it for him if I weren't conscious and shaking with fear. Where are we going?"

The halfling was getting impatient. "To Robert Friar."

Even before Al killed the bitch who'd killed his Sarah, he'd lost some of that shine. The job took it out of you, and he'd gotten hard, cynical, willing to cut corners. Then he lost Sarah, and he went crazy. Maybe he was still crazy, because he couldn't regret killing Martha Billings. Not exactly. But he hadn't given the law a chance. He'd decided his need to kill was bigger and more important than anything else. The law hadn't failed him. He'd failed it. After that, he'd made one bad decision after another.

Lily shook her head. "I mean where in the city. If he is in the city. Will this be a long ride or a short one? How much time do I have left?"

She was still trying to get information. He couldn't see what good that information would do her, but she was doing *something*. She hadn't given up.

"It should take twenty minutes or less to get there. He is in an old warehouse not far from where I captured you. If you do not put your hands behind you back now, I will force you. It would be more dignified to comply."

"I guess I'm not in a dignified mood."

Sarah hadn't deserved to die. Neither did Lily Yu, but Al was even more helpless this time. Condemned to watch it happen. Unable to do anything to stop it. He wanted to bang his head against the wall, but his head would go through the goddamn wall.

Alycithin nodded and said something in her language to the jeans-wearing elf. She handed him the restraints.

Yu tried. She had some moves, too, but the halfling—Al had never seen anything like her. She moved as fast as those damn lupi, and she had the whole package—speed, training, strength. It was over pretty quick, ending with Yu on her stomach on the floor, the halfling straddling her, and the other elf fastening the restraints.

He circled the pair of them, useless and furious and willing to do anything. Anything at all, if only there was something he could do.

The black dragon thought there was.

Send the ghost, he'd told her. Well, Al was the only ghost she had. The dragon had to mean him. He circled the two living people as Alycithin pulled Lily to her feet, unable to stop moving. Maybe the dragon was right. Dragons mostly were, when it came to the woo-woo stuff. Maybe there was something Al could do and he was too stupid to see it. Maybe he was as big a failure as a ghost as he had been as a cop and as a husband. If he—

His ankle brushed against something.

He jumped back. Astonished was way too small a word for what he felt. He hadn't touched anything since he died. He could sort of feel walls and floors and people, but it wasn't like touching them. It wasn't the same at all.

Thin and taut, a glowing cord stretched away from Yu, angling slightly down.

That? That's what he'd felt, the damn cord that ran between her and Turner? It was thinner than ever, as if it had been stretched way out. Tentatively he approached.

Lily's gaze darted to him. The halfling was behind her, marching her forward. "You will not be noticed," Alycithin said. "Do not tire yourself calling out or attempting to draw attention in other ways. Dinalaran, the door, please."

Al reached out and touched the cord—or tried to. His hand went right through it. Disappointment crashed down so hard he could only stand there, staring. But he'd felt it. It had brushed his ankle. Why couldn't he feel the damn thing now? He reached out with both hands—and his left hand touched it. Felt it. His left hand, where his wedding ring glowed.

The cord was thinner than a rope and slick. He closed his hand around it. His fingers gripped. They gripped and held on.

What . . . you doing?

Yu's mental voice was so faint he'd missed a couple of words. He looked at her. "I'm going to try it. Turner can see me. Maybe I can use this to get to him, let him know you're being taken to a warehouse."

Use what?

"Whatever this thing is between the two of you. I can hold it. Maybe I can follow it." Maybe he'd gotten lost in the gray because it didn't have landmarks. This—this cord thing—maybe it wouldn't go away. Maybe he could hold on to it, pull himself along it, even when everything else went to gray.

But he'd better hurry. Once the halfling got Yu in a car, he was going to come apart.

"Don't call me," he told her urgently. "If you do, I'll come back, and I need to try this." He held onto the cord tightly and started running—out the door and right down into the floor.

He felt both door and floor as he passed through them. Not tactilely, the way he felt the cord. Just a vague sense of compression as if whatever he was composed of now reacted to the mass he passed through. He raced through someone's living room, through a wall and a hallway, and out of the building entirely. He was still nearly two stories above the ground.

The cord felt strong and stable in his hand. It stretched out straight ahead of him as he ran. It didn't seem to matter that his feet had nothing below them but air. He grinned, exhilarated. He'd never tried this. When he wanted to move fast, he'd always let himself go misty. But mist didn't have hands, couldn't hang on to a cord.

This was fun.

His grin faded as he looked ahead and saw the way buildings, people, everything faded. Only a few yards ahead of him now, the world took on a gray cast. Beyond that . . . nothing. The cord stretched out and out into the nothing.

He kept running. The world had faded to gray, ghostly shapes, barely seen, when the first vibration shook him.

He hadn't been fast enough. Lily Yu was in a car, and it was speeding up.

He began to tatter quickly, and as he came apart he felt the pull, as if he had a hook set deep in his soul that was yanking him. Pulling him back toward her. He'd only felt a little tug before, not this deep ripping. His hand started to lose the feel of the cord, lose . . .

No. He focused everything he had, everything he was, on his hand, on the hand gripping the cord. On the gold of the ring he wore, glowing like the cord still glowed. Even here where all was gray, here in the heart of the nothing, his ring glowed faintly, just like the cord. He couldn't see anything but his hand, his ring, and a short length of the shining cord. Everything around him was gone. He was gone, except for that hand, but he kept moving even as that hook ripped him.

It hurt. It felt like the hook was ripping open the gut he didn't have anymore.

He focused even harder on his hand, the one part of him that was still real. That would, by God, stay real. And he kept moving away from Lily Yu.

FORTY-ONE

⤙

THAT was the last name on his list. Rule had checked every damn one, and found nothing.

He rubbed his face and looked around. Madame Yu and Mike were still bent over their lists, but the rest were through. Now what? What the hell did they do next? "I guess we pass our copies to the person next to us. Double-check each other."

"We eat now," Madame Yu said without looking up from her pages.

Eat. Yes, it was . . . God, it was noon. Friar had had Lily for about twelve hours. Rule closed his eyes and tried not to think of what that meant. She was alive. She was alive, and she'd managed to contact him once. "Of course," he said, amazed at how level his voice sounded. "Scott, would you order something for us?"

Scott nodded and took out his phone and tapped the man sitting next to him on the shoulder. "I don't know the take-out around here. Where should I call?"

"There's a pizza place two blocks over that's pretty good. I'll get you the number."

Rule's phone sounded. He grabbed it. "Yes?"

"We found something," Tony said. "Pretty fresh, too. It's at the Whole Foods in Potrero Hill. Rick's in the produce section now with his cop. He indicated that the strawberries have a lot of elf-scent."

"Potrero Hill," Rule repeated, jotting it down. "The Whole Foods store." He shoved his chair back.

Bergman came in. "That Crescent Street address is a warehouse. It was leased to Abraham Brown this past November, which is a pretty neat trick, considering he died in May." She stopped. "You found something?"

"Not on the lists. One of my people found elf-scent at a Whole Foods store in Potrero Hill." Wherever the hell that was. He'd been so eager to move that he hadn't asked. "Do you know where that is?"

"Sure." The way her eyes brightened said she was eager to get moving, too. "I'll take you." She stuck her head back out in the hall. "Bill! I'm going with Turner to check out another lead. Get out to that warehouse, see if there's a watchman or someone you can talk to."

"Can we get a copy of the picture on Abraham Brown's license?" Rule asked. "Maybe the elves used that likeness for their illusion. Maybe someone will recognize it."

"Good thinking," Bergman said. "Harris, you're quick with that sort of thing."

"Sure, pick on the new guy." But the young man stood, stretched, and hurried out of the room.

"I will come with you," Madame Yu said, and stood.

Beth popped out of her chair. "Me, too."

Bergman shook her head at both of them. "I need people who can take it door-to-door if we get a hit on Brown's photo. I don't need civilians."

Rule saw the hand first. About three feet away, emerging from the wall next to Bergman—a clear, distinct hand. A man's hand with a glowing gold wedding band on one finger. It was gripping something tightly. Behind it . . . mist. Only mist.

"Rule." Madame Yu's voice was quiet. Worried. She'd moved up to stand beside him. "What is it?"

"Drummond," he whispered.

The moment he used the man's name, the mist began shaping itself. It assembled slowly, painfully slowly, but at last Al Drummond stood there in front of Rule.

He looked bad. He'd been dead for three months, but now he looked like he was dying, and dying in agony. His face was grooved deeply by pain. The tendons in his neck stood out. He seemed to be fighting to stand upright. He looked at Rule and said something.

"I can't hear you. I can see you, but I can't hear you. Where's Lily? Is she nearby?' he asked sharply.

Drummond shook his head and shuddered. Again he said something. Rule watched his mouth carefully, but he'd never learned to lip-read. "Again," Rule said. "Say it again, slowly."

It was no good. He shook his head. "I can't understand you. Dammit to hell!"

"Who can't you understand?" Bergman asked warily.

"Quiet," Madame snapped. "Rule, the ghost tied to Lily is here and trying to tell you something?"

"I can't hear him," Rule said, his voice sinking to a growl. "I can see him, but I can't hear him, and I can't read lips."

"Can he see me?"

Drummond nodded.

"Yes," Rule said.

"And the map? Does he see that?"

Again Drummond nodded. Again Rule repeated that aloud.

"Good." She marched over to the wall. "Mr. Drummond, do you know where Lily is?"

Drummond nodded vigorously.

"He does," Rule said. His hands were fists at his sides.

"We will play the hot and cold game." She studied the map a moment then put her finger on it. "As I move my finger, Mr. Drummond will nod if I am getting warmer and shake his head if I am getting colder. If I touch the place where Lily is, he will speak again. Rule will report this."

Drummond shook his head and began to . . . it looked like he was pulling himself forward with one hand. A hand that gripped nothing Rule could see. He got close to Rule then stopped, his expression obviously frustrated. He waved at Rule with his other hand.

"Wait a minute. I think he needs to be closer to the map."

Drummond waved at Rule again. This time Rule got it. He wanted Rule to move closer to the map. He did. And Drummond followed . . . slowly. As if each step was killing him. When he stopped he was hunched, one hand clutching his middle, the other one gripping nothing Rule could see.

"Okay," Rule said. "Go."

"I begin on the block where our hotel is," Madame Yu announced.

Rule was watching Drummond, not Grandmother, so he didn't see where her finger went on the map. Drummond shook his head quickly. "Colder," Rule said. A pause, longer this time. Drummond nodded slightly. "Warmer, but not hot." Several more heartbeats . . . "Colder. Cold . . . okay, you're back on track. He's nodding. He's . . . there. Stop." Drummond's mouth had moved, but now he shook his head again. "Back up. You were on it, but . . . that's it!" Drummond was nodding and talking up a blue streak.

"My finger," Madame Yu said, "in on Crescent Street. On the block where that warehouse is."

Drummond nodded frantically.

"The warehouse?" Rule said quickly. "That's where she is?"

Drummond nodded again, and mouthed one word, exaggerating the movement. Then he came apart—not just fading to mist the way Lily said he did all the time, but shredding.

"He's gone," Rule said flatly. "The warehouse . . ." It was west of the hotel. Lily had told Rule she was east of the hotel. How could Rule take the word of someone like Drummond over what Lily herself had told him?

"Tell me you aren't seriously considering going there

based on—on whatever the hell you think you saw," Bergman said.

Rule looked at her. She was competent, Lily said. Good at her job. She was probably right. But he couldn't get out of his mind how Drummond had looked. How much pain he'd been in. He'd fought some kind of battle to get here, to pass on what he could. And the last word he'd spoken, the one he'd exaggerated, hoping Rule would understand . . . it had looked like *hurry*.

"Lady," he whispered. *What do I do?*

The Lady had never spoken to him. She didn't speak now. But he felt himself settle into a familiar state. Into *certa*, the battle state, where thought, decision, and action flowed smoothly and icy clear.

He could go to Whole Foods with Bergman, but that was a cop thing to do, wasn't it? Not a Rho thing. Not a lupi thing. "We're going to 44191 West Crescent," he said crisply. "Scott, we need our cars. Special Agent, a police escort would—"

"Forget it. You're nuts, and I'm not going to cater to insanity."

Rule stopped listening as a new thought flowed in. "Never mind. Scott, you'll take the bulk of the men and meet me there. Mike, Todd—you're with me."

"As am I, of course," Madame Yu said.

"Your aid is always welcome."

"You *are* nuts," Bergman said flatly.

Her comment was quickly followed by protests from the other agents. Even Beth looked worried, and his own people were variously alarmed or stony . . . but then, they were Leidolf. None of them had fought beside Madame. But their reaction made him see her for a moment as they must.

She was so small. Small and thin and wrinkled. Madame Yu was an old woman, however large the spirit might be in that erect body . . . which was, of course, far older than the others dreamed. Rule smiled slowly as an idea arrived. He had to assume that Friar would know who Li Lei Yu was, but he had no idea *what* she was. "Madame, I have a part in mind for you to play. It is very dangerous."

She sniffed her disdain of that caveat.

"Will their illusions affect you?"

"I think not, but we shall see."

"Very well. I'll explain en route." Scott, however dubious he might be about Rule's choice of fighting partners, was dutifully calling for the cars to be brought around. Rule started to turn to the special agent.

"I'll go with you, too." That was Jasper. "Unless you're going to run straight at guns again, which I wouldn't be good at because I'd be dead too quickly to be much help. But stealth is usually better in a hostage situation, and I'm good at that."

Rule met his brother's eyes. He saw need there, and determination. What could a human do against such as they faced? He didn't know, and yet . . . "Are you willing and able to follow my orders?"

Jasper nodded.

And yet perhaps Jasper had the right to be there. And try. "Very well. It may get you killed."

Rule took out his phone to make his own call . . . to Cullen. Who had a helicopter. Much faster than cars in San Francisco's appalling traffic.

And Drummond's last word had been *hurry*.

FORTY-TWO

～

SAN Francisco traffic sucked. Lily had never been so glad for a traffic jam in her life.

The gun-toting elf drove the CR-V. The other elf had stayed at the apartment to keep an eye on the sleeping Sean. Alycithin rode in the backseat so she could keep an eye on Lily, who was stashed in the back. They'd added a rope to her ankles to go with the restraints holding her arms behind her back. It wasn't comfortable, but considering what waited for her, she thought she should at least try to enjoy the ride.

Mostly she thought about Rule. Had he been injured last night? Had any of the men been killed? Was Jasper okay? Several times she tried to reach Rule, but she could tell she wasn't budging her dial. Whatever fuel mindspeech burned, hers was used up.

He would come. As soon as Alycithin left and took her damn Gift with her, the mate bond should start working properly again. He'd feel her, and he'd come, but it didn't make sense to just charge in. Plans took time. So the question was: Did Friar want to take his time with her? Or would he gloat briefly, then make her quickly dead in some hideous ceremony?

He might skip the gloating and the ceremony and go straight to the killing. She didn't think so. She didn't think that would please the one he served.

Drummond was still gone. Of course, he couldn't show up when she was in the car anyway, from what he'd said, so maybe he was here but unable to materialize. What did he think he could do? That "thing between the two of you," he'd said. Was he talking about the mate bond? He'd never said anything before about being able to see or touch it.

What would happen to Drummond if she died in the next couple of hours? The thought startled her. Surely they wouldn't still be bound. Even the mate bond didn't endure past death. What would happen to him?

The CR-V speeded up as whatever traffic snarl had had them crawling loosened up.

"I have been thinking," Alycithin said. "If Robert Friar does intend to use you to fuel death magic, he will not kill you while Benessarai is present. Nor will Benessarai allow him to abuse a hostage. However he feels about me, he has too much pride to so abandon his honor. Benessarai will be here at least another twenty-four hours. Our flight leaves at eight in the evening tomorrow . . . unless he has *lied* to me about that, too." She laid a gently sarcastic stress on the word.

"Alycithin, I appreciate you wanting to make me feel better, but why would Benessarai be at this warehouse? Robert Friar won't want him around when you're exchanging the prototype for me. He won't want Benessarai to know he isn't getting the prototype."

"No, he won't be present now, but he will be there soon. This is why I had to hurry you. We must complete the exchange before Benessarai returns."

"And Benessarai is going to jet back to D.C. with you tomorrow without the prototype?"

"Ah, but he will believe he has it. Sadly, it will turn out that the skull used for the device was damaged at some point in its adventures, so it isn't working properly now. Robert Friar will apologize profusely for this. But I am assured your sorcerer does not know how to hide his spells,

so the spellwork will seem to be intact. Benessarai will give
the device to his father, expecting him to be able to dupli-
cate it. Lord Thierath is highly skilled. He could certainly
do so if he were given the actual device."

Lily thought that over. "Wrong skull?"

"I do not have Lord Thierath's skill, but once I have the
original in my possession I can create a close enough fac-
simile to fool Benessarai."

"If this device could destabilize your realm, wouldn't
Lord Thierath know that?"

"Your people have a saying—like father, like son."

"He's a fool, too."

"I am sure I did not say that."

The CR-V slowed. Slowed more, and turned. And
stopped. Lily's heart began to pound.

"We are here," Alycithin said.

She wasn't ready. Her stomach went queasy, and her
mind went blank.

The halfling used the knife on her belt to slash the rope
at Lily's ankles and seized her foot before she could lash out
with it. Alycithin was brisk, efficient, and absurdly strong.
She dragged Lily out effortlessly. Lily barely managed to
get her feet under her in time to keep from landing on her
butt. Dinalaran stood close by with his gun, and Alycithin
seized Lily by the restraints and nudged her forward.

They were parked in front of a bare-bones style
warehouse—concrete blocks painted a dingy yellow, with
a regular door directly ahead and a dock and high-loading
door several feet away. There was room for a semi to pull
up at the dock.

A car drove by on the street behind them. She wondered
what the elf looked like to its driver.

That driver wasn't the only person around. The warehouse next to theirs was bigger and bustling—two trucks
were being unloaded and another waited its turn. Lily had
already tried getting the attention of passersby, though, on
her way out of the apartment building. Alycithin was too
damn good with her Gift.

Alycithin said something in her language.

The people-size door opened. A large, fat man stood in the doorway. He wore a trench coat, T-shirt, jeans, and boots. He was bald with a tattoo on his forehead, and he carried a sawed-off shotgun in one hand.

This wasn't quite the way she'd intended to find Hugo.

"She's here," he said loudly, "with her half of the deal."

Wait a minute. "How come he noticed you?" she asked Alycithin.

"Does your friend not know how to use her Gift selectively? I suppose little training is available to her here."

Hugo moved out of the way, and a second man emerged.

Robert Friar was looking good. His deep tan hadn't faded. The silver in his dark hair was as dramatic and attractive as ever. He wore tailored slacks and a good-quality cotton shirt, open at the throat. It was a deep, rich shade of blue that complemented his coloring. He carried a black bowling-ball bag.

He looked at Lily. Delight lit his eyes. Anticipation. Then his gaze shifted to the woman holding her. "Alycithin, how good to see you again. I hope you will excuse my haste, but we have only a short time before Benessarai and the others return."

"I do not object to haste, but you must take down the wards on the building so I can confirm that we are alone save for our agreed-upon attendants."

"I'm afraid I failed in part of my task. Benessarai refused to show me how to take down the wards."

"Then we will not exchange here and now, Robert Friar. Dinalaran," she said, adding something in her language as she took a quick step back, pulling Lily with her.

Lily didn't see it happen. One second she was being tugged backward. The next a huge, hard shove sent her flying—and a gunshot shattered the air. A second shot boomed almost immediately as Lily landed on her knees, still falling, but she rolled so she ended on her side—and saw Alycithin facedown on the concrete, her back a bloody mess. With Dinalaran standing over her, gun in hand.

He'd shot her in the back. Her own man had shot her.

She'd shoved Lily out of the way. Whatever sense had alerted her, she'd used that split second to save Lily, not herself. The rounds in that SIG would likely have gone right through Alycithin and into Lily.

"That," Friar said disapprovingly as he stepped forward, "was poorly done, Dinalaran. Do you know anything about that weapon in your hand? If Alycithin hadn't quixotically chosen to— Hugo," he snapped. "Get her."

It was awkward to get to your feet quickly with your hands bound behind your back, but Lily managed it—only to be confronted by the elf's SIG Sauer, all too quickly followed by the oversize Hugo, who pinned her to him with a forearm around her neck. He felt a lot harder and more muscular than he looked. He smelled like pizza.

Lily glanced quickly at the other warehouse. It was only fifty feet away, but everyone there continued to unload trucks. No one had heard the shots. No one had seen a thing. Someone was still hiding them. If not Alycithin, then who? She'd thought Dinalaran was one of the body-magic guys. Could he be that good at illusion, too?

Something dropped to the concrete with a metallic thud. She looked quickly that way and saw Dinalaran sink to his knees, tears streaming down his face. He'd dropped his weapon. He looked up and began to sing.

He had a high, pure voice. His song was clearly a lament, the melody simple and haunting.

"Can't have that," someone else said. "It is not fitting that my cousin's murderer sing her death song."

Another person had emerged from the warehouse. He was tall and slim and beautiful and dressed all in white— loose white tunic-length shirt, white leather pants, white boots. His long hair was loose and the color of a new penny. It shone brightly in the winter sun, as if it were indeed made of metal instead of collagen. The tips of his pointy ears poked through that copper curtain. He wore what looked like an enormous blue sapphire on a chain around his neck. One slender hand rose gracefully to touch the stone. He murmured a few words.

Dinalaran hushed and stiffened. Slowly his hand moved to his boot. He pulled a knife from it and closed his eyes and rested the tip of the knife on one eyelid. He adjusted the angle slightly and plunged it up into his brain.

His own body fell across Alycithin's.

"Poor Dinalaran. He has atoned as much as he was able," the copper-haired Benessarai murmured.

"Ah, well," Friar said. "We have a saying: all's well that ends well."

"Time to tidy up." Benessarai stepped away from the doorway and gestured. Four more elves flowed out the door. They wore leather pants in a variety of hues, but their shirts all matched his—white and long and flowing. They had great, long knives sheathed on their backs. He spoke to them in his language and gestured at the bodies.

None of the four spoke. Their lovely faces were serene, unmoved by what was supposed to look like a murder-suicide. But when they reached the bodies, they handled them with great care. Dinalaran was shifted off Alycithin. Both were lifted, moved several feet away, and laid down once more. The elves began arranging their clothing and their limbs with finicky precision.

Benessarai spoke sharply. The elves stopped and backed away.

Friar looked at him and raised one lazy eyebrow. "You do not want the bodies placed in stasis?"

"I must first assure myself that she is dead."

"Ah. You aren't confident your people can tell the dead from the living."

The insult rolled off the thick armor of Benessarai's arrogance. He answered with the sublime indifference of one who knows that little can be expected of the lesser beings around him. "You would not, of course, understand. She was an abomination, but half that abomination was Rekklat. With Rekklat, one always makes sure." He glided forward.

Robert Friar approached Lily. Behind him drifted a white, indistinct cloud.

Drummond was back. It was ridiculous to be so relieved.

Friar stopped in front of her. "Much has changed since we last spoke."

"Yeah, the last time I saw you, you were too busy escaping to stop and chat."

"Strange. I seem to recall you doing the running. You and all your wolfish friends." His stroked her cheek with one finger and lowered his voice. "You won't be running this time."

Lily's mouth went dry. He sounded relaxed. He looked calm and at ease, but his eyes burned with feverish intensity. And with that single casual touch of his finger, he'd let her know he was brimming with power. Overflowing with it, power like nothing she'd ever touched before.

She didn't want to fear this man, but she did. "Benessarai did something to make Dinalaran kill Alycithin. A compulsion spell, maybe."

"Very good," he said, as if she were his pupil and eager for his approval. "He is a wonderfully talented *seurthurin*. That is one who practices the arts of the mind. Benessarai would say that today's events were Alycithin's own fault. She failed to make sure her people took adequate precautions."

"Blame the victim? How very human of him."

"You may not want to say so where Benessarai can hear. I'm afraid he's quite shortsighted about our species."

The copper-haired elf had knelt beside Alycithin's body and was drawing shapes in the air over her open, staring eyes. He uttered some syllables, paused, then nodded with satisfaction, stood, and spoke to his people in his own language.

"Really most completely dead," Friar murmured.

Lily hadn't needed the confirmation. The mate bond was working freely again. She knew where Rule was—and he was close. Very close, but not yet here. They needed to stay out in the open a little longer. "Where's Adam King?"

"Inside." Friar smiled. "I'll introduce you." He raised his voice slightly. "If you're quite satisfied, I suggest we move inside. I'm not happy being so exposed."

Benessarai spoke without looking at Friar. "Patience. Who will attack when none can see us? We will have the remains in stasis quickly, but then the blood must be collected." He waved at his people, who moved close to the bodies once more.

"I am unable to help with that," Friar said, "so I will await you inside where there is more tidying up to do."

"Oh, as you will, then."

"Hugo, bring her along."

The mass of fat and muscle gripping her arms shoved her—and she let the momentum take her to her knees.

"Really, Lily, you can do better. If you don't, Hugo will carry you."

The elves had stopped waving their arms. Two of them bent and tenderly picked up the bodies and started this way. Benessarai spoke to the other two. Lily raised her voice. "Benessarai, he intends to kill your hostage!"

The elf glanced her way. "Hostages are not killed." He waved at the two remaining elves as the two carrying the bodies passed Lily.

She tried again. "He's going to kill me, too, and feed me to his goddess."

"That is true." Benessarai cocked his head, curiosity brightening his eyes. "It is rather a waste. I have never encountered a sensitive. Bring her to me."

Friar spoke softly. "She is my prize, not yours."

"Of course. My apologies, Robert. That was thoughtless of me." He began to saunter toward them.

Out of the corner of her eye, Lily glimpsed movement. A flash of orange. She ducked her head and shook it as if confused . . . which let her look that way without Friar noticing.

A tiger peered around the far corner of the warehouse. Just the head showed—that enormous, orange and black head with green eyes slitted against the sunshine. The tiger nodded at her once and pulled back out of sight.

Grandmother? Grandmother was here?

Thank God she'd ducked her head and her hair was

hanging down, hiding her face. She had a moment to get her expression smoothed out, a moment to try to figure out what that nod meant. Distract them? Be patient? The latter, maybe, she decided. No one was rushing to the rescue right away, so maybe they had more preparations to finish.

Benessarai stopped in front of her. "With your permission, Robert, I would like to try something before you make your offering. It would be too late afterward." He chuckled at his own wit. "Your man will need to let go of her and step back, or he will be affected. He wouldn't like that."

"Of course not." Friar didn't put much effort into the lie. He sounded downright brusque. "If it won't take long."

"Not long at all."

"Hugo, release her but keep her covered."

The big man grunted and dropped his hold on Lily. The smell of pizza retreated with him. Her shoulders ached.

"Hugo won't shoot to kill if you try to escape," Friar told her. "He'll aim for your stomach. A gut full of buckshot would kill you eventually, but not so quickly I would fail in my duty to the Great One."

"Do step away just a bit, Robert. There, yes." Benessarai wiggled the fingers of one hand at Lily.

Magic prickled over her face. It felt like a breeze with feathers in it. "Air magic, only slightly shaped. Mind-magic is connected to Air, isn't it?"

He frowned slightly and wiggled his fingers again.

The gust of magic was stronger this time, more prickly. "Why is it okay for Friar to kill me? I'm a hostage."

"No, you aren't." Benessarai studied her the way a scientist might study a lab rat that was not reacting in the expected way to a stimulus. He started in with more hand waving, this time accompanied by a short chant.

Friar smiled slowly. "Allow me to explain. An abomination can't make a true covenant. If Alycithin was unable to make a true covenant, she has no family. If she has no family, she is not party to the code. If she is not party to the code, then alas, you are no hostage. Only a prize."

"I see. Yet I'm a valuable prize, aren't I? I'm surprised

Benessarai is willing to let you kill me without learning where sensitives come from."

This time the elf answered. "I am curious. Do you claim to know?"

"Oh, yes, I know. You have humans in your realm, right?"

"Your kind are everywhere." He said that the way a New York apartment dweller might speak of roaches: try as you may, you can't get rid of them. "Tell me," he said.

"Make me your hostage so I don't get fed to Her Evil Nastiness and—"

Friar slapped her. Hard. Way harder than he should have been able to. She fell to the ground, dazed, with black fluttering at the edges of her vision.

"You do not—"

He kicked her in the ribs. She gasped and curled around the sudden pain.

"Speak of—" His leg drew back for another kick.

A tiger roared.

Hugo screamed.

Five hundred pounds of Siberian tiger raced straight at them.

Friar's eyes widened. He reached for her. Lily tried to scramble out of the way, but she was dizzy, slowed by the blows. He got hold of her arm and started dragging her, and he should not have been able to do that. Not as fast as he was moving. She caught a glimpse of Benessarai fleeing through the open door of the warehouse, heard the two elves call out something, but she was fighting, kicking, squirming, trying her damnedest to stay out of the warehouse.

She failed.

Friar dragged her across the threshold. Just as her skin tingled from the magic of the wards she heard the raucous *boom* of a shotgun.

Friar slammed the door shut.

FORTY-THREE

～

LILY'S side hurt. Her cheek throbbed. Her hip burned from being dragged across concrete. But Friar had let go for the moment. Cautiously she sat up.

"We need to leave," Friar said. "Now."

"But my people—" Benessarai waved at the door. Someone screamed.

"Are you going out there to rescue them? No? Then we must depart." When Benessarai stood staring at the closed door, Friar snapped, "It saw you. Saw all of us. It looks like a tiger, but I don't know what it is. It wasn't fooled by your illusions. How long will your wards keep it out?"

Benessarai drew himself up, offended. "The wards are strong."

"Good. That means you have time to— No, you don't."

Lily had quietly scooted away and started to gather her feet under her. Friar grabbed her arm again and pulled her up. It hurt. He shook her. "What do you know about that tiger?"

"Do you think," Benessarai said nervously, "that those lupi are behind this?"

There was another scream outside. It ended abruptly.

It was silent inside, too. Lily's heart was hammering, but she took advantage of the quiet to look around.

From the outside, the warehouse hadn't looked very large. Inside it seemed oddly bigger, maybe because of the way the lights were hung on the rafters, pointing down. That left the high ceiling in shadows, making it seem even more distant. Lily gave those shadowy heights one quick glance. A misty white cloud hung motionless up there.

She couldn't see very far into the warehouse because of the way the shipping crates were stacked; the nearest row blocked her view. The immediate area was set up like an office, with short partitions on two sides. There was a counter flanking the door, an ancient vinyl sofa, some filing cabinets, a water cooler, and two desks.

There were also two bodies.

Alycithin and Dinalaran had been laid on the floor in the open space before the rows of crates started. A large, perfect circle glowed around them . . . glowed from the floor up, as if the cement had decided to luminesce. Their dead hands had been folded around the two knives that rested on their chests. Mage lights hovered at the head and foot of each corpse.

No sign of Adam King. If he was here, he wasn't making any sound.

Friar broke the silence. "I believe," he said, "you forgot this." He held out the bowling-ball bag. Lily had forgotten all about it. Friar had remembered even while being charged by a Siberian tiger. The prototype must be in there.

Benessarai accepted it and replied with icy precision. "I appreciate your care for my property."

Friar let his shoulders droop. "I"—he ran a hand over his hair—"I'm sorry for how I spoke to you. I was . . . the beast shook me badly. I admit it."

Benessarai thawed, but only slightly. "Courtesy means little if you possess it only when all is well."

"You are right," Friar sighed, a man who saw his limitations all too clearly. He knew how to play the elf, even if he'd forgotten in the stress of the moment.

The thaw continued. "I suppose we must go. That beast shattered my concentration. Its presence will draw attention here."

"Will you grant me a small boon? My man is either dead or otherwise unavailable. Would you ask one of yours to guard my prize while I retrieve my things?"

"Oh, very well." The fabulous master of mind-magic sounded like a petulant child. "You can fetch my hostage while you're back there. Use the charm so he doesn't give you any trouble."

"Of course." Friar even gave him a little bow.

Benessarai spoke briefly to the two remaining elves— the ones who'd brought the bodies in. One of them—Lily thought this one was female, though it was hard to be sure with those long, loose shirts—headed their way. Her face was as impassive as ever, though she did dart one quick glance at the door when the tiger roared again.

Friar bent close and whispered in Lily's ear, "You have a short reprieve. Behave, and perhaps I won't make you pay too badly for the delay." He shoved her to the floor.

She fell hard. Again. Her ribs ached where he'd kicked her. The side of her face throbbed. When had Friar gotten so bloody damn strong?

When *she* was busy remaking him, of course. When he hung suspended in what had been a gate until Rethna tampered with it. His goddess had given him his patterning Gift. She must have decided to make a few more alterations while she was at it.

While Friar vanished amid the packing crates, Benessarai had moved to the large circle that held the two people he'd killed. He began rolling up his sleeves, paused, frowned, and said something in his language.

Lily's new guard repeated it, or something very like it, and seized Lily by her restraints the way Alycithin had. And pushed. Apparently she was supposed to move forward. She did, but as slowly as possible.

Hurry, she thought. It wasn't mindspeech. She still couldn't nudge that dial. But she thought it anyway.

She didn't feel any tingle of magic when the elf steered her across the circle, which meant the circle wasn't activated. "So how are we leaving?" she asked. "Not via a gate. There's no node."

"A gate?" He smiled at her pleasantly. She'd accidentally stroked his ego, though, hadn't she? Implying he could actually open a gate all by himself. "Not that, but something quite clever. Robert taught it to me, but he can only execute it on himself. I, of course, am able to do much more. I shall send all of us out of phase, and then we may walk out unimpeded."

Out of phase . . . invisible and untouchable, in other words. Like demons could do when they weren't in their home realm. "Friar taught you a demon trick?"

"Don't be absurd. Demons don't exist."

"Could have fooled me. The ones in Dis sure looked real. The dragons thought they were, and I tend to trust dragons on that sort of thing."

He frowned. "You refer to the soulless."

"You could call them that, I guess. We call them demons."

"And you claim to have been to Dis and to converse with dragons." He shook his head. "It is most annoying that I cannot simply cast a truth spell on you. Clearly you are not telling the truth, and yet—but this is not the time for discussion. Sit down out of my way. There," he said, pointing next to Alycithin's body.

The elf made sure Lily sat exactly where Benessarai wanted her and seated herself on the concrete floor, too. Lily found herself looking at the woman who'd captured her and brought her here and used the last split-second of her life saving Lily's.

Exit wounds are always worse than entry wounds, and Dinalaran had shot her in the back. He must have been using hollow points. He'd fired twice, and it looked like they'd both hit her about heart high and blown out a good chunk of her chest on their way out. One breast was gone. The other was pretty torn up.

It made Lily sick and sad. Alycithin hadn't been a good guy by human standards, but by those of her people she'd been deeply honorable. And so alive, so vital and curious. And now she was meat. Lily took a slow breath and turned herself enough that her back was to the corpse. Her elf guard didn't object.

The other elf had knelt near but not at the edge of the circle. Eyes closed, he chanted softly. Rethna's flunkies had done this, too—either adding their power to his or performing an active part of the spell, she wasn't sure which. Benessarai was moving around the circle in a slow, deliberate way. He didn't chant. The circle kept glowing faintly. No magic prickled over Lily's skin. But the look of intense concentration on his face said he was doing something, even if she had no idea what.

He stopped. "Robert, what is keeping you? I cannot finish until you and the hostage are within the circle."

"I'm coming." A moment later he appeared. He carried a large duffel in one hand. With the other he guided Adam King.

Lily knew from the file that Adam King was Caucasian, forty-eight, five-ten, and one sixty. She knew his features were even, save for a crooked nose that had been broken twenty years ago. What the file hadn't told her was how inviting his face was. King had one of those lived-in faces, the kind that says its owner has spent plenty of time laughing or crying, singing and shouting. The kind with friendly creases. His hair was dark and cropped very short. His eyes were brown and dazed. He looked around as the two of them moved into the broad aisle between the packing crates . . . and stopped.

"This is what kept me," Friar said, exasperated. "The charm keeps him docile, but he loses track of what he's doing. Come on, Adam."

"You can't be rough with him," Benessarai warned. "It disrupts the charm."

"Yes," Friar said with heavy patience. "I know."

A dead woman touched Lily's hand.

Lily jerked. She couldn't help it. The dead hand did something, and her restraints, the thrice-damned restraints, fell silently away. Lily's arms trembled as her own muscles took over the job of holding her hands behind her back.

The dead woman placed a knife in Lily's right hand.

Friar got Adam moving again.

"Well," Lily said loudly, "it looks like it's now or never."

A burning man fell from the ceiling.

Flames covered him completely. He fell headfirst, like a diver, but flipped in midair as if determined that his corpse would land on its feet.

Lily thrust to her feet as her elf guard reached for her. She slashed with the dead woman's knife—not trying for a specific target, just forcing the elf back, but she connected anyway. An arm, nothing fatal, but at least she hadn't gotten her knife stuck, and the elf backed off. Lily spun toward Benessarai—who shouted something.

The lights went out.

Lily sprang at him.

Benessarai was many things, most of them repellent. He was heavier, taller, and stronger than her, but he was not a fighter, and his mind tricks did not work on her. Lily felt the knife connect, but in the darkness she didn't know what she'd struck. Benessarai squealed in rage or fear and grabbed her, yanking her to him in a bear hug. "I've got her!" he shouted. "I've got Lily Yu! Stop or I'll kill her!"

Lily's arms were imprisoned. So she used her head.

The cranium near the hairline is one of the thickest regions of bone on the skull. Lily couldn't reach some of the best targets for a headbutt—he was too tall—so she smashed the top of her forehead into his chin. As she connected, she hooked his ankle with her foot and pulled.

He toppled. She came down on top of him, cracking her left elbow on the floor but keeping a tight grip on the knife in her right hand. Mage lights popped up all over the place, and she saw Benessarai's slack face—stunned, she thought, not out, so she pressed the tip of her borrowed knife to the spot right under his chin where a hard thrust would take it up to his brain. Then took the chance of glancing behind her for the guard elf.

Who was several feet away, fighting a wolf.

People were falling from the roof. Leaping down and falling.

One of them was Rule. Her heart exulted even as she turned back to her prisoner.

It would be easy, so easy, to end him here and now. More fitting to do it through the eye the way he'd made Dinalaran kill himself, but she wasn't going to pass up easy to go for poetic.

"Don't! Lily, don't do it!"

It was Drummond. And he was a mess.

He crouched in front of her. One arm hung down. It probably didn't work right because a big chunk of his bicep was missing. Just gone. He crouched on both knees, but she only saw one foot. The other leg ended cleanly about midcalf. His shirt hung open. Skin and muscle were missing from his middle. She could see one of his ribs, the pale curve of it, and the round pillow of his stomach, and the segmented worms of his intestines. Which were also a mess, ripped and ragged.

No blood. Somehow that made it worse. He'd been ripped apart, but he couldn't bleed.

"You've got a choice," Drummond said urgently. "You don't have to do it."

"What happened to you?" she whispered.

He glanced down at his ravaged middle. His mouth crooked up. "I got there, got to Turner, but it was not a smooth trip. I guess I'm finally dying. So listen up. That scumbag deserves to die, but you don't deserve to live with what that will do to you. You don't deserve to end up like me."

His arm was fading. The one hanging down, the one with a chunk missing—it was dimming, going away. She swallowed. "I—"

He leaned closer, scowling. "Promise me. Promise me you won't kill him. Not like this."

She looked him in the eye and nodded slightly. "Okay. I promise."

He exhaled in relief. "Good choice. You're a good cop, and we don't have enough—" Suddenly his head tilted. He looked up and to his right. His mouth fell open. She could swear tears filled his eyes—and joy. He reached up, his face lit with happiness as real as anything she'd ever seen. He reached up with his remaining hand, the wedding band on the third finger glowing softly.

"Sarah," he said. And the rest of him faded away.

Lily felt shaky and weird inside. Kind of hollowed out. Then the body beneath her tensed, and she was called back to reality. *This* reality. Benessarai was looking up at her. She sighed and pressed the knife into his skin slightly to make him pay attention. "So what the hell do I do with you?"

"I can help with that," Cullen said. He limped over, wincing with every step. He was missing half his hair, and he looked like he had a bad sunburn.

"Cullen! That was you falling? You didn't—"

"Didn't burn. Much. I couldn't get the last damn ward down, but it was a fire ward, and I'm good with fire, so I took it down by leaping through it. Landed badly, though— my ankle's got a hairline fracture, I think. It took a lot of concentration to keep the flames from burning me until I could snuff them." He sank down carefully to sit by Benessarai's head. "Good thing this asshole doesn't know about mage fire, or I'd be really crispy. Nighty-night," he said, and slapped his palm onto the elf's forehead.

Benessarai went limp, his eyes closing.

"Sleep charm," Cullen added. "Don't know how long it will work on his sort. You okay?"

"Not . . . long," a breathy voice said on Lily's right.

Lily turned to see the not-so-dead Alycithin smiling faintly at her. She scooted close. "What can we do? How do we help you?"

"Aroglian . . . will help. Give him . . . ring and word. *Thelaisat*." She closed her eyes as if gathering herself. "I bequeath to you, Lily Yu, my . . . rights and responsibilities for . . . Sean Friar, hostage. You . . . accept?"

"I do."

"Say . . . the word."

"*Thelaisat*," Lily repeated. Alycithin's wince might have been at Lily's mangling of her language, or simple pain. "That one . . ." The halfling's gaze shifted to indicate Benessarai. "Best if . . . you kill."

"I can't. I gave my word."

The slightly lifted brows expressed incredulity. Alycithin didn't ask who Lily had promised, though. Instead she said, "Duct tape."

"Duct tape."

"On . . . mouth, hands, feet. Strong. Magically . . . inert."

"Cullen, did you hear that?"

"Mike!" Cullen called. "We need duct tape, pronto. I've got a couple more sleep charms," he added, "which is good, because he's almost burned this one up."

"You shocked the hell out of me when you touched me," Lily said. "And undid the restraints, for which I thank you with my whole heart."

The eyebrows lifted again. "You . . . did not know? Said . . . now or never."

"That was for Rule. I knew he was on the roof. I thought you were dead. You fooled Benessarai, too, when he did that spell."

Alycithin's eyes closed, but her lips turned up. "The fool . . . right about one thing. Rekklat . . . hard to kill. My Gift . . . he didn't notice. . . . I was alive."

"Your Gift doesn't work on me, and I've never seen anyone look as dead as you did who wasn't." She hadn't been breathing. Lily was sure of that.

"Not . . . very alive. More now, but . . ." Very faintly she sighed. "I will sleep."

Outside, a tiger roared. Lily looked up. "Grandmother—"

Rule stepped into view at the end of an aisle between shipping crates. "Let Madame Yu in," he snapped at someone.

"Friar?" she asked, pushing herself to her feet.

"No sign of him. His scent trail ends at the back of the warehouse."

"He knows a spell to go out of phase like—" Rule had reached her and his arms closed around her. Tight. "Ow. My rib." But she held on, too.

He loosened his grip immediately and straightened to inspect her worriedly. "Are you all right? Your face." He touched her cheek gently. "Someone hit you."

"Friar. He's gotten a lot stronger than he used to be. I don't think he broke any ribs, but they're tender."

Rule's mouth tightened. "That would be why Madame rushed things, I imagine. She was to wait for our signal. Cullen took down the first ward—there were only two—but the second was harder."

"Not on Rethna's level, thank all the gods," Cullen said, "but a good, workmanlike job. I couldn't untangle it in the time I had."

"Which is why," Rule said dryly, "he knocked me aside—damn near knocked me off the bloody roof—so he could make his heroic dive."

"Because you were about to do it," Cullen said promptly, "and you are *not* good with fire."

Lily shivered at how close it had been.

"You're all right?" Rule asked again.

"I'm good. Sore here and there, but good. What about . . . do we have any casualties? From last night or now?"

"Minor wounds, nothing serious. I think we managed to keep one of the other two elves in here alive." He turned his head. "Scott? Is your captive going to make it?"

"I think so. He's still out."

"Duct tape," Lily said. "We'll need it for him, too. And we have to send someone to the apartment with Alycithin's ring so Argolian will release Sean Friar and come here to help Alycithin, and—" She broke off to smile. "Grandmother."

Todd had opened the door. The tiger who slinked in was as huge as Grandmother was small in her usual shape. Her head reached Todd's chest. Her tail lashed as she stalked forward. Flecks of blood, drying now, marred her beautiful coat.

Lily didn't ask if any of those outside had survived. Tigers, Grandmother had said once, see no point in disabling an enemy.

The tiger came straight to Lily and rubbed up against her. Firmly. Lily would have fallen if Rule hadn't caught her. "Hey." She grinned and knelt on one knee and ran her hands through the great cat's ruff, scratching where she knew it felt good. Grandmother purred. She was a lot more demonstrative as a tiger. "Thank you," Lily told her.

She got a tiger tongue in her face in return. Tiger tongues are about 120 grit. She laughed and gave Grandmother a last rub along her cheekbone, and the tiger turned and lay down next to Benessarai. She laid one huge paw on his chest—pinning her prey, maybe, but she was still purring, so Lily was pretty sure she wasn't going to rip out his throat.

Lily stood. Rule immediately slid his arm around her waist. He needed the contact, she thought. She did, too, so she leaned into him.

"I have never even imagined seeing anything like that." Jasper had come in behind Grandmother. He watched her now with wide, wondering eyes. "A were-tiger."

"Not exactly," Lily said. "You've been told that you aren't to speak of this? Ever?"

He nodded and tore his attention from the great cat. "Have you seen—"

"Jasper."

Adam King looked a bit wobbly from the aftereffects of the charm, but his eyes were clear. Alan was steadying him with one hand, but he pulled free. "Jasper!"

Lily got to see joy all over again, on two faces this time. The two men were struck motionless by it for a second, then Jasper ran and Adam wobbled forward and they hung on to each other, talking and crying . . . about like she was doing with Rule, except for the crying. Though maybe her eyes were a bit damp. She leaned back to look at Rule's face. "We've got a lot to do. Alycithin needs care we can't give her. We need to free Sean Friar, too."

"I know." But he didn't let go. "Tell me something."

"What?"

"When I . . . when you seemed to want to go to find Hugo, and I . . . did you know what I was doing? Trying to trick you to keep you safe?"

She snorted. "You are not that sneaky, Rule."

Behind her a tiger huffed in what might have been amusement.

FORTY-FOUR

~~

ON New Year's Eve, at three thirty, Lily said goodbye to her new friend of the fifth degree. Alycithin had healed almost completely from her terrible wounds. She was going home via the gate in D.C. The powers that be had decided the least embarrassing thing was to agree with Alycithin that she could take custody of the criminals and return them to their realm.

They might not have come to that decision, diplomatic immunity or no, if Lily hadn't edited her official report carefully. If she had not, in fact, left some things out completely. Sean didn't object. He'd grown to like Alycithin, too.

Sam had returned to his lair without speaking to her.

Lily knew now why he'd shut her out so abruptly. Grandmother had explained. Part of Benessarai's payment to Robert Friar had included three psi bombs—something she'd never heard of—that an agent of Friar's had been taking back east aboard a 747. The man had accidentally detonated them. Sam had foreseen this and reached the plane in time, but he'd had to hold a shield around the blast to keep it from driving everyone aboard insane, including the pilot.

Had he faltered for even a second, the plane would have crashed.

In other words, Sam was a hero and Lily had no excuse for holding a grudge. Four hundred lives had hung in the balance, and she had been a distraction he could not afford. In her head, Lily knew there was nothing to forgive. He'd done the right thing. All of which left her confused and not liking herself much. She didn't know if she was angry or hurt or just pouting, but she couldn't seem to let it go. She couldn't forget that slammed door.

Otherwise, things were pretty good. The day after to-morrow, on the second day of the new year, she and Rule had an appointment. With a real estate agent. They'd be looking for a property with a fair amount of land, some-thing not too far from the city, but also not too far from Clanhome. Toby had been shuffled around enough. They wanted him to be able to continue his schooling at Clan-home.

But Rule couldn't live there anymore. Not now that he was fully Leidolf Rho. They would find a property with land enough for wolves to run and either a really large house or two houses. They'd still need plenty of security, and besides, Rule wanted to bring more Leidolf out here. Time, he said, he started training more of them away from certain habits their old Rho had instilled.

The whole thing made Lily nervous. Rule had consid-ered paying cash, but decided it would leave him with too little cushion. This purchase was on him, mostly. Lily sure couldn't afford the kind of place they needed, Leidolf didn't have the funds, and it was not something Nokolai could help with. So they'd be signing a mortgage. One whopping big mortgage, even with Rule making a whopping big down payment. Land did not come cheap.

Tonight, though—tonight was for Rule. Rule and Noko-lai.

Lupi made a big deal about New Year's Eve. At least Nokolai did. Christmas they considered more of a private time, one you spent with family or friends, but New Year's

Eve was for clan. They had a big bonfire, lots of food, dancing, and music, and everyone came who could. You were supposed to bring something to toss on the bonfire, something that stood for whatever you wanted to let go of along with the old year. People starting adding their whatevers around eleven so everyone would have a chance to finish before midnight, when the Rhej would ring a big old cowbell to let everyone know.

This was Cynna's first time to have that duty. She was kind of nervous about it.

Some of the letting-go objects were funny, like Hostess cupcakes Emma tossed on the fire with a shout of "Junk food!" Some were a mystery to everyone else, like the small rubber ball José contributed. Several lupi gave him a hard time for stinking up the place—rubber smells awful when it burns—but he just smiled. A lot of people simply brought a piece of paper with something written on it.

That's what Rule did. Lily didn't know what he'd written on it, but he'd nodded as it turned black and burned.

Lily brought a stone from her necklace—the one that was supposed to keep ghosts away. It wouldn't burn, but it was the idea that counted, she figured. She knew what she was letting go of as she chunked it on the flames. If she'd had to put a word to it, she would have said, "judgment," but it was both more and less than that.

Drummond hadn't come back.

When Lily was nine years old, a monster had stolen her and her friend. He'd raped and killed Sarah. Lily was alive because of a cop who got there in time. Since she was nine years old, she'd known two things: there were monsters who looked like people. And one day she would become a cop and protect the real people from the monsters. By the time she joined the force, she'd understood that the monsters were real people, too—twisted and warped and bad, but people. But her goal hadn't changed.

When Lily was eight years old, she'd wanted the monster who killed Sarah dead. She'd wanted to be the one who killed him. That was one of the few things she'd been able to say about what happened to her, and it had alarmed her mother. The therapist they'd sent her to had wanted to talk about feelings, not actions. She hadn't known what to say to a child who dreamed of murder.

Grandmother had. She'd patted Lily on the back and said, "Of course you wish to kill him. However, you cannot. Now go kill the weeds in my garden. Pull them out by the roots. Pull out the grass, too. Kill as much of it as you can."

Lily still loved to garden.

It had taken another twenty years for her to understand there had been another reason for her to become a cop. She'd needed the rules. She was capable of killing, and she'd needed to know exactly what the rules were so she wouldn't kill unless it was absolutely necessary.

She stood in the circle of Rule's arm and watched the bonfire, feeling its heat on her face. Two people had brought fiddles and were starting to play. She'd dance in a bit. Her head hadn't been concussed, and if her ribs were still bruised, that wouldn't matter. Rule's gunshot wound—which he had not told her about until she saw it—was fully healed. So she'd dance with Rule, and with others, too. She'd lived, and he had, and everyone here tonight had made it through this year in spite of the war. They would celebrate that.

Some hadn't made it through the year. Too many.

Lily wasn't sure if she would have killed Benessarai if Drummond hadn't shown up to exact that promise, but maybe. Maybe she would. That was not a comfortable thing to know about herself. If she'd killed him, it wouldn't have been because she had to, or even for the pragmatic reason that it was damn hard to imprison a sidhe with his skills. She'd have done it because she could, and he deserved death for what he'd done.

She still thought he deserved to die, but it wasn't up to her. It never had been up to her. That's what she'd tossed on the fire a few minutes ago.

Sometimes the bad guys did redeem themselves, wholly and completely. That's what she'd learned from Drummond. That's why it wasn't up to her.

"This is going to sound stupid," she said, "but I kind of miss him."

"Miss who?"

"Drummond."

"You're right. That sounds pretty stupid."

She elbowed him. "You're supposed to reassure me."

"Can't. I tossed that sort of thing on the fire just now."

She turned in his arms to look at him directly, looping her arms around his neck loosely. "I'm guessing you don't mean you've given up reassuring me."

He ran a finger along the side of her face, which was still a bit swollen. "I gave up thinking I can make better choices for you than you can. Being less than honest with you. And in all honesty, it does sound pretty dumb for you to—"

Rule was really ticklish under his arms. She got him good, and of course he retaliated, so they were both laughing when Cynna rang the cowbell good and loud, welcoming in the new year.

EPILOGUE

~

IN a place that was not quite a place as we think of them, two people were doing what, here, people often do in a bed.

No, not that. Though their reunion had been joyous and prolonged and had included plenty of sex—or something as like to sex as makes no difference, even though they did not have bodies as we know bodies—just now they were sleeping. Or enjoying something very like sleep, but enough of the circumlocutions. We have no way of truly understanding that place, so we'll continue from this point on as if they were here and use the terms we know . . .

He woke first. That was habit and normal and familiar and quite wonderful. It gave him the chance to watch her sleep when he had thought he'd never have such a moment again.

A restless man most of the time, this morning—and it was morning, in all the ways that matter—he was at peace. At least until she woke and smiled at him. She touched his cheek, tracing furrows put there by a life lived hard and mostly right, though when he'd gone wrong, he'd done so spectacularly. As she'd told him tartly at one point, for they'd talked as well as making love. "When are you leaving?" she asked.

He scowled. "What are you talking about?"

"Oh, please. When have you ever been able to relax and enjoy a vacation?"

He blinked. "Vacation? They, uh, said this was a place of rest. I thought . . . it's beautiful here."

"It is. Very beautiful." She was laughing at him now. "Rest, vacation—whatever we call it, this isn't a place to stay forever. Though some people enjoy resting, or so I've heard."

He didn't relax at her teasing. "I, uh, I've been offered a job."

"I felt sure you would be. Come on, let's get up. I'm hungry."

They fixed breakfast together, just as they had for most of their lives. Those other lives, that is, but that's a distinction without a difference. He told her a bit about the job.

He'd been offered it by . . . an angel, he supposed, the same one who had spent time with him when he lost himself in the gray, then had forgotten almost completely. Of course *angel* was the wrong word. He knew that. The wrong word, the wrong everything, for whatever had offered this work to him, it so far surpassed his understanding of beings and boundaries that it made words meaningless. So he thought of it as the angel, and left it at that.

"Whatever it was Friar took out of there with him, it was nasty. And tied to this side of the line in a way I don't like at all. Neither did the, uh . . . whoever offered me the job."

She nodded seriously. "I heard something about that." When he looked surprised she laughed again. She'd always laughed easily, but the happiness seemed to bubble up even more freely now. "Come on, I told you I'd been meeting people. Looking around a bit while I decide what I'm going to do now."

"Yeah, but I never see anyone around for you to talk to."

"Because you don't want to. If you'd been interested . . .

but never mind." She reached across and took his hand. "Al, it's okay. When did I ever kick up a fuss because of your job? I don't want or expect you to spend a few eons sunbathing on the beach with me."

Now he smiled. "You hate sunbathing."

"True. So. When are you leaving?"

His hand tightened on hers. "Not yet. I need more time with you, more time to . . . but when I do take the job I won't be gone constantly. I'll be able to take . . . not weekends, but time here, now and then. Time with you. I won't remember things here when I'm back there, not very well, but I'll know I've been with you." He felt sure of that now.

"Memory works differently there than it does here," she agreed. "But the good things stay with us."

"Yeah." He looked at their joined hands, at the rings that glowed on each of their hands. "Yeah, the good things stay." He grinned suddenly and looked exactly like the wicked twenty-nine-year-old man she'd first fallen in love with. Exactly—because memory did indeed work differently here. "And I've got to admit, I'm really looking forward to seeing Yu's face when I show up again."

CAST OF CHARACTERS

Al Drummond: FBI agent who went bad, he was killed at the end of *Death Magic*—yet remained as a ghost somehow tied to Lily.

Beth (Elizabeth) Yu: Lily's younger sister. Twenty-five in *Mortal Ties*. Roommates are Deirdre (short, shiny blond hair, a nose stud, five piercings in one ear and three in the other; doesn't trust even numbers) and Susan (same name as Beth's oldest sister).

Celeste Babineaux: Rule and Jasper's mother. Bipolar. Deceased.

Cullen Seabourne: Sorcerer and lupus, adopted into Nokolai clan after being expelled from his birth clan (Etorri) and living for many years as a lone wolf. Sixty. Married to Cynna Weaver.

Cynna Weaver: A Finder and spellcaster who follows a Swahili tradition that imprints spells on the skin like tattoos. FBI agent. Thirty-two.

Isen Turner: Nokolai Rho. Burly and bearded, he's ninety-one years old but looks around fifty.

Jasper Machek: Rule's newly discovered half brother or *alius* kin (means otherkin) on his mother's side.

Leo Romano: Laban Rho until forced to step down, passing his clan's mantle to his heir, Tony Romano.

Li Lei Yu, aka Grandmother: Lily's grandmother on her father's side. Much older than she looks.

Lily Yu: Homicide detective in Book 1 (*Tempting Danger*); joined the Unit (FBI) at end of that book. She's twenty-nine in *Mortal Ties*. She was abducted by a child rapist when she was eight. Rule's Chosen, Lily is a touch sensitive—she identifies the presence of magic through touch, but cannot be affected by it.

Michael Machek: Jasper's father.

Ruben Brooks: Head of Unit Twelve of the FBI with an incredibly accurate precognitive Gift. Became both lupus and Rho in *Death Magic*.

Rule Turner: Nokolai Lu Nuncio or heir; Leidolf Rho. The press call him the Nokolai prince. Dark hair and dark eyes, he is fifty-five, but looks about thirty. He was raised by his father at Nokolai Clanhome.

Ryder: Cynna and Cullen's new baby daughter.

Sarah Drummond: Al's wife, killed by Martha Billings.

Toby Asteglio: Rule's son. He's nine and lives with Rule and Lily.

Tony Romano: Laban Rho. Tall, muscular, and gorgeous, he suffered brain damage as a child, and while First Change enabled him to heal the neurological damage, he still thinks slowly—but thoroughly. Often underestimated.

THE LEIDOLF SQUAD

Alan

Barnaby

Chris

Ian

Jeffrey

Joe

Marcus

Mike

Patrick McCausey

Scott White (in charge)

Steve

Todd

OFF-STAGE OR BRIEF APPEARANCE

Arjenie Fox: Benedict's Chosen; a researcher for the FBI; part-sidhe

Benedict: Rule's oldest brother; in charge of security at Clanhome

Brenda: Questioned by Lily; she talked too much to her Laban lover

Carl: Isen's houseman

Carrie Ann Rucker: "Mule" for drug cartel, fifty-nine, a placid woman with graying blond hair and a crooked front tooth

David: Nokolai guard

Hank Jamison: Young Laban culprit

Hannah: Previous Nokolai Rhej

Isadora Bourque: Nokolai's chief tender

Merowitch: Explosives guy

Mick: Rule's brother who died

Pete: Benedict's second

Sherrianne: Questioned by Lily at Clanhome

THE SIDHE

Alycithin: Co-leader of the trade delegation; a halfling with tawny fur, a darker ruff atop her head, and bright green eyes. Muscular and about Lily's height. Came up through the warrior class.

Aroglian: The other elf with Alycithin. An expert spellcaster who specializes in body magic, including healing. White hair.

Benessarai: The other co-leader of the delegation. Son of a sidhe lord, heavily outranks Alycithin socially, which means he's really in charge. Copper-colored hair.

Dinalaran: One of Alycithin's assistants; armed with a SIG, does the driving. Creamsicle-orange hair.

Lord Sessena: Benessarai's mother and Alycithin's sponsor. Powerful sidhe lord in her realm.

Lord Thierath: Benessarai's father.

GLOSSARY

ELFIN OR SIDHE WORDS

arguai: power from an unknown source; not magic, often spiritual

dielgraf: soul-enemy

Rekklat: a catlike race in Alycithin's realm, known for their skill as warriors and remarkable endurance; Alycithin's father is Rekklat

seurthurin: one who practices the arts of the mind (mind-magic, such as illusion) *so'amellree*: one of the sixteen words for enemy; describes one who might be a friend, were circumstances different (fem. form)

so'elriath: an enemy for whom one feels no hostility, one who is simply on the other side

Thalinol: the Queens' realm

LUPI WORDS

Historically, lupus clans in Europe and Britain used Latin to communicate with each other for the same reason it was adopted by the Church—the need for a unifying tongue. Their version evolved, as languages will, into a thoroughly bastardized tongue likely to make classical scholars wince. In addition, there are a few words used by the lupi that have no known derivation. Lupi claim these words come from an ancient language that predates Latin, but since Latin predates 1000 BCE, experts consider this unlikely.

The use of Latin to communicate between the clans is dying out now, since so many lupi speak English as a first or second language, though it's still considered essential for a Rho and his sons, who must negotiate with other clans. Several of the words and phrases remain useful, though, since they have no obvious English equivalent. Below are a few of the words and phrases any lupus would know.

amica: uncommon, but still used. Means friend/girlfriend (fem.); a lupus might call a male friend of the same clan *adun*, from *adiungo* (to join to, connect, associate).

ardor iunctio: literally, "fire of joining." Symbolic fire used at some ceremonies, most notably the *gens compleo*.

certa: "a place of ice and clarity, where sensation is sharp enough to cut and action flows too swiftly for thought." It's a battle state; sensations heightened, thought clear but altered. Opposite of *furo*.

drei: tithe or head tax; it's a percentage of income or wealth given to the clan.

du: honor, face, history, reputation; has magical component. Predates Latin.

firnam: derivation unknown; a memorial for one fallen in battle.

fratriodi: brother-hate. A grave sin among the lupi.

furo: also called "the fury." Battle fury or madness. Clanless lupi are especially subject to it, but it can happen to those within a clan, though it's rare.

gens amplexi: literally, "clan embrace"; ceremony of adoption into clan. From *gens* (clan, tribe, people) + *amplexor* (embrace, welcome, love).

gens compleo: literally, "clan to fill up or complete"; the ceremony in which a young lupus (at age twenty-four) is confirmed as an adult clan member.

gens subicio: *subicio* means "to put under or expose; to subject; to place near or present." When one Rho dies and a new one assumes the mantles, a *gens subicio* is held at which each member of a clan presents himself to his new Rho and ritually submits.

Lu Nuncio: normally, a Rho's acknowledged heir; also acts as enforcer/prosecutor/second-in-command as needed. (Note: Leidolf has separated the heir from the Lu Nuncio.) *Nuncio* is from *nuncupo*—"to name or pronounce solemnly." Derivation of *lu* unknown, but may be short form of *lupi*.

nadia: mate (fem.); from *nodus -i* (masc.)—a knot; a girdle; any tie, bond, connection, obligation; also a knotty point or difficulty.

ospi: out-clan friend or friend of the clan; from *hospes* (host, guest—friend, stranger).

pernato: a lupus who didn't have a lupus father. A *pernato* is lupi because of recessives in both parents' genes. (Also called throwbacks or lost ones, if one occurs that the lupi weren't tracking. Term first mentioned in *Blood Challenge*.)

Rhej: the title of a clan's bard/historian/priestess. Also predates Latin.

Rho: the ruler/leader of a lupus clan. Derivation unknown; legend says it predates Latin.

seco: part of "to call *seco*"—to call the ceremony that removes a lupus from his clan.

surdo: an unflattering name for humans (masc.). From *surdus* (deaf, unwilling to hear, insensible).

t'eius ven: the intimate or informal form of *v'eius ven*.

terra tradis: the private area where a clan's male youngsters go before their First Change and live until they learn control. *Tradis* is a bastardized form of *trado* (to bequeath, to teach), so it means "the teaching ground."

thranga: a form of war in which the clans unite under a single battle leader against a common enemy; traditionally it requires the Lady's summons, but the nature of that summons may be disputed. Predates Latin.

v'eius ven: probably derived from a phrase meaning "go in her [the Lady's] grace," though some sources suggest *ven* may be from *venor* (hunt) rather than *venia* (grace), or even from *vena* (blood vessel or penis). This form is largely ceremonial.

vesceris corpi: a major insult—translates literally as "eater of corpses" and implies taking a certain carnal pleasure in the act.

LUPI: THE CLANS

There are currently twenty-four clans; ten of them are considered dominant. Four of the ten dominants are in the United States; two are in Canada; one is in Africa; one is in Great Britain; one is in Sweden; one is in the Italian Alps; and one is in eastern Europe.

A dominant clan possesses an especially strong mantle. Occasionally a dominant clan will accept temporary subordinate status to another clan, as Kyffin did with Nokolai in Book 1; it's still considered dominant because the mantle is unaffected. A clan loses dominant status—and may lose its mantle and identity—when it loses a Clan Challenge. Clan Challenges are rare and can mean outright war, but fundamentally they are a contest between the clans' mantles and may be settled by individual combat between the two Rhos. All but two of the nondominant clans are subordinated to one of the dominants. Nondominant clans are small, since the size of the clan has an effect on the strength of its mantle, and vice versa. Etorri is the exception. It's very small, yet its mantle is extremely powerful.

The most powerful clans currently are Nokolai and Leidolf, closely followed by Ybirra. Etorri wields great influence based on its *du*, but it lacks direct power because of its small size.

Below are the ten dominant clans:

UNITED STATES

Nokolai: Rule's clan. Rho: Isen Turner. Rhej: Hannah. Originally from the Brittany region of France. Nokolai is the fourth largest clan (Leidolf, Ybirra, and Mondoyo are larger) and has the most subordinate clans—four, with two in the United States (Laban and Vochi)—and is the most wealthy. Clanhome is in southern California.

Leidolf: A numerous clan, traditional enemies of Nokolai, implicated in the attack on Rule's father [Books 1, 2, 3]. Randall Frey is the Lu Nuncio (heir) in the first two books, but is killed in Book 3. The Rho in Books 1–5 is Victor Frey. Victor's other son is Brady Gunning, a sociopath: "tall, blond, and bony; nice chest." Their Rhej is Ella—African American, tall, broad frame, Baptist. Leidolf currently has no subordinate clans.

After Book 3: Randall Frey is dead; Rule is Leidolf heir; Alex Thibodeaux (grizzled, just under six feet, built like a pro wrestler, with skin the color of burnt toast) is Lu Nuncio for the clan; and their Rho (Victor Frey) is in a coma and dying. He dies in Book 5 (*Mortal Sins*).

Szós: Hungarian clan that immigrated to the United States; Rikard Demeny is Lu Nuncio in Book 2. After that, Lu Nuncio is Lucas, third-born son of Rho Andor Demeny. Fierce fighters. One subordinate clan (Czech; didn't immigrate).

Ybirra: Large Spanish clan; the newest clan, founded in 1882 by Tomás Ybirra. Javiero Mendozo is Lu Nuncio; Manuel Mendoza is Rho. Clanhome in New Mexico. One subordinate clan four years before the opening of the series.

Wythe: A midsized clan with a Clanhome in northern New York; the last clan to immigrate to the United States. Originally from England. Lu Nuncio is Brian Whitman, younger brother of the Rho Edgar Whitman. Both Edgar and Brian die in Book 8.

CANADA

Etorri: A tiny clan with great *du* (honor, face, magic, history); Stephen Andros is Lu Nuncio. Previous Rho was William Carr; current one is Frederick Andros. Follows different rules for succession and does not accept subordinate clans. Clanhome is in eastern Canada. Etorri is said to be Greek, though the identity of its founder is one of many secrets kept by the clan. Etorri is a puzzle to the other clans.

Kyffin: The smallest dominant other than Etorri, based in western Canada; Jasper Herron, the Rho, is unusually young (forty) and a friend of Rule's. Subordinate to Nokolai for a year and a day, starting in middle of Book 1. The Lu Nuncio is Jasper's uncle, Myron, as Jasper's son is too young. Kyffin's influence is due largely to their friendly relations with pretty much every other clan.

EUROPE

Ansgar: Scandinavian; Clanhome in Sweden. Ben Larson is Lu Nuncio. Not a large clan, but three very small clans are subordinate to Ansgar, increasing its voice.

Cynyr: A Celtic clan; most live in Ireland and Scotland, some in Wales. Lu Nuncio: Connolly (Con) McGuire. One subordinate (English) clan.

AFRICA

Mondoyo: The only African clan, started by a small group of lupi who went to northern Africa after the Great War. Out of communication with other clans until eighteenth century and have different customs. Lu Nuncio is Ato Tsegaye.

SUBORDINATE CLANS

Laban: One of Nokolai's subordinates; their small clanhome is near San Francisco. Their mantle is unusually strong for a subordinate clan, but they do not do well without a dominant. They like to fight too much.

Vochi: Nokolai's other subordinate clan in the United States, they are known for their financial acumen. Vochi births few fighters.

SHE blinked and swayed, so dizzy she had to reach for the wall to prop herself up. Could you pass out without falling down? That's what it felt like—like she'd blacked out. Which she'd never done, not in her whole life, and all of a sudden she was Sleeping Beauty and years and years had passed. Except she was still on her feet, so obviously years hadn't passed. The ladies' room was right behind her. She was still in the narrow little hallway of . . .

Of where?

Fear struck, quick and hot and dark, flapping its wings in her throat like a trapped bird. Where was she?

She didn't know. She didn't have any idea. She'd been . . . what? She couldn't remember. She remembered going to bed last night but not to sleep, not right away. She always had trouble falling asleep the night before her birthday. She'd sat up past bedtime—a sin overlooked on special nights—writing in her diary, with the light from her lamp warm and yellow on the lined pages and her lavender bedspread pulled up to her waist. She'd told her diary what she couldn't tell anyone, not even Debbie, and for sure not her sisters. Everyone was so "I can't wait" about being a teen-ager, but she'd been glad tomorrow's birthday was twelve, not thirteen. She wasn't ready for thirteen, but that was okay because she had a whole year of being twelve ahead of her. That gave her lots of time.

But that was all she remembered. She didn't remember waking up or eating breakfast or lunch or supper. Was it suppertime? Had they come here instead of going to the roller rink like they were supposed to?

Had she somehow missed her whole birthday?

A burst of indignation burned through some of the fear. That wasn't fair. That wasn't fair at all, and she didn't un-derstand, but here she was in some kind of restaurant. The air was thick with good smells—ginger and onions and fryer fat—and she could see a smidge of the room the hall led to. A man sat at a small, cloth-draped table, leaning forward and stabbing his finger at the air the way men did when they thought they were important and people should listen. The woman with him looked bored. They were both Caucasian, but this was a Chinese restaurant. She could tell from the smells and the crimson walls. Out of sight from her vantage point, someone was laughing a quick, barking sort of laugh: HA! HA! HA! Which made her think of Uncle Wu, who laughed in syllables like that, only quieter, huffing it out: Ha. Ha. Ha.

She was breathing really fast. Huffing like Uncle Wu. She clenched her fists and tried to make herself breathe normal. She needed something to be normal.

She felt tired. Tired and kind of heavy, the way she did when she had a cold. She sniffed experimentally. She wasn't stuffed up or anything. Had she been sick? Maybe she'd had a real high fever. A brain fever. Could brain fevers make you forget stuff? Maybe she'd had a terrible brain fever and got over it, but just now she'd had a relapse—that's why she'd been so dizzy—and—

"Excuse us, please," someone said behind her.

She whirled.

Two women had come out of the restroom. They were

kind of old—maybe thirty—and they were dressed funny. Both wore jeans, which was weird. Who wore jeans to a nice restaurant? One had on a big, sloppy sweater, but the other one wore a tight, stretchy shirt that showed *everything*, like she was a hooker or something. That woman had great big earrings and super-short hair like Mia Farrow and . . . good grief. She had a little gem in her nose, like it was pierced there.

Her mother wouldn't let her pierce her ears, and this woman had pierced her nose!

The two women were looking at her funny. She flushed. She was standing around like an idiot, blocking the hall. She stepped aside. As she did, her foot bumped something. She glanced down.

Someone had left her purse right there in the hall. It was a nice purse, too—black leather, the kind that's so soft you want to pet it. She should tell someone.

She'd taken one uncertain step when someone else came into the hall. A man. He was tall and probably as old as the two women, and he was gorgeous. He looked like a movie star—kind of like Clint Eastwood, in fact, who was still her favorite, and she hated that *Rawhide* had gone off the air. Only this man's hair was all dark and shaggy and he had really dramatic eyebrows that weren't like Clint's at all.

The man looked right at her and tipped his head like he was puzzled. She felt a little flutter in her stomach. Then he spoke to her.

"Julia? Are you okay?"

LILY pushed the remains of her Kung Pao chicken around on her plate and tried to look like she was paying attention to her cousin Freddie, who was excited about implied rates and parity and agio. What the hell was agio? Was that even a word?

She didn't ask. He'd tell her, and God knew how long that would take. It was some kind of broker-speak, though. Probably currency trading, which was his specialty. That was a large part of what he did for Rule these days. Rule's second clan wasn't affluent the way Nokolai was.

". . . not convinced the baht is on the rise, but . . ." Freddie broke off and chuckled. "Your eyes have glazed over."

"Sorry." She and Freddie got along better now that he'd stopped asking her to marry him. She'd even forgiven him for doing so repeatedly without mentioning that he was gay. Turned out he'd been in major denial about that and had only come out of the closet with himself in the past year. He still wasn't ready for the family to know . . . by which he meant his mother.

Lily could understand that. Aunt Jei—who was technically Lily's second cousin, but Lily and her sisters called all their mother's first cousins "aunt" or "uncle"—put the passive in passive-aggressive. She was limp, needy, and full of sighs, a widow with only one child who she doted on, clung to, and controlled ruthlessly.

Poor Freddie.

Aunt Jei was probably the reason Rule had excused himself to go to the restroom. He'd been seated next to her and even Rule could only take so much.

"That's all right," Freddie said kindly, and patted her hand. "You're probably daydreaming about the big day. Only two weeks away now, isn't it?" He beamed at her.

"Two weeks and one day." After which, she thought with a smile, Rule would be officially related to Aunt Jei, Freddie, and everyone else at this table. Poor man.

They were in the larger of the two private dining rooms at the Golden Dragon, where they held most such celebrations, since it was owned by Uncle Chen—another "uncle" who was really a cousin. The party was smaller than usual this year. None of the children were here, and Grandmother's companion, Li Qin, had broken her foot two days ago. While she could get around on crutches, she was still in pain, so Grandmother had insisted she stay home. Also, Lily's younger sister wasn't here, though for a very different reason.

"I attended the wedding of a colleague's daughter recently," Freddie was saying. "Beautiful girl. It was a very modern sort of ceremony. They wrote their own vows, and when it was time for toasts . . ."

Lily nodded and let her mind drift. Her mother had told them firmly they were not to make a fuss: "With your wedding so close, it's too much to ask. Everyone is very busy." Lily's father had wisely ignored her protests. Julia Yu loved being fussed over on her birthday.

That fuss had damn well better include presents, too. Lily's gaze slid to the table behind Freddie. The table held over a dozen gaily wrapped packages. She grinned. Freddie took her grin as tribute to his story about the groom's toast and chuckled and launched into a tale about someone else she'd never met.

Every year Julia Yu insisted she didn't need a thing, not a thing, but they knew better. She adored presents—the bright paper and bows, the whole unwrapping ritual. Lily would miss it if they ever did skip the gifts. Her mother might be picky and perfectionistic about all sorts of things, but presents were different. Her eyes lit with delight. She exclaimed with pleasure over everything, no matter how odd or humble, and held it up for everyone to admire.

"So what did you get Mother?" she asked when Freddie paused.

"Why, I got her a gift."

That meant he was dying to tell, but she was supposed to coax him. She glanced at her watch. Eight forty. "Guess I'll find out soon. She'll be finished primping any—"

The first scream was loud and piercing and terrified. So were the ones that followed. Lily was on her feet and moving before the others got their dropped jaws working. She'd grabbed her purse. She wasn't wearing either shoulder or ankle holster, but she didn't go anywhere unarmed, not these days. By the time she slammed through the door, she'd pulled her Glock from her purse.

Barnaby and Joe were on their feet, faced out. "Hold your positions," she snapped. The other two guards, Scott and Mark, were already on the other side of the dining room and moving as fast as only lupi can. They turned into the hall that led to the restrooms. Lily followed at a quick jog, veering around startled diners and a couple servers. The screaming stopped abruptly when she was halfway across.

Scott reappeared at the entrance to the hall and smiled at everyone. Scott cultivated the geek look. He wore glasses he didn't need and clothes a bit too large that turned his wiry frame skinny. If you didn't notice how well he moved, you'd think he never did anything more strenuous than tote a laptop. "I think she saw a mouse or something."

There were a couple of nervous laughs. Someone said, "Must have been a really big mouse." More laughter as the roomful of people began to relax.

Rule was in that hall. The mate sense told Lily that as clearly as if she could see through the wall. Had some woman with a phobia about lupi seen him and freaked? Could be. His face was well-known. Whatever kind of trouble had triggered the screaming, though, she probably wouldn't need her weapon. Scott had his back to it. He wouldn't do that if something needed shooting.

Still, she kept her Glock in her hand, but down at her side. Scott gave her a odd look, but stepped aside without speaking. As soon as he did, she stopped dead.

Mark stood a couple feet into the hall. He hadn't drawn his weapon, and he barely glanced at her. A few feet beyond him, Rule stood with his arms around Lily's mother. She was sobbing. Her hands gripped his arms. He was stroking her back and murmuring something. He looked up from his soothing to meet Lily's eyes. He looked baffled.

"Mother?" Lily said, stepping forward cautiously. She'd never seen her mother come apart like this. Never. To do so in public . . . "What's wrong? Are you hurt?"

Julia Yu lifted her head from Rule's shoulder. Mascara streaked her face in long black runnels. "I'm old! I'm so old!"

"You . . . you look great."

Julia shuddered and wailed.

"I was coming down the hall and saw Julia," Rule said

carefully. "She looked upset, so I asked if she was all right. She reached up to touch her hair, then started patting her face. Then she screamed."

"Mother—"

"I'm not your mother! I'm not anyone's mother! I'm twelve years old and someone has stuck me in this old, old body!"

The last fifteen months had been difficult. Lily had killed. She'd died herself—or part of her had—and she'd seen someone die for her. She'd dealt with a wraith, too many demons, a Chimei, a crazy telepath, and a couple of really nasty elves. She had literally been to hell and back. But this . . .

For a long moment her mind was simply blank. Then she thought of psychotic breaks. Then she thought of magic. She swallowed hard and put her weapon back in her purse. "You're twelve, you said."

A vigorous nod. "It's my birthday."

Yes, it was. Only Julia Yu had turned fifty-seven today, not twelve. "Do you recognize me?"

"N-no. You look kind of familiar, though. Maybe we met some time?"

"My name is Lily. You're Julia, right?"

Her mother sniffed. "Julia Lin."

Lin. Her mothers' maiden name. "I'm an FBI agent. Would you like to see my badge?"

"A real FBI agent?"

"The real thing." Lily pulled her shield from her purse and held it out. "See?"

Julia Yu released her death grip on one of Rule's arms so she could lean forward to peer at Lily's ID. She didn't reach for it, though. "It looks real."

"It is. Have you heard about—" Noise behind Lily had her turning. Her father and two of her cousins were at the hall's entrance. Edward Yu told Scott he'd better step aside right now.

"Edward," Rule said, "give us a couple more minutes. Please."

"I'm going to see my wife," Lily's father said. "Julia—are you all right?"

"Who's he?" Julia said, her voice wobbly. "He's not your husband, is he? He looks too old."

Lily almost lost it. She swallowed and blinked like crazy and prayed her voice wouldn't break. "Father. Give me a minute. Please. If magic's involved—"

"Magic!" Julia cried.

Edward Yu didn't answer, but he shoved at Scott. Who didn't budge, of course. Neither of them was a large man, but Scott was lupus.

"Edward." The cousins parted to allow a small, awesomely erect old woman to come forward. Her black hair was pulled ruthlessly back from her face and fastened in an intricate bun. She wore crimson satin, lavishly embroidered. Grandmother murmured something in Chinese that Lily didn't catch and laid a hand on her son's arm. "Something bad has happened. Julia does not know you. We will stay back for now so we do not overwhelm her."

Edward Yu frowned hard. His eyes were frantic. "Not long. I won't wait long."

Lily turned back to the woman who didn't know she was a mother. Who thought she was twelve years old. "I'm with Unit Twelve, Julia. Have you heard of that? We investigate crimes connected with magic."

"Someone put a spell on me, didn't they? That's what's wrong!"

"It's one possibility. I can find out if you'll shake my hand."

Julia's eyes narrowed suspiciously. "Why?"

"I'm a touch sensitive. If magic has been used on you—a spell of some kind—I'll feel it when we touch." Her mother was null, with not a whisper of a Gift. Any trace of magic Lily found would have been put there by someone else.

Julia cast a worried glance at Rule. He nodded reassuringly. "I guess that's okay," she said, and held out her hand. It was shaking.

Lily took it in both of hers.

Julia Yu used to play the piano. She had the hands for it, long-fingered and graceful. Her manicure was immaculate, the polish a pale pink. The hand Lily held was covered in well-tended skin and a hint of . . . something.

The sensation was so faint Lily wasn't sure she really felt it. She closed her eyes and tried to shut out every other sense, concentrating on her hands . . . yes. It was like the difference between air that's completely still air and the merest puff of a breath, but it was there.

"You found magic." Julia's voice was high and quick. "You did. I can see it on your face."

"I found something," Lily agreed, opening her eyes. Something that bothered her, but she didn't know why, when she'd barely been able to discern that anything was present at all. Maybe her unease had nothing to do with her Gift and everything to do with whose hand she held. "I don't know what. It's very faint. Would you mind if I touched your face?"

"My face? I—I guess not."

Julia Yu was five inches taller than her second daughter. Lily reached up and laid her palm flat on her mother's cheek.

The skin was soft there, too. Pampered. Had she touched her mother's face at all since she was little? She couldn't remember. Julia was staring at her with such hope, as if she could fix things with her touch. Lily's eyes stung, so she closed them. Her hand. She had to focus on her hand.

Not quite as faint here. Still a barely there sensation, but a bit more present, just as she'd hoped. A spell that tampered with identity or memory should be more concentrated on the head. Only she still didn't know what she was touching. Magic always had a feel to it—slick or rough, intricate or smooth, oily or dry or whatever. This wasn't tactile. More like being in a dark room where you couldn't see a thing, but you knew someone was there. You didn't hear anyone or smell anything. Maybe you sensed the air move or the heat of their body, but you weren't aware of that. You just knew someone was there.

Lily opened her eyes and drew her hand back. Her right hand. Not the one with Rule's diamond. The one with the *toltoi* charm. "I think . . ." God, she could not cry. Not now. She had to be a cop, not a daughter, right now. She made her voice firm. That's what people needed from a cop—firmness, authority, even when said cop was clueless and wanted badly to curl up in a ball. "I did find something."

"Can you take the spell off? Make it go away?"

"No, I'm not a practitioner. We'll get someone who is, though. Someone who knows a lot more than me." Lily tried to smile reassuringly. She was pretty sure it was a sad and sick failure. "Rule—

"I'll call Cullen." He tried easing one arm away from Julia. She clutched at him. "I'm right here," he said soothingly. "I've got you. I need to call a friend of mine, though. He's very good with magic."

Cullen Seabourne was one of a kind, the only Gifted lupus in the world. His Gift was one of the rarest, too. He was a sorcerer, able to see magic much as Lily was able to touch it. He was also a complete geek about magic. He'd have some idea what to do.

Lily sure didn't. She drew a shaky breath. What now? If this had been anyone else, a stranger, what would she be doing right now?

"Lily," Grandmother said. "You will now tell me what you found."

All right. Yes, that was one thing she could do. But first . . . "In just a moment. Rule, I need to give your people some orders."

He had his phone to her ear. He nodded.

"Scott, I need the restaurant exits shut down. No one is to leave. Julia, you'd probably like to sit down. You've had quite a shock. Grandmother, maybe you could take her to—"

"What did you find? What's wrong with Julia?" That was her father, who had waited all he could. Scott had moved away as soon as Lily gave him his orders, leaving defense of the hall to Mark, who also didn't budge when

Edward Yu shoved him. Her father's hands clenched into fists. "Move."

"Father, I don't know exactly what's wrong, but I know this is a Unit matter. I need to talk to Uncle Chen. Will you bring him here?"

His mouth tightened. He cast his wife one long look, then nodded and turned, pushing his way through the crowd gathering at the hall's entrance. It wasn't just relatives now—several customers had decided they needed to see what was going on.

"Everyone else—you will go back to your tables. Now." She whipped the last word out. A few people did back away. None of her family budged. "Mark, keep this hallway clear. Anyone who doesn't go sit down—" Quickly she amended what she'd been about to say. "Anyone other than Grandmother who doesn't go sit down will be taken politely but firmly to their table."

"Don't be absurd." That was Paul, her brother-in-law. "You can't intend for him to lay hands on any of us."

"This is a crime scene. I mean exactly what I said. I need you to go get Susan." Lily's older sister was a dermatologist, so this was way outside her field, but she could at least make sure their mother didn't go into shock or something.

Being given an assignment tempered Paul's indignation. He frowned to let her know he did not appreciate her attitude, but he left to get Susan.

"Cullen's on his way," Rule said.

Thank God. Though it would take him awhile to get here. He was at Nokolai Clanhome, which was forty-five minutes outside San Diego. "Grandmother, can you take Moth—Julia—into the ladies' room so she can sit down?" There were a couple chairs in there.

"Who are all these people?" Julia said plaintively. "I thought I was here with my family, but I don't see them. Is my mother here? You need to call her. Mrs. Franklin Lin. She'll be worried. You'd better call her right away."

Lily met Grandmother's eyes. Her mother's mother had

died forty-five years ago...two months after Julia's twelfth birthday.

Grandmother stepped forward. "You will allow me to worry about that. I am Madame Yu. I am not your grandmother, but you may call me that, if you wish. Come." She slid an arm around Julia's waist, gently but inexorably detaching her from Rule. She was a full head shorter than the younger woman. "You will sit down now. Someone will bring you a glass of water."

"Can I have a Coke?" Julia asked as she was steered into the ladies room.

"A glass of Coca-Cola, then. We will not worry about caffeine tonight."

The ladies' room door closed behind them.